P
THE GRE

"Chase-Riboud shines a literary floodlight on Hannah Elias, one of the richest Black women we never heard of, until now. Whispered secrets, historic intrigue, dashing characters, intimate details, and opulent language all converge masterfully. This book's pages demand to be breathlessly turned until the end."

—Tricia Elam Walker, author of
Nana Akua Goes to School

"Love, murder, race, class, and memory collide in a mesmerizing swirl of licit and illicit desire that was old New York in the age of the robber barons across the pages of *The Great Mrs. Elias*. This is a delicious read."

—Alice Randall, author of *Black Bottom Saints*

"A stunning portrait, developed with artistry, compassion, and depth, of a woman and a society you don't want to stop staring at—one that offers a new revelation every time you look."

—Nana Ekua Brew-Hammond,
author of *Powder Necklace*

THE GREAT
MRS. ELIAS

THE GREAT MRS. ELIAS

A Novel

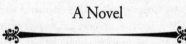

BARBARA
CHASE-RIBOUD

AMISTAD

An Imprint of HarperCollins*Publishers*

THE GREAT MRS. ELIAS. Copyright © 2022 by Barbara Chase-Riboud. All rights reserved. Printed in the United States of America. No part of this book may be used or reproduced in any manner whatsoever without written permission except in the case of brief quotations embodied in critical articles and reviews. For information, address HarperCollins Publishers, 195 Broadway, New York, NY 10007.

HarperCollins books may be purchased for educational, business, or sales promotional use. For information, please email the Special Markets Department at SPsales@harpercollins.com.

FIRST HARPERCOLLINS PAPERBACK PUBLISHED IN 2023

Designed by THE COSMIC LION

Library of Congress Cataloging-in-Publication Data is available upon request.

ISBN 978-0-06-302001-6

23 24 25 26 27 LBC 5 4 3 2 1

Jules Dewayne

David Charles

Alexei Karol

Sergai Giovanni

I am not a woman but a world
My clothes need only to fall away
For you to discover in my person
One continuous mystery.

—*Gustave Flaubert, "Quidquid Volueris"*

A Note from the Author

There are hitherto lost or misplaced documents, court transcripts, newspaper articles, real estate sales, police records, and psychiatric reports included in this novel of turn-of-the-century New York that are not only authentic and historic and hitherto unknown but central to the story and understanding of my heroine. These documents are like a stage set on which her extraordinary life unfolded in plain sight of her invisibility. Most of the names have not been changed to protect the innocent, because there are no innocents; some, however, have been changed to protect the guilty.

PROLOGUE

Well, you might call this whole tale the story of Hannah's houses: the poorhouse, the whorehouse, the workhouse, the jailhouse, the crazy house, the outhouse, the almshouse, the house of ill repute, the mug house, the crimp house, the tenement house, the merchant house, the House of J. P. Morgan, the Metropolitan Opera House, the banking house, the trading house, the Senate house, the house of mirrors, the playhouse, the courthouse, the gambling house, the clubhouse, the parish house, the house of assignation, the house of correction, the dead house, the parlor house, the panel house, the slaughterhouse, the shock-and-fall house, the trinity house, the house of the spirits, the haunted house, the house of detention, the bawdy house, the governor's house, the doll's house, the fun house, the countinghouse, the movie house, the death house, the fashion house, the house of cards, but, above all, the house on Central Park.

August Nanz, Esquire
Barrister, New York City, New York
Borough of Manhattan

1903
THE ASSASSINATION

Sorrow is better than laughter: for by the sadness of the countenance the heart is made better. The heart of the wise is in the house of mourning; but the heart of fools is in the house of mirth.

—*Ecclesiastes 7:3–4*

ONE

Murray Hill, New York City,
November 13, 1903

A brazen Indian summer sun bore down on the carriage lane of Park
Avenue, New York, turning the white granite sidewalk into the proverbial street paved in gold. A man in his late sixties, top-hatted with a
neat gray goatee and bright blue eyes, a copy of the *Wall Street Journal*
under his arm, stepped out of the beautiful amber-glass-domed kiosk
of the new IRT subway at Thirty-First Street, having ridden the fastest,
most modern and chic method of getting from Wall Street to what was
then "Uptown."

The gentleman had left the comfortable, wood-paneled, first-class
wagon, with its blue plush velvet seats and glass electric fixtures, and
climbed the marble stairs into daylight. He passed under the kiosk, lit
a cigar, and then started toward his brownstone mansion at number 91
on Park.

He was a tall, handsome man, hair parted to the left under his beaver-
skin top hat—an authoritative profile that spoke power—and a very
large nose, though nothing compared with that of the famous J. P. Morgan. He wore a dark greatcoat with wide sleeves and a short cape over
the shoulders; a light gray morning coat; a high, white-collared, pale gray
shirt; and striped pants. He carried his newspaper under the same arm
that carried his nobly battered briefcase. His white, spat-covered patent
leather boots strode purposely toward home and the lunch his niece had
waiting for him.

As he approached the low cast-iron fence protecting the flower bed in front of his mansion, another man, nattily dressed in a short tweed jacket, baggy plaid canvas trousers, and a bowler hat, stepped out of the shadows, making him stop short in surprise. Out of the darkness stepped a good-looking man, with a perfect, graying handlebar mustache, clipped wing sideburns, and yellow sunglasses that glinted in the bright autumn light.

"Mr. Green?" he asked politely.

"Yes?"

"Mr. Andrew H. Green of Ninety-One Park Avenue?"

"Yes. What is it to you, boy? Get out of my way."

"You, sir, are a fornicator and a thief. You stole my Bessie from me with your millions! Turned Bessie Davis's head and bought her just like a slave, with your greenbacks and diamonds and furs. If it hadn't been for your slander, I would be a happily married man today."

"I beg your pardon, my good man. I don't know what you're talking about! I don't know any Bessie Davis, and if you don't get out of my path immediately, I will call the police."

"I loved Bessie Davis," said the man, "and you took her away from me and now you must pay."

Andrew Green saw the snub-nosed derringer in the man's hand, lifted to eye level. Green saw the gleam of the polished metal pointing straight at his head, and behind it, the hand holding the gun.

"Damn your fornicating soul," said the shadow, and he fired point-blank.

Green felt a searing pain in his face, heard a momentary crack under the bone of his forehead so that his hand flew up as if to pull something stuck to him. His fingers felt wet. His knees gave away. He stumbled.

Green clutched his now-throbbing head with both hands. Where was his top hat? He had tickets to the Metropolitan Opera that night. No, this couldn't be happening.

As if in answer, the man emptied the chamber of the gun into Green's body—five shots in all. Green fell backward onto the sidewalk, blood gushing from the ruptured artery in his neck, as doors along Park Avenue opened, as the horses of the cabbies parked in front of the hotel across the street reared in fright and shades were lifted, as drapes pulled back and pedestrians turned to look, then ran in panic in different directions.

The assailant then put the gun to his own temple and pulled the trigger. Nothing happened. Men from the cab line bore down on him. The chamber was empty. He had miscalculated. "No!" he cried. "I can't live without Bessie. Bessie, wait up!"

The assassin made no attempt to escape as the cabbies from the Murray Hill Hotel across the street rushed toward the immobile figure, and a shrill police whistle signaled the arrival on foot of patrolman Liam Houghtaling of the Fifth Precinct, his revolver drawn. He could see a man prone on the pavement and a man . . . no, a coon standing over him with a gun in hand, tears running down his cheeks. The officer noticed that a crowd was gathering, and that it might turn into a lynch mob once people realized the killer was Black. A young white woman rushed out of number 91, screaming, "Uncle! Good Lord!" She was now cradling the murdered man's head in her lap.

"Jack!" the patrolman yelled to another Irish policeman overtaking him. "A killing, probably a robbery. Don't shoot unless he tries to run for it."

Liam Houghtaling's gun hand was damp with sweat. Five years on the force and he had never had to face violence—not in this neighborhood.

"Police! Freeze!" He almost fainted when the stone-still assailant turned to gaze in his direction. The murderer now stood over the body pumping blood like an opened fire hydrant. The young blond woman's howls seemed to shake the ground under Houghtaling's feet. He realized, though, it was actually the rumble of the new Interborough Rapid Transit subway, and its tremor had transferred to him.

Both policemen watched, guns drawn, as the weeping killer lowered the cocked revolver from his own temple and began to walk away, then returned to the body, standing over it, cursing it to hell and brimstone.

"There he is," he said. "I done it."

Houghtaling took the murderer's gun away from him gently, and seeing that the Black man made no resistance, holstered his own weapon, took out his handcuffs, and subdued the suspect as he had read in his manual. No one but him realized that his hands were shaking.

The second policeman, Jack Kelly, was not so by the book. He began beating the Negro with his nightstick even though the man was handcuffed. The man did not resist but sank to his knees as the blows rained down on him. His eyes had rolled back in his head and curses fell from his lips, which were drawn back in a grimace that exposed two gold teeth. He was in another world, thought Houghtaling, a world that recognized neither pain nor sanity.

"Jesus, Mary, and Joseph, call an ambulance, get a Black Maria!" Houghtaling said.

The young blond woman held the dying man in her arms, crying, "Uncle, Uncle," looking up at the cloudless blue sky from time to time in bewilderment while her skirt darkened with blood.

"Miss, did you see what happened?" Houghtaling asked.

"No. I heard shots and I looked through the door because they were so close. Please help me!"

The gathering crowd was turning ugly at the sight of a white woman kneeling in grief, her wispy blond hair in a disheveled halo, while a Black man nearby was the apparent murderer.

"We have to get this Negro out of here," Houghtaling told Kelly, "otherwise we're going to have a lynching right here. And call the fire department!"

As Houghtaling knelt beside the girl and leaned over the body, Andrew Green began mumbling, the nonsense syllables of a dying man. The girl wiped the blood from his face with her gown. "What uncle? What?"

The policeman leaned in too. The last words of anyone were worth hearing. If they were, in fact, words. They sounded like gibberish.

Green himself wasn't sure whether he was making any audible sound. He knew only that he didn't deserve the pain he was feeling or the sense of being immobile, of all places, on the ground. He tried to explain the unfairness of it all: "I don't know any Bessie Davis, as God is my witness . . ."

Then he said nothing more.

The patrolman closed the victim's eyes and crossed himself. There had been no time for a good Catholic confession, unless those mumbles were it. Houghtaling thought, living on Park Avenue, the victim was probably a Presbyterian anyway. Still, the cop whispered as many Hail

Marys as possible before the ambulance and the prisoner's transportation arrived. The ethnic names for the vehicles that took prisoners away—the Black Maria and paddy wagon—were used liberally by the police and the members of the crowd. Police reinforcements were a welcome sight for the patrolmen, neither of whom had ever seen a dead body before. The newly arrived police began questioning the gathered crowd, asking if there were any eyewitnesses. The journalists who had been alerted by their informants in the police department arrived quickly too, and started interviewing bystanders.

The orderlies verified that there was no life left in the prone body, then lifted him from the girl's arms and took him inside his house. Houghtaling walked over to the girl.

"Who was he? You know?"

"Why, Andrew Green, my uncle!"

"The Andrew Green?" Houghtaling felt a chill go down his spine. The man was a legend—one of the most prominent elites in New York. Everyone knew his name.

"Yes." The girl was sobbing. "This is his house. His office is downtown. He was just coming home for lunch." She began crying harder.

"Have you ever seen this man before?" the policeman said quietly, hopefully pulling her from her grief. He pointed to the assassin, who was now crouched and still handcuffed. He was praying aloud.

"He's the furnace tender at number 136. He also works at number 130 on the other side of Thirty-Third Street. I've seen him often in the neighborhood."

"Can you think of any reason why this . . . this individual would want to shoot your uncle?"

"None, officer, none, none, none. . . ." The girl's head fell forward and she buckled into sobs again. The servants of 91 Park Avenue had come out of the mansion, and the patrolman guided her into their arms.

Behind him, the crowd grew uglier. Houghtaling heard them shout racial epithets. He turned and saw spectators eager for violence, held back by a tight wall of police. The crowd rocked back and forth as they shoved one another for a better view, a multilegged animal ready to pounce.

"Damned Negro!"

"A man ain't safe in front of his own house!"

"Why wait for a judge to let him go when we can make sure Andrew Green gets justice now!"

"Killed by a damned nigger bastard."

"Son of a bitch."

"Assassin!"

Houghtaling walked up to the spectators and shouted, "Calm down!" He tried again: "I want everyone to be quiet!" Still, no one seemed to hear him over the babble. He pulled his gun and shot in the air. "This is my prisoner. There'll be no lynching on my watch. Now move back. Move on. Nothing to see here."

But not even that got the crowd to disperse. They leered and commented, although at a decreased volume until another police squad car arrived. It parked near the Negro murderer and blocked their view. About fifteen minutes later, two well-dressed men arrived from the newly formed Detective Bureau of the homicide division of the New York City Police Department.

"Crazy bastard," said Houghtaling to the first, a certain Joseph Mc-Clusky. They stood together, shoulder to shoulder, looking at the perpetrator of the crime. The detective hardly acknowledged Houghtaling's words. McClusky's face from the side showed none of his thoughts. His profile was like a statue in the museum. He had a sharp nose and straight lips that displayed few creases, which would have stored a lifetime of smiles. Thick, black, unruly hair demonstrated that the Irish in him ran deep. Overlong sprouts from his hairline drew attention from his most interesting quality, his piercing gray eyes.

Some people said he was the smartest detective in the bureau, a real compliment in this unit of elite inspectors who answered only to the district attorney. Women called him handsome when his face finally opened up and the eyes exposed the possibility of dreams. Most of the time, however, he shut the door on his heart and his imagination, like now.

"Robbery?" he asked Houghtaling. Both men were surprised when the murderer raised his head and answered, "Oh, yes!" He appeared suddenly animated: "That thief stole my sweetheart and ruined my life. The slander he heaped upon me . . ."

"And this sweetheart," asked the detective, "where is she?"

"She's on Central Park West. She owns a mansion at 236."

"You mean she works at 236 Central Park West?"

"No, that's her house. She owns it. She's the proprietor." Then the murderer began laughing, a crazy, jittery sound. "And she got just what she deserved. You'll see . . .," the man continued.

"And who is she?"

Here the murderer's expression changed again. Now his face clouded, and tears filled his eyes. "Why, she's my dead Bessie. My dear dead Bessie. Dead. Bessie Davis. I killed her too."

"And who are you?"

"Cornelius Williams. Cornelius Vanderbilt Williams." The reporters scribbled madly. A sketch artist on the scene moved closer, adjusted his weight to one hip, and started to draw.

The murderer was long and loose limbed, almost comic in his disjointedness. His mixed gray hair was easily depicted with a few brief stabs of the pencil on paper. The salt and pepper of his flamboyant mustache comprised a few wavy lines. His eyebrows made an interesting detail. They ran together, shaping a "T" with his nose. It was less a Negro nose than a classic European one, narrow and sharp, as were his other features. All sheathed in brown skin. The artist paused for a split second, wondering whether to give the portrait an interpretation of the Black man to demonstrate his complete Negroness or to draw him the way he was. Luckily, the murderer's eyes made the artist's decision. They had such a loony expression that the two detectives were now stepping back. In those eyes were the violence and despair of the unloved. This condition was one every man knew and avoided like it was contagious. The brothels and barrooms were full of such men. The eyes, when the artist looked at them as required by his job, communicated pain and frustration. They roamed the crowd for sympathy. They scanned the faces of the two detectives, as if they somehow had the answer to his now-silent prayers.

While the artist had a little empathy for the man, he was not skillful enough to portray the Negro's desperation to the reader. Also, his editors would not want him to be too kind in his depiction. He was a killer and a Negro, so his appearance had to appear sinister. The sketch artist simply wrote a note to himself that the man's eyes were a light chestnut color like his skin tone, as the detectives herded him into the horse-drawn patrol car.

Detective McClusky rolled his eyes heavenward. A Black man had just assassinated a famous white millionaire in cold blood and in broad daylight and confessed in front of two dozen witnesses and two police officers. The Negro claimed he had lost the affections of a rich white woman who owned a mansion at 236 Central Park West, the most aristocratic block on the whole West Side. It was not as prestigious as the Upper East Side, but it was still a neighborhood for the rich. In any case, Negroes were not his cup of tea, crazy or not.

He looked over at Lieutenant Houghtaling, who said in a voice that sounded only half-joking, "We could have shot him just now and put him out of his misery."

McClusky didn't agree outwardly. But if the cops had finished off the Negro, they would have saved the state of New York the expense of a trial and an electrocution.

TWO

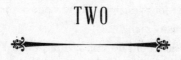

I t was evening by the time Hannah Elias had the strength to sit in the cushioned bay window on the second floor of her brownstone mansion at 236 Central Park West. The leaded Tiffany glass panes threw a mosaic of light on her and her bedroom. At her feet were the late-edition newspapers. Her Japanese manservant, Kato, had deposited them in her room without a word. He may not have known the consequences of the front-page story, not to the extent that she did. But the crowd gathering outside, many of them knocking urgently on the front door, told him that his boss's discreet life was over and pandemonium was on its way.

One newspaper's three-inch headlines screamed:

**FATHER OF GREATER NEW YORK GUNNED DOWN BY
A NEGRO ASSASSIN IN BROAD DAYLIGHT**

His missus sighed before Kato closed the bedroom door.

Hannah was shaken. Cornelius had shaded his face with his hand, but he had addressed her by her real name, Bessie, and delivered a shot that would have killed her had not the steel stays in her corset deflected the bullet, leaving her with no more than a dark bruise. Her butler Kato had summoned a Chinatown doctor famous for treating mob gunshot wounds. She had not called the police. If she had, she thought, Andrew Green, the Father of Greater New York, might still be alive.

Cornelius. Cornelius Williams, a man she had lost track of for a decade, came to her door yesterday. He was one of the most insignificant men in her life of many men.

Now the best she could do was sit up, propped in the window by Kato, her rib cage aching with every inhale. Thank God for good lingerie, she thought. It had helped her make a living. This time it saved her life.

Sitting there, Hannah resembled a Renaissance painting, her head covered with a lace mantilla, one hand raised to her neck, her gaze lowered over the park in reverie. The winter sunlight streaming into the room lit one side of her face and munificent bosom. It was not an especially beautiful face, yet it produced the illusion of great beauty, which she had trained herself to turn off and on like the newly discovered electric bulb. It depended simply on whether she chose to smile, for then her face would open and radiate warmth like the sun parting clouds, confounding passers-by and lovers alike, not discriminating between men and women.

She had learned over the years to orchestrate this power like a musical instrument, and like the expert pianist that she was, could explore its tonality, shading, and pitch in such a way that it was never the same beauty just as it was never the same music. Developing this ability had stood her in good stead all her life, endowing her with a chameleon quality that fascinated her lovers. Hannah realized the events that had just taken place would shake New York City to its foundation as well as endanger the charade she had built for herself out of a windowless rented room in New York's Five Points to this sumptuous mansion on Central Park West.

The enormous bed was overhung by a canopy as high as the room's ten-foot ceilings. Green velvet drapery with silver tassels and buttons edged in silk fringe formed a tent over the elaborate headboard and fell in soft folds on either side. The bed was lifted off the parquet floor by giant silver lion's feet, and the fleece mattress was framed by a delicate hand-chased bronze screen that surrounded it on three sides with an opening on either side through which to enter.

And while Madame Valtesse had received her guests in her bedroom,

Hannah's chamber served only as her inner sanctum into which only her maid or her butler ever penetrated. She had no desire or need to show off her wealth in this way, and although she held this marvelous object in admiration, she didn't worship it or the money it had taken to purchase it. In fact, she slept in the bed almost as an afterthought. To her, it was not a bed at all but an elaborate vessel that piloted the Cleopatrian revenge she had planned as a young girl against the Caesars and Marc Antonys of this world.

It was true, she thought. She had at one time been Bessie. How had Cornelius managed to find her, she wondered, after such a long time? And why, after all these years, had he stood in her doorway and with the words "Farewell, Bessie. I'm sending you to hell," pointed a pistol at her heart and pulled the trigger? Why had Cornelius dragged her whole honky-tonk ragtime life into her vestibule and shot it?

She looked up into the huge antique Venetian glass mirror that faced her bed at what people saw when they beheld the former Bessie Davis. She liked to undress and admire herself in it. She believed herself to be the reincarnation of Queen Cleopatra; her raw femaleness, her approachability, her maternal instincts, her woman warrior exterior were all overshadowed by the one thing she had built her life around: her sex—in all its power and imperialness. She was like a blooded racehorse, born of centuries of interbreeding with other feminine bloodlines, which had finally produced a thoroughbred whose line did perhaps go all the way back to ancient Egypt.

She enchanted onlookers with the serpentine thrust of her hips as she walked. She would turn her back on a visitor, walk away, then suddenly turn around and envelop him in her smile. They had seen her hind parts and posterior, now let them savor her foreparts and cleavage. . . . This cunning power she exercised over all males, high and low, rich and poor, famous and unknown, white, black, or brown. It commenced with the movement of her body and ended with her enigmatic smile—as volatile and dazzling as the life she had led in what New York called the skin trade.

Hannah continued to look into the mirror at what people saw when they beheld Mrs. Elias. Her hypnotic gaze, as mysterious and promising as a saint, reflected her afternoon dress of magenta satin with black velvet trim, silver *paillette* and steel bead appliqué with mint green satin details. It was by Jacques Doucet of Paris. She was still in mourning and had worn only black until yesterday, when for some reason she had decided to wear a lilac dressing gown over a red corset. Hannah said a silent prayer for Green's soul, then for her own.

But she knew that not all people were born to do the right thing. There were natural-born sinners and natural-born outlaws, people who somehow got the short end of luck, beauty, power, and morals, and so made their way as they would, in the underground of life and society. It was their fate and their burden. They were not really to blame. They tried to be good, but they were constitutionally bad. She was one of them.

She was now a woman of independent means. She was as burdened by her past as she was by the pearl choker wrapped around her neck like a noose. She could not run. This was her house. She would not abandon it because of a lovesick fool.

Not a trace of her history showed in the lines of her body or the expression of her face. She could have been born yesterday. Her eyes closed over their deep cast-iron color that, as the saying went, a man could lose himself in. Many, many men had done just this. Some, on the contrary, had found themselves in that gaze. Men had also found their mothers, their wives, and their daughters in those eyes, depending on the hour and her mood.

What's in a face, she thought? Hers was known to be beautiful, but what exactly did that mean? Her eyes were so black they appeared to have no white around the pupil at all, only almond-shaped openings of livid, penetrating darkness that despite their blackness exuded a singular steely light that men took for allure and sexuality but which was merely intelligence. Beautiful, perhaps, but what did that mean when the exact same amalgamation of exotic features would be deemed ugly if the spectator had known her real identity?

If Hannah leaned forward, she could see the entire shaded drive leading north to Harlem, each beautifully hued brownstone mansion marching northward like uniformed soldiers, each facade different yet unified by the color of the stone: a dark gray-brown that gave harmony and unity to the whole street. Across from the row of brownstones ran the carriage drive and the solid granite wall of the park, and beyond the meadows, dales, and carriage roads. The November sunlight streamed through the multicolored Tiffany glass, illuminating Hannah's profile and turning it a dozen different colors.

Was she responsible for the death of a man, she thought? She had perhaps ruined several men's lives, but she had never killed anyone. There was no one named Bessie Davis, she reminded herself. She hadn't been Bessie Davis since 1888.

She groaned slightly as she picked up a newspaper and read. Cornelius, the reporter wrote, had lain in wait for Andrew Green, the famous millionaire, called "the Father of Greater New York" for his feats of urban planning; specifically, joining the separate boroughs of the city under one umbrella. The journalists didn't know that Cornelius had soaked in a stupor of jealousy all night after his attempted murder of Hannah, and that Green was the second victim.

The papers had, however, given an address that would soon connect her to Green, which was the reason men had been banging all day on her door. They said they wanted to hear the other side of the story. They were looking for Bessie. Hannah's dual identity was swiftly being uncovered, and she was being convicted in the press. In this era of newspaper scandal sheets, readers would charge her with the crime of being a "Negress" occupying the posh address among millionaires across from beautiful Central Park. In the eyes of the public, women like her were simply not worthy.

Cornelius had entered her beautiful home and dragged her muddy life across her lush carpets. Her fantasy world had to give way to the reality of a death, one that might send her to jail again.

Green was a very important man, and not the only millionaire connected to her. They didn't want to see her name in the newspapers. They wanted her silent.

The tea Kato had delivered along with the newspapers was growing cold. Hannah picked up the cup with a shaking hand. But it slipped from her grasp and fell onto the parquet floor. The sound of expensive imported china breaking into a million little pieces was deafening.

❧

Leola Pershing saw a crowd of newspaper reporters gathered in front of 236 Central Park West as she leaned out of her carriage window approaching Hannah's house. She decided to descend and make her way on foot to the secret entrance of Hannah's mansion in the alleyway behind the elaborate facade. She held the emergency house key in her hand, which was deep inside her coat pocket; panicked and not knowing what to do, she began to walk more swiftly along the low stone wall enclosing the park. Then she spurted across the driveway and into the hidden doorway disguised as the front of a brownstone underneath the massive stairs, entering the mansion through a secret passage.

No one noticed Leola opening the brownstone door with her key. She walked down to the dark basement and lit the portable oil lamp. The room held Hannah's leftover furniture. Leola tiptoed through rows of floor lamps and bronze chandeliers, wall tapestries rolled up like rugs, and gilded mirrors that flashed back the image of a plain, unpainted redhead under a wide-brimmed hat. She startled herself. How old she looked without makeup or silks swathed around her neck. Her unadorned self, however, had attracted no attention from reporters or cops.

She almost tripped over the extended leg of a claw-foot chair. Hannah loved so much junk. Her basement could have been the wing of a museum—the Egyptian wing. Behind the exit door of the basement, where it met Hannah's house, was a mudroom where the servants gathered to smoke. Instead of the usual butlers' and maids' garb, Hannah had dressed them in tunics, gowns, and sheath dresses—a little bit of insanity that she was wealthy enough to indulge. Leola knocked on the door that separated the two basements. Her key allowed her entrance into only the back building, not Hannah's personal residence.

"Hello," she called. Nobody answered. She pushed hard and the door opened.

White gowns, golden rope belts, and gilded barrettes were strewn on the floor. The servants must have absconded when the newspapers came, and they knew they'd look ridiculous escaping in sandals and robes. Not to mention, they would be cold. They probably disappeared because none of them had citizenship papers. They were less Hannah's minions than rats leaving a sinking ship.

Leola moved quietly up the staircase to the first-floor landing. Had Kato run too? She saw him nowhere. But then she heard shuffling, as if someone walked away quickly, and caught sight of a person in a long black dress. Was Hannah still in mourning? Sadness seemed to follow her in all this opulence.

"It's Leola," she called. The woman's figure quickly disappeared upstairs. Leola followed.

"Hannah, you know I can't get up these stairs fast as you," Leola shouted behind her. "Stop being daft, girl!" But the woman had disappeared.

Leola, in chase, burst through the bedroom door, then caught her breath as the others screamed. There was Kato at Hannah's feet picking up broken porcelain. She was seated in the window in a bright silk dressing gown, clutching her side with both hands.

"My shitting God!" Leola exclaimed. They all looked at one another and then laughed, tears running down their faces. It was the first laugh any of them had had all day.

Leola flopped onto Hannah's bed in relief. It was gilded wood, hand carved from a solid block of mahogany and covered with sculpted bronze garlands, cherubs, roses, lilies, ribbons, fans, palm leaves, and inlaid mother-of-pearl.

Leola called out from Hannah's lair, after she caught her breath. "I didn't know what had happened to you, my girl. But I knew something was brewing. All the papers have your address."

"I know, Leola," Hannah responded. "What am I going to do? Tomorrow everyone will know everything."

Cornelius had addressed her by her real name, Bessie. That was the first problem. The papers said Bessie lived at 236 Central Park West. The reporters had already made the connection to her. They didn't know yet, however, about Bessie's or Hannah's distant past, or even just yesterday.

But the death of Andrew Green had complicated her life. In the public eye, she might be a coconspirator in some way. And she never wanted any innocent person dead. She had perhaps ruined several men's lives, but she had never killed anyone.

There was no one named Bessie Davis, she reminded herself. Her own guilt rose in her throat like bile.

She told Leola, "I hardly knew Cornelius."

Leola held her tongue rather than ask, *Are you sure?* "Tell me what happened," she said.

Hannah went over the events of the night before.

Hannah wondered why, after all these years, Cornelius had stood at her doorway and shouted, "Farewell, Bessie. I'm sending you to hell."

"He is crazy," she described the scene to Leola. "He pulled the gun on me, and I couldn't talk him out of it."

"Look." Hannah told Kato to hand the corset to Leola. As he did, he felt it was still damp, not with her blood but from the tears he had cried over her body when she'd blacked out and he thought she was dead.

Kato fingered the ribs of the lingerie until he found the place where the bullet had made a mark before ricocheting. He picked up the bullet's metal casing and handed that too to Leola.

"And see." Hannah opened her dressing gown to display her rib cage. The bruise from the bullet was splayed from its purple center to its ruddy edges. She lifted her breast to show Leola and Kato the extent of the damage. They looked at the scar, but they also could not ignore her beautiful body. Her breasts were still full at thirty-eight years old. Her body was taut and unmarked. It was the color of wet sand where the sun reached her neck and a creamy pale caramel where her clothes usually covered her. When Hannah dropped to the seat in the window, she looked perfect—muscular at her shoulders and broad at the bosom, with a waist that was impossibly tiny given her pregnancies, including the possible one at this moment.

Leola got up from the bed, walked over to Hannah, and reached out to feel the place where the skin was marked.

"No, don't touch it," Hannah said protectively.

"My poor friend. You're in trouble again. Just like old times."

Leola's words, however warm, all of a sudden felt more like pity than compassion.

"I need you to do something for me," Hannah told Leola.

"Anything," the woman replied.

Hannah asked Kato to help her down from the window seat. A few reporters thought they noticed movement as the window cleared.

Hannah went to her Louis XIV escritoire and took out of the drawer a children's copybook she used to practice her handwriting. For years she had practiced writing until her undisciplined schoolgirl scrawls had become as fine a hand as would have done justice to a lady. It was firm, bold, perfectly slanted, and exquisitely formed.

The blue lined exercise book also held pages of pasted-in articles, menus, recipes, poetry she had copied from books, women's magazines, and architectural journals. It was here that Hannah kept the list of her clients. Her neat writing ran down pages and pages of men's names, addresses, occupations, and sexual preferences. She handed it to Leola along with a packet of letters tied with a blue ribbon.

"I want you to take these downtown with you and, please, put them in the safe."

"OK."

The notebooks were familiar to Leola. She had seen her friend write in them many times. She knew they contained her most private thoughts. The money she had now came from Hannah's gifts.

Leola put the notebooks into her bag and, with a hug to her friend, left the house the same way she had entered. The woman appeared as a plain nobody walking out of an undistinguished house on a side street. She carried a pocketbook full of the most intimate details about New York's millionaires, and nobody noticed.

THREE

The evening of Andrew Green's murder, Hannah Elias studied herself in the gilded mirror of her bedroom after Leola and Kato left. She searched the glass for a version of truth in her reflection. So many people were gone—her daughter Gwendolyn, her daughter Clara, and now Green. But Bessie Davis was dead too as far as she was concerned. The woman who lived on Central Park West, who had arrived in the vestibule yesterday to talk to Cornelius, and who now sat in the bay window, was Hannah Elias.

Bessie Davis was a girl who would have been happy to clean a mansion like this. She was Hannah Elias, the mistress of the house.

The sun setting behind the mansion lit the greenery of the park outside, outlining the passing carriages in gold. She turned from the window and brought the newspapers into her bed. As she pored over the newsprint, she might as well be reading her own obituary instead of Andrew Green's. Destruction was imminent.

Before Leola left, Hannah told her, "The papers will have a heyday, calling the last fifteen years of my life an impersonation. But they don't know the way I feel in my soul."

Leola looked at Hannah a bit strangely as she referred to herself as Cleopatra. She held herself in a dignified quiet, like the still air before a violent storm. She read the papers' accounts of the murder over and over again. There was no mention of a second shooting. Yet it must have been

Cornelius. From time to time, her gaze would lift to the last vestiges of the setting sun.

ANDREW GREEN KILLED BY INFURIATED NEGRO
FATHER OF GREATER NEW YORK MURDERED
NEGRO WILLIAMS SLAYS ANDREW GREEN

Tomorrow, the *Times*, the *Tribune*, the *Sun*, the *Globe*, would have her name in the headlines as well, she knew. Her chest contracted. One day, she was the talk of the town, the next she might be committed to the penitentiary. That was life's way. Bad times came suddenly.

The moment to save Andrew Green's life had come after she had been shot. She should have called the police. If she had, Green would have still been alive.

But her fear of the police—her hatred of the law, her own outlaw life—stopped her. Now, even though she tried to protect herself, she was sinking into her past, as thick as the muck on the bed of the Central Park pond.

Hannah picked up the *Evening Herald*. The papers claimed that Cornelius had sworn that Andrew Green was the man who had stood in the way of his marriage to Hannah. It had been Green who had spirited her away, Cornelius claimed, taking her into his world of wealth far beyond his reach—a world that banned him.

The newspapers spoke of Cornelius as a "furnace tender" at 136 Park Avenue, but she remembered him as a loose-limbed, handsome, laughter-loving, churchgoing caterer with his own thriving business, moving from fashionable hotel to fashionable hotel, inventing, preparing, and serving food to the rich and nouveaux riches of the Eastern Coast. He had known everything about food, luxury, and service. He was what colored people called a tiptoe man—a man who simply tiptoed out of responsible life—a house with a mortgage, a wife, and children—in order to survive the humiliation, discrimination, and hopeless contempt that society served him. He had also tiptoed around her house, on her heels practically, while she was married to Matthew. He asked her too many questions and gave her the creeps.

Was she responsible for the death of a man? She had perhaps ruined several men's lives, but she had never killed anyone. She ruminated on her conversation with Leola that evening.

"Do you think," she'd asked Leola, "that it was my fate not to get murdered and his to die?"

Leola shrugged. She was unaccustomed to having such thoughts.

"Or was it my fate to get murdered because I knew Cornelius, and somehow Green stepped into my destiny?"

"I don't see how you had anything to do with this, Hannah. You haven't seen Cornelius for years. How did he even know where you lived, much less want to murder you?"

But Hannah wondered if Cornelius's insane act was the sign that interest had come due on her long-term loan—borrowed luck at having achieved this much material wealth after doing so many things wrong. Hannah looked at life the way she did banking: there was the piper to pay, the mortgage restituted. She should have been dead a long time ago.

Had Satan really knocked at her door last night, and sent punishment for her sporting life?

Outside, dead leaves blew against the leaded windows like Hannah's own ignored resolutions. Some of the dead leaves stuck to the windowpanes, weightless and useless. Other leaves carried the seeds of another plant. Hannah didn't really understand the difference. In her world, the wicked were never punished and the good were not rewarded.

Hannah told Leola just before she left, "Maybe they will never find out. Cornelius may be dead himself by now. I read they took him to the Tombs. He barely escaped a lynch mob. There may have been another waiting for him at the city prison."

"You don't really wish to have another death on your conscience?" Leola asked.

"Leola, Cornelius tried to kill me. He thought he had! He's crazy. It's been years since I've seen him, and how many words had I ever exchanged with him? He was Matthew's friend—not mine."

"Do you think anyone, especially the police, is going to believe that once they find out who you are?"

"But it's true, Leola. I didn't know him. I have no idea why Cornelius shot me! He just said, 'Farewell, Bessie. I'm sending you to hell.' And then he pointed the gun and fired. If only I had called the police. Andrew Green would still be alive—"

"Well, he didn't say 'Farewell, Hannah. I'm sending you to hell and then I'm going out and shooting Andrew Green.' You couldn't have known. Could you?"

"OK."

"The police, if they come, may come with a search warrant—understand?"

"I understand."

Leola pulled back and studied Hannah. "Remember we've been through worse."

"Not worse—maybe as bad—but never murder . . ."

"Shit, Hannah, we're soldiers—soldiers in the longest, bloodiest war of all—the cunt war. We have more men's blood on our hands than the king of Spain."

Hannah smiled. Was Leola going to give her another lecture on fallen women and the Sisterhood, she wondered? Leola had always tried to protect her. She had always been there in her darkest moments, with her lilting voice, weaving a cocoon of soothing words around her bruises and heartbreak. She had saved her life more than once.

Leola told Hannah, "Green is dead. You can't change that. You are not responsible for what Cornelius took it upon himself to do—a madman . . . It's not your fault, Hannah . . ."

"Not my fault, Leola? I'm the one in the middle, the only connection to them both."

"Call Nanz at least. I'm sure he's seen the papers by now," Leola pleaded.

But Hannah was thinking about a third man. John must have seen the day's headlines too, but she had heard nothing from him. What was he thinking?

1876
BROTHELS

And bring the four hundred and fifty prophets of Baal and the four hundred prophets of Asherah, who eat at Jezebel's table.

—1 Kings 18:19

In no other country is a girl left so soon or so completely to look after herself.

—Alexis de Tocqueville,
Democracy in America

FOUR

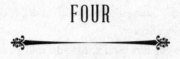

At dawn, Bessie Elias's mother shouted upstairs, "Sugar Pot, are you getting the children up? Hurry them to the table."

Bessie—an eleven-year-old middle child—rose from the bed she shared with her sisters. She was the first of the younger siblings to walk to the outhouse, carrying a stick to chase the last morning rats, and the first to heat the water on the woodstove to bring to the girls upstairs so they could wash before getting dressed for breakfast.

"We're coming, Mam," she called to her mother, who had risen before daylight to take care of her eleven children. Bessie's older sisters and brothers had already left to work in the homes and the hotels of the Philadelphia elite. Once within walking distance, the houses that employed servants were moving farther away, following the tracks of the new railroads. That left Bessie to take care of her younger siblings and help her mother.

Bessie's younger brothers came downstairs. Even in stocking feet, their footfalls resounded on the wooden staircase. Their mother, Marion Elias required all the children to sit at the table together, even for a small piece of bread and a bowl of porridge. She had started teaching them manners early so that they too could find jobs in the mansions now dotting the suburbs, at a time when colored servants were less desired than Germans or the Irish.

Another reason that she had the children arrive together, pray, and wait until she gave a motion for them to begin eating was practical. If the children had the run of the kitchen, getting any food they wanted at any time, the bolder ones would eat as much as possible, and the shy ones would starve. Much like life, Marion reasoned—the weak could hardly maintain themselves, much less succeed. It was her duty, as head of the household, to impose fairness.

When the boys got downstairs, Marion told Bessie, "Have them sit now."

Bessie motioned to all the boys and stared slightly at her twin, David, who returned this greeting with a nod and a smile. She was always a little startled to see herself reflected in his face. They looked so similar even though they were fraternal, born on the day the Civil War ended.

On May 13, 1865, they had pitched themselves from their mother's womb into the hands of the midwife who served the run-down tenements of Philadelphia's Seventh Ward. The "Colored Colony," as residents called the area, had been established by free slaves about one hundred years earlier. Since then, the area had developed good neighborhoods and bad ones just like any other corner of America. The Elias family, in those days, lived at the poorest end of the spectrum. Bessie's father, Monarch, was a groom with the Sixth US Pennsylvania Calvary—a job, but one that paid little and kept him away. But the day that Bessie and her brother were born, the bloody battles ended, and her father made his way home. The Civil War had killed five hundred thousand men on both sides, one man killed for each enslaved man freed. But the most important soldier to the Elias family had survived.

Bessie couldn't remember her infancy, of course, but she knew that her father had nicknamed her "Sugar Pot," like a bowl serving the right amount of sweetness. Her mother liked the name because that was the term her Scots-Irish relatives used to refer to their children.

Bessie was a tiny child with small bones and translucent skin. Her father still carried her on his shoulders at six years old while her brother was made to walk. They both followed behind Monarch once he began working in the nearby stables. They helped feed root vegetables to the horses, throw armfuls of hay into the stalls, and, when they were big enough, shovel manure from various locations in the barnyard into a pail. Then, together, the twins carried the heavy, stinking bucket to a storage area.

Bessie's father taught both children all that he knew about being a stable hand. An expert horse breeder as well, he bragged to his children that they were descendants of the Munsee tribal chief Lappawinzo and an African princess.

"Some people like thoroughbreds," he told Bessie, who never quite believed his whole story. "But I'm partial to grade horses."

Bessie knew that these crossbreeds were less fragile than thoroughbreds and sometimes had unique characteristics. Because of her mother's side of the family, the children were born several shades lighter than their dark-skinned father. Bessie wondered whether that had been his intention given his difficult life. Or did he feel bad when their color did not match his?

Sometimes people asked him, "Whose children are those?" Except when her mother was with them. Then, people in both the Colored Colony and Germantown looked away.

Monarch never said a word to them. But a few days later, nothing would please him.

When Bessie was young, about a decade earlier, the entire family lived in the ramshackle annex to the stables of Monarch's employer. The children slept on straw pallets made out of stuffed horse-feed bags in the hayloft. The elder children took care of the smaller ones—Sadie, Katie, Lizzie, Abigail, and David—until Bessie was ten. The eldest sister, Emma, cooked along with their mother. Emma, Hattie, Sam, Mary, and Maggie rotated in one job at Philadelphia's Belford Hotel so that each had a little money for working one week a month.

Bessie's father periodically lost his job for shouting at his bosses. They fired him and called him "an uppity red nigger" even though he was the best horse whisperer in the district. Bessie knew when something went wrong because he'd come home, sit in a soft upholstered chair, gather the children around, and tell them a story.

"Your people owned so much land here before white people came," he spoke loudly. "So far west. So far north and south. It was all ours, Lenape. We were people who wanted peace. Good people. We were too good. We sell a little land to a man. Then his sons come back and say, that's not what we bought. 'We bought all the land a man could walk through in a walk on a day and a half.' Our people thought, 'That's not much land. When you walk through the woods, you have to break the branches as you go. You're going to stop to shoot a squirrel when you get hungry. You might sleep a few hours at night.'"

The children watched their father although they had heard this story many times. "But the white man's sons cheated. The sons of William Penn cut a path through the woods before the walk started. They drew a straight line so there was no going around bushes or tripping over tree roots. Then, they didn't walk. They got the fastest men in the area to run. Three of them just in case only one could actually finish the race. In a day and a half, with people giving them food and carrying them in boats across the river, one runner went sixty-five miles. In a day and a half they went as far as our land extended. They claimed everything west of it that belonged to us."

Monarch slapped his palm to the arm of his chair, and the youngest children jumped. "Damn it. Don't ever trust the white man. Don't trust anyone."

As the children sat very still, waiting, even though Monarch had finished his story, their mother stepped into the circle.

"Who needs to wash up before bed?" she asked. "Bessie, go set up the pitchers and basins."

The children dispersed, leaving Monarch with his head in his hands and Bessie's mother cleaning around his chair.

The battle to keep filth and dirt from overwhelming her existence was constant. Like other Seventh Ward residents, she was a slave to the house, using pails of boiling water, bristle brushes, soap, lye, whitewash, sawdust, vinegar, turpentine, and ether to splash against the stoop, scrub the pavement, unstreak the walls, and ungrime the floors in an attempt to keep insanity at bay.

Bessie's mother bent over steaming wooden tubs of laundry. She wrapped her head in a canvas sack. She scraped their soaking wet dresses against a ribbed board to remove the stains and wrung the hot water out of the fabric until her arms swelled like a wrestler's. Her mother's raw, chapped hands were so eaten by lye that the skin flaked like the scales of a fish. In the evenings, Bessie rubbed a pomade of chamomile, lard, and honey into her mother's knuckles and across her palms.

"Thank you, Sugar Pot," her mother whispered, with her head back and eyes closed.

Her parents' life revolved around the acid odor of lye from her mother's tubs and the putrid smell of horse manure. Still, the children appeared neat and clean when they stepped out into the world. They had shoes—moccasins cut and sewn by Monarch—one decent set of clothes, and two sets of underpants. One to wash and one to wear. By the time she was eleven, all the Elias children had gone as far as middle school. Bessie wanted to attend school even more. She had her eye on a trade high school called the House of Industry.

For all her young life, her siblings worked at home and, if possible, outside the house for a salary. There were so many of them, and Monarch's presence filled the tiny home.

Finally, his superior skills landed him an offer for a wonderful job. A man asked Monarch to come to Saratoga Springs, New York, where he could groom and care for racehorses during the summer season. And he could bring his son.

Monarch and David made plans. With money sent for the purpose of outfitting a new stable boy, they went to the tailor and had David fitted for britches and a vest. They went to the shoemaker and got him his first pair of boots. All his clothes needed to be sturdy to last through the summer and his long days of work—feeding and watering the animals, cleaning the stables, currying the horses, and occasionally riding them from one part of the grounds to the next. He and Monarch dreamed that this could be David's big break. He was small like his sister, but maybe he could be elevated to warming up horses, even becoming a jockey in a few years.

All these plans were wasted, it seemed, when David came down with scarlet fever just before they were about to leave. They were afraid he could die.

Monarch worried about how he could return the money for David's clothes and whether he would be fired, this time, before he even began working. Bessie spoke up.

"I can go in David's place. I know how to take care of the horses. No one will ever know."

Her mother objected: "No. Girls don't belong with the men in the stables."

"What choice do we have, though?" Monarch said. "We lose everything if we don't take a chance. And she's as good as her brother anyway."

At this, Bessie beamed. She said, "No one will find out."

That night, her mother sheared Bessie's hair.

"Holy Lord!" she said every time a thick plait hit the floor, until the six that had neatly held Bessie's thick curls in place were on the ground.

Bessie's face was still delicate and beautiful, though. So her father handed her a cap and told her to pull it down low on her face. "And never say anything. People might hear your voice."

Bessie had been raised to talk in a polite, gentle voice. Her tone was sweet.

"I'll tell them that you're a mute or have a problem with talk," Monarch added. "I'll figure out something."

On the day they arrived at Saratoga, no one paid Bessie any attention. She followed closely behind her father as she had as a little girl. Once she was told her chores and he went off to another part of the racetrack, she worked silently with her head down.

Luckily, Monarch's boss had his own stable apart so Bessie didn't encounter the other men. And at the end of the day, her father came back if he had been called away. He slept nearby so no one bothered her and she could change clothes without anyone seeing.

This went on for a week, and then there was a terrible day.

One of the jockeys burst into the stable shed.

"You're not Monarch's son!" he approached. "Who are you?"

Bessie, horrified opened her mouth and screamed, "He's my father!"

"And you talk, eh!" The man stared at Bessie. "His daughter, ha, my girl. And getting the pay of a boy and lying about it! And the job of a boy! I could have brought my own son. Uppity nigger son of a bitch! The nerve!"

The jockey started to storm out of the stable, but Bessie ran after him. She grabbed his arm. "Please don't tell."

"Now you've got a lot to say?" he said. He slapped her with all his strength, his shadow encompassing her cutting off light and air. One hand penetrates deep into her while the other hand thrust deep in her throat so no cry for help can escape her. Unable to move or scream under the double bind, thrown to the ground and held there under his suffocating weight. A stranger's male body livid bore down on her. The full specter of hellish rape was upon her.

Vomit burst against her starched vest from her impaled body strangled and skewered like a fowl. Bessie fought him to unconsciousness. Another slap and then another.

"You tell, and your father is fired, bitch! This is what you get for acting like a boy!"

Still mute, peace is all that's left to live for as she fell into darkness.

Bessie was awakened by her own sobs in a pool of vomit. She coughed and threw up again. She got to her knees and pulled up her britches. She wondered whether she was dead or alive except that the mare in the stall glanced back on her in pity as Bessie struggled to pull herself to her feet by grasping the mare's haunches. How long had she been unconscious? She had awakened where she had been thrown; manure and straw clung to her like the act itself. Her heart pounded—what would she tell her father?

She would tell no one. The last two stalls had to be finished with clean straw in twenty minutes. Bessie dragged herself into the neighboring stall. It was dark and empty and there she cried great, gulping, wrenching cries of a child. When she had no more tears, she limped into the next stall and began pitching hay, flinging manure left and right, scrubbing the wooden floor until it shone. Exhausted, she laid down and slept until dark while her father searched for her in stall after stall.

"Sugar Pot!"

Bessie knew something was wrong. When her father said, "Sugar Pot," there was always a question mark at the end—"Sugar Pot, can you do this?" Or "Sugar Pot, fetch me this," or "Sugar Pot, go find your mother." But this "Sugar Pot" didn't have a question mark behind it but a period. Her heart accelerated with the knowledge that something was wrong.

"I'm going to have to send you home."

Bessie burst into tears, and behind the tears was blindness. He knew!

"But why? I worked as hard as anyone—longer and later! I was the best water boy . . .," she sobbed.

"The boss found out you were not a boy. That we had lied. He don't allow no female in his stables except his dogs or his horses. You're to take the first train out. Bessie, he wants you off the premises. Tonight, you'll have to get to the station on your own because . . . all the jockeys are racing tonight. They'll all be missing. I'm sorry, Sugar Pot . . ."

Monarch put his head in his hands. Sitting there on a sack of feeds he looked like an old, old man. Bessie was still sobbing, her fists clenched in rage, her back as rigid as a plow.

"But I didn't do anything wrong—it's not my fault! I am as good as any boy! Stronger, better, smarter . . . I work harder than they do! Why? Why? Why?"

But Monarch remained silent in the deepening shadows of the stable as Bessie, the stark itch of hay in her nostrils, wailed out her pain, her rage, her shame, her heart.

He knew! He knew, of course he did, and her mother would know too when she got home.

"I'm giving you all the money from the job to take home for your mother. Everybody, even the boss, pitched in. It's enough for her house. You be careful with it and hand it over to your ma as soon as you get back. This, here, is a money belt. You strap it on under your clothes and don't take it off for anything or anybody until you hand it over."

But Bessie's tear-stained face had turned as hard as stone, not a flicker of light escaped from her black, fathomless eyes. There was not enough money in this godforsaken world that could make her safe or whole again.

Bessie boarded the train home only to feel like a different person entirely from the one who had excitedly sat next to her father watching the scenes out of the window on the way there.

"Look!" She had pointed out to him a million new sights, from the groves of tall trees in the distance to the sight of deer running along the nearby roads. The apparition that she kept to herself, however, was the sight of the Pullman porters.

Having been raised around rough men—coal carriers, street cleaners, stable hands—she had never seen men with such clean hands and faces who were also colored. She watched them with perfect balance, swiftly moving from the aisle where she sat with her father to the grand Pullman car that carried the wealthy passengers. The men carried big trays covered with white cloths. She could not see the contents under the napkin, but she smelled strong coffee and fresh rolls.

But the stench of the stables she had all over her on the train back to Philadelphia. When she saw the grand Pullman car and the men and women stepping up to their accommodations, she felt bitter. She had seen the same people in Saratoga, lavishing their money on drinks and meals—hot plates in the middle of the day, not cold sandwiches in pails. She saw Commodore Vanderbilt's private railway car attached to their train in Franklin Station, Philadelphia. Arriving in Saratoga, she was dazzled by the spa, the great houses, and the ladies with their hats and jewels. She considered now how impressed she was that first time with thoroughbred horseflesh, the handsome sporting men, the gamblers, the jockeys, the excitement of the races, and the magic ability of her father to cure horses.

On her return trip, though, the world was different. She looked at the Pullman porters as servants to people who had power over them, just like the jockey had over her. Who knew what things they had to do to keep their jobs? She heard them say, "Yes, ma'am" and "No, sir" with a clip that to her had sounded aristocratic when she was innocent. But now that she saw real aristocrats, people with money who could do whatever they wanted, she considered how unfair it was that she could not sit in the Pullman car instead of coach. Why didn't her mother have a feathered hat or jewels on her fingers? Why did her family eat the same soup night after night? Was she born just to be miserable all her life, or had her destiny been stolen like Monarch said, when the English stole their land? On the ride home, the Pullman porters still smiled at her, and a couple winked when they passed her seat in coach. On her trip to Saratoga, she would have been overjoyed to have their attention. But now she looked at them with narrow eyes and considered that she was going to figure out a way to balance out her fate. She was going to ride in first class one day. And if a Pullman porter or any man ever wanted to marry her, she would accept only because he could serve her.

Bessie's mother took the money Bessie had handed over—and purchased a house on Addison Street in a better neighborhood. Called a "trinity house," it was three stories high, one room to a floor: Father, Son, and Holy Ghost. The house faced a narrow, brick alley, and a labyrinth of dark lanes and courtyards filled with festering garbage and outhouses, open sewers, and windowless cellars crowded behind the mansions of the rich Philadelphians of Spruce and Pine Streets. But it was better than living in a stable.

Bessie was bitter. She realized that what had been done to her body was payment for her mistake. She had let a man know that she was not a boy.

The only consolation for her shame was the new house. She had acquired the money to give her family something of value. She couldn't tell anyone she was spoiled now as a woman, but secretly she knew there was some value in what she had done and even a perverse pride.

If she did nothing else in her life, she already had earned a house for her family. The proof was the house on a better street, the beds where her sisters slept separately, and the room her mother and Monarch shared alone. She now called him Monarch, as she had gotten accustomed to hearing the men say in Saratoga. She didn't answer anymore to Sugar Pot.

Monarch made himself busy with new teams of horses, a new equipage, and painting another man's stables. He worked from five in the morning to eleven in the evening for weeks after his return.

FIVE

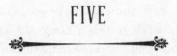

Fairmount Park, Philadelphia,
September 1876

O ne day in September, Monarch decided to take his family to the
centennial celebration in Fairmount Park. The first World's Fair
was almost three hundred acres of exhibitions of commerce and culture
from nations and companies. Monarch made sure that all his children
had new moccasins, straw hats, and picnic baskets containing marma-
lade, biscuits, ham knuckles, and apples. The children followed behind
him like a line of ducks. The older girls were, of course, working long
hours at the grand hotels, which were busting with tourists. The crowds
in Fairmount Park were a veritable sea of bodies into which they marched,
bobbing and weaving on the surface and avoiding eye contact with the
white Philadelphians.

There were displays of machinery and inventions. Luxury products
were exhibited in stalls. Bessie had seen some of these items in Saratoga—
creams for a woman's face and hands, and beautiful clothes. Exhibitors
displayed dresses from San Francisco made of silk, hats and laces from
France, and earrings and furs from shops in Philadelphia that the family
never visited. Bessie was transfixed. She wanted to stay in the clothing
exhibition for hours. The other children, however, made her move along.

When they entered Gallery K in Memorial Hall, the site of the American artists, Bessie was stunned. Her mother hadn't wanted the children
to see this exhibit, because it showed a figure that was half-naked. But her
father insisted that the exhibit was important.

Before they arrived at the statue, there was an illustration of the artist, a woman, as dark as Monarch. He stood proudly next to the description of the artist and read it aloud. She was part Chippewa and named Wildfire at birth. Now people called her Edmonia Lewis. The statue, named *The Death of Cleopatra*, showed a woman draped in fabric and jewels and slumped in a grand, embellished chair. One breast was exposed, and her head had fallen to one shoulder. Bessie could almost see the blood dripping from the side of her mouth. It was as if the artist had seen Bessie herself at her lowest point. Cleopatra looked exactly the way Bessie felt after the jockey had slapped her across the face and molested her. She was limp like a washrag, but beautiful. Even though she was dead, the stone made the woman look strong and full. What was she like before this happened?

The huge, seven-foot seated figure was the most beautiful thing Bessie had ever seen—Saratoga ladies' gowns included.

"Who is Cleopatra?" she asked her father.

"It's the name of a queen who lived in Egypt a long time ago."

"Is that why she is dead?"

"No. She committed suicide."

"What's suicide?"

"When you lift your hand against yourself," said Monarch. "When you are so low you want to die and have the courage to do so."

Bessie's eyes involuntarily welled with tears. She knew how that felt.

Monarch added, "It is a sin against God. If you take your life into your own hands, you have defied God's power. You have exercised your own will instead of submitting to His."

Bessie was blinking away tears.

Monarch turned to talk directly to her. "Life is still life. Life goes on. Never forget that. People make mistakes. But you can't change your mind after self-murder. It is the worst of sins. It's blasphemy to God."

"So she didn't believe in God?"

"I don't know. That's a good question. She believed in herself because by that time she ruled the world."

"Do you believe in God, like Mama?"

"I believe in our Indian gods and in a Supreme God, yes, Sugar Pot," he hesitated.

This time Monarch looked at Bessie in a different way, as if he were talking to an equal. "Cleopatra was a queen, and a warrior. She wanted to take care of her people."

"So why did she kill herself?"

"She also had enemies, and she didn't want to be captured by them and be made a slave."

Bessie studied the beautiful stone figure without saying anything for a long time, until more people came near.

Bessie overheard one woman say to another, "How did these Negroes get into the exhibition?"

"Oh, you know," the other replied. "Negroes. They always want to see a naked white woman. They'd do anything to get in an ogle." Then the women laughed.

Her mother called. Bessie followed, a little overwhelmed by everything she had seen and heard.

Bessie tried to find as much information about Cleopatra as possible after she visited the Centennial Exhibition. About a month after it closed in November, a column in the *Sunday Dispatch* wrote that she was the daughter of a king and born in the year 69 BC. "A woman of physical and personal attractions, she fascinated Caesar and Marc Antony. A good deal of fighting was done on her behalf by the Romans." Bessie could imagine men fighting over her. She read in books later on, however, that the men were lovers and Cleopatra had been in control.

As Bessie approached her teens, her body took on the solidness and the shape of Cleopatra's. Her color was the indescribable color of sweetness itself—peaches, almonds, café au lait, vanilla, depending on the day and the light, pierced by her black cast-iron eyes that had no white around them, only the unfathomable darkness of an endless tunnel lit only by the radiance of her smile. Men now stared at her the same way that their eyes lingered on Cleopatra in the exhibit.

Monarch spent more time in the stables. He was always alone, far from the laughter of his house and his children.

One morning when he was home, Bessie and her mother were arguing over a small chore. Bessie wanted to save it until she came back from a walk. Her mother didn't want her to leave the house.

Monarch left instead, went to the nearby stable, picked up a shotgun that he had hidden there one evening, put it under his chin, and shot himself.

Bessie and her mother heard the sound of the gun going off, but suspected nothing. Soon, however, came a knock at the door.

The firemen from the city came but refused to clean up after a Negro. They made the men from the neighborhood who took his body away do it—cleaned up the brains scattered everywhere—in the rough haystack, the flanks of the horses, the walls of the stalls, the leather saddles, and the shiny new landau carriage. There was no investigation by the police of why the suicide had taken place. It was an open-and-shut case.

Bessie's mother looked at her differently now. Bessie knew the reason: His death was her fault. Her mother thought it was because her father could not stand the arguing. Her mother had no idea of the extent of Bessie's shame.

To Bessie, Monarch's diatribe against suicide had been nothing except empty lies. He had lied. He had not kept his word or God's. Bessie never understood why her father had abandoned them to the mercy of men like the police and the firemen or those of Saratoga or those of the Walking Treaty, men who took whatever they wanted because they could. But she vowed one day to take her revenge.

Monarch's funeral was grand, paid for by the Odd Fellows, a secret fraternal organization he belonged to that from that day on paid her mother a monthly pension for the rest of her life.

As the years passed, Marion Elias became even more rigid. She had been a serious woman before Monarch died. Now she still kept their house pristine, took all her children to Mother Bethel African Methodist Episcopal Church every Sunday, and expected spotless behavior from them. If she had ever had a dream or a fantasy, there was no trace of it in her eyes or her manners.

In spite of her doubts about God and men, Bessie tried to become the person on whom her mother depended. Bessie learned to play the piano, took care of the younger children without complaint, and attended the Philadelphia House of Industry to learn more skills and some academics. After graduation, she was put out to service as a downstairs maid.

Her employers lived in a villa in Overbrook, just outside the city. The Main Line Railroad—known as "Old Maids Never Wed and Have Babies Period" because it stopped at the town stations of Overbrook, Merion, Narberth, Wynnewood, Ardmore, Haverford, Bryn Mawr, and Paoli—had caused a revolution in the Seventh Ward. The rich had deserted their mansions on Spruce, Locust, and Walnut Streets and moved to the "heavenly" countryside, leaving their maids and washerwomen in possession of the center of the city, but they were obliged to travel sometimes two or three hours a day each way to reach their employers' homes. Or they were forced to become live-in maids, abandoning their husbands, children, and lovers six days a week.

Bessie didn't mind the commute. She was able to get up early and help her mother with the younger children. After breakfast, she walked to the train and sat with a library book. The Library Company of Philadelphia, which once had been only for members, now offered the biggest collection in America to the public.

Bessie had found an old book, *Memoirs of Celebrated Female Sovereigns*, by Anna Jameson. The first chapter began with the story of Semiramis of Assyria. Bessie read the book backward and forward, absorbing every bit of information.

Semiramis was just a year older than Bessie "when she assumed the reins of the empire and resolved to immortalize her name by magnificent monuments and mighty enterprises." The most important part of her life was not her death, Bessie figured out. "She built enormous aqueducts, connected the various cities by roads and causeways, in the construction of which she leveled hills and filled up valleys; and she was careful, like the imperial conquer of modern times, to inscribe her name and the praises of her own munificence on all these monuments of her greatness." Semiramis was as capable as any man, more than most.

The book said that she commanded foot soldiers and cavalries. She used elephants to conquer new lands. Once, she was informed that a rebellion was taken place in her city. She ran from her toilette half-naked with her hair flowing behind her to put down the uprising, just by her presence.

Then Bessie read the story of Cleopatra and committed it to memory.

Cleopatra spoke ten languages. She knew philosophy and literature. The melody of her voice and the brightness of her smile captivated men. When her throne was taken from her by her brother, she sneaked into Julius Caesar's room by being wrapped in a bolt of linen and carried in secret. She presented "a strange mixture of talent and frivolity, of firmness and caprice, of magnanimity and artifice, of royal pride, and more than feminine weakness."

The first few times that Bessie read the chapter, she needed to refer to the dictionary. But soon she understood that only with her personality, Cleopatra had captured Caesar with "charm and eloquence." He offered her protection and love. She did the same with Marc Antony. In her first meeting with him, she arrived on a ship, its sails made of purple silk.

At about this time in the text, Bessie's train trip was over. But her imagination was inflamed.

The Jennings family consisted of a husband and wife and two daughters about her age when she entered their house. She imagined herself queen of their ornaments. She dusted, waxed, and polished as if Caesar were going to arrive. She arranged the crystal bowls, china vases, pieces of precious stone, and figurines. She kept them clean and sometimes caressed them, inspired by their beauty and perfection. She kept her patrons' objects, carpets, furniture, glassware, books, plants, draperies, porcelains, marble statues, and tapestries in perfect condition, as if they were her possessions. As a result, she was promoted to ladies' maid and chosen to care for her mistress and her daughters' clothes and adornments.

In 1884, Bessie was nineteen years old with a perfect figure and a weakness for beautiful clothes. She remembered the finery of the ladies of Saratoga and the possibilities of the fabrics from her trip to the World's Fair. She took special pleasure in caring for her mistresses' abundant wardrobe.

She spent the next few months commuting to their home and became an affectionate part of the Jennings family. Then they asked her to move in to save herself the trip. There was no one in the Seventh Ward she wanted to be with, so what was the point of a day off? And there was certainly no place to go except bars, bordels, or church.

She dedicated herself to lovingly caring for the gorgeous dresses Mrs. Jennings and her daughters brought home. She avoided Mr. Jennings, who seemed to seek her out more than the women to pick up cups and saucers or carry his shoes from his chair to the bedroom.

Whenever she could, she would rush headlong into the dark recess of Mrs. Jennings's voluptuous clothes closet, hiding there, burying herself in the cascades of dresses, gowns, and coats, the suspended garments parting at her passage as she caressed the wools, crepes, silks, satins; fingering the textures, inhaling the scents, memorizing the perfumes, drunk on the expensive odors, the smell of crisp linen, the sumptuous weight of the fabrics.

When Bessie's sister Hattie announced plans to marry at Mother Bethel Church, Bessie was overjoyed. It would be a memorable wedding in the Seventh because he was a Pullman porter. Despite her younger cynicism, Bessie knew now that they were men with steady jobs who were generally stable and kind. How many of her new brother-in-law's comrades might be at the wedding, she wondered? More than anything, she wanted to stand out at her sister's wedding.

Months later, she was standing in Mrs. Jennings's closed closet when Mr. Jennings entered. She murmured aloud that she had wished to have even one dress.

"My sister's getting married, and I don't want to look like a frump."

"You would never look poorly, Bessie," Mr. Jennings replied. "You're a beautiful girl."

She blushed at his kind words. She had never felt beautiful except when she buried herself in her books. Then, within the pages, she was bolstered in her imagination, that she had courage or beauty or smarts like the characters.

"Why don't you borrow one of my wife's dresses?" he said. "I'll ask her. She won't mind."

"I couldn't," Bessie replied.

"You could, if you allow me to have a little feel . . ." he said, his eyes searching hers looking longingly with a smile. "I won't hurt you," he said.

Bessie felt sick. She stood shuddering as his hand rose under her dress. "I promise you'll have your dress for your sister's wedding. I'll ask Madame." Bessie squeezed her eyes shut.

She didn't feel right after that as she chose a ball gown of jade green chiffon and taffeta, patterned with amber tea-rose petals, which formed a mermaid train.

Like Cinderella, she arrived at the wedding and was surrounded by admiring beaux. Hattie didn't mind. The Pullman porter was her prize. She had chosen a boy named Frank Satterfield to escort her baby sister.

By evening, word had spread throughout the Seventh Ward of the coming out of Hattie's alluring sister, Bessie. But Mrs. Jennings had made a discovery of a different sort. There was an evening dress worth five hundred dollars missing from her closet. The gown had been made specially for her daughter's wedding, a month away. Also, she noticed Bessie was gone.

She sent the police to Bessie's house. She and Mr. Jennings met them there.

Mrs. Jennings was alternately weeping and shouting. "We trusted you!" she cried. "We loved you and this is how you repay us. How can we trust any of you people again?"

Mr. Jennings was more emphatic: "Maybe this is the best lesson for you, Bessie. You have got to learn once and for all the consequences of your actions, a sense of responsibility, the difference between right and wrong. You're a beautiful and intelligent girl. What's the matter with you people? You don't think about tomorrow but just take what you want."

"But you said I could borrow the dress. You promised! I paid you!"

"Shut up, girl," the policeman said. "You just admitted your guilt. I heard you and so did everyone else." He took her by the arm and escorted her into the Black Maria.

Bessie's mother was dry eyed and just stared at her daughter and the people who accused her. She pushed the younger children away from the open doorway. Sadie, Bessie's youngest sister, strained to see her sister leave in handcuffs.

Bessie shouted from the street in the sweetest voice possible, "Don't worry, Sadie. I'm not guilty. I'll be all right. I swear I'll be home again before you can say 'jackrabbit.'"

Her mother slammed the door.

Bessie was charged with theft and grand larceny. She sat in a cell overnight awaiting trial. She had two visitors before her case was heard.

Mr. Jennings and her mother.

"You made a promise to me," Bessie told him.

"Yes, Bessie, but I can hardly tell my wife that now. She'd kill me. Be reasonable, Bessie." He was the last man she was ever going to trust.

"We have no money for a lawyer," her mother said. "You're going to have to do the time."

"Can't you try the Odd Fellows?" Bessie asked.

"I'm too ashamed. What would I tell them? 'Monarch Elias's daughter is a felon and is going to prison unless you intervene'?"

"I'm innocent!"

"No, you're not. You coveted that dress, and you stole it."

"It was Mr. Jennings who said I could borrow it."

"Well, then why didn't Mr. Jennings step forward and say so?"

"He's afraid of his wife."

"Afraid of his wife and someone's going to the penitentiary!"

"He said his wife wouldn't mind, but she did."

"But he didn't say you could go into his wife's closet and take the dress off the hook without telling anyone, did he?"

"No."

"Oh, Bessie, Bessie, what am I going to do with you? I'm glad your father isn't alive to see this."

Bessie turned her back on her mother. "Don't mention Daddy to me, Mama. I don't want to hear it. Just . . . just let me be."

Bessie lowered her head, knowing her mother had no idea why her father had been given the money for their house. She, Bessie, had paid for it, with her body. Her father had bartered his sacred right to protect his daughter and avenge her violation. Monarch had sold his daughter for a fistful of dollars. And he had been so ashamed of himself he had defied God by committing suicide.

Their family home, the trinity house, their miracle shelter, was in fact her house. Her violation had bought it. And now a similar act had put her in jail. There was no winning.

Her body, her father got paid. Her body, Mr. Jennings was free.

There must be a better way.

Although the judge agreed that Bessie had had every intention of cleaning and returning the dress, he sentenced her to three months at the Moyamensing Prison, already known for violent criminals and periodic executions.

Bessie approached the prison on Eleventh Street with tears in her eyes. Then, seeing the front door of the women's annex, she began to laugh. The escorts looked at her as if she were crazy. She had been seeing pictures of buildings like this, it seemed, half of her life. The main entrance to Moyamensing Prison looked like an Egyptian temple. Maybe she did belong there.

SIX

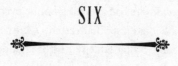

South Philadelphia,
1884

Bessie began her sentence at Moyamensing. The prison had been built in the 1830s, and now, fifty years later, it was a vast, rat- and roach-infested stone facility. The women's annex held eight hundred inmates in a building built for four hundred. Forty individual cells housed four prisoners each, and the other 640 women slept in high vaulted dormitories with no dividers. There were no indoor toilets.

Bessie was assigned to a cell with three other inmates: a prostitute, a shoplifter, and a killer, all younger than twenty. The other inmates called their padlocked cell the "nursery." Bessie spent all her time trying to keep clean, the shoplifter spent all her time reading pulp fiction and comic books, and the assassin sat staring at a blank brick wall all day. She had murdered her husband and lost her mind.

The prostitute spent her time selling sex to the guards and other inmates for food, soap, and clean clothes, earning a seemingly endless supply of dollar bills. She didn't seem affected by the jail at all. She managed their little cell like a housewife, carving out places for the girls to keep their things and suggesting games for them to pass the time.

The inmates rose at five for no special reason, and lights went out at eight. There was no recess, no exercise, no fresh air or hot showers. The prison uniform, issued clean once a month, was a rough, gray smock that reached the ankles, with a bonnet to cover every strand of hair. The prison guards made the rules as they saw fit, and the warden never visited the premises but summoned young girls to his office.

The prostitute's name was Leola; the killer's, Mary; and the thief's, Charlyne. No one used family names. Bessie found the killer quite beautiful in a fragile, luminous way, and when she asked how she had killed her husband, she replied she had poured gasoline over him while he slept and set him alight. She had also, inadvertently, burned down the house, barely escaping herself, so that larceny had been added to the charge of homicide. She had done it, she said, because he beat her and burned her with cigarettes and held her breasts and buttocks to a hot stove, but most of all, because he had killed her dog Barney by poisoning him with arsenic—a long and horrible death.

Bessie was interested in the murderer's story, but it was the prostitute, Leola, who fascinated her the most, for she was the funniest person she had ever met. Leola was a year older than Bessie. She had been in the Sisterhood, as she called prostitution, for six years.

"You're a lucky duck for getting a cell, Bessie," said the red-haired beauty. "I've seen them take the new girls straight to the dormitory. You wouldn't have survived the night."

"Why?"

Leola laughed as if everyone knew. "Rape."

Bessie's eyes went wide. *In public?*

"Remember this," Leola told her. "To the guards you say you've got syphilis or the clap. To the queens and lesbos, you say you've got The Curse. To the gangs, you say you belong to 'Dresser's gang'—they won't bother you even on the inside if you say that—and there's no way they can check. There're too many 'Dressers' and they use false names. Try to get on the good side of Guardian Swartz in cellblock C. She's the only human being in this whole penitentiary."

Delores Swartz was indeed human and compassionate. She took a liking to Bessie and kept her out of the clutches of the Cockers, a lesbian gang who ruled cellblocks A and B. She also allowed her to frequent the prison library by giving her a job cleaning books in the stacks.

"You're a smart young lady; you should try to go to high school when you get out of here. You could be lots of things: a librarian, a nurse, even a teacher. I have a friend in the Philadelphia school system who is in charge of hiring for the public library. Maybe he could get you a job as a cleaning lady, when you get out."

But Delores Swartz never got a chance to help.

One day, Bessie got into a fight with another inmate and did as the other inmates were telling her. To save herself, she bit off the other inmate's ear. Bessie was remanded to the hole, where she was doused in cold water with fire hoses every four hours for five days and then thrown into solitary confinement for another two weeks. By the time she emerged, she had no interest in prison guard promises, cleaning books, water hoses, and the law in general. She took up with the Cockers, who were impressed with her survival.

She still managed, however, to stay friends with Leola, who winked both of her big, gray eyes at Bessie and smiled on the day of Leola's release. And one of the other girls passed Bessie a note that Leola had left with the name and address of a brothel in South Philadelphia: Mrs. Truitt's.

Bessie knew Leola would return to prostitution. She had said as much many times when they shared a cell.

"If you ever need me, you can find me at Mrs. Truitt's."

"You're going back there after all this . . ."

"I have no other place to go. I have a police record. You'll see when you get out and try to find a job . . ."

And so, to Bessie's despair, Leola left her there among the madwomen, the thieves, the killers, and the abortionists.

Bessie returned home to Addison Street only to find the house barred to her.

Her mother cracked the door open to give her a lecture. "You have substituted prison for slavery," said Marion Elias, who seemed to have become grayer and older. "Don't you know that with a prison record and no references, you'll never be able to get work as a domestic again? No one will have you! What else can you do?"

"I can play the piano in church," Bessie replied. "I have a diploma from the House of Industry . . . I can be a cashier."

"Do you think anybody would let you play the piano in a church? Or work as a cashier? A jailbird!"

"Then," she announced, "I'll play the piano in a brothel."

Her mother struck her in the mouth with all the force of her six-foot frame, drawing blood. But Bessie didn't flinch or step back out of range. She simply kept her head lowered. When she heard the bang of the door, she lifted her head. For a moment, she stared at the trinity house as if memorizing it. She turned her back and walked away.

❧

To avoid the streets, Bessie went to the address given to her by Leola: Emelyn Truitt at 726 Minister Street.

Mrs. Truitt took one look at Bessie and invited her to stay. Her brothel sheltered eleven prostitutes: Ellen, Charlotte, Anastasia, Adeline, Eleanor, Susan, Rebecca, Julia, Nettie, Eliza, and Leola, all between fifteen and thirty years of age. Mrs. Truitt considered herself a teacher, not a madam. All the women called themselves "Sisters." Their profession, Bessie learned, was called "the Sisterhood." Every afternoon, Mrs. Truitt had the girls come into the parlor, where she discussed what she called "Rules of Relationships."

"Girls, what are the rules for survival?"

The older prostitutes were excited to be called on. "Never kiss or indulge in intimate gestures," one said.

"Never disclose your real name," another added. "And never discuss your personal life."

The youngest one raised her hand. "Always ask for payment in advance and never extend credit."

Mrs. Truitt reminded them, "Always set limits on perverse or 'unnatural' acts and make a signal that means Stop if he wants to continue the infliction of pain."

"Always demand a condom and cash only," Leola said.

"How do you remember all this?" Bessie whispered to her.

"Here, read this." Leola handed her a piece of cardboard that had obviously been passed around many times.

The list continued. Bessie read as Mrs. Truitt next told the girls the news of the day, so that they would have something to talk about that night.

The list read:

Do not indulge in sex for free except with your boyfriend.

Do not indulge in sex for pleasure except with your boyfriend.

Never accept invitations.

Never meet outside working hours or outside the brothel.

Listen to confessions without offering advice.

Moan at the moment of the client's climax.

Do not drink, smoke tobacco, or indulge in cocaine or opium. (Laudanum is acceptable.)

Always tell the client he is the best lover you have ever encountered.

If you tell any man in the world he is the most handsome, the most intelligent, the most virile, he will believe it.

Protect your health and your body with fresh air, exercise, and cleanliness.

Never fall in love.

Bessie slept in Leola's bed that night after her shift ended. The next day, they went out and purchased a handgun for Bessie to put under the mattress.

Within a week, Leola had taken Bessie to the doctor and to get her hair done. This had never happened to her before.

"You know what Mrs. Truitt says: 'Cleanliness is next to godliness.'" Leola cackled and Bessie smiled. Maybe that was true.

Mrs. Truitt quickly invented a specialty for her new charge that she said stirred the four senses: vision, taste, smell, and touch. Bessie would emerge from the unveiled copper bathtub in her bedroom, naked but covered from head to toe in a veil of confectioner's powdered sugar under which shimmered her skin, incandescent and comestible. She would then lie on the couch, her arms crossed, or would be trussed up, hands over her head, feet hardly touching the floor, hanging from a bar suspended from the ceiling. The client could remove the sweet, delicate film of sugar in any way he wished: lips, mouth, tongue, sponge, hands, feather duster, boa, belt, chains, razor, or with any other instrument, including his own. It caused a sensation among the clients. Mrs. Truitt's purse got fatter.

One day Leola showed Bessie Mrs. Truitt's closet of sexual accoutrements: dildos, whips, chains, handcuffs, clubs, hoods, blindfolds, masks, corsets, chastity belts. Bessie burst into laughter. Men were insane!

"Well," said Leola, "Mrs. Berkley just up the street specializes in flagellation. You ought to see her closet. She doesn't want for clients, believe me.

"She has a huge supply of birch that she keeps in water so that it is always green and flexible. She has shafts with a dozen whip thongs on each of them. She has twenty different sizes of cat-o'-nine-tails, some with needle points worked into them. She has a choice of leather straps like coach traces made of thick sole leather with two-inch nails run through, used to docket and currycomb the toughest of hides—rendered callous by years of flagellation." Bessie laughed.

"You have never seen it all—holly brushes, furze brushes, bouquets of prickly evergreen called 'butcher's bush'; and during the summer Chinese vases are filled with a constant supply of green nettles with which she can restore the dead to life." Leola was breathless.

"Whoever goes to her whorehouse with enough money in his pocket can be birched, whipped, fustigated, scourged, needle-pricked, half hung, suffocated, strangled, holly-brushed, furze-brushed, sting-nettle-massaged, currycombed, sodomized, and generally tortured until he has a cock full!

"That"—she sighed—"is Mrs. Berkley's vocation . . ."

Mrs. Truitt had precise ideas about men and how to treat them. According to her, a courtesan should always pretend to be in love with her client and behave like a wife.

A whore should learn to read a man's mind and gauge his moods so that she can mold herself perfectly to his tastes.

A hooker must estrange the client from family and relatives; she should also tell her client that before she met him, life had no meaning and the only thing she desires is to bear him a son.

If her lover catches her with another man, she should pretend to commit suicide and make sure he hears about it.

She should feign jealousy if he looks at another woman.

She should hate his enemies and praise his friends.

She should praise his good qualities even if he has none.

She should be willing to return any money or jewelry he has given her.

When a lover has no more money, he should be dumped. The best way of doing this is to make fun of him, show indifference during love-making, insult him in front of servants, or publicly humiliate him.

If somehow he manages to regain his fortune, she must then win him back by passing all her evil antics onto the shoulders of her madam, just as a king passes his evil deeds onto the shoulders of his prime minister.

These rules were Mrs. Truitt's catechism. She had her principles, and they were carved in stone. No mother superior could have been more vigilant of her inmates. She supplied shelter, food, clothes, jewelry, doctor's care, and protection. The girls supplied fresh and beautiful flesh. When Mrs. Truitt considered a girl too old (around thirty), she usually married her off. She was very successful as a matchmaker. The girl's past was totally erased, and she entered the gentry a virgin.

Mrs. Truitt was also very good at creating virgins. She had done so in Bessie's case several times and sold the sequence to the highest bidder. She was a specialist in fetishes and had closets full of women's steel and whalebone corsets, garrets, silk stockings, garters, shoes, boots, bloomers, gloves, stomachers, petticoats, peacock and ostrich feather drawers, hats, fans, handkerchiefs, leggings, masks, wigs; as well as powders, paints, and cosmetics of all kinds, which served both the transvestites and perverts.

The madam herself was a tall, plain-looking, and plain-speaking woman with a beautiful voice resembling a chic saleswoman in a haughty dress shop. Her warm peach complexion was topped with a magnificent head of thick auburn waves. She was a stickler for manicures and pedicures. Hands and feet, she insisted, were everything for a courtesan. She considered herself an artist. She sold perfection as well as happiness.

A young, ambitious man born into poverty, Mrs. Truitt lectured, perhaps an immigrant or the son of an immigrant with dreams of wealth and power, had a number of choices if he was hardworking. He could find a job, practice thrift, save his money, buy a store, make it a success, buy another, and borrow money to buy one even larger. Or, since acquiring the means to buy just one store could take decades, he could become a burglar, a footpad, a shoulder-hitter, a gambling house shift, a numbers runner, a swindler of immigrants, a poisoner of horses, a mayhem specialist for hire, a strikebreaker, a river pirate, a crimp, or a killer. Then with enough skill, luck, and drive, he might come to lead his own gang, rob a bank, or extort money, and from there, if he didn't get himself killed, launch himself into politics or real estate speculation or the business end of the entertainment industry, able to play the stock market and use Wall Street to earn his fortune. Or he could marry the boss's daughter.

But a poor young woman in the same situation had only one route open to her: sex. If she started as self-employed, opportunities were plentiful for a comely young woman in her teens or twenties. There were men on the street or on the trolley or at the amusement park who could spare a dollar or two. Perhaps a girl could get away with doing it for money every now and again and not think of herself as a whore but merely an occasional flirt. But any girl alone and out after dark was fair game. Too often, however, there were grave hazards.

And to Mrs. Truitt's credit, she spelled out the dangers to everyone during her class sessions: A girl could contract a venereal disease from a man who got around, or a pregnancy. Syphilis or gonorrhea could make her a walking dead woman. No one in conventional society would even look her way. She could never marry. She could be blacklisted from any job she tried to get, or pimps would use her up. The fresh quality that had made her attractive to men would spoil, and she would be forced to enter a brothel—not as nice as hers, Mrs. Truitt added—but somewhere where her earnings would be taken by a madam who would pay her a meager allowance and control her movements as if she were in a nunnery.

And if she was ever turned out into the streets, a girl would be worth less than nothing. Criminals would rob her, beat her, and demand favors for free. Cops would arrest her. Rapists would poison her until she went to the narcotics wishing she were dead. Before then, she'd be hooked on

opium and morphine, and probably get tuberculosis and be malnour-
ished. This was the path—going from district to district—downward,
ever downward from the choice corners to the side streets; from the side
streets to the slaughterhouse district and from there to the Schuylkill
waterfront and the wharf, which was the end of life. Mrs. Truitt's advice
to all her boarders was to save their little money, stay as clean as possible,
and leave the Sisterhood before they turned thirty.

Bessie took the rules and lectures to heart, writing them down in a
little blue notebook like a good student along with comments, which
were more appropriate to a novice in a convent than a courtesan.

She seemed enhanced, enchanted, and empowered. And, given
Mrs. Truitt's daily lessons, Bessie became good at her job. Very soon
Mrs. Truitt's best customers took to asking for her by name. She began to
receive offers to be kept by rich men. Mrs. Truitt fended them off as best
she could, because she didn't want to lose Bessie's services yet. She was a
good investment.

Plus, Bessie wasn't interested in being kept. She had more freedom in
Mrs. Truitt's house than ever before in her life.

Often in the early hours of the morning, she and Leola would crawl
into bed together and fall asleep in each other's arms. Leola was the only
person Bessie told her true story to. "I have a twin, David," she told
her. "I was jealous of him for having a penis when I didn't have one—
otherwise we were exactly alike. So why did he have this thing in front
and not me? It was so strange to see myself as him in the mirror in everything except this, but even stranger to see what a big difference a dick
made. He was male. I was not."

Leola held Bessie tight and said with a straight face, "The dick is
overrated." The young women laughed until they fell asleep.

Bessie treated the other young women the way Leola treated her,
and they began to come to Bessie with their problems. At these times,
she found the Cleopatra that she knew to be inside herself. She would
sit tall in her chair and sometimes even adorn herself with a sparkly robe
that she bought—not for her clients—just to feel good. Then she would
answer the younger girls as if she were a high priestess. Bessie closed her
eyes and crossed her arms over the top of her chest and whispered with

the same mysterious smile she had once seen on the face of an Egyptian statue illustrated in one of her library books. The girls asked her advice for everything from accepting the offer of a benefactor to a new hairstyle. Her pronouncements always had a majestic ring to them, as if she'd received messages from the beyond. An aura of Egyptian hairstyles and clothing entered the whorehouse. Mrs. Truitt's fortunes soared.

What surprised Bessie the most though was how ordinary Mrs. Truitt's boarders were except for Leola. There was not a Salome or Sheba or Jezebel among them. They were mostly small-town, country, or slum girls like herself. They were poor, not only in money but in thoughts. Few of them had ever sat alone to read a book. The absolute poverty of their dreams matched the deficiency of their persons. They were paupers in imagination, courage, and self-love. Where, she wondered, were the infamous, fascinating members of the Sisterhood? Where were the shameless hussies of eternal damnation? Why was everyone so afraid?

Young as Bessie was, she burned with ambition, becoming the wisecracking, cigarette-smoking, bawdy goddess of Minister Street, the prophetess who was afraid of nothing. Every incident became an omen, every omen Bessie filled with her own imagination. She was rewarded with adoration. Even Mrs. Truitt liked her style. Everybody wanted to sit at the table when she ate.

Bessie lectured them in the morning before breakfast as Mrs. Truitt did in the afternoons. She told them that they had lives beyond the sale of their bodies. She wasn't sure that she believed it herself. But she had heard sermons like that in church. They all had, and they were grateful for the pep talks, especially after their families had thrown them out.

"You are valuable as well as beautiful," Bessie said to the plain faces around her, especially weary as the paint smeared the eyes and mouths. "Life," she explained, "is more than a bordello and the dicks." Sometimes when she spoke, she would get flashes of the girls she saw when she entered Saratoga, hopeful and full of aspirations. But when the young women around her table asked what they should do with their lives to make them better than they were now, Bessie just smiled, her mysterious smile, her Sphinx smile. She really didn't know herself.

"Bessie, you are one smart son of a bitch," said Mrs. Truitt one day.

"You remind me of myself at your age. Stick with me and I'll show you how it's done. There are all kinds of prostitution in this world, not just our kind. Prostitutes run the universe . . ."

Bessie seemed to be in her element, swimming easily in this current of female closeness. She never asked for favors in return for her advice, but the other women took to bringing her little gifts and offerings as if she were really able to ask God's intervention into the affairs of their little community of sinners. Even Mrs. Truitt sometimes came to her for advice.

Sometimes Bessie sang or played the bordello piano, making up rags, and sometimes she would dance, making up steps. But, people would say, there was always something otherworldly about these performances, as if Bessie were indeed connected to the ages or the long-ago past.

Bessie's style was to make men wait for her like Cleopatra did to Marc Antony. She sat them in her empty room while she got ready down the hall. The bathtub steamed, and so did her clients. There were two kinds, Bessie had learned: those who waited quietly fully dressed, and those who took off their clothes immediately. Those who had already undressed could be serviced without trouble. They came quickly and they went quickly. Those she had to undress were more complicated. Sometimes all they wanted was a sympathetic ear or an ample bosom. Then there were those with long stories to tell or perverted or strange desires. Bessie felt sorry for them all, but her expression revealed none of her thoughts, animated only by her best smile as she advanced toward them. Men would sigh as they gazed into her black eyes and laid their head on her bosom.

SEVEN

Philadelphia,
March 1885

Bessie had been at Mrs. Truitt's for several months when she became one of her own predictions. Her twin brother, David, rescued her. He and her old beau, Frank Satterfield, the boy who had escorted Bessie to Hattie's wedding, found her after searching all over the city. They appealed to Monarch's Odd Fellows association for help, and seven armed men had quietly entered the bordello one day in December, badly frightening Mrs. Truitt and her pimps, but even more so the afternoon clients, who fled half-dressed, their clothes slung over their arms. The vigilantes threatened to have Mrs. Truitt arrested for kidnapping a minor, and although she had several judges and the whole police force in her pay, she decided all things considered to release Bessie without a fight. Nine furious Odd Fellows with their sawed-off shotguns standing in her front parlor were an impressive persuasion.

Mrs. Truitt had, after all, already made a great deal of money off Bessie. She had sold her virginity for a fortune—four times. She had, she protested to the vigilantes, been like a mother to Bessie, affectionate and protective. Bessie was free to leave if she chose. Leola as well. But Leola decided to stay.

Bessie refused to leave Leola behind, but David and Frank finally compelled her. As Frank Satterfield had been her securer and her brother's friend, she accepted his offer of protection.

The same month, Frank and Bessie took lodging in a courtyard off

Tenth Street between Vine and Callowhill Streets. There they half-starved on his meager salary as a stevedore in a dark, cold-water shed. Without any references and with a police record, Bessie could not find domestic work. One day, she surprised the landlady rifling through the small wooden chest that contained their few belongings. Bessie called the police and had the woman arrested. But she paid off the judge and got a suspended sentence, walking out of court a free woman. This was Bessie's second lesson in justice and her first in corruption.

Now Bessie hardly left the house for fear of encountering the woman again.

Bessie knew almost immediately when she became pregnant. She had seen it happen in the bordello. Like the women there, she felt sick in the morning and listless during the day. When she was awake, though, she was extremely happy. She began cleaning the house more and arranging their small room to make it cozy. She didn't tell Frank anything.

One day, he came home, and she said, "I have good news."

Frank looked at her as if good news was never possible.

"I'm going to have a baby," she announced.

He answered quickly, "For who?"

She was shocked. "The baby is ours, Frank. You and me," she said.

"I don't know," he mumbled, then he picked up his hat and left. She didn't see him until later that night. "It's good news," he said, then added, "right?"

"Yes, Sugar, of course it is."

Frank behaved the same way throughout her pregnancy. One day he was happy the baby was coming, the next day he was out of sorts.

Bessie herself felt a range of emotions, not the least of them being that she had no one to depend on. Thankfully, Leola stopped by occasionally to bring her some food or to make her laugh.

One night, Bessie tried to find out from Frank the reason that he was so unsure about being a father.

"Well, maybe it's just not mine," he said.

"We've been together for the whole time," Bessie answered.

"We're not married though," he said. Then he picked up his hat and coat and he left again.

Bessie waited up all night. She was weak when the sun rose. Frank hadn't returned. He never came back.

She was too ashamed to tell Leola that she hadn't been woman enough to keep Frank, or to return to Mrs. Truitt's after leaving there in a blaze of glory. Bessie certainly could not run home to her brother, who might side with his friend. Men always did.

But she couldn't pay the rent and she didn't trust her landlady at all. So Bessie applied as destitute to the Blockley Almshouse.

Blockley was not only a poorhouse, but also a public hospital, an orphanage, and an asylum for the insane. Like an English castle, it sprawled on lowlands that sloped down to the Schuylkill River, across the Market Street Bridge in West Philadelphia but in an area that had few residences. The land was uninhabited.

The nearby waterways and marshy meadows, teeming with malaria-infected mosquitos, were also ideal hideouts for shadowy characters and criminals who traversed the river in skiffs after thieving or smuggling jobs in what was known affectionately as "Philly." The widest waterway was Beaver Creek, which flowed through the almshouse grounds and emptied into the estuary. The banks of the river were intentionally flooded in winter, so that ice could be cut for the hospital's use, which the director described as being "richly endowed with bacteria." There were four three-story buildings, which housed three thousand inmates, of whom two hundred were orphans and three times that many were insane. Behind the compound was a potter's field, where many of Blockley's hapless occupants were eventually laid to rest.

The poorhouse was worse than prison, Bessie discovered. If it was terrible to be a criminal, it was even worse to be a pauper—and to choose between the two meant that a poor person was a born criminal even if he never committed a crime. In dormitories of thirty to forty people in rags were added vermin and cockroaches, like those she had fought off at Moyamensing Prison. Instead of uniforms, the indigent were left in their own rags.

The walls were damp, and mildew sprouted everywhere: climbing the walls, into one's clothes, the bedsheets, the bread and crackers they served with the soup. Well people and sick people lay side by side, and many suffered from malaria, which attacked in the summers when the mosquitoes rose like a gossamer curtain over the pond and the river. The inmates died the following winter, weakened by the racking fevers.

Bessie was terrified that she or the baby would die there and be buried in the potter's field. Some inmates, feeling sorry for her, gave her bits of their lunches and sips of condensed milk. Bessie promised herself that if the baby was born alive, she would escape this holding pen as soon as she could walk across the river. Bessie had been poor all her life, but until now she had never felt less than human, even in prison. Punishment, humiliation, cruelty—all crept into her consciousness like winter invading the bones through the seeping walls, dirt floors, and black, leaking ceilings. She was relieved when the sole doctor got her into the hospital ward early so that she would have extra nutrition, more heat, and a clean bed, and there her first child was born. She named her Clara.

Bessie's release day came with no fanfare and no visitors, even though the Addison Street house was a half-hour walk away. She hadn't told her family about Frank or the baby, but the Colored Colony was small. She assumed they'd heard and sided with him: Clara was the child of a stranger.

Monarch had often used the expression "The horse is out of the barn" to refer to girls in the neighborhood who had grown up too fast. At the time, she, her mother, and the other children had laughed.

The others now, like Bessie's sister with her reputable husband, were well on their way to middle-class respectability. Bessie knew she was the family shame, the escaped horse, running wild and never to be tamed.

Maybe she could save Clara. She didn't want to condemn her offspring to a life of misery.

Bessie strapped Clara to her chest under her coat with a wrap made from a scarf, and she began to walk across Philadelphia in the cold. A snowstorm loomed as she headed to the Market Street Bridge.

It was the morning of Christmas Eve 1885, when Bessie stepped through the gate onto Derby Road carrying two-month-old Clara in a sling on her chest. Bessie told herself Clara would not spend the holiday in the asylum. She walked along the Schuylkill River. Its water was mottled with ice. A fifteen-minute walk and she was on the bridge, looking down.

She was shivering in the coat she had brought to the almshouse, and, as she had worn it the whole time she was inside, it was ragged and dirty. The baby was warm, and Bessie wondered how, if she jumped from the bridge, they would die first—from the cold or from drowning? If she stood looking long enough at the water, the air would freeze the both of them even before she made the leap. She hadn't planned to jump or throw her child. But the snow began to whip against them, and the rest of her life before her seemed dismal and endless.

The ice floes moved swiftly under the bridge. The snow crusted on Bessie's face and eyes. She moved toward the railing and stared down. She felt the ground shaking under her. The bridge itself trembled. Then she heard the sound of the railroad crossing from one side of Philadelphia to the other. She thought of her first ride on the train, the ladies of Saratoga, the Pullman porters and the Black cooks who probably inhabited warm houses with well-fed children. Clara could have that. She stepped out of her frozen dream, left the rail of the bridge, and rushed to the safe riverbank before the train even arrived.

She would stick to the plan she'd made when she was sane in the insane asylum. That plan would protect her baby the best.

A rumor in the hospital was that a respectable colored couple had lost a child and one of the orderlies had helped with the burial. The husband was an elevator operator and the wife remained at home in a tidy little house on Wood Street.

Bessie had gotten the information from the orderly with just a little conversation. He was so accustomed to the screams and moans of the insane that an overture from a pretty, young mother was a relief. He was happy to describe the house and the beautiful nursery that the couple had decorated.

He had given her enough of a description that when Bessie walked about fifteen minutes more, she arrived at the street and recognized the house immediately.

The snow was heavy now. She knocked on the door loudly, then again. While she waited, she unwrapped Clara from her chest. She held the baby in her arms.

"Mr. Hudson?" she asked the man who came to the door.

"Yes," he replied.

She kissed Clara quickly on the forehead and thrust the baby at him.

"My name is Bessie Elias," she blurted. "Please take her. I heard that your little baby died recently, and I have one I can't support. I thought you might take her and bring her up to work for you. She needs a good home and I can't provide that. I can't provide anything. She will starve with me. I've just gotten out of Blockley." Her voice was so low now he could hardly hear over the howling wind. She whispered, "I promise never to return for her. You are safe to consider her your own child. Her name is Clara."

Before the astounded man could protest, Bessie turned away in shame and left, leaving the baby in his arms, wrapped in sackcloth. She disappeared into a night of light crystals and drifting snow.

From this moment, she vowed, Clara was dead to her, as dead as if she had thrown her into the river and jumped in after her. But now, separately, they both had a new life.

Freezing and dazed now, Bessie tried going home to Addison Street one last time.

"They let you out today?" said Sadie, Bessie's younger sister by several years, as she peeked out of the half-cracked door of the trinity house.

"Yes. Aren't you going to let me in?"

"Can't. Mama says you're not to set foot in this house."

This was my house, Bessie thought. *My body paid for it.*

Sadie's voice was shaking. Bessie had always been good to her. They had slept in the same bed not two years ago before Bessie got in trouble. Bessie prepared Sadie's clothes, helped her cipher her lessons, and showed her the way to style her hair.

There was also the matter of their resemblance. Both petite and full figured, they had the same sand-colored skin and big, dark eyes. Sadie loved Bessie more than anyone else in the family, including their mother.

Sadie opened the door wide and remembered the way Bessie had looked in that pale green dress of gossamer the day of their older sister's wedding. No one in the family would forget it—for different reasons.

Bessie started to ask Sadie to hide her somewhere in the house. Then she laughed. Where?

"I can hide you," Sadie insisted.

"This house is too small," Bessie said. "A trinity house is really too tiny to save anybody or anything. Who's home?"

"Only me tonight. Everybody else's working at some hotel or another."

"Well, since Mama's turned her back, I suppose everyone else must too—the whole family."

"I suppose . . ."

"Suppose? You know it's true! You're just too scared to tell me."

"Mama's disowned you. She forbids the mention of your name in her house or in her presence."

"And I suppose that includes David and Sam and Abigail."

"Yes. They say you beget misfortune—that you are unlucky and it rubs off on everyone. They call you little miss jailbird."

"Do they? What about you?"

"Not me!" replied Sadie stoutly. "Except we're not supposed to even pronounce your name."

Bessie could survive the physical pain of the almshouse, but her heart could hardly beat hearing Sadie's words. Bessie was nothing to her family now. For a moment she wished she hadn't been born in the same way she imagined they did. Bessie stood at the door, her mouth open with no words for her emotion. She imprinted the line of Sadie's smile and identical body to memory. It wasn't hard to remember—at least there she saw a reflection of kindness. For a moment, she felt Sadie's love, at least. Sadie's eyes were wide with her concern and admiration. Her compassion was perhaps the last love she would ever appreciate.

Sadie insisted, "No, no! Come in, it's snowing! It's Christmas. Ma's working. She's not here."

"I'm working too," Bessie said. "I've got to go."

"You look terrible."

"I've been in the poorhouse, honey. It's a place you never want to be." Bessie said nothing about Clara. If she did, she might fall into sobs. As sure as she had been when she made the plan to give the baby away, now she was as confused as when she was on the bridge. She had only one way forward now if she didn't want to return to her horrible sadness—to be brave. She told Sadie, "No. I swear I'll never set foot in the poorhouse again."

Bessie added, "I'll come back for you, Sadie, I swear. I will rescue you from this . . . trinity house and from Addison Street and maybe from Philadelphia. But you have to be ready."

"I'll be ready," whispered Sadie, her voice full of conviction.

EIGHT

Philadelphia,
Christmas 1885

Bessie returned to Mrs. Truitt's on Christmas Eve. Leola screamed with joy when she saw her.

"Girl! Where have you been? It's been donkey years!"

"The poorhouse."

"What! What about Frank? And David?"

"Lost," Bessie murmured. "Dead to me. Like my poor sweet baby."

"Dead?" whispered Leola. "You lost a baby?"

"I really don't want to talk about it."

Leola remained silent—as was part of the code in Mrs. Truitt's house.

Bessie went to work that very night on the corner of Vine and Broad Streets in borrowed clothes and a bearskin coat. She was not the only streetwalker working on Christmas Eve. There was plenty of loose money on the holidays.

For the next week, men came tumbling into the house.

Bessie worked like this until the spring, losing herself and letting her mind go flat.

The Thirty-Fifth District in Philadelphia stretched from Broad and Vine to Callowhill Street and was patrolled by several Scots-Irish plain-clothesmen as well as two officers in uniform: Michael Kelly and Rufus Doty, who were not only partners but partners in crime. They demanded kickbacks from all the streetwalkers in their district. As Bessie became known, they put her on their blackmail list.

"You're doing all right for yourself, Bessie," said Doty. "We've put your name down for a kickback of thirty dollars a night or half of what you make," he added.

Bessie narrowed her brow, and before she could voice her disagreement the second policeman moved closer to her. "You've got a police record . . . One more arrest and you will be back to your loser self in Moyamensing."

"Take it or leave it," said Kelly. "We don't give a damn; but this is our precinct . . . You work here and you take your orders from us. Clear?"

"And free tricks as well," added Doty, and left Bessie silent but furious.

Bessie received another lesson in police corruption and blackmail.

She went to Leola's door and knocked. Her friend peeked through the door with a face smeared with dark eye makeup and lipstick that bled to her cheeks.

With a flustered look Bessie told Leola, "I've got to get out of here. I'm being extorted."

"What?"

"Officers Kelly and Doty backed by the mob. They want half . . . if I refuse, it's the mob—a beating once and then disfigurement. I won't do it. I'd rather die. I have to escape Philadelphia . . ."

"What about New York?" said Leola.

Two weeks later, Leola and Bessie, unaccompanied, drew stares as they entered the new Broad Street Station and gawked at steel beams of the building's interior. They wandered the walkways in feathered hats and clothes that were too tight and flouncy for a serious trip. Men throughout the building asked if they needed assistance.

"Everybody is so nice here," Leola observed, before they found the right location to board.

"It's how they treat you when you got money," Bessie explained. She overtipped the porter who brought them to their seat, as well as the waiter who personally served them. The good treatment they received was a result of Bessie's generosity, but also the engineer, who feared that the women would wander through the cars soliciting customers. If the staff attended to the women, there was no reason for them to get out of their seat.

The train left the station with smoke, noise, jolts. It chugged through Philadelphia, which the women already saw as a distant memory. The train crossed the Schuylkill River, where Bessie had almost committed suicide.

They traveled for hours over meadows and marshland, occasionally seeing a barn or a small hamlet from the window. Leola would sigh: "Green as me mum's home in Derry."

Bessie said, "You went there?"

"Everyone told me."

After a while, the women slept, leaning against one another, waking only when the train arrived in Pennsylvania Station in New York. The porter brought their overnight bags and set them in the underground walkway.

"My goodness," Leola said.

Gigantic columns held massive archways. The ceiling above them was open and enormous. Even the lamps lighting the corridor were as tall as three men standing on one another's shoulders.

"This is grand," Bessie said. She felt smaller and less important than she ever had been, and in a way, freer. She understood what one of her regular clients who frequented Philadelphia, because of her, had told her. She could become someone else here. After all, who would come looking for her?

Bessie threaded her arm through Leola's, as they marched through the terminal's glass-roofed arcade, along with the footfalls of hundreds of others, emboldened by their place in the vast, modern crucible of humanity.

Standing in the sun outside, near the giant Corinthian columns of the building, the women stared at the address Bessie's John had given them. They hailed a carriage and handed the driver the piece of paper.

"Are you sure you want to go there, ladies?" he asked.

Bessie, now full of confidence, said, "Of course."

"Satan's Circus it is," he said.

They didn't know quite what he meant. And they were giggling and ogling at all the sights in the city as they made their way to the address in the open carriage. The buildings were cramped together, and each one seemed to hold a new excitement. As they crossed Seventh Avenue, Bessie noticed a number of elegant people of color. The carriage driver saw her staring and called out, "You are crossing African Broadway."

"Look, Leola," Bessie said.

Bessie stared at the neat dresses with shawls and spring coats the women wore. She noticed the way their men walked with them on their arms. She could actually make a new life here, she thought, maybe even with a husband.

When they turned the next corner, piano music lifted from the windows of all the buildings. People sang loudly, sometimes almost like a shout, trying to bring business to the sheet music sellers.

As the carriage slowed to a stop, however, waiting for its turn to cross the avenue, Bessie heard one man standing in a window singing sweetly:

> "She lives in a mansion of aching hearts,
> She's one of a restless throng,
> The diamonds that glitter around her throat,
> They speak both of sorrow and song;
> The smile on her face is only a mask,
> And many the tear that starts,
> For sadder it seems, when of mother she dreams,
> In the mansion of aching hearts."

"Isn't that beautiful, Leola? I think New York is a magical place." The carriage jerked and they proceeded a few blocks more across town.

"Ladies, this is your address," the carriage driver said, taking their small bags to the sidewalk.

The building was narrow like all the rest, with steps that led to the second floor and other steps leading to an entrance a few feet below the sidewalk.

Leola looked around at the buildings all closed tight during the day and a few policemen lingering on the corners.

Bessie climbed the steps as Leola waited at the bottom. She wasn't eager to go into new places. New York itself was enough. For as much as Bessie thought its sounds were musical, Leola thought it was loud. For Bessie, it was exciting. To Leola, it was dirty. She could find the same in Philadelphia, and she didn't need to look far.

Bessie knocked loudly several times, and finally a heavyset woman in a housedress and a scarf came to the door.

"What you want in the middle of the day?" she asked.

Bessie gave the name of her customer: "Is this the house of John Fooler?"

"Ha!" The woman laughed and slapped her leg. "They is all Johns, ain't they?"

Leola caught her breath.

"Honey, you at Madame Paree's place. Come back tonight, they'll be Johns aplenty and dancing too. Standing up and laying down." She laughed again at her own joke.

Bessie realized the man had given her the name of a city brothel.

When the housekeeper saw that the women were obviously from out of town, and young, she told them that the action took place at night. They should return and meet the madam of the house. In the meantime, they should look at the "better" parts of New York.

She asked, "You ever seen Central Park? Get you a carriage and go uptown. See something different. Leave your bags here."

Leola said no immediately. She said aloud, "We don't mind carrying them."

Bessie smiled and said, "OK. We'll be back."

She hailed another carriage and told the driver that they wanted to drive to Central Park.

Bessie had never seen so many rich and happy people. Elegant women rode in expensive carriages and C-spring barouches. Alongside her and Leola trotted thoroughbred saddle horses. In one section of the park was a pond with sailing boats and children running with hoops. Bessie marveled at Central Park's hills and dales, its rocky promontories. Its lake and open places and beautiful woods made it in every way delightful to her.

This carriage driver, like the last, wanted to brag about the city as the women stared in wonderment.

"This park was laid out by a man named Andrew H. Green," he said. "He was the head of the park commission. It is pretty great, isn't it?"

Bessie nodded. Leola was suspicious.

"This is a park for the people, the ones that want to be nice." He explained that before the park existed, this was one of the filthiest and most dangerous spots in the city. "Miserable Black and Indian shanties. Children playing in stagnant water. Must have been three hundred people. All cleared out for the park."

Bessie fell in love with this park. It was so much like her life—where there had been barren rocks, unsightly swamp, and pitiful poverty, there were now velvet lawns, flower beds, and statuary. She was inspired. She actually felt empowered.

The carriage turned onto the Mall. Colorful foliage spread out on both sides of the driveway. Reds and oranges mixed with evergreen, burnt sienna, and the batteries of planted flower beds that stood on the still green lawn or climbed up artificial rock formations.

"Isn't it wonderful?" the carriage driver called out. "I don't care how long they were living here—those niggers and Indians needed to take their slum living somewhere else and let civilized people make something beautiful."

Leola looked at Bessie, who didn't flinch. If that's what it took to improve her life, she'd change that part of her life as well.

———

When Bessie and Leola returned to the Tenderloin bordello, the street was alive with people. Elegant men and women in formal clothing pulled up in carriages. Streetwalkers boldly rubbed themselves against men along the side of the building while the police stood at the corner. Somewhere Leola thought she heard gunshots.

Leola turned toward a building that said "boardinghouse" and found that she could rent a room for the evening.

"With or without gentlemen callers?" the clerk asked.

"Without," Leola replied.

Bessie turned to look across the street. "I think she's expecting us."

"Don't fool yourself," Leola answered. Still, she could see that Bessie was enamored with the music, the lights, and the facade of beauty that was so carefully arranged.

She was already out of the door before Leola could say "Goodnight." She didn't return until morning.

"I just had to dance. I didn't have to do anything I didn't want to," she said. "I'm not going back to Philadelphia."

Leola had already anticipated that decision. The next morning, she went back to Mrs. Truitt.

Bessie became one of Madame Paree's girls by night, and by day, she wandered the streets of New York. She investigated the fabric shops and dreamed of the beautiful dresses that she could get sewn just for her. She walked up and down Twenty-Eighth Street listening to the music coming from the windows. Occasionally one of the salesmen would let her sit at the piano and play a song. She fancied herself progressing toward her ambitions of marrying a nice colored man like the ones she had seen on Seventh Avenue or becoming a singer in one of the clubs or a dancer or spending time reading books from the New York Public Library.

But Madame Paree, while paying her top dollar, charged just as much for her accommodations and her food. Bessie hardly had anything for herself. She also found that if she put her money in her drawer every day, a few dollars would disappear. So she began to keep her money on her body in a money belt attached to the top of her cotton stocking or hidden inside her corset. Still, all the things that made living in New York so good were expensive and out of her reach.

She had promised Sadie and herself that she would never return to the poorhouse. But it looked as if that were where she was headed. Her sister didn't need to know. Bessie wrote to her:

> *Dear Sadie,*
>
> *You're probably wondering why I haven't been in touch since moving to New York with Frank. But I have been so busy with my job as a ticket cashier in Grand Central Depot which takes all my time and energy. I have strange hours and sometimes spend all night at work. So I am forced to be very careful about traveling or visiting anybody because the Pinkerton railroad detectives keep close watch on all employees entrusted with receipts or money as I am here in my little cashier's cell.*
>
> *Pa is no longer with you, but you have Ma, Emma and Hattie, Maggie and Sam, Abigail, David and Lizzie, Mary, and Katie I love them all, even as I write their names so as not to forget them. I cannot believe I will never see you again. I will not believe that. But you all must forgive me and forget me. I want to better my condition. I must. You may ask, Sadie, why this is so important to me. I can only say that one day I intend to have my own house, which will be my refuge and my safety from the world, which is a damnable place, Sadie. I want to better my condition in life.*
>
> *Your loving sister,*
> *Bessie*

The letter, which was addressed to Marion Elias, came back to Madame Paree's address unopened. There was a large, black-edged post-office stamp on it, which read, DECEASED. RETURN TO SENDER.

One day, Bessie was walking down Fifth Avenue to Fourteenth Street. She found herself staring at an elaborate emporium of carved marble and colored glass with a large sign above the entrance: DRUGS AND AERATED WATERS. It was a beautiful sight.

Inside was a soda fountain, a spectacular machine that spewed carbonated water out of gleaming brass spigots. The one Bessie stood in front of was at least ten feet tall. Her mouth fell open in astonishment. The apparatus stood like an altarpiece of a church, made of Italian marble, brass, and zinc.

Bessie had seen a soda fountain like this one with her father at the Centennial Exhibition in 1876. These cathedrals to soda water were manufactured in Philadelphia by Charles Lippincott and Company. Some of them were so famous, they had names like people. This one was called the Minnehaha and was trimmed in green-veined white marble with pillars of burnished zinc pipes that resembled a church organ, placed in a fluted basin held up by bronze dolphins. Atop a stone arch stood a glass vase capped with a silver crown, enclosing a marble statue of a nude woman. The four corners of the roof held handsome brass urns on pedestals, and in a polished niche a bronze draped figure—Cleopatra—reclined, holding a lion's head from which spouted the carbonated water. It flowed into a wide zinc basin under which hung a brass plate with the words "Cold refreshing soda water flavored with pure fruit syrup."

Then she saw an even more astonishing sight: the father of Clara. The bile rose in her throat. She had heard that Frank had left Philadelphia when he left her.

Now she didn't know how she felt when she saw Frank. It certainly wasn't love or reminiscence. She felt sick. Her stomach started to knead itself, and her head spun.

He had walked out on her in her time of need. And what she had suffered as a result! The almshouse insane asylum. The pregnancy alone. A near suicide. Her baby given away. Being turned out from her own house. He was the cause of it.

Yet there he stood near the soda machine. In a neat white shirt, clean hands, and a shaved part in his hair. Looked like he ran a hot comb through his moustache to make it smooth and turned up on the ends.

He looked so neat and calm while she was forever at wit's end, trying to figure out the way to get from one day to another, to change herself, to forgive herself. He had abandoned her without a second thought. She had been left to fend for herself. The litany of wrongs ran from her head to the tip of her fingers. Her small hands knotted into fists.

The white jockey who took her childhood from her. The "head" of the Jennings family, who lied to his wife and sent her to jail. Even Monarch spilling his brains where she would be sure to see them. Blockley and Moyamensing Prison. Clara gone forever. All melded into a zigzag bolt of lightning, which struck her from the top of her head to the soles of her feet. Bessie lost all sense of time, space, and her own physical body. She lost her sense of sight and smell.

She rushed toward Frank to tell him all of it but instead made a lurch at his head, punched him in a fury, then chased him, overturning tables and smashing crockery, and pummeling his back when she caught up to him. She screamed curses at him that she had learned in prison. The air shriveled. Patrons dispersed to the street. Bessie didn't know if it was day or night, New York or the Seventh Ward.

She felt as light as a hummingbird as she flew around the fountain, released from all sense of gravity, freer every moment with this outburst of hurt and humiliation. Freed from these horrible men of her past with her screams. She slipped and Frank was on top of her, holding her down on the cold marble floor. Her screams and punches were ineffective. She felt tired now and, strangely, a little happy.

She went to sleep, actually blacked out with a smile on her face. When she came to, she was laying on the floor in the back of a Black Maria between two Irish policemen facing Frank.

The drugstore owner had called the police and had both her and Frank arrested. Frank swore out a complaint against Bessie for disorderly conduct. The police van took them both to the Jefferson Market police court, where Bessie explained that Frank Satterfield was the father of her dead child and that he had deserted her.

"Sure," one of the cops said.

But Frank went free while Bessie remained in jail. When the case was recalled three days later, Frank submitted an affidavit:

CITY OF PHILADELPHIA

Personally appeared before me, Israel W. Dunham, Magistrate of Court No. 6 of the said city, Arthur Gale, who, being duly sworn according to law doth depose and say that: he has known Bessie Elias for ten years past and known her to be a common woman, and that he has met her in the house of ill repute of Mrs. Evelyn Truitt, No. 726 Minister Street.

Sworn and subscribed to before me on the 17th day of September 1887, Israel W. Dunham, office No. 12 South Sixth Street.

After examining the affidavit, the magistrate turned to Bessie with one question: "Are you Bessie Elias, of the affidavit?"

"Yes, no, I'm not that Bessie Elias. I'm not Bessie Elias."

"Can you show proof that you are not Bessie? Proof that you are not a hooker?"

"No, sir."

"I sentence you to one hundred twenty days on Blackwell's Island for disorderly and lewd conduct and for disturbing the peace. And fine you twenty-five dollars."

It was all the money she had. Bessie was sent to New York's Women's Penitentiary. Bessie didn't know the Arthur Gale who had signed the affidavit, and Arthur Gale didn't know her. He was a Pullman porter, running out of Philadelphia on the Philadelphia and Reading Railroad. Perhaps he owed Frank a favor and had paid it with the false affidavit that denounced her as a prostitute and freed Frank as her common-law husband.

This was Bessie's third time in an institution. They were getting worse.

Blackwell's Island housed not only a women's prison but a madhouse, a smallpox hospital, the chapel of the Good Shepherd, and, on its northern end, a lighthouse. Barren and windswept, it rose out of the East River of New York. The gray gneiss stone fortress perched on a narrow strip of land two miles long, in the middle of the river. It had been built to hold three hundred prisoners, but a thousand human creatures swarmed like maggots within its walls. Among the prison's various and famous tortures were "cooler cells," where dousing by means of 120-pound-pressure fire hoses had earned it its underground nickname, "the Cooler." The warden was a cousin of the mayor and a believer in the death sentence, corporal punishment, and mental and physical torture. Many of the prisoners went from the almshouse to the prison to the madhouse without ever leaving the island.

This time there was no Leola, and Bessie had to fend for herself. She sat on her haunches in a cellblock filled with two hundred ranting, raving, profaning harlots of all ages, her hands over her ears to smother out the sound of screams, imprecations, and filthy language and to convince herself she was not one of them. The women climbed the walls, tore at their clothes, and fought among themselves. There were many nights that Bessie thought she too would end up in the asylum at the northernmost point of the island. When she complained, she was branded a troublemaker and shut up in solitary confinement with no heat or light, or toilet, only bread and water once a day.

She had no tears left. Her sentence had been augmented by two months when she was sent to the cooler for having gotten into a fight with another inmate. She moaned softly as she sought a way out of the vision she had of herself. A jailbird. A disgrace to her family. All she wanted was to begin again. That's the reason she stayed in New York. It wasn't easy.

There was one common denominator, though. Each time that she had no place to live, her plight became more desperate. She needed a roof over her head that was not controlled by her mother, her employer, and never again the state. What would that take? She didn't know. She only knew that if she had to live in one of these places again, it would kill her, if she didn't kill herself.

A few weeks before her release, she had a visitor. Leola appeared. It seemed the story of the Minnehaha soda fountain arrest had circulated all over Philadelphia's Seventh Ward. People reported that Bessie's screams had been so terrible that the druggist, fearing the total destruction of his beautiful new fountain, had called out the riot squad. Bessie had been arrested for disturbing the peace, resisting arrest, and attempted murder. Frank had lost his job and fled back to Philadelphia, where the story spread widely.

Bessie had also grown into a hero to the girls in Mrs. Truitt's house. One of the girls had made her way to a friend of Frank's who said that Bessie was in the women's prison, and word of mouth among the hookers had led Leola there. A guard now led Bessie to a holding cell so the women could talk.

"Don't act surprised and don't make any noise," Leola told her. "Wipe your face and knot your hair back. Then follow me."

Bessie did.

"OK, guard!" Leola called, and when he came near, he unlocked the holding cell. Leola touched him as if they were shaking hands, but Bessie could see the edge of a roll of cash move between their palms.

The women walked quietly into the sun, taking the ferry across to Manhattan together, silently. When they got a few blocks away, Bessie sprung to Leola's neck, hugging and kissing her.

"How did you do that?" Bessie asked.

"It's your money," Leola said. "Mrs. Truitt said she had been saving some of your earnings for you, and the girls wanted to help you out. We're so proud of you."

"There's more. I bargained him down. Guards go cheap in New York." Leola laughed. She handed Bessie an envelope of cash. "Please don't spend it in one place."

"My foolish days are over," Bessie promised.

With the money, she got a decent hotel room for herself and her friend. They took bubble baths and lay under the bedcovers and talked.

Leola tried to convince Bessie to return to Philadelphia. But she said no. She still believed she could be reborn in New York. This time she would be smarter.

The next day Leola went with Bessie to rent a room where she could stay for a while. It was still in the Tenderloin district. But she wouldn't sleep where she worked, in Madame Paree's brothel. Instead, she found another girl who had just arrived in New York to share the room, and she charged her almost the same price as the room itself, with just a small discount. They cooked in the room and slept at different times so that the bed was never unused. Bessie still earned money at Madame Paree. But occasionally, she took "private clients" into hotel rooms.

Bessie was twenty-three years old, had been once in the almshouse and twice in prison. The relief she felt beating up Frank had made her feel clean, left her unremorseful.

"One day, I'll take care of you," Bessie promised Leola.

"You'll take care of me!" Leola shook her red curls in despair.

But Bessie had a plan now. "I'll never be a beggar again. I'll never go to prison again. And I'll never work for anyone else except myself."

1888
THE SISTERHOOD

I am a woman sir,
And this is my house,
Please excuse me if I leave you
More for your sake than mine.

—*Giuseppe Verdi,* La Traviata

NINE

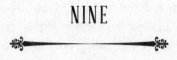

Lower East Side, New York,
December 8, 1888

Was there any place more exciting than New York or as dangerous? Bessie knew only that she was as free as she had ever been. She was a girl in her twenties, still as pretty as a teenager. Her perfect figure had been made even more voluptuous by her childbearing. She was also more knowledgeable than she had ever been.

New York, unlike Philadelphia, was a big city. There was no one to watch her behaviors. No one she could embarrass or who shamed her. No one knew her enough to place her anywhere or with anyone. She was a chameleon, not only by the clothes she wore but also by the ethnicity she presented.

She still dreamed of meeting a colored gentleman, a real gentleman—not one who frequented the brothels when no one was looking. And she was learning, little by little, to act like a lady.

She went to the tailor and had her dresses made just a little looser than she would normally wear them. She bought beautiful dresses with white pleated bibs where she would normally just leave a plunging neckline. Bessie learned to wear her hats straight on her head and not cocked to the side.

But her biggest change came after she observed the musicians on Twenty-Eighth Street—the place people soon would call Tin Pan Alley for the cacophony of sound that came from the windows, like kitchen pans beaten with wooden spoons rather than piano hammers hitting their strings. She saw men, thick-haired, dark-complexioned men who she learned were Jewish descendants, introducing themselves to others on the street as Gentiles. Monroe Rosenfeld called himself Mr. Belasco. He wrote the song that she adored: "With All Her Faults, I Love Her Still." The music, romantic and earnest, matched the perception she had of her future. Someone would love her despite her past. But she didn't have to show them everything at once. She would first introduce them to her new self. A person with a new name.

Everyone in this city of beginnings had the same intention: Fuch became Fox, Bauer became Brown, Barberi became Barber. However, she liked her last name, Elias, while her first name sounded servile and southern. She wanted something that had an ancient and respected history.

She considered Cleopatra, Delilah, and Salome, but it seemed that every brothel had one. That would mark her for sure. She wanted a name that she could take to church when her respectable gentleman came along.

One name lingered in her imagination like a bell, so sweet she knew it would draw people to her: Hannah.

Hannah was a biblical name from the First Book of Samuel. Hannah had kept a promise to the Lord, who had cured her of infertility. She had vowed to give her firstborn back to God if she conceived. Her child Samuel became great, someone who made her proud. She now imagined that her daughter, Clara, might now have a wonderful life with people who fed her and raised her like their own.

Bessie was gone. She imagined that she would never answer to Bessie again. Hannah was the name the twenty-three-year-old took. Hannah was a respectable woman by day, and by night, a demimonde, in the city that had the best of the best and the worst of the vile.

Soon she established herself as a member of the Sisterhood at the most successful of the New York concert saloons, Harry Hill's at Houston and Mulberry Street. It was a fake den of vice to which cab drivers steered middle-class tourists in search of a thrill, but at the same time, it was indeed an authentic brothel. Outside, there hung an enormous red lantern. The hall had two doors: a free entrance for women, and another for men, for twenty-five cents. The main hall was made up of a series of rooms from which the walls had been removed but which retained different height and floor surfaces. At one end was a bar; at the other, a stage where farces, Punch and Judy shows, and boxing matches took place. On most nights, however, the stage held an orchestra, and clients were expected either to dance with paid female partners or to leave.

Other streetwalkers were present but invisible. Arrangements were made in private, and Johns were taken elsewhere. This suited freelancers like Hannah perfectly. There were no exceptions to the dancing rule except for big spenders known to the management, who were permitted to congregate with the drinking crowd at the bar. The sporting crowd often contained celebrities—the rich, the famous, boxers, jockeys, actors, entertainers, songwriters, and opera singers. The public also included high-stakes gamblers, politicians, off-duty policemen, society figures, authors, journalists, and gangsters.

Harry Hill himself was the referee of status and the protector of peace, backed up by two bouncers. Sometimes roughhousing was staged for the tourist trade. Rules were posted on the walls. They forbade drunkenness, profanity, lack of chivalry toward women, and stinting on drinks. Meanwhile, in the basement, games and knockout artists reigned.

Sex did not occur on the premises, and, in fact, it usually did not occur at all. Since prostitutes did not receive wages but worked on a percentage basis, the client would be encouraged to buy numerous drinks for himself and his companion, who drank colored water costing twice the amount of the man's drink—from fifteen to twenty-five cents. In an hour or so, the client would be too inebriated for anything else. The real money came from house-controlled gambling and thievery. There was a new knockout drink called the "Mickey Finn," named after the proprietor of Chicago's Lone Star Saloon. Its recipe supposedly came from a voodoo witch doctor in New Orleans and was effective only when mixed with alcohol. The result was more volatile, lethal, and effective than chloral hydrate.

There were seventy-five concert saloons in the Bowery, employing almost a thousand "waitresses." If Harry Hill's traded in sham vice, real vice lurked all around. On Hester Street was Billy McGlory's Armory

Hall, perhaps the worst dive in New York. Open twenty-four hours a day, its double doors led into a long hallway through which customers had to make their way in darkness. Murder was an everyday occurrence. Transvestite singers and dancers doubled as waitresses. Waitresses of either sex immediately sat on the laps of the paying customers. For a quarter, they would go away. If not, the couple could go to one of the curtained boxes in the balcony. In either case, nobody left in possession of his wallet.

It didn't take long for Hannah to get to know all the proprietors in the area. The American Mabile on Bleecker Street was run by Theodore Allen, who was known as the wickedest man in New York, having been raided 113 times without a conviction. From him, she learned how important political connections were.

Frank Stephenson was another operator who specialized in exotica. He ran the Slide, a homosexual concert saloon on Bleecker. He also ran the Black and Tan right beside it, where all the women were white and all the men were something else: Black, Indian, East Indian, Chinese, Malay, Arab, Turkoman.

One of the worst of Harry Hill's competitors was within sight of the police precinct building on Mulberry Street. It was run by a fence named Mike Kerrigan, who, when asked about the location, replied, "The nearer the church, the closer to God."

"Nigger" Mike Saulter, who was Jewish, not black, owned the Pelham on Pell Street, which featured a pianist called Blind Tom, who was not blind. The Callahan Dance Hall Saloon was noted for its singing waiters, which one day would include the two Yoelson brothers (the youngest was Al), who changed their name to Jolson, and Izzy Baline, who changed his name to Irving Berlin. At Crosby and Houston, the House of Lords and the Bunch of Grapes gang had their headquarters. Owney Geoghegan's Hurdy-Gurdy on the Bowery was the first to introduce boxing matches—known as "free and easys"—which took place in a small canvas ring in the middle of the dance floor. And then there was the Morgue, headquarters of the Whyos gang.

The Whyos were the most powerful downtown gang in New York, a large Irish group originally from the Five Points district, with operations in different locations throughout the city. New Yorkers called them the Whyos because of the way they communicated by whistling. The Whyos' going rates for crime and mayhem were the lowest in New York, and they were posted menu style at their club:

Punching $2	Nonfatal Shooting $100
Both eyes blacked $4	Poisoning $50
Nose and jaw broke $10	Ear chewed off $15
Slash in the cheek $1–$10	Leg or arm broken $1–$15
Shot in the leg $1	Stabbing $25
Bomb $5–$20	Arson $10–$200
Murder $10–$500	

Then there was Johnny Camphene's bar, whose specialty drink contained camphor, oil of turpentine, varnish solvent, and lamp fuel. One would be lucky to escape with his eyesight.

Before long, a landlord named William McMahon had recruited Hannah, attracted by her youth and stamina, with a formula that would make her a fortune. His establishment on Sixth Avenue, just south of Thirtieth Street, featured good music, and was a rendezvous for middle- and upper-class married men. To attract the straying husbands, McMahon fostered an atmosphere of respectable vice. He threw out "trimmers" (prostitutes who stole from their clients), prohibited close dancing, and expelled women for showing their ankles and customers for using foul language. The three-story edifice was painted yellow and, like all such places, admitted women free and men for twenty-five cents. It provided curtained-off tables, and a tunnel ran from its basement to an adjacent hotel. McMahon paid $250 a week to the mob for protection; not a large sum, probably because police officials were his biggest customers. It was there that the cocktail was invented by the famous bartender Jerry Thomas, who created the Blue Blazer and the Tom and Jerry, and made use of a half-eggshell to measure portions, thus the name "cock" tail.

Socialites from uptown immigrated downtown to siphon off the raw energy, music, vice, liquor, drugs, mayhem, and sex of the new music. The Mafia ruled, with pimps and sporting men who became the landlords of the suddenly profitable business of brothels, houses of assignation, and concert halls. Actresses, singers, circus performers, magicians, electromagnetic doctors, alienists, hypnotists, memoirists, and confidence men all congregated at the tip of Manhattan.

In the late 1880s low life began moving slowly uptown, red-light district by red-light district. Broadway was electrified, and the elevated train sped by over the rooftops of tenements and factory buildings. The stock market expanded until it was about to burst. Then it did burst, in the Great Wall Street Panic of 1890. Men won and lost fortunes. It was the golden age for invention: the radio, the telephone, the telegraph, the phonograph, the X-ray, the magnetic third rail, the moving picture, and the automobile. People raced everything that had legs: dogs, horses, men, and then bet on them. People fought anything that bit: dogs, cocks, mice, men, and they bet on them as well.

Immigrants flooded into Little Italy, Chinatown, the Lower East Side, Five Points, and Battery Park. They couldn't speak English and they couldn't read any language. They gathered in ethnic groups, changing whole neighborhoods. Hannah moved throughout the city with her mysterious smile, and the brains to keep her mouth shut.

With her newfound wealth, Hannah dressed herself in fashionable, expensive clothes, and spent all her money on hats and House of Worth dresses. The Gilded Age thrived; twenty tabloids kept a chronicle of the city's highs and lows, nobodies and celebrities, carefree rich and homeless poor.

One evening near Christmas 1888, Mrs. Miller of Pop Miller's Saloon asked Hannah to help her out. She had a delegation of visiting firemen from California attending a convention in the city that had booked her entire house. This would be prominent but rough trade, she explained. Hannah agreed to work in-house as a favor that night.

She entered the smoky saloon with a regal walk, a style she invented called her Cleopatra sway. A pall of cigar smoke overhung the room—a table with food, and a few people clinging to one another on the empty dance floor.

A tall, slender, white-haired man in evening dress approached her. He had piercing blue eyes and a short-cropped, salt-and-pepper beard. He had wide shoulders and held himself erect like the military man she supposed him to be. He was staring at Hannah in astonishment, as if she were a religious manifestation.

Hannah asked his name.

He replied, "John. Pleased to meet you."

Hannah always smiled when a client replied with the name John. They were never telling the truth, so that was the name all the "escorts" used—"John"—to refer to a client. He placed his hand on her elbow and they moved over to the wall.

The couple on the dance floor had been replaced by an act. Six male and female strippers removed clothing from one another with their hands and teeth until the women wore only stockings. Then one woman placed a lighted cigar in the private opening of another who was lying on her back with her feet elevated to her head. Simultaneously, the other four pretended to have sex by means of a dildo.

The firemen were excited and amazed.

Turning his gaze from the floor to his date, the man at her side asked, "And your name is?"

"Hannah. My name is Hannah."

She could tell that his eyes were wide, but that he looked uncomfortable and wanted to focus on her instead. Perhaps as a distraction, perhaps for the night.

"You are not obliged," she said.

"Oh, it's not that. I want to, I really do. I just don't like the spectacle."

"Well, we can leave then. You don't have to watch. No one should be forced to do anything they don't want to do. I certainly would not force you to."

"Do you do things you don't want to do?"

"I do nothing but things I don't want to do." Hannah laughed.

He smiled and took in the melodic tones of her voice, a vibrato that promised illicit, mysterious, and hitherto unknown pleasures. It was a laugh with slow-as-molasses intimacy that no man had ever resisted.

Rising, she took him by the hand. He followed her quietly, making neither protest nor plea.

After that night, John began to meet her at Mrs. Miller's regularly. Their affair continued, profitably for Mrs. Miller and Hannah, night after night for the next several months. Sometimes he was exhausted but didn't want to leave her presence, so they spent the evening quietly playing dominoes and talking. She knew only that he was a businessman, married, with children, whom he refused to describe. She really didn't want to know.

When John visited, she steered the conversation to New York—places that he thought she should see or food he had eaten at fancy restaurants. Hannah was not jealous. One day, she told herself, these things would be part of her life. Mrs. Truitt had said that all her girls should settle down by the age of thirty.

One night, as John waited for her, Hannah didn't appear. She had decided to leave Mrs. Miller, who was angry that Hannah had left no forwarding address. She could have at least pimped her out of another place. "I got lots of whores. Get another one. Younger, prettier."

John shook his head. "No." There was something from Hannah that he wanted. He just didn't have a name for the feeling yet. She meant something to him. He felt a little empty thinking he'd never see her again.

The night Hannah didn't come back followed the day she realized she had saved enough money to rent a house of her own, not just two rooms that she shared—now with three other girls to cut expenses. To celebrate, she stuffed her purse with dollars and began looking for a place.

She put on her low-heeled shoes and one of her looser dresses, powdered her face lightly, and took a walk.

Union Square was rich in expensive, high-class brothels in the former brownstones of upper-class New Yorkers who had all moved to Fifth or Park Avenue. She thought this was a good place to begin.

She headed toward a building with a sign reading FOR RENT BY OWNER. She walked up the steps to the parlor floor and knocked.

A pale, freckle-faced maid in a black dress with a white apron and dusting cap answered. "What can I do for you, misses?"

"I'm interested in renting the building," Hannah said.

"One minute," the woman answered quickly. She shut the door, leaving Hannah on the stoop.

An older woman returned. "Who sent you?" she asked.

"I saw your sign and I'm interested in taking the building," Hannah answered.

"Who are your bank references?"

Hannah blinked. She didn't understand.

"Who is your banker? What can he say about you?" the woman repeated. "Your papers?"

Hannah knew that the woman meant something legal. She had never needed this to rent a room. She just showed the cash, and the room was hers. Maybe Union Square was still not for her.

"Can I see the house?" Hannah realized that she hadn't even seen the inside of the building. Maybe she didn't even want to live there.

"Ha!" The woman laughed and closed the door.

Hannah didn't want to appear as if she had been rebuffed, as she clearly had. So she descended the steps of the brownstone and walked about a half block to the corner, and then wondered where next to go.

If she walked south, she could arrive in Greenwich Village, at an area just below Bleecker Street near Minetta Lane called Little Africa. The buildings were easy to rent there and a little run-down. As a result, she could easily operate a bordello too. The "black and tan" whorehouses invited people of all races. She could rent to white and Black girls too because the streets were integrated. There was also the district at Twenty-Third Street and Eighth Avenue where the Grand Opera House stood. Booth's Theatre once stood two blocks east as the most handsome theater in the city. There might be houses there.

People grumbled as they passed Hannah, who was blocking the path as she stood on the corner. She considered walking uptown to Madison Square Garden, the sumptuous creation of McKim, Mead, and White's architectural firm, which housed all kinds of spectacles, such as boxing matches. Lots of men went there.

She didn't want to go to West Forty-Second Street, where practically every house was a brothel, many of them known for French girls who indulged in unnatural practices.

She returned to the Tenderloin that she knew, but a few blocks to the north. Her first house stood at 136 West Thirty-First Street.

In this area, her color hardly mattered. The girls who rented her rooms were known to take customers all day and night, any color, any gender. There was an orgy in one of the rooms every night. The parties were so wild that the costs of replacing furniture sometimes exceeded the income from the sex.

Hannah quicky tired of living in the area. She was tired of pushing past half-dressed women standing in the doorway fighting over the latest sporting man.

She and a few of her tenants changed houses to 215 West Fortieth Street, where she remained only a few months. Sex shops were rampant at this time in New York, with some men claiming that without prostitution, rape would become rampant. Hannah wondered if rape wasn't rampant anyway. At least now the girls earned money for what might happen to them. She found herself guiding the younger streetwalkers as she had at Mrs. Truitt's and turning less tricks, finding being a landlady much less hard on her body—and sometimes even easier on her mind.

She moved her house again, to near the East River on Water Street. This was Corlears Hook, called simply "the Hook," located at the easternmost end of Manhattan at Grand Street. It had the highest concentration of commercial sex workers in the city, which had given the name "hooker" to the prostitutes who plied their trade there. The police never ventured there except in groups of six. The Slaughter Houses and the Daybreak Boys gangs had once established themselves in dives like the Tub of Blood, Hell's Kitchen, and Swain's Castle. But the last of the gangs had dissolved and the meeting places had closed, leaving a glut of cheap real estate. Finally, Hannah found a house she could purchase rather than rent.

She had talked to a man in one of the saloons who told her that he owned a building in the Hook and if she could come by at the end of the week, they could make the sale.

She walked through the street pulling a suitcase like many of the poor downtown immigrants, except inside her bag were stacks of small bills. She went to the office of the building's owner, who was a small man with a large belly and pants held up by suspenders. He opened the door for her very politely and had her sit. He sat on the edge of a desk facing her. They were alone.

"So you want to live here?" he asked her. "You been here long?"

"I'm interested in buying," Hannah answered. She didn't want her inexperience to show. She remembered the embarrassment she felt when she tried to rent her first house.

"It's not the Ritz." He laughed.

She was well dressed, obviously alone. But she could take care of herself.

"So what you going to do here?"

"Do you want to know what I'm going to cook for dinner too?" Hannah responded. She wasn't going to look like a fool even if she had to act as cagey as him. "I'm here to buy and you said you were selling."

"I'm selling like you're selling," he said. And he suddenly became less polite. He lurched over to her and brushed his hands on her chest.

"Nice!" he said.

Then Hannah did something she hadn't planned during the time she counted the twenties and tens, stacked them, and tied them with string. She balled up her fist, stood, and punched him in the jaw with all her might. "Do that again, and I'll slice you from appetite to asshole." She pulled her knife from her boot and began to walk out of the room.

Just then, a small-boned, slick-haired man opened the door, accompanied by a tall, good-looking blond.

"I'm Mr. Fiorello and this is Mr. Nanz," he said and pointed to the younger, more attractive partner. "You'll have to pardon my assistant, Mr. Grunn. He screens my callers."

Hannah straightened herself and sat again. "Are you selling this building or not?"

"Of course we are," Fiorello said.

Nanz had papers, which Hannah and Fiorella signed. Hannah opened the suitcase and the men gasped, then laughed.

"I can see you are an astute businesswoman," Fiorello said.

Hannah took this comment as an insult, thinking he was referring to the suitcase. She began to get angry again.

"Madame, we are happy to do business with you," Nanz explained. He asked her to leave the money and walked her and the paperwork to a nearby bank. They went into a back office and she received the title to the house.

"You may reach me here through Mr. Symthe, my banker, at any time."

She had done it. This time, she had a house without being abused and humiliated. And now she had a banker for a reference.

Hannah recruited a few ambitious girls as discreet whores who received discounts on their rooms if she received a part of their payments. She kept the first-floor apartment all to herself. She lived in the back and in the basement. She offered the front to a psychic who used a bright sign and any number of exotic outfits to lure customers in. She would predict men's impending death if she saw a good mark, and they would return again and again to get glimpses of their dead relatives in the old country. They wept to go back to Europe. If she had smarter customers, she'd send them to Hannah to get cured by her healing powers.

Hannah set herself up in business as a masseuse. She also advertised her services in the tabloid newspapers. Sometimes she just gave massages. Other times, she gave more intimate services.

For three years, Hannah and a revolving door of young women plied their trade. Her money increased and she understood two ways New York prospered: sex and land.

✤

On January 1, 1892, Hannah found herself at Harry Hill's annual fancy dress ball. The hall held more than seven thousand people. She stood at the top of a staircase and peered down. Crowds of splendidly dressed partygoers surged down the wide, curved staircase around her. The ceiling blazed with chandeliers. Soon she would be part of the herd, but for now, she savored the moment of eminence, like a queen surveying her minions.

She wore a ball gown of blue French velvet with machine-made Alençon lace, trimmed with silver ribbon chenille and silk roses that climbed over one shoulder from girdle to backless plunge. The dress had a wide train edged with three tiers of silver braid in a garland design. She wore long white opera gloves and carried an ostrich feather fan, which she waved languidly as if she were Cleopatra on the Nile. Hannah's shining eyes were framed in a silver papier-mâché mask.

She swayed slightly along with the fan as if she were on the deck of a moving ship, her legs apart for balance. It seemed to her that night that she was not standing in Harry Hill's but in the midst of rowdy, sexy life itself. But she wanted to look like a pro, not an ingenue around wealth. She was already twenty-seven years old. So she squared her shoulders and lifted her head, unlike the young Bessie racing down Addison Street in a pale green chiffon dress, the whole world waiting to crush her. She thought for a second she had a sudden whiff of fresh horse manure like home, but it was really the scent of burning hashish.

Hannah inhaled, drunk with emotion and excitement, thinking that all this elegance could be hers one day. Her soul, her ambition, her love— all seemed suddenly to exhale into the vast space below, which writhed with the tumult of bodies in motion.

Hypnotized, Hannah leaned forward, swaying, her arms reaching out toward it. Then holding up the train attached to her wrist, she pranced down the red-carpeted staircase to Scott Joplin's "The Entertainer," played by a full orchestra in frock coat.

Every class and social category, from kept women to respectable society matrons, from Wall Street businessmen to drag queens, was present, looking for a bit of vice. There were professional prostitutes, successful madams, questionable mistresses, adventurers, call girls, actresses, and singers; many of them, like Hannah, alone. Sporting women mixed with nabobs, bachelors, and visiting firemen. Underworld figures mingled informally and fluidly with the overworld figures of politicians, police captains, businessmen, industrialists, and Tammany Hall bureaucrats.

Hannah recognized several policemen to whom William McMahon paid protection money. She recognized prominent madams like Eliza Pratt and famous lesbians and bawdyhouse proprietors such as Mollie Dix and Rosie Hertz. There was a smattering of celebrities such as the political boss Big Tim Sullivan, and big-time gang leaders like Monk Eastman and Paul Kelly.

Public women like Hannah were the new celebrities. Hannah glanced at a nabob, a wealthy, single New York male, as he made his way through the maelstrom of swirling dancers. She was alone, but she knew in minutes she would soon have a trail of suitors behind her. She felt happy. She felt secure. It seemed to her that because she had been born the day the Civil War ended, she belonged in this new gilded age not as a victim, but as a victor. Softly, she hummed a line from a pulp novel she had read that afternoon:

"Go tell the raving maniac not to be crazy. Tell the serpent not to bite, tell the lion not to play with the lamb, tell the childless widow not to weep, but don't tell me to remain wretched."

Hannah began to move through the crowd, flashing her smile.

Heat and noise rose from the packed bodies. There were three thousand of the best men and four thousand of the worst women in the city. From lowly clerks to aristocratic merchants, from respectable housewives to fifteen-year-old streetwalkers, everyone was in motion looking for sex, drugs, and dollars. There were the Bowery Boys in their flashy outfits, rings, watch chains, and leather boots. There were gentlemen in swallowtail coats and white cravats and vests. There were knaves and rascals, bankers and merchants, rich men's sons and bank cashiers. What they all had in common was disposable cash and lust.

Hannah sniffed the air. It smelled of male sweat, tobacco, and cocaine. There were bachelors, widowers, and married men ready to commit adultery. There were the out-of-towners, men of moral excellence at home but sinful in the anonymous city of their dreams—the small-town Don Juans from Cincinnati, Birmingham, and Wichita. On the outside they all looked as if they knew everyone and were comfortable everywhere, but in many ways, like the crewmen, pimps, and Bowery Boys, they were all foreigners to themselves and strangers in America.

Hannah had never before heard Scott Joplin in person. People swooned over his rags. She found herself swaying, drugged by the music.

"Are you here alone?" asked a deep, uptown New York voice. The words were well-articulated, each syllable slowly pronounced to project calm and wealth.

Turning, she gazed up at the tall, impeccably dressed stranger in white tie, and smiled.

"Yes."

"My name is Edward," he said.

"I'm Hannah."

The last of "Leader Rag" spiraled upward and hung in the air above them as the orchestra swelled, the lights blazed, the warmth of thousands of bodies surrounded them in an ocean of sound and scent, talcum powder and rosewater. Champagne, bourbon, and bare skin that emitted the odor of sex converged into a frenzy as Joplin played and played and played. He sat at his grand piano on a revolving podium wearing a white tie, his wild hair like a flame flickering in a draft. There were rubies on his fingers and a diamond in one ear. His fingers were only a blur as he drew incredible sounds from his piano, his hands racing across the keys in fabulous combinations of inexhaustible musical invention.

Hannah knew that Joplin had begun playing as an orphan in a bordello in Missouri. She didn't know that the syphilis he got there would cause him to end his life in an insane asylum. He was here now and so was she.

This smiling, joyful music man, like her, was an icon of the century: she as a most desirable, beautiful loose woman, and he as an entertainer who would help usher in jazz.

The audience went wild. Hannah was weak with excitement and squeezed Edward's arm so hard, he looked down, surprised.

A beautiful young woman startled the crowd by announcing in a loud voice that she would dance the cakewalk without any underwear. She lifted her skirts between her legs with one hand, kicked away a chair or two, and pranced around the hall in spectacular kicks. The men craned their necks to get a look at her. The people in the balcony hung over the railings. More figures moved onto the floor and went reeling around in a mixture of dancing and byplay as frenetic as the melodies Joplin kept on playing.

The majestic sounds at blinding speed went on and on as the fiddler wove a counterpoint. The clarinetist elaborated a riff that sounded like a steam engine whistle. The dancers' movements grew increasingly rapid and licentious. Heels kicked in the air, legs and thighs and sexes were exhibited in wild abandon. Hats flew off. Exhibitions of nudity abounded. Abandoned were furs, hats, scarves, and outerwear, as more and more performers joined in. The females on the floor, egged on to delirious movements by the men, did acrobatic splits. The scene climaxed with a dozen girls denuding their lower limbs and raising their skirts above their waists to go whirling round and round in a lascivious mix of cakewalk and cancan, while Joplin's music hung in the air like a narcotic.

Hannah approached the podium, her eyes blazing. To play like that! She could hardly believe she beheld the Great Joplin. She had always dreamed of loving a genius. A man so extraordinary Hannah felt her soul was his vessel.

She felt Edward's eyes on her. Hannah heard everything any man had to say. And what he said was, "Hannah, Hannah, how did you get that smile?"

She transferred her joy to him.

They danced the waltz, the quickstep, and the foxtrot, and ended the evening together. He brought her to a beautiful hotel. She lay in bed in the morning and listened to him talk.

Edward Estel was a banker who enjoyed his work. "Who wouldn't like to be around money every day?" he told her. He talked about walking into a vault surrounded by gold and serving men who opened bank accounts with thousands of dollars in cash. He talked to her about compound interest as if it were some godlike miracle. "The more money you have, the more money you make!"

He said even someone as young as her—he guessed about seventeen years old; she didn't tell him she was ten years older—could start investing in stocks, first with pennies, then in utilities that were "burning up."

Hannah listened greedily. It was the first time she understood the way men got ahead who didn't work with their hands.

She encouraged him to talk that morning and the other times they were together. She behaved as Mrs. Truitt had taught her, except with a little twist. The madam had said to always tell a man he is handsome. Hannah told Edward he was so smart.

He seemed amused talking high finance with a woman—moreover, a *fille de joie*. He could of course tell her anything and everything about anyone without harm. Whom could she repeat it to? No one.

One day she even walked into a bank by herself and opened an account. She didn't tell anyone, not even Edward, her plan. She didn't want to be embarrassed if she wasn't allowed to put in a little cash.

"Hannah Elias. Yes. Single." She responded to the questions of the clerk who set up the service. As proof of her identity, she showed him the deed to her house. Even though the address was in a terrible part of town, he was impressed.

As her intimacy progressed with Edward, he got into the habit of dropping confidential information or passing along investment tips.

"You mean that I can buy railroad stock low and sell it when its value climbs?" Hannah asked.

He turned and actually looked in her eyes. "Hannah, you have a financial mind." This gift surprised and delighted him to no end. He could be Pygmalion and Hannah his creation come to life.

"Remember, Hannah," he said, "money is easily made in New York. Fortunes are acquired daily—families go from a shanty on a back street to a brownstone in upper New York." He smiled. "But they carry with them their vulgar habits and disgust those who come from social positions above them and who are compelled to invite them to their houses.

"If a man has money, he has a passport to high society. He may come from Botany Bay or Saint James with a pass from a penal colony, but if he has a diamond ring and a coach, all doors will be open to him."

Hannah wondered if he meant women too, but she didn't ask for fear of cutting him off and losing this lesson.

"New Yorkers are invited according to their bank accounts and their standing on the exchange," he added. "Someday, you will go to a fashionable party. In this city, those events are made up of representatives of all nations and all citizens, men and women who speak English and those who cannot—Jews, gentiles, Irish, Germans, Hindus, Asians—everybody except Negroes."

It was at this moment that Hannah realized that as much as Edward had been with her, he still didn't know who she was. She nodded as if it didn't matter.

TEN

Lower Manhattan, New York,
December 1892

H annah's favorite place in all of New York, besides Central Park, was Delmonico's Confectioners and French Restaurant, where she was now seated facing Edward. It was one of four sister establishments in the city and the first public dining room to open in the United States. In its early days, it had laid the foundation for the entire American restaurant industry, beginning at 2 South William Street in Lower Manhattan. Delmonico's operated on the policy of only the very best ingredients prepared in the best manner possible for quality. Cost be damned. The brothers offered their customers the best wines, like vintage Château Margaux and rare Champagnes. It was rumored that the wine bill of the millionaire August Belmont at Delmonico's was $20,000 a month. The service was splendid, the waiters noiseless, the dishes served on the finest china. They succeeded each other with fidelity and beauty, like a well-composed painting or symphony.

But above all, it was the best club for women of Hannah's profession in the city. "The Resort," the New York *World* newspaper had written, "has more native and foreign notables than any other place in the city." There were distinguished literary and political persons sipping the mutational cocktail, the anteprandial sherry and bitters, and the evening "poney." Wall Street magnates dropped in on their way home to sip insidious mint juleps or Champagne cocktails. Frenchmen, Spaniards, and Italians stopped to have their absinthe, Americans their straight bourbon, the Englishmen, their half-and-half. Every evening it was alive with chatter, gossip, and good-natured imbibing of domestic and imported wine, along with celebrities—young women of exceptional beauty and questionable morality.

In the demimonde to which Hannah now belonged, she was expected to wear all her best and most elegant clothes and jewels to be seen and shown. Hannah reveled in this act, prancing past the endlessly reflecting mirrors between the sparkling white silver-dressed tables wearing gowns and furs, hats and gloves, trains and ostrich-feather boas, pearl dog collars and diamond bracelets. There was even a cocktail named after her made of honey, Champagne, bitters, and raspberry syrup. Men strode to the bar and asked for "Hannah's Gift."

They didn't know she was sitting nearby listening. She wished that her image was hanging on the restaurant's wall like the paintings of elegant women, except she would be captured by the newest technology: photography.

The Delmonico's at Twenty-Sixth and Fifth Avenue drew the society crowd; the one on Chambers Street drew the politicians, merchants, lawyers, and foreign aristocrats. The so-called Citadel at Williams Street had Pompeian granite columns that drew bankers and shipping magnates, and the Broad Street establishment catered to stockbrokers and market specialists.

One night, Hannah and Edward were at Delmonico's on Broad Street, where in the first-floor restaurant, silver chandeliers hung from the frescoed ceilings. Mirrors lined every wall, and massive mahogany furniture dominated the room, in which huge bouquets of fresh flowers bordered the working fountain, which stood at its center. On the second floor, there was a ballroom decorated in red and gold and four private dining rooms, each a different-colored satin. The third floor held more private dining rooms and the kitchens. The cellar included vaults stocked with 16,000 bottles of French wine. The restaurant offered the newest food and cuisine, unknown in the homes of even the wealthiest New Yorkers. The Parisian à la carte menu allowed customers to choose and pay for as much or as little food as they liked instead of the set price, time, and meal served in American taverns and inns. The restaurant where Edward met Hannah that evening had grown into worldwide fame, with its distinctive "D" embossed on its linen, silver, and china.

They dined alone in one of the small private rooms. In the past year, their friendship had evolved into weekly assignations, which often ended (or began) in the dining rooms of Delmonico's. Edward had not only introduced Hannah to Delmonico's, but he was spending more and more of his time tutoring her in business, while she showed him the sexual arts. He was having the time of his life, although he was wondering sometimes which one of them was Pygmalion. When he gave the role to himself, he rationalized a virtuous excuse for their trysts. Nevertheless, Hannah was teaching him a thing or two about life in the real world in exchange . . .

"A bordello is exactly like a bank," Edward told Hannah now, in his well-modulated voice, his hands behind his head, lounging on the ottoman sofa in their private salon. "It is a place of commerce with a source of supply and demand. You, Hannah, are the supply and I, Edward, am the demand. As long as I want what you're selling, we have a business deal. Your body is real estate, like real property—a brick and brownstone building. It is a solid commodity that one can touch and that exists in space. It doesn't need to be sold to achieve revenue. It can be rented—like when you appear at a party to brighten up the place—or borrowed against, when a person like me wants to offer you jewels or hand you my cash, because I know you'll make more money with that beautiful face and return my investment. Just never sell your real estate, Hannah. Just never let the life ruin you when you're all you've got."

One night when a similar evening had just ended, Edward asked Hannah, "Why does a whore become a whore? Can you tell me? There must be as many reasons as there are strumpets. For example, it is one of the few ways, short of being run over by a Rolls-Royce automobile, to meet a man of a higher station—except"—and he smiled—"at Harry Hill's annual fancy dress ball. It gives the appearance of independence you all seem to clamor for. It avoids the drudgery of the factory, the farm, the sweatshop, and marriage, and it obtains the outward trappings of a better life: jewels and clothes and perhaps even pleasure."

Hannah's reply was not the wisecracking, cynical one he expected.

"I don't know what is at the heart of being a whore; all I know is that no one is born a streetwalker, and despite what reformers and doctors say, there is nothing in the blood that predicts you will sell your body just because someone was born poor. But it seems to me there is always some great loss or emptiness in fallen women—and it usually has to do with a man."

She kept secret the abuse by the jockey, the loss of her father, the abandonment of her common-law husband. Still, she spoke honestly. "There is always a feeling of being alone in the world and a little anger in that." She gave an involuntary smile that chilled Edward. "Some people need to rebel. Others feel like life should give them more of what they deserve, that earth or God or somebody had planned a life for them that they did not want and they alone could change that."

She saw from the way Edward looked at her that he was amazed.

She continued, "Yet, to be a whore is a choice. Even if force and violence and need entice a woman into being a harlot, there has to be that one moment when she, she herself acquiesces—unless she's a child."

At this she paused. Edward searched himself for the right thing to say, but he had nothing.

"There is always an alternative to rape: death. Every whore knows that prostitution defies death. So, we are drawn to that power too." She thought maybe she had gone too far with her lesson, so she tried to disguise Edward's understanding of her. She didn't want to lose him because she was too serious. She turned her voice and manner into that of a coquette. "It is not entirely inconceivable that a prostitute could flourish by becoming a madam, as you suggest. Maybe she just needs a patron." She puckered her lips and batted her eyelids at Edward, who laughed at this obviously fake performance.

"As for me, Edward, I entered the life for none of the reasons I told you," she lied, then admitted, "I learned from listening to other women. I was tired of having to kowtow to weak men's power over me. I wanted my own power. In this war, my body is my weapon."

"And such a wonderful weapon it is!" Edward gave her a hug.

Hannah kept inside the thoughts that her body gave her the military equipment, like Cleopatra, to reinvent herself and to turn the men she seduced into the stereotyped Johns. They looked at her, a young woman, and saw an adulteress, courtesan, whore, prostitute, strumpet, tart, hustler, chippy, harlot, Lorette, streetwalker, hooker, fallen woman, demimonde, slut, public woman. So she would see not gentlemen but bankers, merchants, princes, railroad kings, tycoons, and politicians—all dirty words to her—men worth only what they could give her.

She was staring into the distance and not at Edward, she realized, because he was looking at her in a new light.

"After all," Hannah added, "there wouldn't be any prostitutes if there weren't men willing to pay them. There would just be a lot of dead and battered women, and the world would look on in total indifference."

Edward leaned back and took her face in his hands. "If you were in Paris, my dear, you would have a great future as what they call *une grande horizontale*, a lady of high market value and intelligence who makes a career lying on her back gazing at the ceiling, being what every man dreams of—a virtuoso of sex and the art of love, the exquisite maestro of the carnal act. I can see you now, in the Paris stock market, investing your earnings. What a picture you would make!"

Hanna smiled; she had begun getting good interest on her bank account already.

"These women make their living as demimondes lying on their backs, but their minds never stop working, not for a moment, just like yours. They make their fortune from men and then retire to country houses and chateaux and marry some marquis." He laughed.

"You're my marquis." Hannah laughed, trying to reveal a little more of herself.

"No, darling, you are the queen of the service industry. Just remember to never borrow too much and invest everything that you don't need to operate from day to day. Don't spend on restaurant meals and stockings, things I can buy for you. Put your money into things that will appreciate—have more value—in the years to come—real estate, jewels, gold."

Hannah then had a revelation. Every story she read said that Cleopatra adorned herself with gold, lived in beautiful palaces that artisans decorated with precious artifacts. She knew as much as the banker. She knew the way to get value and increase it. This was the reason everyone knew about her. She was an expert in love and money. Hannah, without knowing it at the time, had chosen her mentor wisely.

Every night after Edward left, Hannah pulled out two notebooks. In one book, she wrote all his financial advice. In the other notebook, she wrote his name, the date, the amount she received, and his preferences—of her services. She did this for all her clients. The fee became higher if the act was more complicated. Most of the men didn't give their real names, so she described them in every intimate detail—scar on the thigh, one testicle, raised mole on the hip. If she needed to sing to get out of jail, the police could locate many of New York's finest citizens with their eyes closed.

On the mornings that Edward's wife was out of town at her relatives', she lingered in the soft Egyptian cotton sheets in the good hotels that Edward liked to book. As he shaved and brushed his teeth, she asked him questions about finance: "What if I really need money one day?"

"Like what if you don't have a John? Or you get older?" he asked, only half-joking.

"Yes." She dropped her eyes, a bit afraid at both scenarios. She had in mind buying an expensive sequin and beaded dress.

"Use your house."

"Sell my house for a dress?" she exclaimed. "That doesn't even make sense to me."

"No, Hannah." Edward spoke to her now as if she were not the smart

Horizontal but a child who couldn't learn fast enough. "You take your house, which is worth a certain market value agreed upon by a bank, and you take a loan against it. You basically remortgage to use your equity."

He could see Hannah's mind working; he didn't realize she was trying to commit his words to memory.

"It's like this: You have capital—your house or your body—you borrow against it for a sum that you're going to pay back. In the meantime, you use the money you get to buy something worth more—a bigger house or younger whore who will work for you. Now you have two properties. You have two houses to bring you rent. That money goes back into paying the original loan. Or you have two fine asses—yours and the new girl's—to get paying clients."

She smiled, although she wasn't interested in putting on her Lorette's mask just then. She realized now the way Mrs. Truitt ran her bordello. She owned the building and practically owned the young women who worked for her. They certainly paid her almost as much as she paid them. Lucky for Hannah, Mrs. Truitt cared about her charges by teaching them and helping them find suitors so that they could take care of themselves.

And Edward was helping her now.

"Remember, Hannah. Your checking account in the bank does not render you interest, but your merchant bank account pays you a percentage to use your money to make them more money, you see? Never borrow more than twenty percent of your capital. More than that is speculative and dangerous; you risk losing everything. Stick with insurance, US Treasury Bonds, bank stock, and interest-bearing accounts."

Hannah, by now, was ahead of her teacher, though. There were certain things that she would not do. Yes, it was like sex. She did not indulge in several perversions and sent those men uptown to the Forty-Second Street bordellos. She also did not spend more than was safe. She didn't use checks either. She had cash and, since her run-in with the woman in Union Square, she made sure she had bank references.

She went from bank to bank, opening new accounts with bank checks—one banker to another. She made friends with the clerks, who knew her by name and respected her business acumen. She carried

herself as a gentlewoman, and although the bankers probably knew better, they treated her in the same way they did a respectable wife from
uptown.

In this way, Hannah began to acquire a few Manhattan properties.
They were run down, but they were capital. They would never abandon her.

Hannah put her money into property instead of lavish cars and rent payments. She did not drink or gamble away her tips, as Edward advised.
Within a few years, her several bank accounts accrued interest at high
percentage rates. She was well on her way to becoming a financially secure woman.

She even learned about stocks and bonds, mortgages and loans, insurance and savings accounts, interest rates and dividends. She began to
read the stock exchange pages in the *Wall Street Journal* and once visited
the exchange herself, and was shocked to see other women circulating,
buying and selling. They were respectable women, Edward had explained,
heiresses and widows with fortunes to protect.

"But I don't think you should invest, Hannah. It's too dangerous," he
said. "Like horse racing, you have to know the jockeys and trainers, the
owners, and the track to parlay a good bet. And even then, you can lose
because the horse just isn't happy that day."

Hannah knew more than she wanted to about horses. So she decided
to stay clear of the memories that haunted her still.

"And get good advice," he warned. "Employ the best to guard your
money and make it grow, but remember the only person with a real
interest in your money is you. Information is the key to wealth. Money
is not these banknotes I leave beside the bed when I've consumed your
merchandise, money is only what it can buy—status, influence, power,
loyalty. And what is power, influence, loyalty? Independence—and what
is independence? Freedom, Hannah, freedom."

On July 25, 1893, Hannah rose earlier than usual to meet her bankers before two p.m. She made the rounds to five places where she had savings and mortgages on her properties. She was bringing the weekend profits from the girls in her properties; almost all the women turned tricks.

At the first bank, her clerk nervously accepted the money to put on her housing loan.

"You should maybe talk to your lawyer," he said. "There may be changes in the market, and you'll need his advice."

Hannah suspected nothing, although she thought that the bank was busier than usual. The clerks and tellers did not look happy.

At the second bank, the doors were shut. She looked at her watch. It was just after noon, so everyone should have been there. The same happened at the third bank. The building was dark and securely closed. This was a place one could not enter if security refused. There were no people outside or, undoubtedly, inside. The walls were thick cement and steel. The windows were high above a man's head. Still, she saw no lights.

Finally, when she got to the last bank, the clerk told her that they were still open only because J. P. Morgan sat on the board. He was a wise and cagey investor. But everyone else, he told her, is getting scared.

"They say there's not even enough gold in the US Treasury to insure money," he said. Hannah remembered the lesson that Edward gave her, that cash was worth nothing unless it had value and use. "You know that the Philadelphia and Reading Railroad went bankrupt, yes? Today the Erie Railroad failed too. They had too many tracks, not enough business, and they were in debt up to their ears."

Hannah listened, knowing that men sometimes just needed to talk when they were overwhelmed. He looked flustered.

He whispered, "People are taking their money out. I can't tell you what to do."

But Hannah saw the message in his eyes. And following his nod to the teller window, she took her bank book and asked for all her funds. As she hesitated, people were lining up at the door. Now the guards were letting only a few enter at a time. Hannah removed all her money except one hundred dollars. She stuffed the cash into her purse.

Before she had left the clerk's desk and walked to the teller, she asked, "What about my houses, my capital?"

He responded, "They're not your houses unless they're all paid off."

She had leveraged one house to pay off the next. So they all had liens. The banks foreclosed on her. Some banks shut their doors altogether. Hannah wasn't the only one to suffer in what the newspapers began to call the Panic of 1893. People lost jobs, and one-third of New York became unemployed.

Still, while the banks lost and the conspicuous consumption of the earlier years of the Tenderloin district operated now under the eyes of reformers who felt that excesses—of vice and money—were leading the nation astray, the business of selling women's bodies hardly diminished. So while Hannah lost everything except the money she carried out of the bank, she still had a job.

She returned to the district and her plan of renting two rooms with three roommates, as desperate as she was. She put an ad again in the penny press with an illustration of Cleopatra, her name, and the offer of relaxing massages.

One day, opportunity knocked.

The Christmas holidays once again approached. Still, following the financial panic that year, Hannah felt dispirited. She had cautiously spent her money, but who could have predicted the banks themselves would disappear? She needed another plan.

She answered a knock on the door early one evening and there stood a tall, white-haired John. The thin, clear complexion, thin lips, and high cheekbones looked very familiar. She searched her mind for his sexual preferences. The eyes, then, made her remember. They were still bright and sincere. It was the John from Pop Miller's, the one with the soldier's bearing whom she left suddenly when she bought her first house. He spoke excitedly as a young cadet.

He had searched all over New York for her, he said. He had hoped that "the Cleopatra Hannah" was "his Hannah." He was beaming and he smelled of expensive cologne. His beautifully tailored coat showed that he had survived the bank panic.

"Is it you, Hannah?" He laughed. "Is it really you? I thought I'd lost you forever!"

She smiled, not sure about his idea of possession. Was he crazy? Could he be jealous? "His Hannah" was "her Hannah." After all these years alone, she knew that much. Edward had said that money would give her freedom. It did, in a way. For a little while, she had the confidence to walk into banks, talk to financiers, and mingle with people wealthier than she had ever seen. When the money went away, though, she wasn't ready to lose the feeling of knowing that she was capable. She was sure about her self-reliance now. She knew the value that she possessed.

Hannah invited the John into her small apartment, but she didn't rush him to bed. She let him talk. She found out that his name really was John, and he didn't mind telling her. He was now seventy-four years old.

"My wife is gone," he said, as if he was repeating it once more for himself. When he said it, Hannah saw real emotion. His voice trembled a little. He floundered as she had when Frank walked out on her so many years earlier. He was not pregnant and broke like she had been, but he was lonely. That was the feeling that drove him to find her.

"It happened when everything was going crazy, you know. The summer past. Everybody I knew was losing money and scrambling to stay afloat. I was too. She went into the hospital. I was there when she passed." He looked at Hannah as he spoke. "Hannah, money doesn't mean anything. Life is short."

She took his hand and felt it go weak a little. The muscles were flappy, but she could feel the memory in his muscles from a robust youth. She could feel the energy return to him as she stroked his palm and encouraged him to undress. She washed him and took him as he sat in a chair. It was almost impossible, but she didn't let on. After she had finished, he was exhausted.

She took him to the bed, and he slept a while. When he woke, he gave her so much money, she didn't need to work through the holidays.

"My wife was sick for a long time, Hannah." He held his hat in his hand just before he departed. "It has been years since a woman has moved me. It's been a lifetime since I've felt joy. Thank you." How old are you, Hannah?"

"I'm twenty-eight."

"A nice age to be," said John Rufus Platt.

John came to visit her frequently in her apartment. After a while, he was paying her so much that she dismissed her roommate so they could have privacy. She still rented the second apartment and filled it with poorer girls who shared the rooms, so Hannah was still able to make a profit on her own.

She was still seeing Edward at hotels in the area. He hadn't been destroyed by the panic either. And now, the city was coming back. As they sat eating breakfast from room service, the newspapers on the silver tray said that J. P. Morgan was buying the government. Edward said Morgan was saving the nation by financing its debt.

"Banking is one of the surest professions in the world—besides yours, of course—because it is founded—also like yours—on universal vice. Not sex, but greed. Greed, like death and taxes, will always be with us." He sighed. Hannah thought he liked talking about money more than he liked sex.

"What I'm saying is," he continued, "that bankers are prostitutes and prostitutes are bankers—that's all to remember, Hannah. We are all selling something to someone—a part of ourselves, even if it's our own brain—to survive. It's just that women have a narrower field of operations than men, and poor women—as you have often pointed out—have even less."

Hannah hadn't told Edward the number of buildings she lost or the bank accounts. She was sure he didn't want to know. They were intimate in certain ways but not confidants. He was the conduit between her and her knowledge of a privileged world of money and power—a place he entered every day at six a.m. as a member of his social class.

"Men and women can sell their time on the free market all they like, but they can never buy it back again. Never. Remember, Hannah, you can never buy back the time you've sold, but you can reinvent the time you have left. Americans do it all the time. August Belmont's father, for example—he dropped his Jewish name, his family . . . We are, as they say, a nation of immigrants—of nobodies, of no-names, know-nothings. We all come from someplace else and dream of being somebody better. We hardly know our grandparents. We change our names, shaving off the unpronounceable syllables and substituting clean Anglo-Saxon vowels—no more *-ski*s, or *-burg*s, or *-vich*s, *-stein*s or *-leoni*s, just the nice, round vowels of James, Smith, Brown, Belmont . . . We can get away with bigamy, murder, and bankruptcy, simply by walking away, by changing states, moving West, choosing another name, ignoring the past, erasing our ancestors.

"My father used to say that there is a second act for all Americans—that perennial clean slate, new start, born again. He was talking about white people, of course, not Negroes. Negroes are the only people in which there is no reinvention, because their only identity is there on that black skin—they can change their names, become millionaires, invent the goddamn wheel, and they're still only one thing: a Negro."

Hannah was shocked. After all the time they had spent together in the restaurants and the clubs, in the bed, he still didn't know her at all. They were always in the bordellos and celebrity parties. But in there, no one paid attention to color. They wanted exotics. She wanted to laugh. The whole time, Edward still thought she was a tawny white woman.

He continued speaking aloud, as he was prone to lecture on banking, and now on race. "Negroes are the only Americans that cannot do a disappearing act—because they're already invisible. They can't change their skin color. It always comes out. The Black blood defines them, their children, and their children's children down to the last generation. Poles, Lithuanians, Slavs, Danes, Turks, all become American in a generation, blending into the landscape, staking a claim to it—but three hundred years hasn't made one Black man a white American. On the contrary—the longer Negroes stay, the more foreign they appear as history passes them right by—the march of time . . ."

Hannah hid her feelings. She wondered what he would have thought of her sisters and brothers, of Monarch Elias. Or Marion for marrying him. Her neighbors or the people who worked in the houses, the Pullman porters. Did he think they would always be beneath him?

And if he knew the truth about her, would he still think she was so smart, or would she be doomed to be a toy to him all her life? Hannah felt herself going flush.

"Am I getting you excited?" Edward asked. "All this talk of Negroes . . ."

"Actually, I was thinking about getting you excited," she said.

He smiled.

Edward began to tell her about all his friends who were buying up property. So many people lost their homes in the panic, now was the time to buy.

Hannah already knew. The Sisterhood was rampant. A brothel in the Tenderloin district averaged more than $2,000 a month, almost $25,000 a year at a time when a bookkeeper earned $1,000, a secretary $700, and a worker $300. Police captains cost only about $50 a month. She rattled off the numbers to him. But he offered no financial assistance to her, only a pithy pronouncement: "Behold how one becomes rich in America."

It was John Rufus who gave Hannah the loan to buy a new house at 145 West Fifty-Third Street, which belonged to Mr. X, a society slum landlord, who, despite his illustrious family name in tobacco, made his fortune in vice. His specialty was renting his tenements, whorehouses, casinos, and dance halls. The area was a little better than where she was. She opened a boardinghouse for permanent guests, ordinary working people. One of her tenants was a quiet man named Cornelius Williams. Hannah also rented rooms by the hour to eight streetwalkers, who would become permanent inmates eventually: Fantasia, Eur, Lydia, Charlotte, Augusta, Swan, Tropez, and Cornelia. Her boardinghouse, little by little, became a house of assignation. She hired some workmen to dig a passageway leading from the basement to a nearby gambling and opium den.

Clients entered through her front door but never left. From the gambling den, Hannah received a kickback that more than covered her payments to the local police.

Rather than quickly return the loan to John, she banked the money to get interest. He didn't seem to be in any rush. He showered her with gifts. They fell into old ways. He lingered sometimes to play cards alone with her or to talk. He brought her copies of magazines from his house— *Munsey's Magazine, Architectural Record, Harper's New Monthly,* and *Town and Country*—from his wife's subscriptions, only tearing off the label with her name and their address.

Hannah saw the possibilities of bigger and better homes. Still, she was happy to have a house of her own again. When she placed her foot on her own floorboards and stamped—she crushed the memories of prison cells, the humiliations of the stables, the trinity house in the Seventh Ward, and the maid's room on the Main Line.

Not long after living in the new house, Hannah heard from Leola. She left Mrs. Truitt in Philadelphia and joined Hannah in New York. Their old and affectionate friendship was renewed. They would escape by day to Central Park. Shaded by parasols, in an open landau, the trotters would canter down the wide, tree-lined Mall. They laughed and gawked at the elegant clothes and equipages on this daily promenade, gossiping like schoolgirls. The smell of the Life and Sisterhood would disappear among the fresh breezes and the scent of cut grass.

Leola would hum "Six Feet of Faith" as they flew up the causeway toward Harlem. As they drove along one day, Leola rambled on excitedly about a sporting man named Charles Quinn, and his new panel houses. All the other brothel owners, she explained, had jumped on the bandwagon. "You must do the same," she exclaimed. A panel house, Leola explained, was a con game that blended prostitution and larceny. The success of the operation depended on the strict observance of the method. First, the woman had to be an intelligent, neat, good-looking woman of color, because the men who were robbed in this manner, especially well-to-do family men from out of town, did not want it known they kept company with mulattos, so they would not go to the police. If they did, when asked their name and residence by the police as a matter of public record, they always reneged on their accusations. This was what the panel houses thrived on.

"You find a basement apartment in a quiet, respectable neighborhood," said Leola, "and it's rented by an anonymous tenant not known to anyone in the building. A panel is cut into the wall, fitted to slide softly. The bolts and locks on the door are made to seem to lock on the inside, but they really fasten on the outside so that the client thinks he has locked all comers out whereas he has really locked himself in. Once the client is inside, lured by a sad story of a respectable woman driven to the streets by a violent husband, the price agreed upon is paid in advance to evaluate the entire contents of his wallet.

"The room has only one chair, so the gentleman, supposedly her first client, has to put his clothes there or on the floor. The chair is quite a distance from the bed, the only other piece of furniture in the room. Once the man is undressed and engaged, at a given signal the panel slides open and the accomplice creeps in and searches the trousers for the wallet. Not all the money is taken so that in court, he cannot say he was robbed and still had money. The wallet is filled with fake newspaper dollars so that its aspect stays the same. When this is done and the thief has crept out of the room and closed the panel, a loud knock is heard, and a furious husband arrives in the room. The gentleman takes flight. If he feels for his wallet, it is safe, he thinks. It is usually not until the next morning that he realizes he's been robbed. If he goes back to the house, everything is packed up and gone; if he goes to the police, they have little sympathy for a fool and his money, and he is more a figure of ridicule than concern. So, he remains silent." Leola sighed, shaking her head and smiling.

"You mean you rob your client?" exclaimed Hannah, shocked.

"Well, yes," said Leola.

"I am not a thief! I have never stolen anything in my life and never will! The idea that you would take more money from a client than he has already paid you is . . . dishonest! You have made a legitimate bargain—a promise to be met—and you'd steal from him? Shame on you, Leola. Shame! The Sisterhood is not that!"

All the burning shame of her pale green dress came flooding back. "To steal from a client is dishonest."

Leola muttered under her breath, but didn't know how to contradict Hannah. Leola's scheme made Hannah realize that she was not cut out for the Life in which she could still be expected to perform such tricks. She owned a house where only she made the rules, the first rule being never to return to prison. The second was to consider Clara dead and buried. The third was never to be poor or at the mercy of any man again. Moreover, she had finally realized that sex was not a matter of sex at all.

1896
THE CAPITALIST

The aggregations of great sums of money are absolutely essential for the conduct of human affairs.

—*John Moody*

The three most expensive words in any language are "unique au monde."

—*J. P. Morgan*

ELEVEN

Upper West Side, New York,
September 1896

Hannah and Leola stopped at the boathouse in Central Park and hired a boat to row around the lake on Sundays. Hannah dreamed of traveling to London one day on the Cunard Line. In the magazines, she saw pictures of elegant women standing on the decks of the great ships. They wore white tailored suits and bright hats with veils, and carried lace handkerchiefs. They visited the residences of Her Majesty the Queen and glided down the Thames.

Hannah removed her glove and trailed her fingers in the water just under the surface. The lake was not very deep. She could see the bottom. There were smooth rocks stuck in the mud, visible as the water rippled over their surface. Hannah sometimes felt like that. She felt unmoved by the flow of men that traversed her body, who never once left a trace on the surface of her soul.

The sporting life ran in rivulets through her fingers without meaning, exiting to a larger world day after day. She thought about Sadie, the only person in her family who tried to communicate with her. Every once in a while, Sadie would walk to Mrs. Truitt's, the last place that she knew Bessie lived, to ask Leola if she had any news. Then Leola of course had left Mrs. Truitt's for New York.

Hannah lived as if each day were her last—the balls and parties, the sporting men, the clothes. She didn't feel used or weak. She leaned over and took the oars from Leola, rowing the two of them swiftly and with strength, stretching her muscles with the effort. She had always been a

strong girl with an iron constitution. For years she had employed a physical education teacher from the Red Lantern gym in Chinatown to teach
her Chinese boxing. Hannah was no longer afraid of any man. Men had
that one vulnerable spot, which she did not. Hannah had no vulnerable
spot. And men's own power could be turned against them with the swift
bend of a knee. She rarely needed to fight now. She saw dangerous men
as soon as they stepped into her parlor. She sent them away. She kept
only the ones she knew she could manipulate—like the oars in the water.

Every year when the fall season opened, Central Park was thronged
with splendid equipages. There were new paths, new trees, more ingenues
preening, both female and male. And unlike men's clubs or opera boxes,
Central Park posed no entrance barriers based on family background,
source of wealth, or race.

They would come out in force, these golden girls with their equipages and new clothes, singly or in twos and threes. Being seen on the
Park Mall was part of the job of fashionable New York courtesans. Assignations were made or redeemed, cards and notes exchanged. Desperate young women arranged hurried trysts that ended often with a trip
to the notorious abortionist Madame Restill, never a marriage proposal.
And while their lives ended in calamity, fashionable New York proceeded
without a ripple or a mention of them. The rich took fresh air and stock
of one another every year. They recognized each other's carriages and
nodded or paused to talk. The social climbers saluted them like royalty.
Leola and Hannah were recognized but never acknowledged. Such was
their social class.

After their trip to the lake, Leola and Hannah stopped at the Minnehaha soda fountain on Fifth Avenue to enjoy ice cream sodas. The
owner didn't recognize Hannah. She looked nothing like the poor, hag-
gard woman who had burst through the doors years earlier.

The Italian marble fountain still impressed Hannah. In fact, the edifice lifted her spirits when she remembered the way she had screamed out
of her past life and even gotten Frank fired.

This one Sunday afternoon she spied an elegant couple drive up in
their polished landau and enter the ice cream parlor. The woman was

dressed in lavender silk with dark blue trim and a white rose-decorated hat with a veil. She lifted the train of her dress as she passed through the door, aided by her gentleman. The couple was so lovely, so elegant, so clean. Hannah stopped sipping her soda to stare at them as they brushed by her. Then she recognized the man. Edward Estel. This was, then, his real family, his wife. He was cheating on this impeccable, beautiful woman, with her beautiful lavender dress and her beautiful carriage.

Hannah wanted to shout, *Your husband is sleeping with another woman! Me, Hannah Elias!* She felt the bile rising in her. She whispered to Leola, "That's Edward." She had told Leola about her banking friend and regular customer.

The woman was young and blond. Her hands were soft and pale. Her skin was like a porcelain doll. While Hannah was thirty-one years old and looked ten years younger, this woman actually seemed ten years younger. Edward's wife laughed at his conversation with an intimacy and comfort that showed they loved one another. This was his real life. One thing was sure: he didn't talk finance trusts or banking with his wife.

Edward saw Hannah sitting at the table. But he looked straight through her as if she were invisible. And perhaps she was. Hannah stared at him and put on her mysterious smile. But Leola stood up and sashayed over to the couple sitting near the fountain, waiting for their soda. She put on her most aristocratic English-accented voice and said, "Edward? Edward darling! . . ."

Edward looked over Leola's shoulder into the eyes of Hannah. The blood drained from his face and he automatically crossed his legs.

"Oh," said Leola, her voice rising, "I'm so sorry! I mistook you for someone else! A London acquaintance . . ."

"Miss?" Edward's wife said.

"Excuse me," Edward said, his uppity voice becoming shrill.

Leola turned and came back to sit with Hannah, who was mortified but also a bit happy. The two women rose and left the place as Edward and his wife discoursed animatedly.

Edward did not return to Hannah after that incident. She was a little disappointed that their friendship ended, such as it was. But she was ready to release him anyway. The day in the soda parlor, she wanted the role of Edward's wife, not his concubine. Or anyone's wife now.

A few weeks later, she stopped again at the Minnehaha fountain after a drive in the park alone. A man began a conversation with her. He was a Pullman porter for J. P. Morgan's New York Central Railroad. Hannah took one look at the good-looking, debonair, already smitten Matthew Davis and decided he would do nicely. She would make her childhood dream of marrying a Pullman porter come true. Thanks to judicious speculation, she was now the proprietress of a boardinghouse on Fifty-Third Street, a tax-paying landlord. She deserved, she reasoned, a husband commensurate with her new status.

Hannah had no trouble getting Matthew Davis to propose. It took her eight weeks. He couldn't get over his good fortune.

They were married at City Hall with Leola as a witness. Hannah wore ivory lace over chiffon and a silver-trimmed Turkish turban with a knee-length veil and carried a bouquet of lilies and white roses that set off her happiest smile. Her birth certificate had "Bessie" on it, and that was what was on her marriage certificate: "Bessie." And that was the name her husband knew her by. But her millionaires all called her Hannah. She decided not to tell her new husband about her old lover, or her old lover about her new husband. She would tell them, she vowed, in good time.

She was happy with her Pullman porter husband. She read a news article in the *New York Age* that there were eight lawyers, thirteen undertakers, twenty-three doctors, and seventy-three schoolteachers who were colored in New York City. Matthew's job as a Pullman porter was as close to success as a person of color could rise.

There were other fields dominated after the Civil War by ex-slaves, such as horse racing and catering, but the new eastern European immigrants were moving them out. Of course, there were no Black firemen, policemen, postal workers, or magistrates. But over twenty thousand males worked as Pullman porters—the largest number of men in any field outside sharecropping except for Hannah's profession. The Pullman

Car Company had hired only colored men from the very beginning. The company needed workers as waiters, butlers, valets, concierges, and shoeshine boys—in other words, work these men had done as house slaves all their lives.

Porters worked 400 hours a month or 11,000 miles—whichever occurred first—to receive full pay. A porter's tips could be ten times more than his monthly salary. Hannah tried to convince her new husband that his tips should be saved or invested, as Edward had taught her to do, and that they should spend only his regular salary. It was windfall money, she explained, rather than budgeted money, but Matthew wasn't interested. Tips were to gamble away, to spend on food, drink, clothes, and sporting life. He was on the road twenty-nine days out of the month, he said. He needed amusement and comfort when he got home.

The boardinghouse over which Hannah now reigned was a neat-looking, anonymous three-story redbrick house with a stooped awning shielding the front door, which hid from view anyone who might be entering or leaving the house. The windows were high and narrow, with green shutters. On the parlor floor, the windows were french with flowered drapes looking out onto an inner courtyard. The carpeted parlor was furnished with a score of small cherrywood tables and upholstered armchairs. On the sideboard, there was always a bouquet of fresh flowers, and above it hung a large, framed painting she had bought at auction. It was a scene of woodlands, dales, and waterfalls, with mountains in the background. In the foreground, almost lost in the rocks and greenery, were tiny figures placed here or there, walking, working, picnicking. And on the road that curved into the picture and its perspective was a postilion with a dozen hounds chasing it. It could have been Central Park, and the carriage could have been Hannah's making a getaway.

Matthew spent most of his time away from home on the rails. Hannah ran the house, served the meals, collected the rent, and made sure the help cleaned the rooms and didn't steal anything. Her roomers were of both races; mostly honest working-class people mixed with a few musicians and music hall actors. She rented only to very discreet ladies of the night. The hourly roomers were mostly gone.

Hannah still kept her connections to the gambling den. Matthew didn't mind. His vices were more convenient now when he returned to town.

Cornelius Williams, the caterer who had moved in, became a permanent fixture, somewhere between a gatekeeper and a butler, lurking around the house when he was not working and spying on the comings and goings.

Matthew took a liking to him because he was another Black man whose watchful presence might protect his wife and home. But there was something about Cornelius's silent scrutiny that disturbed Hannah and his looks gave her the chills. That he was fascinated by Hannah was evident; even Matthew joked about it.

"The doorman to Hades"—as Matthew had named him—"has a crush on you. Why don't you get him a job as a bouncer for the gambling joint?"

"They have a bouncer," she replied. Hannah treated Cornelius with polite distain.

"He's your personal eunuch, Cleopatra," Matthew joked.

"What's a eunuch?" she asked.

"A eunuch," Matthew explained, "is a castrated male who guards a potentate's harem of wives and concubines in places like Constantinople and Baghdad. Their balls are cut off so that they cannot have sex with the women that are imprisoned under his care and over which he has complete power of life and death . . ." He smiled acidly. "Like me."

"How do you know about eunuchs and things?" Hannah asked, not laughing.

"What else do I have to do?" Matthew said. "All of us know about the world. We see a lot. Rich people, strange people. All of the vices of humanity come through those Pullman cars. The better class of people leave books for us too. I read about harems and eunuchs and the sultans of Turkey, the slaves of Cairo, the concubines of Baghdad in a book . . . someone left on the train."

"Did Cleopatra have a eunuch?" Hannah asked.

"She did actually. Ganymedes."

"Say that again."

"Gan-ya-me-des," Matthew enunciated. "This one book said he was a rival to Julius Caesar. I don't see how a eunuch could compete with a man."

Hannah could imagine it.

"It's amazing what you can learn about people from the shoes you shine. A foot is a whole world, from a Pullman porter's point of view. People talk on long trips, and if there's nobody else to talk to, they talk to me, about the damnedest things, about their love life, about politics, about sports and sex, their wives and children, philosophy, poetry, music. I've learned a lot from the rich and powerful and smart people who ride the rails. I've served tycoons and criminals, professors and politicians, judges and actresses, people who count in this world."

Sometimes Matthew seemed more interested in riding the rails than in Hannah at home. She thought his feeling was much like the desperation of the men who rode J. P. Morgan's freight trains, the men who were called hobos. In one of her magazines, she read that after the Civil War many soldiers returned home by hopping freight cars; thus the name in the South meant "hopping boxcars" or "homeless body." But to a New Yorker like Hannah, it meant Houston and Bowery, where the homeless people of the city gathered. The magazine said that the word may have come from the Japanese word *houbou*, meaning "a lot of places." Whatever the origin, these were men who were escaping from a reality too heavy to bear: no money, no home, no wife, no work, six children, no paycheck, a prison record, the landlord, a lost love, the police. Whether Matthew had the heart of a hobo, she wasn't quite sure. She knew, though, that her life seemed less perfect than she first imagined. She was still lonely.

One day, Matthew brought a man to the house whom he had served on the Pullman train between Chicago and New York. Granville T. Woods was an inventor and patent holder of some sixty titles, so he said. His inventions, he explained, included the electrical apparatus that gave the trolley its name, the trawler, and which provided electric traction to rail vehicles by transmitting power from overhead wires. Even more important, he had invented the third rail, a revolutionary method of distributing electric power to the subway and elevated trains. The genius of these electrical magnetic inventions had changed the face of public transportation. Thomas Edison's company had bought several of his patents. In all, he told them, he had sold more than thirty licenses.

"Gran' here's a genius," Matthew had said one night at dinner. "I was proud to serve him. I told him to come on home and meet the missus."

Granville Woods was put together with fine elegance and no less strength. He was tall, and like Commodore Vanderbilt, nobody passed him on the street without taking a second look. He was as erect as a Mohawk Indian. His shoulders were broad. His arms hung loosely, and he moved with masculine, feline grace. He had nut-brown hair, a high forehead, and dark, almond-shaped eyes full of sweetness and fire. He had a wonderful smile, with big, bold, even teeth and a rakish military mustache that framed his full lips. He was clean shaven except for that, and he wore long sideburns to his chin line.

Granville dressed entirely in black, always the most eloquent color at all times, which gave him an aristocratic air that impressed people. Hannah imagined that he could understand her many identities because he passed himself off as an Australian Aborigine instead of an American Negro, because he believed he got more respect as a foreign Black man than as an American.

His appearance belied the hard life he had endured as a child in the cotton fields of Mississippi and as a young man digging ditches in Georgia. His skin was unlined, smooth, and plum black. Hannah had seen such a face only on Egyptian statues. He was so dark his face seemed a bottomless well of softest night, deep and abiding, pierced by bold black eyes of candescent intelligence, which held secrets too dangerous to reveal.

Woods was forty-one years old, he told them, a Christian who had never married. He was a country boy, born free in Columbus, Ohio. There had been Black Laws that had prohibited Blacks and mulattoes from entering the state without a $500 bond, serving in the militia, attending school, or testifying against white defendants. Granville had managed to attend school until he was ten.

He had then been instructed in the mechanist trade as an apprentice. At the same time, he had attended night school, and by sheer willpower and ambition, he had chiseled a higher education out of rock and stone. He had traveled west, worked as a fireman and finally as a railroad engineer. In his spare time, since saloons and easy women were not his cup of tea, he had taken up the study of electricity. He had left for the North at seventeen, where he had attended college for two years in Rhode Island, specializing in electrical and mechanical engineering, working six half days in a machine shop and spending the other half days in school.

The turning point in his life had come when he had been hired as an engineer on a British steamer, the *Ironsides*, and had set sail around the world, visiting almost every country on the globe. When he returned, he settled in Cincinnati, and he founded his own company in 1884. Four years later, he had filed his first patent for a system of overhead electricity for railroads in cities like Chicago, Saint Louis, and New York. A whole slew of other patents followed: an improved steam boiler furnace, an electric railway system, a multiplex railway telegraph, which allowed communications among stations and moving trains. When he moved into Hannah's boardinghouse, he had just sold his rights to a telegraphing machine to Alexander Graham Bell.

The first night at the boardinghouse, the three of them had gathered around the kitchen table. While the men joked and laughed together, Hannah sat silent, unable to speak, unable to breathe, unable to take her eyes off the inventor. She had risen and reseated herself a thousand times, it seemed, unable to comprehend either her shame or her happiness.

The impulse that squeezed Hannah's heart was more than infatuation. Even she knew that. She who had been such an expert in love had no idea what to do now that she had come face to face with her feelings. All Hannah knew was it felt like music. It felt like religion. It felt like ragtime. Granville's every glance, every gesture, evoked unbearable commotion in her: his way of walking, his way of talking, his measured, languid movements, the way he held his shoulders back as if he were meeting a storm, his laugh, his eyes, the echo of his step, the way he moved his hips or held a cigarette. Each cast its spell.

After Granville moved in Hannah's life began to revolve around him and his wild stories about his life and his inventions, his struggle for recognition of his genius, and his repeated rejection.

But Granville's travels fascinated Hannah the most. His stories of Athens, Barcelona, Malta, Paris, London, Saint Petersburg, Cape Town, and New Delhi made her head spin.

"Yes, I've seen the pyramids in Egypt," he answered Hannah's question one day as they sat together in the parlor. Matthew was on the road. "The Sphinx is a magnificent statue in the desert. A crouching animal with the face of a man."

Hannah was so excited that she excused herself so that she wouldn't betray her feelings. She rose and returned with tea and a tray of cookies to make him linger and talk.

"Did you ever see Cleopatra's tomb?" Hannah asked. Her voice trembled even though she tried to control it. Granville's knowledge was so extensive and true, not like Matthew, whose knowledge came from reading and stories overhead while shining shoes.

"No, not me. Not anyone, Hannah." He sensed her excitement. Matthew had told him about Hannah's obsession. He wanted to please her, so he told her about his trip.

"I did travel to Alexandria and a nearby site called Taposiris Magna. It's like an amber-colored city of stone. The ruins are under the modern city of Alexandria. People have found cisterns and churches, pyramids and columns. There's even an old lighthouse and another monument where people think burials took place."

Hannah was practically in a swoon. All her years with madams and hookers, bankers and millionaires, were nothing compared with the education that Granville afforded her in the afternoon tea that followed when Matthew was home or when they were alone. He told her about her greatest interests simply out of his generosity. What kind of man was this?

Nights she could not sleep for thinking of Granville. She imagined the day that they could travel the world together, visiting city after city in eternal movement. Was it possible that she, a convict, a prostitute, and a married woman, could possess such a man?

Meanwhile, Cornelius, the silent, invisible boarder, watched her growing infatuation with Granville and became consumed with jealousy.

Into her boardinghouse had walked the perfect man—no matter that he arrived with her husband. She took that first fatal step by breaking Mrs. Truitt's rule about falling in love. She made no attempt to resist her enjoyment of Granville's company. This destroyed the equilibrium Hannah had established between business and pleasure. From the moment she laid eyes on him, her life transformed itself into the pathos of an abiding passion. Her chest hurt. Her heart pounded and her pulse quickened in his presence. Hannah was terrified.

✤

Hannah felt as if she were once again that young girl in the green chiffon Worth dress running down Addison Street to her sister's wedding. She remembered the thrill of being beautiful and pursued, not for the sex she would trade for money, but for her genuine self. Granville had returned her to a state of innocence, and she remembered how clean she felt. Vital and pure, she remembered the joy that the future portended.

She wondered whether she could reinvent her virginity for him, as Mrs. Truitt had done. She couldn't see the incongruity in that notion, because she was married. He would have certainly known that. That's how large her fantasies grew. Could she offer him a kiss? Give him the very breath in her lungs, or sweep his mouth with her lips? All Hannah knew was that she would love him forever. In her blue-lined copybook, she wrote and rewrote: "I love Granville Woods."

She told her secret to Leola one night when she visited.

"You know better than this," Leola admonished her. "You know this is the last thing in life you need, especially now. Besides, that is the one rule you must not break—"

"I can and I will," Hannah insisted.

"Granville is a gentleman, a Christian, and Matthew's friend. He's an honest man. You cannot convince him, and you cannot deceive him. It is a losing proposition on all counts."

"But think of Granville. I can help him on all counts."

"You think he would accept that? Never! It goes without saying he's too proud. Besides, he's the kind of man who doesn't need a woman— even a woman he loves. He's married to his own mind, and you can't change that."

"I don't want to change him. He is perfect."

"Indeed? And what makes you imagine you deserve him? Your spot-lessly clean and devotional life? He is beyond, far beyond your reach, Hannah. He is a walking, breathing catastrophe for you."

"He's worth any catastrophe!"

"Oh, Lord, Bessie." Leola tried to return her to reality. "Granville is another one of your famous missteps that will land you in jail, again. Or killed. He is the most dangerous man you have ever encountered because he is good. I see it here, in the cards. He's a good man who loves you."

Leola got up from the table where they were sitting. She went to get her hat and coat. She was fighting a losing battle with her cruel words. Hannah was already lost.

On January 1, 1898, New Yorkers celebrated the unification of the five boroughs of New York. Andrew Green, who had executed the plans for Central Park, had led the drive to bring together the metropolitan region as one entity. The *New-York Tribune* headlines read, "The New City's Greatness: It Outrivals the Cities of the World in Area and Water Front-age." Green had persevered through the ridicule of Brooklynites—who wished to remain autonomous—who called the plan "Green's Hobby." Voters and a new commission, however, approved. On New Year's Day, metropolitan New York was born. Green became known as "the Father of Greater New York," a title he would hold for the rest of his life.

The day was monumental for Hannah too.

Her husband, Matthew Davis, herself, Granville, and Cornelius all spent the day together just like tens of thousands of other New Yorkers. They assembled along a four-mile parade route down Broadway to the sea. Hundreds of American flags flew from buildings. Public offices were closed. The strains of "The Star-Spangled Banner" filled the air. Hannah and the men watched the parade, then moved to the harbor, where they watched a procession of three hundred sailing ships. They came slowly down the Hud-son to form a crescent at the foot of the Statue of Liberty on Bedloe's Island.

Ships fired salvos in the statue's honor. Cheers rose from the crowd. The noise of whistles and sirens filled the air. Hannah stood between the man she loved, Granville, and the man she was married to, Matthew. The man she hardly knew existed, Cornelius, stood alongside. He sang "God Bless America" as loud as possible in honor of Lady Liberty. The group laughed, and then joined in.

Hannah sang heartily, liberty being her goal. The great accomplishment of Andrew Green marked a turning point in her life that day. She had no idea that Green would also make a profound change in her future.

Matthew left that very evening on the Chicago Special out of Grand Central. Hannah had been given a ticket to a grand ball of the New York Odd Fellows in Greenwich Village to celebrate New York City's birth. She asked Granville to escort her.

"But I don't own a frock coat, or a tuxedo," he protested.

"You can fit into Matthew's," Hannah said. She flew to her apartment and brought back the jacket to his room.

"Try it on!"

Granville put on the frock coat, which fit him perfectly. He went into another room to try on the pants, and when he appeared again, she assisted him in fastening the scarlet cummerbund. As her arms circled his waist, a current of electricity pierced her, lodging in her stomach, spreading warmth through her body that stopped her breath and knocked her dizzy. She had never experienced such a sensation. She knew what lust and carnal desire felt like, but this new ache was more illumination than lust, more thunder than desire. She had wanted only to dissolve into his tall, narrow body. She looked up and met Granville's eyes, and realized he too had felt everything she had.

"Is this, sir, what you call your electrical magnetism?" she whispered.

"Bessie," he said, "My God . . ."

The yearning in his voice, and the desire and awe it expressed, fused them in an embrace. Their mouths sought out one another, and Hannah allowed herself to feel the sensation, the movement of lips and tongue to reach her in other places deeper inside herself, to lose her thoughts in a way she had been warned against. An irresistible force moved her, created a yearning that weakened her knees and lightened her soul.

Granville too decided to give in to the feeling, although not very far. He took her hand and said, "Let's just have an enjoyable evening." He sent Hannah off to get dressed, which she did, more excited to go to this dance than any ever.

That night, the noisy, joyous cotillion of a hundred couples dressed in finery and silks could have done justice to Mrs. Astor's ballroom. The movement, heat, and excitement mirrored their own commotion. There were waltzes and gallops, cakewalks and rounds, in perfect imitation of the elite of New York society, at which the very same colored musicians and caterers served. The men all wore Mason or Elk or Odd Fellow signet rings, and the women all wore the latest fashionable gowns and diamond, jet, and garnet jewelry, hair coiffed in feathers and plumes, their bodies encased in corsets and sequins. It was a time to forget the cold hostility of the outside world, to forget the pain and the precariousness of life as colored people in New York City in 1898.

Hannah and Granville danced far into the night, blazing with joy at expressing their infatuation in public, yet anonymous in the throng. They were not aware of Cornelius's watchful eyes or the sadness with which he followed them—from dance floor to punch bowl to balcony to dance floor again. It seemed to Hannah that her exhilaration and happiness had reached a point of no return. She waited for some kind of declaration of love from Granville. Her breath was shallow, like an innocent girl. Could a married madam elope, she wondered?

They could live in so many cities where she would go unrecognized.

"Men like me should never marry," Granville said without prompting when they took a break from the dancing. "I am married to my work. Would any wife be happy playing a secondary role?"

Hannah knew that she could. Her jealousy would never be the result of another woman, as she lived now.

He added, "Scientists make terrible husbands and even worse fathers."

"I can't imagine you being a bad father." Hannah knew about that.

"But you *can* imagine me as a bad husband, can't you?"

"You mean . . . always thinking of something to invent or to prove. Never thinking of anything or anyone else—"

"Exactly. Besides, if I were going to marry anyone, it would be you, and you're already married to my only friend. I would never betray your husband."

"I would gladly devote my life to your happiness. A man like you, a man of genius, is sacred, sacred to posterity, sacred to science, sacred to the souls of Black folks. You should be cherished and honored by any woman you deem to love. She should be your rescue, your helper, your servant, your slave, really. The reason why she's put on earth."

For the first time, Hannah imagined helping someone other than herself. In her future with Granville, she too could help humanity she thought. Granville would make a difference with his mind, his inventions; she wanted only to serve that mind.

"Can't you see that?"

"No, I don't see that, Hannah." He fell silent.

Still, Granville didn't want the evening to end, and neither did Hannah. They strolled along the streets for a short while in the a.m. hours; then they took a carriage ride to the ferry terminal at the foot of Manhattan. They waited at the nearly empty pier for the boat that would return filled with hotel cleaners and rich businessmen starting the day. Granville appeared as a tall, stately man, a black-garbed figure in a bowler hat and white scarf. Hannah wore a pearl-gray flannel suit with a pleated train, a white silk blouse, and a wide-brimmed red fedora hat with ostrich feathers. They sat close together, holding hands. When they boarded the ferry, listing from side to side with the winter sea, Granville put his arms around Hannah. She lay her head on his shoulder. For the ride to Richmond and back, they were in a world of their own, in view of the Statue of Liberty. Lady Liberty was their only reminder of reality.

They returned to Fifty-Third Street when most of New York was sitting for breakfast. Cornelius heard the two pairs of feet climbing the stairs. He stood near the side of his front window, in the clothes that he'd worn to the dance. He had not slept, not wanting to miss their return. His chest felt as if it contained a spring that was being wound tighter and tighter. He trembled as he peeked out the window and saw them entering the building, and then stood by his door listening for their footfalls. It took them a while to part, he knew, probably kissing as they stood in the foyer. Cornelius wanted to swing the door open and say "Ah-ha!" exposing their infidelity. Unfortunate for him that he never had the chance.

Hannah returned to her house with the knowledge that her husband would be gone for almost a month. She considered that by the time he returned she may have eloped with Granville.

She undressed slowly, smiling, and fell into bed with Champagne dreams and the memory of the soft, swaying ferry.

Hours later, after she performed her toilette and put on a beautiful day-dress, she knocked on Granville's door.

It swung open. She walked in.

Granville was gone. He left a letter.

> *To my demon of pleasure,*
>
> *By the time you read this, I will be on the train to Cincinnati, which I fear is the safest place for a poor, deranged man like myself at the moment. I will not betray Matthew, and if I remain anywhere in your vicinity, what happened last night will happen again and again, and I do not have the will power to resist. Once is an accident of fate, or a poor sinner's stumble, twice is treason. I do not want to know anything more of your life with him. Since he is your husband and not I, he is my enemy. Nor do I wish to know anything about the sporting life you lead behind his back. A life you have never revealed to me, but which I have guessed. You are not an honest woman. I don't care anymore, since you are not now, nor ever will be mine. Yet I mourn for Matthew, as I mourn for myself. We are not lucky in love. I will never forget you. I will never love you. I do believe I despise you—at least more than I love you.*
>
> *Since both are sins, the safest emotion for a Christian soul to have is indifference. But the violence, the emotion I feel for you, is so close to love, you might as well name it that. The reverse, my hatred, however, is my fortress. I will never let you in and I will never crawl out, for if I did, I would be obliged to kill you for what you are.*
>
> *Granville*

Hannah never believed Granville was gone for good. She had believed she could have any man on the planet she desired. Granville was no different from all the others.

She rushed downstairs to her room and wrote a letter in response.

To my beloved inventor,

Do you know what it's like to be imprisoned in an asylum for the destitute? I don't mean barefoot, empty-stomach dirt poor. I mean kill for a crust of bread, fuck for a sliver of soap. I can, because I have been a pauper. I had no place to go. My daughter Clara was born in the poorhouse. Should I have raised her in a brothel or an orphanage, which are both jails? I abandoned her, yes, just like my father abandoned me, just like my twin deserted me, just like you have left me.

My mother couldn't wait till I was out of Blackwell prison to punish me by dying. I don't write this as an excuse. It was the poorhouse, the whorehouse, or death itself. I chose the Sisterhood. I've never regretted it until you. Now I can say I should have chosen death rather than endure your renunciation. Please don't leave me and never come back. Please don't hate me and never come back. Please don't kill me by never coming back. I love you, Granville. With all my past, my present, and my future—the breath that keeps me alive—I love you. Don't deprive me of life itself. I beg you. Don't never come back. Don't do it, Granville. For the love of God.

Hannah

She sent the letter to Cincinnati, where she guessed he had gone. She waited weeks, pacing the floor and growing thinner. Then the letter came back unopened and with a black-edged stamp like a death notice that read, UNKNOWN AT THIS ADDRESS RETURN TO SENDER.

The return of her unopened letter sent her into total collapse. She could not keep food down; she ran a fever that eventually forced her to take to her bed. Her suffering was monstrous. For so many years her iron will had fought against her total defeat, which only made her heartbreak more terrible.

Matthew came back from the road and couldn't figure out the source of her ailment. He would enter her room and contemplate her prostrate state. He was sure she was going to die. What would he do then, he asked her?

Hannah finally lifted her head and whispered, "I'll be up tomorrow, rain or shine . . ." Months passed before she was as good as her word.

TWELVE

West Fifty-Third Street, New York,
November 6, 1898

Matthew contemplated Hannah like a man struggling for breath while trying to survive in the ocean. At times he caught himself gasping if he contemplated too long on Hannah's past, and what he suspected was the occasional release when he left town. But he was too afraid and too weak to protest. Instead, he chose a path that would reduce his suffering: staying away on the rails for as long as possible.

He turned to drinking and gambling with his Elk and Odd Fellow friends when he returned home. When he excused himself from the card tables occasionally, they whispered about him because some had seen Hannah and Granville on New Year's Day. Others had heard about her reputation and her occasional forays to the downtown bordellos. When Matthew came back, they smiled wanly in his direction, feeling sorry for his dilemma, of which he wasn't even aware.

He and Hannah went together to church on Sundays. Often Cornelius was there, sitting a few rows behind. They heard him praying a little louder than the others around him and saying "Amen" in a very strong voice when the minister mentioned the word sin.

Sometimes Cornelius moved so that he was so close behind them in church that the boa feathers on Hannah's hat would stir with his breath.

Matthew wondered about the reason that Granville left. But he didn't want to ask Hannah. After she recovered from her depression, she still didn't seem right to him.

Except for the time that Granville lived in the house and Hannah suffered depression, she continued to see John Rufus Platt. Several times a week when he was home, she told Matthew that she was going to pay a bill. As a boardinghouse owner, he knew she collected rents and put them into the bank. He knew about her deposit account when they married. He believed that she went to the bank, to promenade with Leola, and to get herself a piece of jewelry a few times.

Matthew didn't question the enormous, expensive rings that seemed to come her way and appeared on her dresser when he had returned from the road. Nor did he ask her the reason she owned so many ball gowns. They went only once or twice to a fancy-dress dance.

Cornelius had followed her one day when she took public transportation to the Upper East Side, across from Central Park. He was detained by a policeman who saw him rushing behind Hannah, then stepping to the side of a building so that he could peek at her.

"Hey, buddy," the cop said. "What's going on with you? Are you all right?"

Cornelius nodded wildly in the affirmative.

So the policeman took him aside and patted him down to make sure he had no weapon. By that time, Hannah had gone.

Platt knew Hannah was married. She had started to wear a ring on her left hand, much plainer than the others he gave her. She twirled for him in shiny necklaces and undergarments.

When Granville lived in her house, she told Platt, "I think I'm in love."

"I thought you were married," he said.

She ignored him and chose not to elaborate.

After Granville left and Hannah didn't contact him for weeks, Platt went to her house. He missed her so much. The person meeting him at the door, however, was Cornelius.

Platt asked, "Are the folks in?" He took Cornelius for Hannah's doorman.

Cornelius didn't like his tone, too familiar. Or his appearance, too rich. Or his face, too white. As Hannah's self-appointed protector, Cornelius said, "She is not here and she is not coming back anytime soon so there's no sense of you hanging around here.

Platt says, "Who do you think you're talking to Boy, telling me what I can and can not do. Your Boss will hear about this!" When Cornelius told Hannah that evening, expecting to get a compliment, Hannah's voice rose. "You have no right! No right at all to police my associates, billers, or bankers. Who told you to make decisions about my life?"

Hannah told Cornelius that he had to leave the apartment. He had one week to get out or she was going to call the police.

Cornelius realized that the white man could have been a policeman at the door seeking Hannah to pay her "insurance policy" for protecting the gambling house. He became contrite. But she would not hear his apology.

"You get out of my business and get out of my life," she told Cornelius.

One Sunday night, August 13, 1900, Hannah strolled over to "African Broadway," Seventh Avenue from Twenty-Third to Fortieth Street. There she saw young men wearing the latest fashions—silk hats, patent leather shoes, diamonds on their fingers, conspicuous pocket watches or the newest fashion, wristwatches.

Some blocks of Seventh Avenue were like the other parts of the Tenderloin near Madame Paree's, because streetwalkers sashayed slowly near the buildings and men lingered waiting to make assignations.

There were so many Black men in New York who had left the labor and oppression of the South and were now alone. Many just wanted free, friendly talk. Others asked for more.

But this night, after she had worked and lived for years in the Tenderloin and the Bowery and knew all the comings and goings, at about two in the morning she saw a white man grab a woman by the arm in front of one of the brownstones.

A Black man walked up right behind him and stabbed him and ran off with the girl. It wasn't that unusual. Fights like this happened all the time when pimps robbed a white John. But by morning, Hannah knew that this hadn't been a John but an undercover cop—the son of a police captain—who had died in the hospital.

Whites, many of them Irishmen who were friends of the policeman, trolled the area where she lived and the Black man was last seen. Within a week, a fight between two men—one white and one Black—took place, but rather than the usual, mutual pummeling that ended when one slinked away, a white mob descended on the Black man involved.

He was beaten almost to death, and afterward Blacks throughout the West Edge of the Tenderloin were threatened constantly. Some people were beaten as they left their jobs. Some of the neat young men Hannah admired no longer stood on the street waiting to give her a smile and some conversation.

The cops came into the area seven hundred strong and picked up random Black New Yorkers, brought them into police custody, and beat them almost to death.

For a month, August through September 1900, the race war continued. White gangs surfed through the streets. Blacks threw garbage on them from the rooftops. The Black Citizens' Protective League armed themselves with guns for battle. Their presence may have quelled the random beatings. The murderer was caught and sent to jail. Black people who had come from the South started to move out of the area and uptown to Harlem.

Hannah reconsidered whether she wanted a partner at all. How could he ever protect her? The woman whom the undercover policeman had grabbed had been the girlfriend of the murderer, not a hooker at all, going into her own house. By defending her honor, this man would live and die behind bars.

"Marriage is not for me," she told Platt. She mimicked the words Granville used, but instead of being tied to genius as he was, she was tied to her business.

Platt was overjoyed. He now could have more of her time. To celebrate, he helped her sell the building where she lived with Matthew and where Cornelius boarded.

They knew nothing of the sale. They only woke up one morning and Hannah had disappeared.

However, while Platt thought they had gotten rid of the building, Hannah was no fool. Edward told her never to dispose of real estate or let anyone know everything about her finances.

All along she had been working with August Nanz, the lawyer she had met in the Hook for her first building. And she even consulted him when the banks went bust. He seemed always to land on his feet. And they had that in common.

August Augustus Amadeos Abraham Lincoln Nanz, Esq. (his mother had used the encyclopedia his father sold from door to door to name him) was Hannah's jack-of-all-lawyers, a young, ambitious, cold-blooded, two-faced ambulance chaser and Tombs barrister. But she needed him. He ran errands, did dirty work, and collected and paid bills, and was a stand-in escort, janitor, decorator, and confidant.

August stood out in a crowd of hunchbacked lawyers. He was a very tall, athletically built, fair-haired, ice-gray-eyed man with a long, handsome, brazen face shaped like no other person. He could just as well have been Scottish or English. In fact, he was third-generation Swede; his great-grandfather had been a ragpicker, his grandfather a stonemason, and his father a door-to-door encyclopedia salesman. He had been the first in his family to attend college. His mother had weighed him down with famous names at birth—she couldn't make up her mind and seemed to have stopped at the As—sure he was destined for great things. He had worked his way through New York University, waiting tables, singing in brothels, and selling Bibles. He had managed, despite a total lack of connections, to land a job as a law clerk in a prestigious Wall Street firm. His great-grandfather had changed the spelling of his name from the Swedish "Nöng" to "Nanz" to sound more Anglo-Saxon. His employers had been satisfied enough that he was a WASP and considered him their experiment in poor, smart white boy acquisitions.

Hannah met him first at her building transaction, then ran into him a few times in the downtown bordellos. She invited him into her home some nights when she was alone. They sat painting their nails and talking about the ways to get boyfriends for money or love, while neither really expected a payoff. Nanz had become a legitimate, if detested, lawyer. He kept Hannah's secrets as no one else could, because she knew his.

When Hannah found a new house away from her husband Nanz made the arrangements for the down payment on the house, with the rest deposited into Hannah's savings account and his commission. She kept the title on the Fifty-Third Street building and let it evolve fully into a bordello as Matthew left.

Hannah's bigger and better building sat on West Seventy-Third Street. Neither Matthew nor Cornelius knew the location.

She took Leola with her, leaving thirteen whores and a heartbroken husband. John Platt had given her enough money to cross the line from simple commerce to American industry.

The facade of the new brownstone house on Seventy-Third Street had a dark blue door under a vaulted cornice of sculpted limestone, supported by a ribbon and tassel-tied wreath. It went unnoticed on the quiet side street. The foyer was round and rose three stories to a domed, multicolored skylight, from which hung a forty-eight-branch crystal chandelier. The hardwood floors were set with large star-shaped medallions of parquetry, and in the center was a huge, plush ottoman with ferns. There was a butler named Richard Smith, a cook named Mary Scott, and a large staff of Chinese servants.

She filled the house with ladies of every hue and nationality for every taste: Lulu, Xaviera, Josie, Lorie, Polly, Chica, Imperia, Chiyo, and Leila. There were bouncers and bodyguards who were retired policemen and a regular physician, Dr. de Kraft. There was also gambling on the premises: roulette, blackjack, bridge, poker, *trente et un*, in separate saloons reached through the cellar. The inmates could look down from the sweeping staircase and gilded balcony that surrounded three sides of the foyer as the men entered. Two six-foot incense burners flanked each of the doors that led to rooms served by narrow staircases. There were no saloons, parlors, or reception rooms where clients and inmates might accidentally be seen or overheard by other customers. There was only one room where entertainment, spectacles, and exhibitions occurred, and this was the only place one man might meet up with another. Hannah rarely appeared and was known to both inmates and clients as the Capitalist.

And that was her identity, as far as anyone could ascertain. She had passed the financial barrier of small-time madam into the realm of big-time courtesan servicing the rich and well born with appropriate concern and savoir faire.

Her boarders included Eurasians, Indians, Burmese, Madagascans, native Black and native white, and the mix of both. They were all specialists in the art of massage. This skill made Hannah's fortune grow. She advertised discreetly in newspapers and journals, and her clientele was just as discreet and more than a little grateful for the lavish interiors, the Turkish baths, the sumptuous meals, the lit candles, the soft music, the opium pipes, the incredible cream colored to deep maroon bodies who did amazing things with their hands and feet to one's senses.

Hannah was a generous madam and a silent one, who guarded the names of her clients with her life. She was soon catering only to upper Fifth Avenue, Sutton Place, and Park Avenue clientele. Black tie was mandatory, and coachmen lined both sides of the street.

All of a sudden, Hannah had large amounts of cash. Her name became known for her toilettes and expensive gowns designed by Worth and Doucet. Her money flowed fast and freely. The dresses arrived by the armful as if she had decided to smother the memory of the stolen Philadelphia dress in the yards of silk and satins, lace and velvet it took to make just one of her gowns. Hannah's fashionable Parisian clothes became her signature.

John Rufus sent his friends around, and her reputation as proprietress of the best and most discreet house of assignation on the Upper West Side flourished.

As fame had its price, Hannah was soon discovered by Matthew. The Odd Fellows now told him the whole story once his wife disappeared.

A process server came to the door and asked for Hannah Davis. It was a name she never used. So her doorman called her down to see the visitor. He handed her the paper to say that she needed to appear in New York State District Court. The suit sought divorce and named John Rufus Platt as the co-respondent.

Hannah had planned her divorce for more than a year but not like this. Shocked, Hannah rushed to the offices of Warren, Warren, and O'Beirne and explained her plight to Nanz.

Still delusional from love, all Hannah could think was that her divorce was a relief. She would be free to marry Granville. After reading the summons, August peered over his gold-rimmed glasses, now in his legal mode, trying to appear older than his twenty-eight years.

"The complaint is for alienation of affection," said August.

"Well, what is that?" she cried.

"Mr. Platt," said August. "Any relation to the *Social Register* Platt?"

"I don't know."

"Well, Mr. Davis has filed a complaint against Mr. Platt naming him your lover, which is grounds for divorce in New York County."

"What! But I never told Mr. Davis anything about Mr. Platt. How could Mr. Davis have found out?"

"Through your real estate, Hannah. Your house on Fifty-Third Street was underwritten by Mr. John Platt. Those records are public. Your husband is very angry, Hannah, especially since you never told him about Mr. Platt before marrying him. Your husband thinks that is where all your money comes from."

"The boardinghouse!" she exclaimed.

"A house of assignation," corrected August.

"I have real boarders!"

"Madame, as you are a married woman, the house on Fifty-Third Street is communal property. Mr. Davis can demand half of it as his. He *is* demanding a settlement, and he can demand alimony, Hannah. If this goes to trial, both Mr. Platt's name and yours will come out in divorce court and I fear in the newspapers. Is Mr. Platt married?"

"A widower."

"Well, at least there's no betrayed wife to contend with."

But it was Hannah who felt betrayed. How could Matthew have gone behind her back like this? Why hadn't he simply confronted her, Saturday-night style? She conveniently forgot that she was the one who had left.

August removed his spectacles and considered his client. She had introduced herself to him as a Cuban national, hence her suitcase of cash when they had first met. But he knew now that Matthew was a Pullman porter and Black—everyone knew there were no white Pullman porters. There was a huge enigma here, thought August, not just a matter of a cuckolded Negro husband. As long as he had known Hannah, she carried herself as a white woman. Of course, they had entertained one another in mixed company—didn't everyone downtown mix? Negroes and white, foreigners and Americans, men with men, women with women. Hannah to him was a white woman who had crossed the color line with a Negro and then betrayed her husband with a white man. There was no law against interracial marriage in New York State, almost alone in the United States where it was against the law and a felony punishable by prison or a fine in the rest of the country. August was fascinated.

"I want you to go see Matthew Davis and find out what he wants from me," Hannah said without any other explanation.

"He wants money, Hannah."

"Well, I want you to say we will settle with him for a thousand dollars and a divorce. Then I want you to go to Mr. Platt and tell him you, Mr. Nanz, are prepared to act as his adviser and attorney in this action, which must be kept out of the newspapers. Can you take care of this?" Hannah reached over and touched August's hand. "Of course, it will be Mr. Platt who will pay you."

August's eyes lit up. He put his glasses back on. Hannah had finally cut him into the source of her money. With a client like John Platt, in an affair like this one, he could rise in the firm from a lowly clerk to a case lawyer.

"Please, Hannah," he pleaded, "don't have any further contact with your husband or Mr. Platt. I believe Mr. Davis has moved out and is living on Lenox Avenue."

"If that's what the divorce papers say."

"What about the other properties?"

"Nobody knows my business but you, August."

"Well, don't buy anything else until you are legally and officially divorced."

"Yes."

"And you will need to move out of the house on Seventy-Third Street as long as you're still doing business. You can't be seen with suitors, gentleman callers, or clients."

Hannah booked a room at the Waldorf. There was no date for the checkout.

1902
THE MANSION OF
ACHING HEARTS

She lives in a mansion of aching hearts,
She's one of a restless throng,
The diamonds that glitter around her throat,
They speak both of sorrow and song;
The smile on her face is only a mask,
And many the tear that starts,
For sadder it seems, when of mother she dreams,
In the mansion of aching hearts.

—Harry Von Tilzer and Arthur J. Lamb,
"The Mansion of Aching Hearts"

THIRTEEN

Upper West Side, New York,
March 1, 1902

John Platt was overjoyed to have gotten rid of Matthew once and for all. Now Hannah was his alone, he claimed happily. The young lawyer, Nanz, from Warren, Warren, and O'Beirne, had represented her and disposed of her husband. Platt gave the lawyer carte blanche. Once Nanz had obtained Hannah's divorce, he finished paying off the house on Seventy-Third Street as he had promised. She returned to the floor in the building that was hers alone. Platt paid her visits whenever he wanted.

Little did he know that Hannah felt free enough now to finally search every district of New York City and the eastern seaboard for the man she loved, Granville Woods, all the time buying more houses on the West Side. She was never very far from Central Park. The area symbolized her release from convention and a return to herself.

From the money she made now mortgage free, Hannah purchased a house at 73 West Sixty-Eighth Street in 1899 and then 166 West Seventy-Second Street, which she bought from Adeline Widmayer and her husband for $49,500 in 1902.

She expanded her budding empire as the proprietor of four high-class brothels of impeccable reputation and safety, some connected to private gambling casinos. She still visited the soda fountain. She still took her daily drives through Central Park with Leola. On one of these drives, they passed a magnificent brownstone mansion for sale facing the park. It had been built by the famous architectural firm of McKim, Mead, and White, and it had belonged to a millionaire ironically named Blackwell, the name of the almshouse where she stayed, which in double irony had changed its name to Roosevelt Island.

Not long after that, August Nanz's detectives found Granville living in Harlem, near the construction site of the new subway stop at 125th Street. Hannah, confident and joyful, took a public cab to the address August had given her. She stood trembling in the long, barely lit hallway in front of his door.

When the door opened at her timid knock and the love of her life stood there in the flesh, Hannah had a moment of hesitation. The hallway light cast a long shadow and illuminated the soft boa feathers on her hat, which was shaped like a huge gardenia and draped with a heavy gray veil. The train of her dress swept the bare wooden floor: it was long sleeved with a pearl-gray satin skirt and matching chiffon bodice, the black Chantilly lace collar setting off her jet and diamond necklace and earrings. Her hands shook as she lifted her veil and raised her eyes to his.

"Bessie!" He stood frozen in the doorway of the room, eyebrows lifted, studying Hannah.

"I've searched everywhere for you," she whispered.

"I've been fighting the Thomas Edison Electrical Company, among other things . . ." His voice trailed off as he stared helplessly at her. It was one thing to make a vow and quite another to keep it. Despite himself, he grasped her hand and led her inside.

She removed her hat.

"You can keep that on, Bessie—you're not staying."

"I'm free, Granville. I've been divorced from Matthew almost two years now. I've been looking for you all this time."

"To do what?"

"This"—and she kissed him.

"Bessie, this—"

"Is not right? Can you truly say that?"

"I detest you, Bessie, everything you stand for."

Hannah took off her gloves and undid her waist clincher and the short cape that hid her décolletage. She loosened her hair and let it fall around her shoulders. She had been doing this all her life. To her, Granville was no different from any other man.

He turned his back on her.

"Bessie, please don't do this. It's embarrassing. I don't want you."

"I know you haven't forgotten our love. I know it. I have never forgotten you. I've never stopped wanting you. I've waited to find you. I love you. I'm making you an offer of marriage. I'm a rich woman with a dowry. I can build you your laboratory. Marry me, Granville."

"I don't want your money, Bessie," he said, turning to stare at her, his eyes wide, so black she could see her reflection in them. At the same time, his face was distorted with the effort of holding himself back. "How can you imagine that I would consider matrimony with a hooker and a divorcée?" Granville continued without any consideration of her feelings: "You're truly a whore, Bessie. You'll never change. I know Matthew divorced you for adultery. I am thankful that I wasn't the source of his pain or your cuckold. You're a born liar, Bessie.

"Trust me now. Money changes people, mistakes, too."

"Yes," said Granville, "I know. Money corrupts and a lot of money corrupts completely. There are no mistakes, Bessie, only consequences. You are not made for matrimony. Neither am I. I've told you that."

"We are made for each other."

Granville groaned. He wished for a moment that he wasn't a Christian. "No, Bessie. We're different. You are made for your millionaires," he said harshly. "They spend their lives stealing a fortune from men like me, and then with one foot in the grave decide to give some back in philanthropy—or spend it on people like you. I'll have none of it, Bessie. Your money comes from misery—their last days and a trail of people they've cheated."

"No, I make happiness. They want to follow me. I deal in dreams."

"They're still conquerors—climbing over you and anyone else."

"It is mine to give, isn't it? Is it wrong to give them what costs me so little and makes them happy?"

"Is it right to steal from the rich just because you don't steal from the poor?"

"I'm not a thief! I'm a woman of property!"

"That's right, Bessie. It's people like you and your friends who put up fences, dig mines, drill oil, and turn it into private property—just like yourself!"

"I've never stolen anything from anybody. Never! Not even that dress, that wretched dress. The money I have, I've earned, every penny!"

Granville shook his head sadly. "I pity you, Bessie, I really do."

"But you still love me, Granville." She lifted her skirts.

Granville caught his breath. He passed his hands across her hips. She came closer.

"Bessie. You're going to condemn us both. It's not love I have for you."

"But I love you," she whispered, her voice breaking.

"No, Bessie. We're not evenly yoked."

"I divorced Matthew for you. I left Platt for you . . ." she lied.

Granville pulled her toward him so roughly she lost her breath. She edged into him and kissed him. He began to run his hands over her figure, pressing her curves. Then, roughly, he began to undress her, silently pulling her from the layers of her expensive gown. Their kiss was like dawn rising from the dead black embers of bitter loneliness to a blazing high noon sun. Hannah in her happiness believed Granville had been restituted to her at last as he picked her up in his arms and laid her on the plain celibate army cot of a bed. Only the gas lamp from the street outside outlined his broad-shouldered, sculpted body. He took her until he brought her to sobs. He returned to her several times over the course of the night.

At sunrise, she felt a chill, and the lightness of his warm body disappeared. She sat up. "Granville?" Hannah called out to him. "Granville! Granville!" Then a scream. *"Granville!"*

Her voice only echoed in the empty apartment, *"Granville! Granville!"* She could only call his name hopelessly, the sound rising from shrillness to a scream as she heard the door shut. At once she was on her feet, running. One barefoot step slipped on a scattered pile of greenbacks on the floor as she raced after Granville's shadow. She chased him out into the hallway only to see his back disappear into the stairwell, like a shadow in the shape of a man.

She returned barefoot and shivering, stumbling across the wooden floor. Her trembling hands picked up the packet of dollars. She examined the stack of five-dollar bills, which bore the portrait of Benjamin Harrison, Civil War general and the twenty-third US president. If she took the money, Granville would become just another client who had paid for her services. In this way she could be free of him forever, having chosen her own destiny, by her choice. But if she left the money lying there, their affair would be unfinished, because she'd never know his response. She would be crushed under the weight of unbearable longing.

Hannah's pain was so all encompassing she went blind for a second as she stood immobile as dead. Her body had learned to shut itself down in the presence of unbearable pain. She came to with the bills, crisp and hard in her hand. *The panel scam*, she thought. Then she placed them in a tin plate she found in the kitchen and set the greenbacks on fire. She watched them burn black as their smoke curled to the ceiling. There would be nothing left of their transaction except ashes. Granville would see them when he returned and realize what it meant. After she dressed, she dipped her finger into the warm cinders and encircled the skin around her eyes like eyeliner. Ashes were the poor hookers' substitute for makeup. It marked her occupation now and then.

She surveyed the room and etched in her mind every image of what Granville owned, lived with, and touched. She found her hat and left the apartment, closing the door softly. She expected he was watching the building's front door, and he wouldn't come back until he was sure she had gone. It was not until she was in the cab, when she recalled his smell, the feel of his flesh on hers, that she broke down and wept the bitter, racking tears she had not wept since Moyamensing Prison.

She had drowned and died in Granville. He put an end to the woman who took so many men into her body, who had come and gone, thinking only of themselves and their own gratification, harboring their pitiful dreams: erotic, romantic, domestic, repeating the same old words, the same stupid phrases. She had been the perfect whore—the perfect public woman—the perfect Horizontal.

She cried for a long time until she couldn't anymore. Then she lifted her head and looked out at the trees swiftly moving past along Central Park North and the people rushing to destinations. Life pulsed around her. The horses clopped by in carriages in the park. Children ran alongside the ponds. None of them knew Granville. And yet, they went about their lives. Maybe, she thought. Maybe soon, she would too.

She rode a little while longer and thought more clearly. As with the death of a loved one that makes life all the clearer there was purity in rejection. She understood that she could continue to become herself even without him, in the same way that life went on. One didn't die of love, she thought, one died of the absence of love. She still had Granville.

And if she still wanted to love him, it was her choice; it was no business of his. Her capacity for love did not die, she thought. She didn't need Granville to love Granville.

No one "lost" anyone, because no one "owned" anyone. Men came and went as they wished because they knew they could. Now Hannah realized that she could too. But the pain would never stop.

Within the week, Hannah had bought the house she had seen on Central Park for $45,000 from the Washington Life Insurance Company. She did so without soliciting any advice from anyone. She didn't even tell Nanz as she did the paperwork with the lawyers from the insurance company. This was her answer to Granville, to all the grand and powerful men—the capitalists, the Marc Antonys, the inventors, the bankers, the generals, and the caesars—from a whore who serviced them and into whom they poured their precious seed. But more than that, her house was a monument to herself.

The time had come for Hannah to claim her throne. And she lavished her new house with all things Cleopatrian.

She and Nanz visited the antique stores and auction houses, estate sales and country fairs, looking for Egyptian pieces that were authentic, or interesting reproductions.

Hannah plunged into the world of furniture and fabrics, tiles, colored glass, and fine woodwork, of chandeliers and fireplaces, bookshelves and palm trees. Like her heroine's palace, her house would mock the double standard that demanded chastity for one sex and allowed freedom for the other.

The mansion at 236 Central Park West would be her refuge and asylum, a mansion equal to those of her merchant bankers and captains of industry.

Hannah was rich. She dealt now in real estate, city bonds, treasury stocks, futures shares, wheat, coal, and steel. What was she now? A capitalist: a woman unashamed, her very own benefactor.

FOURTEEN

Upper West Side, New York,
1902

Hannah now kept Platt as a visitor of her choosing. Only when the house was complete did she allow him to visit her.

"My God, it's bigger and better than my mansion on East Fifty-Fourth Street."

"Well"—she laughed—"that was the idea."

"Well, if you're finished with this one, why don't you buy a property on the subway line? The exact locations of the exits and entrances to the stations will increase real estate values just as Central Park did a generation ago."

"What do you mean?"

"I mean that the value of real estate along the route of the new IRT subway is going to skyrocket very soon. You can get in on it, Hannah. The consortium headed by August Belmont owns the rights to the whole subway system for ninety-nine years."

Hannah was silent. This was awesome. Granville used to talk about the subway and his new third rail system all the time.

She contacted Nanz shortly after, and he bought two more houses for Hannah's growing portfolio. He followed her real estate sales and paperwork. But she recorded her profits and losses and her many bank accounts by herself. Mrs. Truitt had taught her that a female head of household has to look after her own money.

Hannah now possessed one of the most beautiful houses in New York. She lived on one of its most aristocratic blocks. Each day, Max, her Swiss driver, splendid in pale blue livery with gold trim that glistened in the sun, drove her equipage onto the Mall to savor the gift of Central Park. And Platt assumed she was happy. And he was happy because he believed he owned her. He glowed with possession and good health. He seemed to have shed thirty years. He laughed and ate and drank and made love like a man almost forty years younger—considering some techniques. His melancholic ways and somber demeanor disappeared. He actually moved joyfully around Hannah's bedroom, singing and talking, arguing and flashing silly jokes while Hannah descended into the decorum of an Upper East Side matron.

Often Hannah visited her favorite spot in Central Park, Cleopatra's Needle, the small Egyptian obelisk that had been erected in 1880. She sometimes crossed the park on foot, shaded by her parasol, and sat in front of it, and contemplated the hieroglyphics on the somber granite surface, marveled at its age stretching into time like a dagger.

All those centuries, and nothing had changed. People still fell in love, still betrayed each other; women still prostituted themselves and men still killed each other over them. Hannah knew the stone hadn't really belonged to Cleopatra. She had read somewhere in one of the ladies' magazines that all the queen's monuments in Egypt had been demolished after her defeat because the Romans believed that a person could be erased with a few blows of a hammer—erase the inscription on a tomb and you annihilated the person as well as his memory. She sat there thinking about the white marble statue of the dying queen: mother of twins, prostitute, victim of men, and possessor of her own power. Antony had been nothing but a tiptoe man, a flimflammer, a sporting man. Caesar? A man without testicles, Hannah decided.

She wasn't recognized by strollers at the park, shaded by her black parasol; in street clothes she was as anonymous as someone's housemaid stealing a few minutes of rest from an errand. It was only her spectacular millinery that tipped people off that she was a woman of means.

When the weather was good, she even removed her hat and sat bareheaded, face lifted to the sunlight. Her life was no longer about sex.

It was about wealth. It was about living under a false name and false colors, as if indeed a sledgehammer had chipped away her name, leaving only blank, uninscribed stone. She liked this anonymity.

Still, who was she now? What would she leave behind? The unmarked gray stone didn't notice her. The nurses with their baby carriages, the top-hatted merchants and bankers, the veiled and bonnet-shaded ladies out for a stroll, all passed her by. She was just as invisible to the poor people: the newsboys, maids, matchstick girls, errand boys, telegraph messengers, city men, and occasional policemen. It calmed her that they knew nothing of her secrets.

Hannah sat, back straight, staring ahead, and a second veiled lady in every way identical to her came to join her. She was wearing the very same hat. She took her hand and leaned against her shoulder because she knew Hannah. She was a silent witness to a past so bare and ugly, there were no words necessary.

Hannah had finally sent for Sadie. The young woman had been so carefully watched by their mother after Hannah left that Sadie was still an innocent young woman in her twenties. She had no desire to become the wife of a Philadelphia porter or blacksmith or even a colored doctor. She saw the way relationships and family could easily be severed.

When Leola told Sadie that her sister was now established and wanted her to come to New York, Sadie jumped at the idea. Leola sent the money for the train ticket, and Sadie was installed in Hannah's mansion. They lived as sisters, mother and daughter and aunt and niece, catching up on the many years they had lost together.

Sadie watched silently as John Platt came and went. So she was not surprised when one day in the park her sister revealed that she was pregnant. Hannah was thirty-seven years old, though she had lived many more lives than thirty-seven by then.

Sadie suspected that Hannah had dealings with the underground, but Nanz kept her in the dark. Seeing Hannah having difficulties because of her fragile pregnancy, Sadie herself came up with the idea of helping

Hannah by substituting her person for Hannah. "There is no difference between us that I can discern," she said. "We look alike, we talk alike, we hurt alike . . . I am you and you are me."

The doctor told Hannah to be very gentle with herself. At her age, a pregnancy was dangerous if not fatal. He also advised Hannah that if she herself worried about the pregnancy, the baby would suffer.

When Hannah was six months and showing, she finally revealed the pregnancy to Platt. "I have something to tell you," she said. "I'm going to have a baby."

Platt was speechless. She could see his mind working. He tried to count back the months.

"Why did you wait so long to say anything?" he asked. But as soon as he had spoken, he knew that the question was rhetorical. He knew, given her past, that she trusted no man. Their affair would have ended if he had said the wrong thing. He was sure of that.

Still, he wasn't sure whether he was happy. His other children were already adults. This would complicate their inheritance. There would be lawsuits and scandals.

"Hannah, you must understand—" he started to speak.

"No, you," she said. "You understand that this is what I want, and I will have this child in a few months."

Hannah sounded sure of herself, but the decision had taken months for her to resolve. She couldn't imagine the consequences of the child's birth either. Platt pushing a baby carriage?

Her feelings were similarly mixed because she thought of Granville. He could be her child's father. But she knew he would disown it.

Now Platt stepped closer to Hannah. He took Hannah in his arms. "Of course, you want the baby. You will have this child. I want it too. I will love it."

They both knew that the child would have a more difficult time in his society as his bastard child than as the nonfathered child of a wealthy woman. Hannah could make herself anew, but Platt could not.

The old man pulled Hannah closer to him, and they held one another. For a few moments, they both cried, tears of joy but also sadness.

Roosevelt Hospital, New York, October 1, 1902

Hannah's pregnancy did not last.

She thought she was safe, until one day when she drove out to Central Park with Leola. Something was wrong. The baby, almost seven months then, began turning and cramping in Hannah's womb.

Max raced with them both to Roosevelt Hospital. The loyal coachman could see she was in terrible pain. She hadn't been in the hospital long when she miscarried. There was no way to tell who the father was or the real color of the baby—except that it was a girl.

An older nurse held Hannah's hand. "You're young. Life is long," she said, wiping Hannah's forehead with a towel. "You'll have more children."

The nurse didn't know that Hannah had a daughter already. Hannah howled at the thought that she had given away Clara.

Leola went home to tell Sadie and sent word to Platt. He rushed over while Sadie stayed out of sight.

Platt made sure that Hannah would get the best treatment in the hospital. Everyone treated him as the grieving father.

When Hannah came home, Platt stayed at her bedside, sleeping in a chair and feeding her soup that the servants brought.

He sat there, patiently, and let all of Hannah's anguish wash over him. As a passionate man, he prized Hannah for the difficulties he had experienced in winning her—the struggles, efforts, and uncertainties he had experienced in possessing her all these years made her all the more precious to him—his uncut diamond, his secret painting, his love.

"What is it, Hannah?"

"I want to see Gwendolyn. Take me to see Gwendolyn." This was the name she had given the child.

August Nanz had arranged through Hannah's orders for the miscarried infant to be taken to Woodlawn Cemetery and buried. Neither Hannah nor Platt ever saw her face. Nanz took care of the body, ordering the elaborate tomb to be built.

"Soon," Platt whispered to Hannah as she fell asleep.

The rain had stopped. Hannah's veil clung to the contours of her face, engraving it with transparent roses. She looked up at Platt. He never knew what to say at such a moment, especially to someone like her who had seen it all.

So while Platt searched for the appropriate words in his conscience and the right sentiment in his heart, Hannah knew in her mind that Platt was only what he was.

The wind rose out of the valley of Woodlawn, nudging the efflorescent cypress trees. Droplets of the earlier rain hung from Gwendolyn's sleeping angel atop the crypt. There were just the two of them, alone, thought Platt, standing beside this monument to lost love.

Platt and Hannah found themselves perfectly in sync. Both getting soaked by the rain, bowing and grieving. The cemetery was now their eternal meeting place. And why not? They both believed that the experience of loving and losing was the single inevitable feeling in life.

FIFTEEN

Upper West Side, New York,
March 30, 1903

Hannah's body recovered in a few months, but her spirit was despondent. When spring returned to New York, the time when Gwendolyn would have been conceived, Hannah decided to let Sadie watch the house while she went out of town.

Leola was ensconced in the Fifty-Third Street house, so if anything went wrong, Sadie could always reach her.

❧

Hannah rented a cottage for the season on Cornaga Avenue in the heart of fashionable Far Rockaway, Queens. The cottages were actually two- and three-story mansions with wide porches, large enough to host outdoor parties, and covered carports for carriages or, occasionally, newfangled automobiles.

The negotiations for the rental house had been conducted through the National Bank of Manhattan. No one in Far Rockaway saw her face. She was heavily veiled as she drove along the beach road in her Studebaker Spider Phaeton. Her new purchase was a pleasure carriage made of French goatskin, painted a maroon color. Her horsemanship allowed her to drive, although she had a local man strap the surrey to the horse every afternoon for her outing. Hannah did not entertain and accepted no invitations, but everyone knew who she was.

Surrounding the houses were large, green yards, not overplanted, but tastefully decorated with young trees and square, even bushes. Flowers mixed their sugar scent with the salty smell of ocean water.

Hannah's nearest neighbor was Lillian Russell, but even her coveted white-and-blue invitations were politely declined.

During the week, almost every day, packages from New York and Philadelphia would arrive at Hannah's door. They were either presents from Platt or gifts she bought herself. The puritanical WASPs of Rockaway frowned at these extravagances, but she didn't care. The presents made her feel better. So did the thought that society people cared enough to envy her.

Hannah had a hairdresser who came early to do her hair, and a masseuse who attended her after she had worked out with her physical education teacher, Jack Cooper. Lillian, whose own gentlemen guests seemed to change every weekend, closely observed all this with jealous eyes. Hannah complained about Lillian's large, noisy parties, sending a note to the actress through Kato who came down from the New York mansion with his mistress to spend the summer.

Lillian sent word back through Jack Cooper, who was also *her* physical education teacher, that it was for professional reasons only that she was obliged to entertain every weekend, and, since she could not accommodate Hannah's request for silence, the only solution was for her to join the party. Rumors had it that J. P. Morgan had competed with Diamond Jim Brady for Lillian's affections. What the local WASPs didn't know was that she had acted in some of the Rialto's and the Tenderloin's most notorious and noteworthy music halls.

Lillian Russell's music hall life had begun in the same district of New York as Hannah's: the Bowery. Her career had begun in the sex district of West Broadway, the most racially mixed milieu in New York, which was why Russell recognized Hannah from the best-known dance hall on the West Side, Dickens' Place, operated by Pete Williams, a colored saloonkeeper.

One afternoon, Hannah decided to accept Lillian's invitation to cocktails. But she took one look at Hannah when she walked in and recognized her from their dance hall days. Outraged, Lillian informed

Hannah's landlord that his tenant was not a bona fide Caucasian. There was no mistake.

"That woman is not Cuban, she's a Negro."

"Mrs. Elias," replied the landlord, Mr. Althouse, "is an excellent tenant and has impeccable references."

"But you oblige me to live next door to a Negress!" Russell cried.

"Madame, think of Mrs. Elias, who is obliged to live next door to a vaudeville actress."

The real estate agent who had rented Hannah the cottage let it be known in the town that Hannah's bank references were such that she had on deposit a sum that drew from $20,000 to $30,000 a year in interest and that her credit was unlimited. As far as Far Rockaway was concerned, Hannah was a deceased Spanish general's widow known as the "Veiled Empress."

Hannah sent word to her neighbor that if Russell didn't stop carping about who she was, she would tell Far Rockaway just who Lillian Russell really was. For the rest of the spring and summer, the actress and Hannah vied with one another to see who could spend the most money.

Every Friday morning, Hannah sent for her C-spring carriage, a large, new purchase that had eight springs so that the compartment floated above the wheels. The ride was smooth and felt elegant. She went with the carriage, a coachman, and a footman to the railway station to retrieve Platt for the weekend.

Hannah always dressed carefully for Platt's visits because he liked to see her in different afternoon and dinner gowns. She greeted him in a morning dress, and then changed to a dinner gown for supper just before he took his train back to the city. This day, she had on a dress of cream chiffon edged with a shawl-print border, and machine Alençon lace. It had a long train, a seafoam satin sash, and a high collar of lace, over which she wore her pearl necklace. The gossamer chiffon shifted like the sea waves outside as she moved about the room.

Platt's eyes followed Hannah's every gesture adoringly. She always made sure there were large bouquets of fresh flowers, plates of sweets and fruits, and peach iced tea. He might have stayed the night or left for the city after dinner. He never knew what surprises Hannah had prepared for him or what humor he would find her in.

"But what do you care what Lillian Russell thinks of you?"

"It's not that I care, it's that I don't like people putting labels on me, or making judgments or snooping around my house and my servants. Who does she think she is? She is only a tenant, just like me. I don't have to answer to her!"

"Of course you don't. So why do it?"

"Because of what I know about her past, but also because of what she knows about mine!"

"Well, then, isn't it tit for tat? Shouldn't you both just shut up about each other?"

"I would, but she keeps on running off at the mouth and bringing her sporting crowd up for weekends."

"Well, she likes company."

"They play ragtime and generally make a lot of noise, drink and stay up all night."

"You sound like one of Mrs. Astor's four hundred complaining!" He laughed.

"I don't like my past catching up with me," Hannah said.

"Well, run faster, dear," said Platt, his eyes brimming with affection.

"I can't, Papa"—she laughed—"not in this long train."

He could see that she was coming back to herself. The ongoing quarrel with Russell had taken away some of her grief.

Platt looked around the drawing room with satisfaction. "You've chosen well," he said. He picked up a porcelain doll that was lying on the couch. Hannah always traveled with a great many of them.

When Leola first told him about Hannah's lost pregnancy, his eyes had welled for his poor mistress. He had wanted to make the memory of all her pain disappear, although he couldn't change her past.

When they slept together sometimes, she had a recurring nightmare. She screamed and thrashed on the bed. Platt shook her awake, her wild cries still ringing in his ears. She clung to him and told him that she was in a trotter sulky on a strange, endless racetrack, being pursued by a gang of jockeys with demon faces who kept gaining on her no matter how fast she drove. They screamed curses as she sped faster and faster until the wheels fell off the chariot and it overturned. She fell into a spiral, which sucked her into the heaving bowels of hell.

Platt tried to comfort her, but he realized he could do nothing for Hannah except buy her another house or another necklace. Hannah's demons were her own.

❧

Hannah was enjoying the last days of vacation in the Rockaways when the cool weather brought a chill, and the ocean had a beautiful cast of fog in the morning. She felt refreshed, almost ready to go back to the city, prepared to entertain. Hannah asked August to help her organize a ball to celebrate the completion of her house.

August found an obscure Spanish aristocrat in whose honor he invited New Yorkers who mattered. Most had closed their summer houses and sought invitations to events. The lavishly printed cards came with a handwritten note that the party was exclusive and secret, a surprise affair for the hostess and the Spanish aristocrat, an honored guest.

Nanz spent wildly on floral decorations, plates of gold and silver, and china from Hong Kong. He hired servants in livery to wait on the guests. He employed a fine orchestra to play in the foyer under the great dome.

On the night of the party, after Hannah had returned to Manhattan, the guests chimed, *"Sorpresa! Feliz cumpleaños!"*

August Nanz had truly surprised her. The Egyptian rooms had been thrown open. An unending number of people came through the front door, chattering loudly and gawking, obviously impressed by the opulence. They milled through the public rooms of the house.

In a splendid ball gown of ivory and yellow satin damask trimmed with pearl appliqué and silk fringe by Worth, she moved like a phantom through the rooms, listening with incomprehension to the lilting Spanish. Her eyes scanned the faces, the chattering mouths and envious eyes. She searched for a friendly glance, some sign of recognition, some evidence that she was still not invisible. But she was. No one really cared who the party was for. The preoccupied guests, happily eating, drinking, dancing, and conversing, were all engrossed in their own affairs. Hannah was stranded at her own ball, her dance card empty, a foreigner in her own house as the orchestra played Scott Joplin's latest rag.

The hammers of the artisans were already at work repairing damage even before the festivities had ended and the mansion's great oak front door closed on the last departing couple.

Hannah's copy of the *New York Times* came that morning with the story of the party at her house in the society pages. "The rich Cuban socialite," she read, "Hannah Elias honored New York's finest company in a grand party . . ."

This was all that Hannah desired.

August had invited all of Hannah's neighbors as a courtesy. Even Andrew Green attended with his cousins, who lived next door to 236 Central Park West. As a result, Hannah had a stack of thank-you notes and invitations on the front room table. They would talk about that too. And that would become her reputation, not her past.

That evening, Hannah and Sadie had dinner alone together, face-to-face in the formal dining room. They had both worn dinner dresses—imported silk gowns with velvet robes, held at the waist by satin belts. They laughed about Philadelphia and the old trinity house on Addison Street.

1903
THE DETECTIVE BUREAU

Thou portal—thou arena—thou of the
myriad long-drawn out lines and groups!
(Could but thy flagstones, curbs, façades, tell their inimitable tales;
Thy windows rich, and huge hotels—thy side-walks wide;)
Thou of the endless sliding, mincing, shuffling feet!
Thou, like the parti-colored world itself—
like infinite, teeming, mocking life!
Thou visor'd, vast, unspeakable show and lesson!

—*Walt Whitman,* "Broadway"

SIXTEEN

Lower Manhattan,
November 14, 1903

"The Tombs" was the location where Detective McClusky and Officer Houghtaling had taken Cornelius Williams. The building was located at Center and Elm Streets, squashed among the other structures. The prison was built on a landfill in a once beautiful area called Collect Pond. The pond became polluted, however, and then was filled in for construction projects. The official name for the prison was the Halls of Justice, but no one called it that. New Yorkers had nicknamed the ominous building "the Tombs" because it resembled an Egyptian mausoleum, with its granite columns, black marble, brownstone, and onyx fittings.

Murderers, armed robbery suspects, gangsters, and dangerous felons had all passed through the Tombs' ornate entrance, and many successful escapes had been made over the years by these same criminals via stolen Black Marias, broken windows, delivery vans, forged papers, fake prison guards, chloroform, mayhem, and even a gaggle of red-coated fox hunters from New Jersey.

On his way to the Tombs in the horse-drawn Black Maria, when Cornelius lifted his eyes, a nightstick broke over his shoulders. He "accidentally" fell on the floor of the cab when he was shoved from the seat. Blood oozed from his nose, and one eye was swollen almost shut. His mustache and sideburns were caked with blood.

However, once the transport rolled through the gates of the prison, the guards opening the back door of the car allowed him to raise himself from the car's seat and step out on his own. Their extremely polite manner could have suggested that his murder of the socialite Green had somehow given Cornelius his victim's social status. More likely, they didn't want anyone from the press noticing what they planned to do to him.

After Cornelius had been secured in an adjacent room, Chief Tim Hurley brought Houghtaling and McClusky into his office.

The burly detectives in shirtsleeves and shoulder holsters were not amused. The department of detectives was brand new. The old adage had been "send a rogue to catch a rogue," but the modern theory was that integrity, tact, industry, and a scientific attitude were the best qualifications of a good detective. Actually, the bureau members were named after a set of men in London known during the previous century as the Bow Street Runners. They were remarkably shrewd officers, more than a match for the criminals they stalked, and could outwit the sharpest villains. When the London metropolitan police system was adopted, the men were called detectives because they seemed to have a gift for detecting crime. They could sniff out a murder, track a perpetrator over oceans and across continents, unravel mysteries, and altogether bring to light things of darkness. In New York, they were also known as "shadows" because they silently and persistently followed their prey. The force was small, about fifteen men, and they answered only to the district attorney himself—William Jerome, an ambitious and socially prominent Harvard man whom the men in this room would all need to report to.

The headquarters of the detective squad was an elegant marble building on Mulberry Street adjacent to the Tombs. Tim Hurley, the chief of detectives, was a stocky man who had an immense head with outsize features, curly, sandy hair, and a solid look about him. Only his eyes indicated that he was the bravest and most able detective in the Western world. His home was a rooming house on Water Street, furnished and unsightly. He was unmarried but did have a Cheshire cat named Rat. He never seemed to be doing anything or to have anything on his desk, which was immaculately clean. He didn't seem to be interested in Andrew Green's murder, although he and the entire police force were expected to attend Green's funeral in two days.

The chief's associate detectives, a dozen or so men dressed in plain clothes, sat around on benches, straddled chairs, leaned up against the wall, talked, smoked, and chewed gum. To the uninitiated, they seemed a far cry from the talented, persevering, sharp-sighted, successful criminal investigators they were supposed to be. As a group they could be summed up as a silent, secretive clan who never spoke about their current case. They spoke only of work accomplished in the past—past crimes, past arrests, past errors, but never the present or future. They all had incidents under their fedoras more thrilling than any dime murder mystery novel, and they took no bets on Williams's future.

Hurley said to Houghtaling, "Tell me what you saw and heard."

"Well," Officer Houghtaling began, "we arrived just after the shooting took place, and found this individual standing over Green's body with a gun. This guy's going to fry, that's for sure . . . the electric chair."

"Wheee!" called Cornelius from the other room.

"He's right," said detective McClusky. "First-degree homicide with premeditation." He paused. Under his feet, the new subway rumbled by, vibrating the building.

"What's this world coming to when a colored man can kill a white man in broad daylight and not get strung up on the spot?" asked the patrolman.

The detectives all looked to the direction where Williams sat. "What an idiot," one of them said. Why would he shoot someone like Andrew Green? Everyone knew him. He was as familiar to city dwellers as J. P. Morgan, Andrew Carnegie, and President Teddy Roosevelt.

Every New Yorker had memorized Green's biography from the frequent news stories about him: he was a bachelor, a visionary, and New York City's leading citizen. There hadn't been an urban scheme in the past thirty years in which he wasn't involved. As city comptroller he had conceived and planned Central Park with the landscape architect Frederick Law Olmsted. Green had straightened out the finances of the city after the Tweed corruption scandals. He had helped found the Metropolitan Museum of Art, the American Museum of Natural History, and the Metropolitan Opera House. Moreover, his vision had brought about the

creation of what was now called Greater New York: the consolidation of
the five boroughs of New York County—Manhattan, the Bronx, Brooklyn, Queens, and Richmond—into one great metropolis. The Central
Park Zoo and the marble arch were all his projects. What could this
poor colored bastard have to do with a member of New York's four hundred, the number of people, it was said, who could fit comfortably into
Mrs. Astor's ballroom?

"I don't know why Green—" Houghtaling began to say.

"He's the devil!" shouted Cornelius suddenly. "He's the devil's dog,
damn devil, damn him! He got what he deserved. I'm not sorry for what
I did. He can burn in hell."

Now Cornelius sang a lullaby. He had completed his task from the
Bethesda angel. He had seen her fly out in a flash from the end of his
derringer at Bessie's house.

"O Prophet," the angel said, "peace is yours as your hand doth strike
down the fornicator."

Even as he sat in the adjacent room, Cornelius saw the angel as clear
as day, with Satan seated on the floor in the guise of a red-eyed black dog.

The devil said, "You have done right to send Andrew Green and Bessie Davis to hell. We have a place for them. Thank you."

Cornelius kept his head down, looking at his scruffy shoes rather than
peer through the open door at the lawmen, which might have brought
them over to give him another wallop.

Then the detectives were ready to leave. They escorted him calmly, by
his handcuffs, over the rough cobblestones outside the Detective Bureau
to precinct headquarters, located on the ground floor of the prison. Here
were five or six comfortable cells overlooking the street where famous inmates such as Henri de Rothschild of the English Rothschilds, who had
stood trial for fraud, had been confined. Prisoners were allowed to bring
their own furniture and rugs and have their meals catered.

They walked Cornelius past these rooms and down the steps to the
very lowest level, deep in the bowels of the prison: "Coon's Row," where
only Negroes were kept.

Cornelius was taken to a large room, stripped down to his underwear,
handcuffed again and chained by his ankles. He was sweating despite the

cold. He stood between police detective Joseph McClusky and Chief of Detectives Hurley. A clerk stood in earshot, holding a pen and paper.

Cornelius faced a battery of detectives and a doctor called an alienist, who could hardly believe his luck.

Dr. Flint had been hired by the city to adjudge Williams's sanity. Alienation was now the new religion of criminology. Its practitioners were physicians who treated mental disorders and who were accepted by a court of law as experts on the mental competence of prisoners or witnesses appearing before it. The insane were thought to be alienated from their normal faculties, explained Dr. Flint to Detective McClusky.

"The word's Latin root comes from *ali enore*, 'to make strange,'" he stated.

Hurley couldn't care less about the explanation. He just knew these alienists ran like cockroaches all over the place.

Flint continued: "You know, there are a variety of opinions about executing the insane, so we come to help. Some people have questions about the morality of the death penalty."

"I am the hand of God," began Williams. "Mr. Green is the sinner, the fornicator, the thief who has paid with his life for his infamous thefts. What was I supposed to do? Sit back and let that man destroy me? I told old Satan, or rather old Satan told me, that he would work with God's angel. She wanted peace. He would take them where she couldn't. I was ordered to smite sinner Green at his home, the home I never had with Bessie because of his millions."

"Are you making a plea?" Hurley said to the man.

"I plead not guilty and you won't get another word out of me without my lawyer being present." This was another incongruous statement, because he had just confessed.

"What makes you think you're going to get a lawyer?" said one of the detectives, suddenly more interested in Williams than the doctor was.

"You'll see," said Williams mysteriously. "Got to get a court-appointed lawyer, but I've got friends in high places."

"You confessed to the arresting officer who witnessed the crime, did you not?" Hurley said.

"I killed Andrew Green—everybody knows that and I'm glad I did.

I'm glad I did it. Glad I killed Bessie Davis too." The court clerk in the corner swiftly copied Williams's second confession and underlined it twice.

"You say you killed Bessie too?" asked Chief Hurley.

"Yes, last night, at her house."

"There has been no report of any other killing."

"She's dead. I killed her. How is she going to tell you? What sense does that make?" Williams began to laugh.

McClusky explained, "Mr. Williams, you may think you killed another person, but there is no record of it, or a body. There were three homicides last night, none of them Bessie Davis."

Williams's eyes rolled back in his head. "But I did kill her! I shot her dead. I saw her fall. I know I killed her—that was my *aim*!"

The alienist and Hurley exchanged glances. Detective McClusky had already checked the residence at 236 Central Park West. It belonged to a certain Hannah Elias, a rich white widow who was known to be alive. Occasionally she was visible in the window of the well-appointed brownstone.

McClusky shook his head. He had never heard of an assassin who didn't remember whom he had killed and whom he hadn't. A person didn't need to be a doctor to see that Williams was insane.

"I can't justify myself before Man, but the Angel and the Devil know they called me. Killing fornicators is my salvation. It took me a long time, but I knew I'd get the two of them one day. They been cheating and fucking and fucking and cheating since I was a caterer and making good money. Then they threw me out on the streets in 1890.

"One-eight-nine-ought," he repeated for emphasis. "I'm only a furnace tender now on Park Avenue because a lying woman's tongue ruined me! Just like that new rag." Williams straightened his back, and as he swayed side to side he sang:

> *"I've got a ragtime dog and a ragtime cat,*
> *A ragtime piano in my ragtime flat;*
> *Wear ragtime clothes from my hat to shoes,*
> *Read a Sunday paper called the* Ragtime News.

Got ragtime habits and I talk that way.
I sleep in ragtime and I rag all day;
Got ragtime troubles with my ragtime wife,
I'm a ragtime killer living a ragtime life . . ."

Cornelius danced around the room as the men watched. When he pulled the trigger and saw Bessie go down, he had ceased to be the same Cornelius he had been until that point. His long search over, he could now be what he had always wanted to be—what had been his goal in life—the Sword of Justice for Bessie Davis's sins, an avenging angel. He was the annunciation.

She was only good company for the devil, and there was only one place for her: hell.

Williams shook his bottom at Chief Hurley and the alienist, as the guards took him away to a cell. They left him locked up as he danced to the ragtime music in his head but now added the lyrics, "I want a lawyer. I'm going to get a lawyer."

"Whew!" murmured McClusky when the men got to the first floor again. "He's crazy as a loon."

"Or smart as a fox," said Houghtaling.

"That Negro has got to be insane," McClusky added.

"Or a very good actor," replied Dr. Flint.

The policemen turned to look at him.

The arresting officers, the alienist, and the city detectives were sure of one thing: this was an open-and-shut case of first-degree, premeditated murder. The cops imagined the Negro was going to fry for murder of the prominent Andrew Green. There was now a redoubtable instrument for executing criminals in New York State that had replaced the gallows: the electric chair. Thanks to some newfangled technology that Thomas Edison had dreamed up, New York had been the first to adopt electrocution as a method of execution, which Edison argued was clean, progressive, and humane. And although the *New York Times* called it "an awful spectacle worse than hanging," the state commissioner saw it as "the grandest success of our age."

McClusky had seen it work recently: a man was seated in a sturdy throne-like oak armchair, his body strapped to its arms and legs, his head crowned with a band of metal like a medieval king. Electrodes were attached to arms, legs, and cranium.

As he was being strapped in, the guards had a discussion as to whether the better current was AC or DC.

"I think Edison got it right," said one. "He made it, so why wouldn't we use Edison Electric Light Company?" He pronounced the name slowly almost as if he were bragging to the prisoner.

"Because Westinghouse is all around better," the other guard replied.

Then one pulled a switch, and a current of electricity was sent coursing through the prisoner's body. Thirty seconds and one thousand volts later, the victim was dead.

"Cleaner than the French guillotine, prettier than a firing squad," said one of the lawyers observing the punishment. Like the brand-new Detective Bureau, the electric chair was a great step forward in modern criminology.

"Ya see?" One of the guards called McClusky over. "The thousand volts of electricity boil the blood. It turns them as hard and black as coal. Or niggers." He laughed.

"Yep," said the other man. "They fry."

It was a word that became part of New York's coinage.

"I ain't crazy!" Williams yelled, as he watched the backs of his tormentors disappear down the long, pale green corridor. "You guys can't beat a confession out of somebody who's already confessed."

"He has a point," said Chief Hurley with a laugh when they returned to the office.

"OK, McClusky, what have you got?" Hurley asked.

"We know a woman lives alone at 236 Central Park West. It's a Mrs. Hannah Elias. She lives in a brownstone mansion of five stories and twenty rooms. Her neighbors hardly ever see her. She is supposedly a Cuban refugee of aristocratic Spanish origin living more or less as a recluse. She has a large staff of French and Asian servants. She owns a carriage that is the envy of the block, a team of magnificent horses, and a Swiss coachman. A couple of years ago, she gave away fifty fancy gowns for a charity banquet. One of the women on Mrs. Elias's block told me that she'd have paid Elias herself for the dresses from Paris. The neighbor saw some of them being worn by streetwalkers on Broadway. Currently, Mrs. Elias stays in her home. Rarely does she leave. Which is really strange, because she gave a big party last week, which was in all the newspapers."

Chief Hurley thought about the information. They were a strange bunch, these rich types.

McClusky continued: "The neighbors also tell me that Elias has only one regular time that she leaves the house. Wearing a big veil, she uses the victoria and rides into Central Park.

"We tried to ask her butler, a Japanese, I think, but he's a shut trap. All of her people are well paid. The neighbors have complained that she gives them too much."

McClusky got some of his information from people living adjacent to 236 Central Park West, the cousins of Andrew Green. "They said her only regular visitor was an elderly man, and the one thing they agreed on was that Mrs. Elias is filthy rich."

Dr. Flint had followed Hurley and McClusky back to the Detective Bureau, while in his mind's eye he evaluated Cornelius Williams. He did not rule out Williams's acting ability; Negroes were known to be great actors. But the doctor did have an initial diagnosis.

"Williams," began Dr. Flint, "in my opinion, is suffering from a form of mental disease called 'paranoia.' The older term for this is 'monomania.' The characteristics are: one, an intense egotism or conceit; two, the possession of a dominating idea or belief that is not real; and three, the evolution of this idea associated with an ever-increasing self-delusion. There is a perfect intolerance of the opinions of others or of opposition from others upon matters relating to their delusion. And they are prone to periodic losses of self-control with attacks of rage or excitement especially if opposed, like Williams.

"They hear imaginary voices or see visions. These hallucinations are often projections upon the sense of sight or hearing of the person and relate to the dominant delusion. Such phenomena may be explained by the sufferers as supernatural events such as ghosts or spirits and are frequently regarded as messages from a divine source such as Christ or, as in Williams's case, an angel and the devil."

The detectives didn't care what the alienist said. Williams was a doomed man: a celebrity killer, an assassinator of power. Green's case would be a godsend to tabloid journalists and newspaper editors. There were already headlines and editorials and reporters crawling all over headquarters and Central Park West. All over one crazy Negro. Williams was to be arraigned in Court of Special Sessions tomorrow. The detectives weren't buying Williams's insanity despite Dr. Flint's lecture. It was difficult to deceive a criminal detective. They could read a man at a glance. They could tell a bogus story from a real one. Williams was now back in his miserable cell—a disgrace to the New York penitentiary system, as they all knew. But what did a Negro expect when he committed a crime? The Waldorf?

Dr. Flint turned toward the detectives. "Well, gentlemen, I must take my leave—I have a report to hand in to the district attorney's office. I will be meeting with Dr. McDonald, my colleague, who will make his own independent examination. Good day, gentlemen."

Hurley began talking as soon as the door closed. "The district attorney is making noises as if he doesn't want this case to go to trial. That's why Flint was here to declare Williams insane. Jerome doesn't want any noise that isn't his."

"Can Williams really afford a lawyer, anyway?" asked one detective.

McClusky answered, "He's getting one from the Legal Aid Society. They're always butting in."

Hurley added, "The DA wants another doctor to examine Williams before the arraignment. You know an alienist named Dr. Carlos McDonald?"

"Yes, of course."

"Well, he is in the building with Williams right now," Hurley said.

"If you ask me," said another detective, "if Jerome wants an insanity plea for a nigger who shot a white man in cold blood and should be strung up, he has a damned good reason."

"It means Williams can be put away quietly without more newspaper headlines and inconvenient stories by reporters about why he shot Green and this white woman on Central Park West," Hurley continued. "I mean, look at Jerome. He doesn't want headlines that he didn't make.

It makes him and the bureau look lazy. Not to mention Green was a big player in Jerome's world too, a decent guy. Jerome doesn't want more bad headlines about good people. Might make people lose faith in government. They won't be able to tell the good guys from the bad.

"He certainly doesn't want the public to be any the wiser. I know the Green family wants justice. But a trial isn't necessarily it. It could drag on for years."

McClusky thought that the alienists all had a stake in the new criminological theories grounded in the splendid discovery of irresponsibility in pathological cases. To him, this meant simply that there were no criminals left, only sick people. He wasn't buying it. A murderer was a murderer, a thief was a thief, and a whore was a whore.

"Yeah, but what the hell does Jerome have us for?" McClusky exploded. "A bunch of clowns out here to do the *Social Register*'s bidding? I want to get to the bottom of this case. Something smells fishy. I have a feeling that this Central Park West woman knows this Negro, Williams. And I'll bet she gets around. Let's take her on. She could even be a Spanish agent or spy. Remember the war of '98! She's said to be Cuban. We took Cuba from Spain."

The other detectives nodded.

McClusky worked under William Jerome and his pin-striped English suits and English boots, his upper-class accent, his Harvard tie, his cottage upstate and his apartment on Fifth Avenue. As far as McClusky was concerned, he was an ambitious prick who didn't know shit about solving, preventing, controlling, or prosecuting crime.

Good government and honesty in public office were Jerome's ultimate goals. Still, he reveled in spectacular, front-page articles on his prowess. His antigambling, antiprostitution crusade and his Tammany Hall exposés in 1899 had led to Governor Roosevelt's removal of the Tammany Hall district attorney and Jerome's election in his place in 1901.

Then Jerome drafted a statute for the state legislature that created the Court of Special Sessions. The mayor appointed him as chief justice of the court, and "Justice" Jerome had formed this Committee of Fifteen. McClusky enjoyed being part of a band of young, zealous, and incorruptible detectives who had the authority to conduct investigations and to issue warrants and summonses. Jerome used their combined power to break up gambling, prostitution, and vice rings that the police themselves protected. He led his raids in person, while McClusky and the other men chopped down doors with axes, blew up barricades with dynamite, and hauled the inhabitants off to jail. The gamblers, keepers of disorderly houses, and prostitutes in these roundups exited the premises in a long, forlorn rabble of overstyled suits, sequins, and feathers.

"Well, we do carry out Jerome's orders, if we want to keep our jobs," Hurley said.

"Yeah. But I'd sure like to know what he was up to," said McClusky.

"For one thing, the doctors are prepared to find one of their cherished neuroses or psychoses," Hurley said. "That's their damned bread and butter! If there were no psychosis, there would be no alienists making thousands of dollars!"

"I have nothing against Flint or MacDonald," Hurley added, "except that they wouldn't recognize a genuine criminal brain if they fell over one. Williams, I am convinced, is faking insanity. He is intelligent, and Jerome wants him quiet as much as the Central Park West set does too."

If Cornelius hadn't been a Negro, mused Hurley, he would be tempted to say that the murderer had probably looked into an alienist's manual, picked out a few typical cases, and imitated them. Except that everybody knew Negroes weren't capable of that kind of cerebral trumpery. Either Williams was a genius or, more likely, a complete moron.

However, if the alienists did find that Williams was insane, he calculated, the DA's case could be presented at once before a grand jury, and the killer could be declared mentally unsound and locked away before any of the secrets of this case—secrets that might tarnish the Upper East Side magnates—came to light. And this, Hurley had the impression, was what Jerome and his cronies wanted.

"That means there would be no investigation," Detective McClusky added.

"Exactly!" said Chief Hurley. "We're out of the picture. We can get around that. We'll interview this Hannah Elias. See if she knows anything about Bessie Davis. This way we get the truth and won't stir Jerome's feathers, not in the least."

He turned to the man who had brought in Cornelius. "McClusky, I want you to stake out the mansion at 236 as of now. Hang around outside, observe any unusual activity, who goes in and out, the comings and goings of the servants. Try to talk with some more neighbors discreetly. Follow them too. If there is a Bessie Davis, so much the better. Note what time the lights go out. Check the stables and the coachmen."

"Right, chief." McClusky was already putting on his jacket and coat. He hesitated a moment.

Chief Hurley added, "Take a man with you and go armed. And get a fuckin' gun from the quartermaster for him."

McClusky smiled. As if he would go any other way. He had a Colt in his shoulder holster, a derringer in his leg brace, and a bowie knife strapped to his left thigh. He already had the house staked out with a few freelancers among the reporters.

Hurley turned away. He had other worries, like the funeral. He had ordered some 360 policemen and plainclothesmen to handle the crowd. It wasn't every day that one of New York's luminaries got bumped off and several hundred millionaires gathered in one place to wave him goodbye.

SEVENTEEN

H annah sat in her carriage behind the police lines under the driving rain and watched the procession of the high and mighty enter Brick Church on Fifth Avenue for the ten o'clock funeral of Andrew Green. She observed several of her lawyers, six of her bankers, and a dozen of her clients through her rose-embroidered black veil as they marched over the wet red carpet leading to the arched entrance.

She was hoping to get a glimpse of Platt. What else can a mistress do when all the wives are in attendance? She probably wasn't the only one in the crowd, and she reconsidered whether the isolation she experienced was worth the acquisition of money, clothes, and shoes.

John hadn't contacted her since she returned to town. She knew he must have seen the newspaper about the party at her house. He must have wondered if she was running a two-timing game. She had to tell him differently. She was becoming more dependent on him since she lost the baby and he had sat by her side so patiently and listened to her wails and cries.

Nanz recognized Hannah's carriage parked just behind the police lines, established to contain the crowds who wanted to gawk at the celebrities attending the funeral. He was her attorney, damn it, Nanz thought, and he had warned Hannah to stay away from the funeral now that her name and address had surfaced in the press in connection with the murder, but there she was. He ground his teeth at the recollection of the previous day's headlines.

FAMILY DENIES CONNECTION OF GREEN
TO MYSTERY WOMAN MRS. HANNAH ELIAS
JEROME TO QUESTION MRS. ELIAS

She apparently didn't realize the trouble this could bring. The worst part was that he'd read it in the newspaper before she'd even told him. Had Jerome reached out to her? Or was he sending a message by telling the newspapers first?

Nanz didn't realize that Hurley had called the newspapers. He felt the truth needed to come out and said that the detectives would interview Elias since Jerome wouldn't. Of course, Jerome put his name at the top of that story.

Now Hannah was a celebrity for the press. Nanz thought she needed to stay inconspicuous. What if a nosy reporter found out—or even worse, a photographer got a photo—that the woman connected to Andrew Green's murder was here, sitting in a carriage? Nanz wanted more than anything to walk right over to her and send her home.

He also was perturbed that he had to look after his client when he had come to mingle with the Wall Street moguls who had turned out en masse for Green's funeral. The *Times* that morning had published a second full-page obituary of Green. It read as if Green had died peacefully in bed without a shred of violence, mystery, or scandal. That's how New York big shots were supposed to die, he thought, not by the hand of a crazed Negro. The *Times* had also published the guest list:

W. K. Vanderbilt
Endicott Peabody
Andrew Carnegie
Thomas Edison
John D. Rockefeller
August Belmont Jr.
Henry Clay Frick
Archbishop Farley
Chancellor Henry M. McCracken
John Jacob Astor

The rain slid off Nanz's top hat and the shoulders of his slicker despite the partial protection of his Bond Street umbrella. The memories of Bessie Davis flooded his mind. She had first been his client, then a friend when he was a Tombs lawyer and an ambulance chaser.

Then she gave him her divorce case. It had turned out to be a stroke of luck for him. As her wealth grew, she had given him other legal chores; in particular, banking and real estate.

But she really mainly needed him to tell her the place to sign. Hannah Elias was a genius. Those black, black eyes held such native intelligence they dispelled his fear of her character. Hannah had never hired an accountant. She kept the balances, withdrawals, and deposits of her bank accounts, stock quotations, municipal and federal bond interests, oil, cotton, and corn prices, rents, taxes, assessments, and the price of a pint of gin in her head.

He was able to leave the firm where he never would have made partner in any case and strike out on his own. Her chores paid the rent on his offices at 488 Broadway. And when Mrs. Bessie Davis had chosen to take back her maiden name after the divorce and become Mrs. Hannah Elias, he prospered further.

Nanz spotted an elegant, elderly man in a top hat making his way through the crowd in the direction of Hannah's carriage. He was unbent and tall in a sealskin coat. He disappeared into Hannah's carriage. Nanz couldn't believe Hannah was having another assignation in public, as public as any event could possibly be.

There were dozens of reporters, photographers, and illustrators in attendance, looking for a story. Hannah's name had been linked with Green's on the front page of the *Times*. Didn't she know that everyone was watching her?

What kind of trouble did she want? He bolted toward the carriage, his open umbrella attacking dozens of others as he fought his way through the milling crowd of spectators and mounted police. People were packed so close that it took him several minutes to reach the police barriers only to watch the carriage slowly draw away. Frustrated, he turned to see the district attorney, whose department had sent 360 policemen to protect what the *Times* had called "the entire gross domestic product of the

United States of America," walk up to one of his plainclothesmen. He eavesdropped on the conversation William Jerome was holding.

"President Roosevelt coming?" asked Detective McClusky.

"That's all I need," Jerome said. "No. He's sent his secretary of state as his representative. Isn't it enough that Andrew Carnegie, Cornelius Vanderbilt, and J. Pierpont Morgan are here? See no evil, hear no evil, and speak no evil—the code of Wall Street."

"And old landlord John Jacob Astor as well. I read in the *World* that Astor's real estate could line a thoroughfare seven miles long. Walk two hours and you would pass fifteen thousand dollars' worth of property with each and every step."

William Jerome and Jack McClusky noticed that August Belmont Jr., president of the Rapid Transit Commission, had stopped to talk to John D. Rockefeller. Belmont the elder, who had changed his name from Schonberg in a vain effort to hide his Jewish ancestry, had at least succeeded in gaining his son's entry into the social elite. August Belmont had inherited the presidency of his father's bank, a seat on the stock exchange, and close relationships on a first-name basis with the Rothschilds (who did not hide their race). He lived like a prince and owned seven homes, any one of which would have made an ordinary millionaire happy.

Carnegie, Vanderbilt, and J. P. Morgan walked like a troika of horses in tandem as they followed the casket. They seemed not to have much to say to one another, thought Nanz, who noticed that each man clutched a copy of the *Wall Street Journal*. Perhaps they all felt their mortality on seeing the deceased. Although he was worth only a paltry million, they seemed to contemplate that they couldn't take all their wealth with them. Everyone died poor.

Nanz moved away from the district attorney and the detective, who nodded to him in recognition of his former days as the kind of Tombs lawyer who didn't mind if his clients squealed.

Nanz was able to squeeze behind the last pew, where he stood unashamed alongside the aspirational New Yorkers.

Brick Church reeked of camphor, candle wax, and wet fur. The massive organ loomed over the assembly, flanked by a gold Gabriel and his trumpet of doom on one side and a silver Archangel Michael holding his harp of heavenly salvation on the other. Everything was, like the age it-self, gilded, thanks to the generous donations of the richest congregation in America.

"Themistocles," the pastor began, "is quoted as saying, 'I know how to raise a small and inconsiderable city to glory and greatness.' It may truthfully be said that no other man has labored more in and for New York City during the last fifty years than Andrew Green. The city itself, in some of its more beautiful and enduring features, is a monument to his love: the New York Public Library, the Metropolitan Museum of Art, the IRT, the consolidation of Greater New York, and his crowning achieve-ment, Central Park. The city may well cherish his honored name with the undying gratitude that is due to a citizen who has made it both a greater and a better city than it was."

Everyone nodded in agreement while several fumed inside that their contributions weren't mentioned. Still, they didn't want to die just to hear about them.

The choir then sang "As When the Weary Troubles Reach a Com-manding Height." As the mourners filed out, they looked curiously at the district attorney, impeccable in his black oilcloth cape slicker, galoshes, and cap, in deep conversation with two of his detectives. Nothing had been said during the ceremony about the murder. It was as if, as in the *Times* obituary, Andrew Green had passed away at a tea party rather than in a pool of blood like a mobster on a New York sidewalk.

As the photographers' cameras snapped and the reporters jotted down quick descriptions, Platt had gotten into Hannah's carriage. He hadn't seen her since he left her in the Rockaways at the beginning of the fall. He had been caught since then in confusion of whether to reach out to her and how. He didn't want to be discovered. But he wanted to see her badly. He was angry that she gave a party without his knowledge. No one had told him it had been a surprise party she had known nothing about.

Now, seeing her carriage and knowing that she was only a few feet away, he didn't care. What was the use of all his money if his reputation controlled him? She obviously needed him now.

The many freelance photographers and amateur journalists couldn't figure out who he was. All the professionals were following the cortege taking Green from the church to the hearse. Platt resembled all the rich men and lovers Hannah had entertained in the Tenderloin. All of them carrying on dual lives of perfect citizenship and terrible corruption. All of them husbands and sinners. They seemed to have heads that were made to be struck in bronze, profiles that reeked of power, history, and capital, which all seemed to issue from the same die. Features that would be fashioned into busts, coins, and monuments. Their chests seemed made for wide sashes and governmental decorations. They all had receding hairlines, high foreheads, big noses, silvery hair, and white beards. They modeled unfettered Christian materialism.

John Platt's face was a sharp map of wrinkles spread across a handsome, adolescent bone structure. The white hair had remained healthy and abundant and fell in a hank over his still clear-blue eyes. Seated in front of her, he held his top hat in his lap, and covered it with one signet-ringed hand. His umbrella, with its silver carved knob, rested between his legs and dripped onto the floor. Through the window of the carriage on Platt's side, where the curtains had not been drawn entirely, the dull light streamed across his distinctive features. His chilly whiteness glowed like a lantern, in contrast to Hannah's impassable silhouette. His knees stuck out at right angles, and his large, patent-leather-booted feet splayed out like a ballet dancer's in the cramped space.

Hannah raised her eyes to his and held them as they sat, in a kind of speechless, domestic silence, as they each waited for the other to speak. As usual, Platt wanted to do nothing except look at her. As with most men, he had long given up the effort of resisting her prowess. Hannah had revolutionized his outlook so that the attributes of womanliness attached to his own class had been eradicated. Her dark eyes and round nose, her tawny skin and strong hands, her beautiful figure, made the women around him on the Upper East Side seem like papier-mâché by comparison. It was amazing.

Platt's blue eyes surveyed his mistress with a mixture of pathos and pride. He was as attracted to her now as he had been sixteen years ago, when he had found her in Pop Miller's and had been surprised at the commotion raised in his heart by a public woman. Even now he found himself sitting with a gaping mouth.

He pressed his lips together and clenched his jaw. His neat white beard hid the lower half of his face, which made it impossible to imagine how good-looking he had been as a young man. But his languid, self-assured eyes were the eyes of a man who had gazed with satisfaction at his own image in the mirror for most of his privileged life. He now studied his reflection in the eyes of his mistress.

He placed his hand on Hannah's gloved, bejeweled fingers. He was surprised she did not wear mourning. Her dress was deep purple under the cashmere shawl, and she had on diamond earrings.

Maybe the party had done her good. He was about to ask when Hannah began to explain that Nanz had given her a surprise. She didn't know about his plan, only that he told her to come home immediately.

Platt found this explanation hard to believe. Hannah tightly controlled her environment. But he was with her again, in the carriage, and he wasn't going to argue about anything that had little meaning when life was so short. He knew that now more than ever.

"What about this man, Cornelius Williams? How does he know you?"

"I think you met him once, Papa. When I lived on Fifty-Third Street, he was the man who argued with you."

Platt made a point of not remembering Hannah's past, especially her suitors.

"It doesn't matter now, does it?"

"Not at all. He's been arrested."

Hannah didn't let on that the police were coming to her house the next day, to look for Bessie. Platt had found out about Bessie at the time of her divorce. But Bessie was dead as far as either of them cared. And Williams hadn't been the one who'd killed her.

Platt now spoke in almost a whisper, as if there were someone present to overhear them. There was an aura of authority in the set of his shoulders that was not simply due to the impeccable cut of his greatcoat. He gave her an order:

"I want you to get out of New York for a while. I want you to leave town. You're sitting there right under the district attorney's nose. Didn't they state in the papers you knew Green? What are you doing here?"

"I hoped I'd see you. I knew that the people at the funeral were your neighbors and friends. Did you read what Cornelius said in the papers? He had killed me."

"But that was obviously a figment of his imagination, right?"

"No, Papa, he came to my house and shot me."

Platt looked stricken. He reached for Hannah while she retreated, straightening her back against the carriage seat.

"Are you all right?"

"Only bruised where the corset took the bullet," she said. "The red one that you liked." Hannah laughed, but Platt didn't find anything funny.

"When Cornelius shot Mr. Green, he thought I was already dead. And Cornelius Williams thought he was shooting you. It's all a terrible mistake."

"I don't know what to believe, Hannah. It's so shocking, Green's death. And then you, being involved—this Negro man being acquainted with you—being obsessed with you. "

Hannah was the one to look surprised now. Platt didn't mind that she was living with Negroes, married to a Negro, or that she had Negro blood herself. But now he mentions "Negro" with a tinge of disgust.

"Oh, God, this is so awful." Platt wasn't thinking about her at all now. "This Cornelius man thought he was shooting me! If he gets out, he'll want to try and shoot me again. Good God! You've said nothing to the police, Hannah?"

"Nothing," she responded.

"And has the murderer said anything about shooting you?"

"He's told everyone that he shot Bessie Davis. But it's only a matter of time until someone connects us both."

John Platt put his head in his hands. This was a nightmare that seemed to have no end. How, how had things come to this? Sitting opposite her, even now wanting to put his hands on her, he was riddled with fear: fear of disclosure, of disgrace, of the contempt from everyone in his circle—his friends, business acquaintances, even his children, who now lived with their elitist standards. They would reject someone like Hannah immediately. He thought he was ready to declare his love. But it was to be on his own terms. Now his hypocrisies ate at him from his stomach to his groin.

"If anyone asks, Hannah, I will deny knowing you. And you should do the same. I'll stay pat if you stay pat."

Hannah gave him her Cleopatra smile, which he took to mean that he had her assent.

The roar of the city's voice and the tempo of its rain could be felt inside the quiet of the carriage. The Borough of Manhattan, New York, in 1903 held more than a million people, of which over 20 percent were Black and 60 percent were immigrants, which meant that 80 percent of the city's population were nonwhite or foreign-born. Only 20 percent were white. Platt was not only a member of that 20 percent, but also a member of the famous four hundred—the rich, white Anglo-Saxons—and Yale educated. He had a stock exchange seat, sat on the board of the Pennsylvania Railroad, and was a member of the city's most exclusive clubs: the Century Association, the Union Club, the Racquet and Tennis Club, and the Metropolitan Club.

His city spread out over sixteen square miles, starting at Wall Street and the Battery to the south and Harlem to the north. Broadway ran through it from Water Street to 102nd Street. There were a million New Yorkers, and 800,000 of them lived in tenements. Five hundred thousand immigrants passed through the cavernous hole of Ellis Island every year, strangers in a strange land, but not like Blacks or the Native Americans who were strangers on their own land.

Thus, the two New Yorkers seated in the carriage—the seductress and the seduced, the grand horizontal and the slave of love, the courtesan and the eunuch—had started out very differently. In her way, Hannah was quite fond of Platt, called him Papa, and was faithful to him in her manner. He was the foundation and the originator of her harem of rich men who had transformed her from a public woman into a banker. She was now richer than several of them and equal in wealth to a dozen more. She had become more like him as the years went on.

Platt looked at Hannah. She seemed calm and regal. Not only was Hannah untouched and unconquered by what Platt considered a sordid, dangerous, and unscrupulous life, but her spirit seemed to have survived, pristine and untouched—without consequences. She seemed concerned by neither favor nor discrimination, neither justice nor injustice, but existed in her own time and in her own element. She was now The Capitalist, a woman who wanted to be left alone and then the host of a grand party. She always seemed to be two different people.

Suddenly Platt felt as if there was no more space to breathe in the carriage. Hannah had a feline way of stealing all the oxygen around her. She always had the ability to walk into a room full of people and simply appropriate all the attention until there remained only Hannah. She had walked into the empty room of his heart and filled it completely. He personally didn't care about Hannah's past or any of her former lovers. Her gift had come to him and made him new. Right then at the site of death, the funeral of a peer, when he felt his own demise imminent, he appreciated her mastery more than ever.

"So you think we're being punished, Hannah? First with Gwendolyn and now this. Two men's lives destroyed: Andrew, and this Williams fellow that you knew."

"Cornelius isn't a bad man, just a bit slow. How could he have been turned into a murderer?"

"He says in the papers it's your fault." He simply reported the facts, but Hannah gave him a quick, angry look.

"We're both to blame. We're all to blame. Who knows?"

"You will leave for a while," Platt said, after a long silence. "Take Kato, so the police can't get to him."

"I intend to leave. In a week, Papa."

"Where?"

"I'll contact you when I get there."

"Good. I—" He could not help but smile at being called "Papa," and he accepted this not-so-exaggerated description of his age.

Still, both had a dim and indefinable vision of what could happen if their liaison were to be revealed, such that no words could describe it, so they sat there. Hannah already imagined the fury of a venomous district attorney who stood outside somewhere in the crowd. She listened to the sound of the rain on the roof of the victoria.

"My ribs still hurt . . . from the bullet."

"Poor Hannah. At least he's caught."

"Yes, and so are we. A man has died in your place. Your place!"

"I believe the question of our connection with Andrew Green will never see the light of day."

Hannah dropped her eyes and looked out the steamed-up window at the sea of top hats and black umbrellas moving away like the Hudson River's low tide, except up Fifth Avenue. The men formed both a mob and a procession. To Hannah, it seemed not only familiar as an auditorium full of theatergoers, but also ominous as a gang. She sat still as a cat.

Platt spoke first. "You must, please, leave town as soon as possible."

"I promise. I'll telegraph you as soon as I get there."

"Where?"

"Saratoga."

"Let me know if you need me. Or need something done. But, of course, you have Nanz for that—your right-hand man."

Hannah heard a little irony in his voice. He was trying to trust her lawyer, but after the party, she could feel that Platt was not entirely comfortable with the relationship.

The carriage drove down Central Park West when Hannah knocked on the ceiling and said, "Let's go see Gwendolyn. I need to see Gwendolyn . . ." Turning to Platt she said, "I need to see Gwendolyn. Let's go see her together."

The coachman, Max, had taken the Eighty-Fifth Street exit. While Platt looked at the scenery, Hannah considered the conversation she'd had with Leola the last time they had been together, the day Green was shot.

"If the police figure out that I'm Bessie Davis, they'll find out that I have a prison record."

"Perhaps not," said Leola. "You're a great liar."

"You know that I'll be a suspect even if I never pulled the trigger. They will want nothing more than to catch two colored people plotting to kill a white man. You know it, Leola. I'll be convicted in the newspapers before I ever get to a jury."

"Oh Hannah, we'll have to figure out something. We'll tell the same lie together. Whatever it is."

Hannah made a gesture of exasperation. "That's perjury. That will send me to jail right away. I'd rather be dead."

"Hannah," she said softly, "you actually still believe there's a right way and a wrong way to deal with the law? You're always thinking that being good will change anything. We are what they call us. Fallen. Women."

"I don't believe that, Leola." Hannah felt stronger and better than ever.

But her friend's mind could not be changed. "Men can reform. Society welcomes them with open arms; the world accepts their apologies, their promises to change as a miracle, hails their confessions of transgression with unmitigated joy. But for us, for women, there are no calls to come home and all's forgiven, no welcoming arms, no acceptance of repentance and promises to men. We are cast out forever. We are fallen for eternity. I still don't see how you still dream of redemption, of a daddy returning to save your reputation, give you money, take care of all your woes."

Hannah had given her a hurt look. But Leola had continued, "All this shit is real."

As Hannah recalled, she had been silent. Leola did not have the answer.

Hannah and Platt stood before the Romanesque white marble mausoleum, which was almost the height of a one-story building and was adorned with elaborately carved sleeping cherubs and sculptured garlands.

HERE LIES

GWENDOLYN CAMILLA ELIAS

BORN OCTOBER 1, 1902–DIED OCTOBER 1, 1902

BELOVED DAUGHTER OF HANNAH KATHARINE ELIAS

HERE SLEEPS BEAUTY AND INNOCENCE AND PURITY.

John Platt's right hand clutched Hannah's elbow, steadying her. Her sobs stirred the black gossamer lace of her veil. He looked away, touched yet helpless. Her body rocked as she cried. It was strange for him to see Hannah off balance. She was physically as strong as an athlete. At one time she had performed the grueling work of the skin trade: on her feet longer than a factory worker, except in high heels; on her back, like the repairman of a train's chassis. Most of her life, she needed the stamina of a stevedore. Hannah was indestructible, he thought. That indestructibility made her irresistible. He had fallen in love with her, as so many others have. But he had lasted, and now he saw her vulnerability. This also made her desirable. He decided to take care of her forever.

Upper East Side, Fifty-Third Street

Almost at the same time that Hannah was thinking of her, Leola was thinking of Hannah. She sat in her apartment on Fifty-Third Street, one of Hannah's bordellos, and picked up a newspaper beside her on the sofa. She read Andrew Green's obituary in the *Times* over and over again. She studied the details of the murder, looking for a mention of a second shooting—Hannah's incredible corset story. Luckily, there was nothing.

She went over to her safe and clicked the lock until the door sprang open. She removed the pale blue copybook Hannah had given her. She hesitated and then opened it to the first page. Hannah's elaborate and beautiful handwriting, full of scrolls and flourishes, filled page after page: accounts, magazine articles, quotations from novels, poems, and notes to herself. An undated letter from someone called JRP exclaimed, "I am highly gratified at the promptitude with which you have responded to my desire to form your acquaintance, the more so, because if I am to believe you (and as yet I have no reason to doubt your sincerity) it is a favor which has not been granted to all who have sought it."

Poor JRP, thought Leola. The world of commercial sex was a world of playacting far more than sincerity. Women like her and Hannah faked names and faked pasts, faked emotions and pleasure, and paid debts with ill-gotten gains—money that was stolen from a grandmother's drawer, from a wife's purse, from a drunken man at the gambling table. A rich man and his money were soon parted. Leola couldn't remember where she'd first heard it. But the saying was implanted on her soul, although she probably misinterpreted its meaning.

Foolish money had given Leola a home and Hannah her riches. And she wasn't going to be foolish anymore. Hannah was a millionaire because she had given herself many lessons in the rituals of upper-class manners: to read and write love letters, poetry, and thank-you notes; of insisting on expensive gifts, gallantry, and flirtation; and of course the house on Fifty-Third Street, which she had parlayed into several more buildings. Leola read no further. It was after all none of her business beyond its safekeeping in the vault. The pale blue copybook, of which there were many, she knew, revealed someone who had made important sacrifices. Ambition in a woman, thought Leola, was always tragic.

Now she wondered whether Cornelius's insane act would turn into a tidal wave of retribution for Hannah's past. Maybe she wasn't rich enough to cleanse herself, as Nanz had told her was possible. But Platt was.

EIGHTEEN

Five Points, New York,
November 17, 1903

Detective McClusky had seen August Nanz rushing toward a carriage as it drove away. When Nanz left the church and walked toward the rich peers whom he sought to associate himself with, McClusky intercepted him. Nanz was deeply embarrassed as was possible for only a formerly poor boy.

He had reluctantly agreed to meet McClusky in Paradise, the day after Andrew Green's funeral. It was an area that Nanz had avoided since his and Hannah's early days. Paradise was a square in the center of Five Points, a district famous for theft, prostitution, and drugs that people called "hop." The area could be entered from five main streets—Leonard, Orange, Anthony, Bowery, and Centre. They radiated out like a five-pointed star, linked by honeycombed dark passages and crooked, narrow lanes. It was a district where Black and white mingled without barriers and where three-quarters of the Black population of New York lived. Twenty-seven of its forty-three city blocks housed the Sisterhood. These were the suburbs of Hannah's past, although as far as Nanz knew, McClusky wasn't aware of this.

McClusky knew Nanz's reputation from the old days in the Tombs, so Nanz knew the detective's choice of location was an effort to intimidate him.

As Nanz stepped from the carriage, he crossed the intersection where a thousand homeless children roamed the avenues. Some streets were only as wide as a dead man's body is long. On the wooden steps to the tenements, women sat, stood, and smoked. They loaded the air with obscene imprecations, assaulting passersby. There were, according to certain reports by the legions of new vice reformers, twenty thousand whores, thirty thousand thieves, three thousand saloons, and two thousand gambling houses situated in Five Points.

McGurk's Suicide Hall was located at the most easterly section of the docks. John McGurk, an Irishman, had arrived from Boston in 1883 and had opened the Mug, an establishment that specialized in waiters armed with knockout drops. When the police closed it down, he opened up a clip joint called Sailor's Snug Harbor. When this too was shut down, he moved up Third Avenue and opened the Merrimac, but it also fell under the hatchet of District Attorney Jerome's vice squad.

Then, in a burst of inspiration, he opened up McGurk's on the waterfront: four stories high, separate entrances for men and women, singing waiters, southern food, a small ragtime band, and a head waiter called "Short-Change Charley," who carried a vial of chloral hydrate to render unruly customers unconscious. The bouncer's name was "Eat 'Em Up Jack McManus," and biting off people's ears was his trademark. McGurk's was the lowest rung for prostitutes, hence the frequent suicides that gave it its name and notoriety.

In one year, six people had killed themselves there, and seven people had tried and failed. Among them were Blond Madge and Big Mama, who bought carbolic acid at the drugstore a few blocks away one night. Blond Madge managed to swallow hers, but Big Mama hesitated at the last moment and spilled most of it on her face, which so horribly disfigured her that she was barred from McGurk's on the basis of scaring away customers.

If Short-Change Charley suspected an attempt in the making, he would form his waiters into a flying wedge and wrestle the girl out the door before she killed herself on the premises. But if a woman did manage to do away with herself within its walls, John McGurk would pronounce an epitaph over her lifeless body and pay for her funeral. This was one reason that death was so popular at his club. Women knew that they would get a good send-off.

McClusky was already waiting behind the Chinese screen used for celebrities who wanted to taste McGurk's cooking in private.

Nanz didn't smile but briskly walked through the thick, spicy atmosphere as he made his way past a dozen people who might have remembered him as an ambulance chaser.

McClusky believed Nanz knew Hannah's secrets. He had orchestrated her introduction into New York society with his bogus ball for an obscure Spanish vice-consul. He was known to have accompanied her to architects' offices, bankers, and uptown house decorators—which while not being McClusky's milieu, were known to the foot-patrol officers. Although McClusky wasn't aware, Nanz had procured her divorce when she was Bessie Davis, and he had helped Platt with the arrangements for the funeral of Gwendolyn. McClusky knew Nanz was Hannah's guardian angel, but he couldn't figure out why.

The Nanz known to McClusky was a product of the East Side tenements, under the "El," the elevated trains that roared over Second Avenue in a slum not much better than Five Points. McClusky knew Nanz's origins because his accent had changed considerably since they first met. Nanz's disdain for poverty now showed since their last meeting. It was true that Nanz's childhood neighborhood had been overrun by Poles, Italians, Lithuanians, and Russians. And as a child he had hated them all, felt overwhelmed by their accents and incomprehensible languages, their illiteracy, their poverty, dirt, and smells. He had fought to extricate himself from this quagmire of foreigners by passing for a White Anglo-Saxon Protestant, and he had succeeded. But McClusky remembered Nanz from his years of transition.

When he began to practice law in the lowest rungs of society, the principles he observed were those of the Civil Code. He did anything within the law's outer reach or not specifically forbidden by law, and he advised his clients accordingly.

This often brought him into conversation with many of the city's unscrupulous police, whom McClusky knew but abhorred. Nanz worked on the outside perimeter of the letter of the law, and the space between that letter was a no-man's-land, a little like lower Broadway. One flowed with the rhythm of the traffic, even if harrowing, as long as one stopped short of running over pedestrians. Speeding through the yellow light was his specialty, so he excelled.

Nanz was obsequious to his betters, contemptuous of those he felt beneath him. He detested the rich and hated the poor. He read the *Wall Street Journal* and the *New York Times* faithfully. No sooner he had been hired by Warren, Warren, and O'Beirne then he had begun to scrape up acquaintances with his trust-funded, well-bred brethren, who made him despise his former life even more. He prided himself on not swearing, drinking, or indulging in any of the other genteel vices like cigar smoking. He listened to opera and attended the performances at the Metropolitan when he could. And he said that he was a perfect match for a rich girl. This is the area in which McClusky suspected a ruse and aimed to play Nanz for information.

Nanz was smarter, funnier, and more refined than any of the young men at Warren, Warren, and O'Beirne, either in frock or out. McClusky saw that Nanz now dressed the part of the young well-born Wall Street jock. His hair was cut in the newest fashion and carefully groomed. It was a magnificent head of blond hair, a lock of which was always falling appealingly over one eye. He would marry his future bride, he said aloud often, in Brick Church.

McClusky, however, noted his indifference to any specific woman. Nanz also proclaimed that men like himself were very long to fix their hearts' desire, but once done they were more susceptible to true affection and fidelity.

McClusky didn't know if this was true, not being much of a catch himself, but he noticed that when a lady happened to like Nanz, all of a sudden he stopped seeing her, he said, for the sake of her "virtue and reputation"—as if he couldn't resist her. McClusky theorized it was not due to the woman but to Nanz's sexual preferences.

"The district attorney and I are going to Hannah Elias's house tomorrow. Will you be there?" McClusky asked.

Nanz stammered uncharacteristically. He had only read about the interview in the paper. He didn't know what to say.

"There are certain client-attorney privileges," Nanz finally told McClusky.

"So, what can you tell me about Mrs. Elias? Where is she from? How did she get so rich?"

"You're asking me to do your job for you?" Nanz replied. At this point, he felt he had the upper hand, since McClusky obviously didn't know much.

"I remember you, Nanz, from when you first started working in this town. You grew up around here, didn't you?"

"What's your point, detective?"

"So you want me to be blunt? It seems to me that someone from these slums would know the ropes. You know, understand how a dust-maid becomes Cinderella. We know there was no fairy godmother that gave her those jewels. Who is she fronting for? Maybe she's laundering money? Maybe that's why Green had to be shot? He's got such a great reputation, but who in this town is above graft? I'll bet you know the score, Mr. Nanz. You know who has the information, and you know where to get it."

Nanz squinted when he heard his childhood neighborhood called a slum. That's exactly what it was. But he had moved so far away from it. Why would McClusky throw it back in his face?

Nanz hated New York, the harshness of it all. He had struggled so hard to get to the place where his reputation was good and his money was regular. Now he had to fight to keep it.

"Mrs. Elias is my client. That's all. If you want to subpoena her for information, you can go right ahead." Nanz played his trump card, because he figured if McClusky had any good information, he would have subpoenaed Hannah already and not tried to get dirt on her in this back-handed way, and at the last minute before her deposition.

"I'll be there tomorrow, Detective McClusky, you can be sure."

McClusky knew Hannah was involved in some way. He just couldn't figure out how. Even the papers knew that something was going on in that mansion, although none of them had been inside. His detail of cops, now relieved to be off crowd control after the funeral and back on surveillance, saw nothing unusual about Hannah. The strangest thing was that Cornelius kept saying that Bessie was hiding at 236 Central Park West and was dead. Was Mrs. Elias hiding the body?

Nanz had given him nothing, but McClusky gained a little insight into the man whom he hadn't seen since he was a young lawyer who hung around the Tombs to take a little money for having his clients confess and save the state money and time. Nanz was a little ashamed of his roots, as McClusky suspected. If he was that easily scared, Nanz could really be compromised by his sexuality, if necessary.

The music of the piano player drifted from the corner to the place where McClusky sat. The song was called "The Mansion of Aching Hearts." McClusky listened to the words through the haze of smoke that filtered out into the night:

> "She lives in a mansion of aching hearts,
> She's one of a restless throng,
> The diamonds that glitter around her throat,
> They speak both of sorrow and song;
> The smile on her face is only a mask,
> And many the tear that starts,
> For sadder it seems, when of mother she dreams,
> In the mansion of aching hearts."

NINETEEN

Upper West Side, New York,
November 18, 1903

S eated uneasily on Hannah's French Empire drawing room side chairs were District Attorney Jerome, Detective Hurley, Assistant District Attorney Appleton, a stenographer, Detective McClusky, and August Nanz.

Nanz had sent a messenger to Hannah's mansion early in the morning to tell her that he knew she was going to be interviewed and that she should have called him. And he insisted that she should not do this alone and that he was going to be there.

None of those present in Hannah's house except Nanz had ever seen or even imagined an interior like the one in which they found themselves. It had disconcerted even Jerome, used to upper-class residences, who was speaking now in the hushed tones of a conversation being held in a cathedral.

Earlier, the door had been opened by Kato. The detectives noticed several other Asian servants moving quietly between the rooms. The foyer and the winding staircase leading to the upper floors were decorated, as was the saloon itself, in Retour d'Egypte, a style that had made a comeback among the nouveaux riches of Saratoga, New Rochelle, and Fifth Avenue. But even this did not explain the perfumed fountain, the servants dressed in Egyptian togas, the opulent profusion of rugs, or the mammoth chandeliers and Tiffany lamps. McClusky felt he had wandered into the *Arabian Nights*. The stenographer was so unnerved that her hand shook over her spiral notebook.

That there was a great deal of speculation connected with Hannah was evident from all the inquiries Maloney and McClusky had made in the neighborhood. Her neighbors, the Greens, said that nobody had had a good look at Mrs. Elias since her uncharacteristic party.

"She keeps to herself," Mrs. Green had said. She was the wife of Andrew Green's brother. She was still horrified about the crazy man who shot her brother-in-law and implicated her neighbor. "I know for a fact that she owns the mansion she lives in, free of encumbrance, and enjoys considerable luxury. As for the white-haired man I've seen there, I don't know his name. The first and only time Andrew went there was when we went to her party. You can't blame us for being curious. He came along. I think all of the time, dear heaven, was that the reason Andrew was targeted—because that lunatic implicated him in some way?"

Everyone rose when Hannah swept into the room in a reception dress of blue and black Pekinese stripes made of gauze and moiré over yellow taffeta, with revers and cuffs of coralline lace with jet edging. A choker of diamonds and pearls accented her décolleté. She exchanged greetings in her soft voice, a little hoarse from a declared cold. She arranged herself on the sofa and smiled, showing deep dimples, taking in the entire assembly. With her eyes, she directed Kato to serve tea from a silver samovar in delicate porcelain cups.

Jerome summarized her first admissions: "Mrs. Elias, allow me to reiterate the facts of your deposition. Your maiden name is Elias and you were born in 1865 in Philadelphia. You are a willing witness and that you will answer all of our questions frankly and truthfully.

"Have you ever met or seen Andrew H. Green in the past two years that you have been living here?"

"No, I haven't," Hannah said politely.

McClusky knew that he had been at her recent party. Lie one.

"And Cornelius Williams, do you know him?"

"I know he is the coal man. He deals with the furnaces in this neighborhood. But I must tell you that I was married once, and Cornelius was a friend of my husband's."

Nanz groaned. She didn't need to admit anything that they didn't ask her. When did she begin to be so damn honest?

"Your husband's name was—?"

"Matthew Davis." Hannah decided to tell the truth. If she was going to jail, it wouldn't be for lying.

Leola had advised her against it: "Hannah, just be the new you. Don't go back to Matthew. No one will make the connection. You're just innocent of the whole affair and soon it will be done."

Hannah had responded, "Leola. I'll tell the truth if they ask me. I am tired of being ashamed." Hannah had come to a place in her life where she wanted to be understood for who she was. That's what the sleepless nights since Green's death had taught her. When Leola said that women like them would always be disrespected, Hannah had wanted to disagree. She wasn't sure at the time. But in the days that followed, she considered: Why should she be anything but a rich courtesan? People had done worse.

In fact, all those men at Green's funeral were millionaires because they cheated and lied, took property from old women, and constructed buildings that charged four times the rent. The poor were pushed farther and farther into the slums, which would inevitably be razed for more construction. Hannah came from the slums and she became rich—not from hurting other people but from giving men pleasure.

"Did you say Davis?" Jerome repeated.

"Yes, Davis. I was Mrs. Davis and Cornelius met me as Bessie."

The stenographer wrote furiously.

"You know, Mrs. Elias, we'll need to bring this to court," McClusky said. This time Nanz groaned. But Jerome perked up. He had to forgive McClusky and Hurley now for forcing him into the interview. This case was suddenly becoming interesting. At first, he didn't want any publicity. The case was open and shut—a crazed man and the mistaken identity of a white woman and her socialite friend Andrew Green. Jerome had hired the alienists just to get Williams sent to jail without any more headlines. But now there could be a larger corruption, something he could sink his teeth into—and he could garner the interest of the New York reading public.

Hannah Elias was Bessie Davis. Her identity was key to the murder. The new headlines would distract from Green's misdeeds and stick to hers.

This might give Jerome more publicity for his crusading efforts against corruption. The good city fathers and the gutter scum would be back in their respective places again.

"So, you were married to Matthew Davis. Your first name was Bessie. Cornelius was your boyfriend?"

"Oh no," Hannah said.

Nanz shook his head. Everybody had warned her. She just wouldn't listen.

"I hadn't seen Cornelius since before my divorce. I put him out of my home in 1898. I moved here two years ago."

"And the reason you moved here was?" Jerome asked.

"Well, sir, gentlemen, look around. Do you blame me?"

This comment provided a moment of levity.

"So can you tell us why Cornelius Williams believes that you're dead?"

"Sir. I only know that I am alive. You can see me. I can't search the mind of a crazy man."

"Of course not," Jerome said, continuing his questioning with this new information.

"Are you the sole owner of this property at 236 Central Park West, as well as two other apartment buildings at 145 West Fifty-Third Street and 73 West Sixty-Eighth Street, and that your tax assessment for the year 1902 was sixty thousand dollars?"

"That's correct."

"Your ex-husband Matthew Davis owns none of this?" Jerome waved his hand over the ornate room behind him. "He hasn't tried to threaten you to get money? You have created your fortune from real estate speculation and a small inheritance."

At this, Hannah began to perspire. She did not have rich parents to give her money and school. This estate was hers, all right. She gave herself an inheritance.

"That is correct," said Hannah. Her voice had turned rough. She leaned forward. McClusky's hound-dog nose caught the scent of her perfume—Jicky by Guerlain—a scent so ambiguous and troublesome, it was sold only as a men's perfume.

"And have you had any contact recently with your ex-husband, or do you know where he is?"

"I have had no contact with him, and I don't know where he is. Just as I have no knowledge of Mr. Williams or his activities since 1901, except to say that his crime is incomprehensible to me and can have nothing to do with me, or my ex-husband."

"Why do you think Williams has this fixation on you?" Jerome circled around to a previous question. He wanted to catch her in a lie. He was sure there was more to this story now.

"I don't think Mrs. Elias can speculate on that," interrupted Nanz. "As she has told you, she has absolutely no ulterior knowledge of this affair. It is most shocking to her."

"Do you think he is a madman, Mrs. Elias?"

Nanz interjected again: "Mrs. Elias is no alienist. Williams is obviously crazy. He boarded in Mrs. Elias's house for several years and saw her every day in all kinds of circumstances. Perhaps this artificial intimacy encouraged him to create a fantasy life around Mrs. Elias that had no basis in reality."

"Well, yes," said Jerome. "That is the psychological conclusion. Good for you, Mr. Nanz. Thank you for your cooperation and your deposition, Mrs. Elias."

Detective McClusky said nothing. Nanz, he thought, acted like a big-boy lawyer, enough to interrupt Jerome's questioning. Nanz knew where Hannah got her money and whether Green was possibly blackmailing her. Hannah could well be making money as a slumlord and cut the developer out. It was the only explanation he could think of while looking at the surrounding wealth and appointments. Many New York fortunes were based on the ownership of the miserable tenements in Little Italy, the Bowery, Hell's Kitchen, and the Lower East Side. Slum landlords raked in millions in exorbitant rents and sublets, sweatshops and illegal alien hideouts. He decided to let it ride, but he wanted to know one more thing.

It was really the information he wanted to use and set Nanz on edge, to let him know the depths that could be achieved by dragging his reputation into the mud.

"Mrs. Elias," said McClusky, "are you a colored lady?"

"I beg your pardon?"

"Are you a mulatto, Mrs. Elias?"

"You obviously hadn't heard that I'm Cuban, a Spaniard."

"Oh, I see, excuse me for asking," McClusky said, while Jerome kept his face expressionless.

"It's quite all right."

"Of course, if you *were* colored, you would be the richest colored person in the United States of America," McClusky added, trying to flatter the truth from her.

"Indeed? I'm not one to follow statistics."

"You own no other real estate—downtown?"

"No, Mr. McClusky, I am not a slum landlord, if that's what you mean. I am a land speculator and investor, working through merchant banks and brokerage agents, as you can surely ascertain."

Nanz didn't like the turn of the conversation. "Please tell me how this is relevant to Mr. Green's murder?"

McClusky ignored him. "Could we possibly have your accountant's name, please?"

"I have no accountant. I do all my own bookkeeping."

"No accountant?"

"No."

"But you're a millionaire, ma'am," said McClusky."

"Indeed, Mr. McClusky."

"I do believe that's all, Mrs. Elias," blurted Jerome, uncomfortable that McClusky had taken the lead in going down this road. "Again, thank you for receiving us. If you will just sign here. Thank you. My card, Mrs. Elias—if you think of anything else you can telephone me."

But Hannah knew it was far from over. If the alienists did not convince the grand jury that Cornelius was stark raving mad, he would go on trial for first-degree murder and more would come to light in the newspapers—not just about her properties, but their purposes. The city's readers would also find out about Platt—who seemed ready to reveal their affair, but even he couldn't guess the cost of his lost reputation.

"Williams claims he shot you and *estabas muerta* the night before his assassination of Green," interjected McClusky casually.

"Pardon?" Hannah laughed, catching only a few words of the sentence.

"Crazy as a loon suffering from delusions, according to his alienists," explained Jerome, leaning forward to scrutinize Hannah, who shook her head helplessly.

"Tragic man. Tragic, tragic man . . ." Nanz said.

When Hannah was asked whether she wished to add anything to her deposition, she simply nodded no. She hated the law. The courts worked only for the people who owned them.

McClusky rushed to the record office to find the marriage certificate of Matthew and Bessie Davis. He found that they had been married in 1896. He also found Hannah's third lie—the one that mattered the most to him. Matthew was a Negro. His Negroness didn't make him a murderer—although he was more likely to be a criminal. And if Matthew Davis was a Negro and Cornelius Williams was too, then probably so was Bessie Davis. They had their own little gang. He would bet there were numbers, gambling, and prostitution at the heart of their activities.

When McClusky returned to the office, he went to Jerome's room.

"Well, there's one more thing," said McClusky. "Here's what I found from the neighbors."

He began to read from his notes in his lilting Irish voice.

"It seems that the murdered man visited close friends on both sides of 236—the Hasbroucks at 235 and the Greens at 237, Andrew Green's relatives. This supplies a plausible explanation of how Williams came to select Andrew Green as the target of his hatred. The sight of his equipage standing outside what Williams supposed to be 236, not 237 or 235, must have led Williams to suppose that Andrew Green was visiting Mrs. Elias and was therefore the man he associated with his so-called sweetheart Bessie Davis, alias Hannah Elias. And this twist of fate may have caused the death of an innocent victim.

"The neighbor, Mrs. Hasbrouck, had this to say: 'To all appearances Mrs. Elias is a woman of considerable wealth. My husband had tried to purchase 236 but the price was much too high. The deposit was twenty-five thousand dollars, besides whatever balance was due. I don't know my next-door neighbor, but until now I believed her to be perfectly respectable in every way. She has always conducted her household in an orderly manner. Mrs. Elias moved into her house about two years ago. She came as a perfect stranger to us and none of our household has ever held any conversations with her. Sometimes we have noticed different men calling at her house. These have always been white men, but I have never seen a Negro in her house; she has no Negro servants. Personally, I am absolutely sure the late Andrew Green *never* entered that building.'

"But," McClusky continued, "Andrew Green had been in the house, and recently seen inside at a party." McClusky did not tell Jerome the remainder of this winding story from Mrs. Hasbrouck about Green:

"We knew him so well. He was to have made a speech next Wednesday at the Murray Hill Hotel before the Knickerbocker Chapter of the Daughters of the American Revolution, of which my husband, Mr. Hasbrouck, is regent. We think it shameful that Mr. Green's illustrious name should be sullied at such an hour by these scandals. Even supposing a man of his character was involved in such behavior, which is preposterous to suggest, would he have been likely to select a house for Mrs. Elias right between the residences of two of his intimate friends? I cannot state too emphatically that the fact that we are living next door to her is purely a coincidence."

McClusky hated spending time with women who just wanted to talk about how important they were.

"Mrs. Hasbrouck broke down in tears at this point," he concluded, closing his notebook.

One thing he knew for sure was that Mrs. Elias, whoever the hell she was, was no damned Cuban. She didn't understand Spanish. When he dropped in a couple of words, she was confused. He had also referred to her servants as *camararos*, to her husband as *esposo*, to her dog as *perro*. He had even ended a question with *no verdad* and gotten only a blank look. He had misused the word *comer* ("to eat") for *comir* ("to travel"). No knowing smile or correction had escaped her lips.

She had been as cool as a cucumber when he had mentioned race, but he was sure she was Negro passing as white and that Nanz knew this. McClusky practically twitched with speculations. What she was hiding certainly had something to do with Green and his fortune.

Meanwhile, she had twisted Jerome around her little finger. The DA had taken one look into her fathomless eyes and fallen under her spell. *"Yes, Mrs. Elias." "Of course, Mrs. Elias." "If you say so, Mrs. Elias." "May I clarify that, Mrs. Elias?"* He had practically groveled at her feet like a damned *perro*. Had Jerome really been impressed with the gaudy, sinister mess of that mansion? Or had he received a phone call from Green's family, who didn't like seeing their name in the tabloids?

And Nanz, a small-time bail-mongering lawyer, was known as a shyster by the Detective Bureau. What was he doing sitting in Hannah Elias's drawing room as her counsel? He was out of his league. He had been there only to deflect the DA's questions. Jerome was going to rue the day he let Elias get away with that fake deposition, he thought.

He had also discovered that there was still another "Mr. Green" who paid Mrs. Elias's millinery bills and bought her expensive lingerie from B. Altman and Saks Fifth Avenue, a third Mr. Green with no first initials. Could it be AHG, he wondered? He scratched his head. There were also several "Mr. Xs" who paid for Mrs. Elias's purchases at Tiffany and Lord & Taylor and who sent fresh flowers on a regular basis to 236. Mrs. Elias was certainly not alone in this world, thought the detective. She had friends, many of them, and mostly male, rich, and in high places, thought McClusky. Lucky sons of bitches, he mused.

It didn't occur to him that Jerome was as interested in Hannah Elias as he was. Jerome, however, wanted the credit.

Hannah Elias was colored. Hannah Elias knew Green. Hannah Elias had been Williams's girlfriend. Hannah Elias had friends in very high and very low places. Had she put a contract out on Green's life? But then why choose a Negro assassin? And why an amateur like Williams who was going to get caught? Had Green actually known Hannah Elias in a previous life and was blackmailing her? Or had Williams been blackmailing her? Did she decide to get rid of two birds, Green *and* Williams, with one stone?

According to Jerome, Cornelius insisted Hannah was dead and that he had killed her. He didn't even believe the newspaper articles that proved Elias was alive and well. Williams had screamed that "Bessie" was a demon and had a rock where her heart should have been, that she was a vampire impossible to kill except with a silver stake. He had sobbed then, like a child, and said that he was haunted by both Green and Hannah and that their ghosts made love together right there in his cell, under his nose, like two harpies every night. That's when Jerome decided it made no sense to confront her.

The stenographer had stopped shaking now that they were outside the mansion, and was going on and on about Mrs. Elias's palace, Mrs. Elias's jewels, Mrs. Elias's pearls, Mrs. Elias's silver tea service, her paintings, her rugs, her window drapes. She couldn't wait to get back to the office to gossip with the rest of the stenographers' pool.

"Irene, shut up!" McClusky snapped.

But even Jerome had been unable to stop staring at the diamonds and rubies on every finger of Hannah's small hands, which made the gems look even bigger, or the spectacular necklace of pearls that nestled so quietly around her beautiful neck. McClusky bit down on his cigar and then lit it, blowing smoke rings, which he had not dared to do in Hannah's drawing room.

Hannah was like clear water. She reflected each and every man who believed he was her only reflection—her only desire. That she and only she had the power to make him really, really happy. McClusky sighed. He had seen this and the saps who fell for it before. The strange, heady combination in Hannah's perfume, which he had pinned as vanilla and bergamot, was still in his nostrils, and her lies still rang in his ears. He had discovered Hannah was like no one else in all of New York, perhaps even the whole East Coast, and more than likely the entire damned United States of America. If she fancied herself a reincarnated queen, perhaps she was to some people. Not him.

Now that he had her real name, McClusky checked the police files to see if Hannah had ever run afoul of the law or had a prison record. Hannah Elias had a clean record—but Bessie Davis was another story.

1903
THE ALIENISTS

Lusts and wickedness are acceptable to me,
I walk with delinquents with passionate love,
I feel I am of them—I belong to those
convicts and prostitutes myself,
And henceforth I will not deny them—
for how can I deny myself?

—*Walt Whitman, "You Felons on Trial in Courts"*

A man always has two reasons for what he does—a good one,
and the real one.

—*J. P. Morgan*

TWENTY

Downtown, New York,
November 20, 1903

The district attorney's offices more resembled the inside of the Brooks Brothers haberdashery than they did a law enforcement bureau, so great was the sartorial elegance of the men seated around William Jerome's mahogany desk. The spacious suite was the point of a pyramid of warren-like cubicles that housed the bureau of the district attorney and his assistants and deputies. Below were corridors, interrogation rooms, libraries, stenographers' pools, picture archives, and the morgue. Among those seated in Jerome's book-lined, wood-paneled office were District Attorney William Jerome, Assistant DA Appleton, the two alienists, the coroner, and Detective McClusky.

William Trevor Jerome, elegant, socially well connected, and rich enough not to have to live off his $12,000 annual salary as a city official, had two nicknames. He was "Cigarette Willie" because of his chain-smoking and the "Owl" because of his round, gold-rimmed glasses. His Brooks Brothers suit hung on his wide shoulders like the hand-stitched, made-to-order garment that it was. He wore a Windsor tie in burgundy with a wing-tipped Egyptian cotton shirt in pale gray with onyx studs and a gold watch chain stretched across a matching vest. He swung around in his swivel armchair, crossing one ankle over his knee, exhibiting his handmade English walking shoes in fawn-colored calfskin so soft the other men could see the imprint of his arch.

Besides smoking, the district attorney drank when he felt like it, played poker regularly, and swore so violently at the head of his police raiding parties, he even embarrassed the proprietors of the bordellos he destroyed.

Jerome had eradicated the system of police protection that tipped off raids, and he held "John Doe" investigations based on information given to him by the informers of his Committee of Fifteen, so that the regular and corruptible police would be unaware of the time and place of his attacks. He held an improvised court hearing right there on the premises, removing a Bible from his hip pocket to swear in the witnesses.

The district attorney's assaults were wildly popular with the public, and he shrewdly exploited his newsworthiness and public image. "Justice Jerome" not only made arrests and took evidence on the spot, he also seized furniture and equipment, which he put into the government's coffers. His storerooms at the Tombs were piled high not only with equipment for faro, red and black, Klondike, and baccarat, but also luxurious furniture, carpets, rugs, and art objects including Old Master paintings, which he sold at auction. Gaming tables were turned over to poor families for firewood. Poker chips were burned by the thousands.

"I gamble a bit myself," he liked to say when criticized for his Wild West justice, "but not like that."

He swiveled his armchair to face the men in his office now. He was very much the master of the situation. Detective McClusky's nostrils flared at the smell of something rotten in the Williams case. A Negro murdering the wrong man, if it was the wrong man; a Negro woman who claimed to be a real-estate speculator, but who surely had more going on. Who knew what other gems there were to be recovered?

McClusky listened as the coroner read his report, which confirmed that Green had come to his death from a bullet inflicted by the revolver discharged by the hand of Cornelius Williams. That was a fact.

Jerome now turned to his assistant Howard Rand, also the scion of a wealthy family. Rand was dressed in a Prince of Wales plaid three-piece suit sporting his inevitable Yale tie and gold watch and chain. His salary from the county was hardly enough to keep his expensive $8,000 automobile with its chauffeur in repair. However, no one worked harder in Jerome's office than the young society lawyer.

"I have been Mr. Green's intimate friend for many years," said Rand,

"and I would like only to point out again the absurdity of the charges made by Williams and their inconsistency with Mr. Green's whole life.

"When I saw Williams this morning, his face struck me as familiar," continued Howard Rand. "Later, I identified him as a Negro porter on a Pullman train on which my wife and I traveled from Montreal to New York some time ago. I am as convinced that Mr. Green did not know either Williams or Mrs. Elias as I am that I'm sitting here talking to you. Williams is either insane or he mistook Mr. Green for someone else bearing the same name. From what I was able to judge from the murderer's demeanor, he is as coolheaded and collected as you or I, except his indifference as to his fate is quite peculiar."

"There is even conjecture that Mrs. Elias is colored," said McClusky.

"Well, McClusky, is she colored?" asked Rand.

"I don't know whether Mrs. Elias is Black or white," said McClusky. "She says she's Cuban. I doubt that. She doesn't speak Spanish. My report states that Hannah Elias, as she is now known, is about thirty-eight years old, and is white. She has lived in New York for about seventeen years. She came from Philadelphia. Her birthplace and family connections, as far as we have been able to discover, are unknown to everyone but herself. The rise and transformation of Bessie Davis into Mrs. Hannah Elias is one of the marvels of life in New York City. For two years, this woman has been a mystery to her Central Park West neighbors. Before that, we know that she lived in a house on Fifty-Third Street, where she rented a room to Williams. The place is a bordello now. About three years ago, she divorced her husband and reverted to her maiden name, Elias. We know she has lived these two different lives with two different names.

"I have the testimony of a woman," McClusky added, "who does not want to be identified for the moment, who used to be employed in the millinery department at Simpson and Crawford department store. She has testified that Mrs. Elias was a good customer, buying millinery to the amount of several hundred dollars a year. The bills for Mrs. Elias's purchases were invariably taken to the cashier's office and charged to a 'Mr. Green.' Just who this Mr. Green was my informant didn't know, as she had never seen him in the flesh."

"I believe that this is not our Andrew H. Green," answered Jerome, "and I am determined to protect his reputation. We as upper-class white men should stick together."

"Mr. Rand, you say you recognized Williams as a Pullman porter. Could he actually be Mrs. Elias's former husband, whom we know was a Pullman porter? Is this some kind of conspiracy?" McClusky asked.

"To do what?"

"To assassinate Green for money or for the mob or because of some imagined wrong?"

"Well, that's a little far-fetched, but I suppose it is possible," said Jerome.

"Now, Dr. Flint, what exactly do you think?" Jerome asked.

"As a specialist in brain disease," the alienist replied, "my opinion is that Williams is clinically insane and should not stand trial."

The handsome, gray-haired physician in the gray tweed suit, black silk vest, and yellow silk tie took out his notes of that morning.

"Dr. McDonald and I have examined the suspect and find him to be suffering from delusions as well as hallucinations and dementia. He is a manic-depressed schizophrenic who has no conception of reality and does not live in the real world," said Flint.

"Evidently he did know Mrs. Elias at a certain moment in his life, but the acquaintance very quickly became an obsession and a fantasy," said Dr. McDonald, "when she disappeared from his sight and made her way into society. When Williams had no access to her, his dream world became a mania—thus the compulsion to blame any and all rich and powerful white men for his troubles and humiliations.

"His state of mind is alarming," he added. "Williams announced to me that he was now the devil's angel because he had sold his soul for a chance to kill Green. The devil, he said, appeared to him first as a bear, then as a giant snake. He described in detail how he bargained with the Evil One. Williams says he is quite happy to die in the electric chair and go to hell, where he expects to meet his own father, and that he is not crazy, because he knows something crazy people do not. The devil, Williams claims, is 'the smartest personage I ever met.' He can speak all languages and Williams could understand him in whatever language he spoke: a textbook example of delusional paranoia."

"I agree," said Dr. Flint.

"There is another story that Williams insists on," McDonald added. "He says he saw two Bessies at one time."

To this, Jerome laughed. "I suppose he could only kill one; that's how we got to talk with the other." There was sometimes no point in making sense of evidence that was clearly misguided.

McDonald told the men seated in the district attorney's office, "Williams said that he had seen Green at Bessie's boardinghouse, when she had once offered him a peek at the 'old fogey,' as she used to call him. The man was asleep on one of her parlor chairs. Soon afterwards, Williams says Bessie 'slandered' him. When he accused her of fabricating things about him, she told him that 'Green would pay her lawyers and take care of her suit if he began one,' and it made him 'mad to think that a man like Green was shielding her.' Then, according to Williams, Bessie disappeared. He searched for her for years he said until he found her in Central Park."

Dr. Flint added, "He still believes he shot and killed Bessie Davis and that Elias is her ghost."

After listening to arguments for and against, Jerome finally decided to allow the case to go to the grand jury and let the jury decide on the insanity defense. It was cheaper to do that than to organize an insanity commission. Jerome's frustration was palatable. On the one hand he wanted Williams electrocuted for murder. But in order to achieve that, there had to be a trial, something he dreaded because it compromised his class, New York society, and the Green family. That, and he hadn't gotten enough evidence to make Hannah into the liar that she obviously was. But there was no crime in changing her name or even having two names at the same time during her married years. If only he could prove that this woman and her Negro companions were at fault, and not someone like Andrew Green. But the newspapers would probably drag all of them through the mud.

"What a commentary on the mutability of fame!" Jerome ranted. "By the word of a crazy murderer, a great reputation counts for nothing. How true it is that the only thing a man can safely work for is his own self-respect! Andrew H. Green was the last man in New York against whom an insinuation of private baseness could ever find any justification!"

Jerome's outburst evoked raised eyebrows from the alienists and surprised yet sympathetic looks from the detectives as they contemplated their boss's flushed countenance, tearful eyes, and trembling voice. He had never reacted so emotively to any crime—no matter how horrible. The hardened detectives wondered what had gotten into their hard-boiled and ruthless DA, who had closed forty-five brothels and sixty-nine gambling dens wielding an ax. For some reason, the murder of Green had hit home this time. Jerome obviously identified with him and his honorable reputation.

"There is a lack of knowledge," Dr. Flint continued, "about certain phases of mental science, which if understood will lead to a much better administration of justice."

"The time is coming," he said, "when there will be less crime because its causes will be studied and prevented. Lawyers will be able to consider the best interests of the community at large, yet still do justice to their clients."

Jerome leaned forward as if there might be a clue to the murder and mayhem Hannah had incited.

"Man is the result of myriad influences," Dr. Flint continued. "Many of these inherited qualities are vices in humans but not in the animal kingdom, where they originated. Ancestral thought survives in the form of intuition. The law of differentiation steps in and gives variety to the individual. Man has superior mental powers: conscience—of which there is some evidence in brute creation—love, and reason. Although he may be influenced by unsuspected causes.

"The law holds that if Williams realizes that his act is wrong, he is sane enough to be amenable to the law. But it is shown that one may know an act is wrong and yet be powerless to resist committing it. This relates to unpremeditated crimes. A criminal may feel the murderous impulse coming on without being able to stop it."

"There are moments," interjected Dr. McDonald, "when passion so dominates someone's nature that every fiber of that person, every cell in his brain, becomes a slave to that instinct. Psychopaths are like that. Psychopaths and prostitutes. Take Cornelius Williams: What can be done with such a man? We cannot afford to have him at large, but I do not believe in putting people to death for any crime."

"New York is the first state to adopt electrocution as the most humane method of execution," said McClusky.

"Humane! Have you ever seen an electrocution gone wrong? It's worse than hanging. It is horrible!" said Dr. Flint.

"We are not here to argue capital punishment, sirs," interrupted Jerome, "but to decide if Cornelius Williams is sane enough to be sentenced as a sane man to death." Jerome was already tired of their chatter about the nature of man. Should Cornelius get fried or not? Everyone knew he committed the murder.

"The tools of science will ultimately not only unlock the mysteries of the criminal, or rather, psychotic mind. Surely, by the end of this century, we will be able to speak of a crimeless society as well as a more just America," summed up Dr. Flint.

Jerome drummed his fingers on the desk as the doctors spoke. He wanted to agree with them. He just didn't have time. While they waited for a crimeless society, what would go on? There were men and women genetically engineered for crime—born felons. All the scientific reconversion in the world was not going to change that.

"There are natural-born criminals who are not insane," interjected Jerome. "Look at the whores."

Dr. Flint answered as his colleague nodded: "These women are, in fact, alienated from the female psychology, which is based on purity and domesticity. Prostitution is contra nature, a perversion."

"But a criminal part of corrupt, capitalistic society," interjected Jerome, not able to contain himself.

"Yes. Commerce, that intersects psychosis, nevertheless," stated Flint.

Fuck you, thought Jerome, but he held his tongue. *And fuck Hannah Elias*, he added. She was the cause of all of this.

Jerome couldn't understand why his detective squad hadn't found more information on her. If she was that rich, there must be a way to trace her friends and family origins. But Hannah remained a mystery; he was being outsmarted by, as far as he could see, a shady woman with millions to burn and no visible male authority in her life. He really wanted Hannah ten times more than he wanted to send Williams to the electric chair. No doctors could tell him that she shouldn't go to jail too.

While the detectives, the doctors, and the DA held their discussions, and police officers and reporters stood outside the front door at 236 Central Park West, Hannah readied to leave for Saratoga. This time, she gave her sister very specific instructions.

As Hannah told her, Sadie rose early and came into the bedroom. She opened the curtains so the press could see through the front window, sat there, and took her morning coffee.

After she sat a long time in the window, enough for the reporters and cops to feel comfortable that she was inside, she put on a beautiful dress and a hat with only a half veil so that her face would be visible. She had Max come around front with the carriage. Then, off they went for a long ride through the winding paths of Central Park as the reporters and cops hurried to follow her.

She made enough distraction for Hannah to slip out the back of the house through the secret exit.

In a small, inconspicuous carriage, Hannah visited all her bankers and told them she was moving to London. She laughed with them and charmed them as she had been doing for years. She cashed in her stocks and moved her money abroad. Edward had been a good teacher. He told her how to make her money grow, to be shrewd, to be worthy of trust—even in the biggest circle of liars. Now Hannah used all her powers to empty almost all of her accounts. She had diversified, although each banker had felt as if he were the only one looking after her welfare. It was a technique she learned in the bordellos. All this business took her beyond banking hours. The last personal banker she saw met her at nightfall.

After she finished the banking, she boarded the train to Saratoga, the place where her trouble began. After the death of Andrew Green, she needed to reevaluate her life. Platt wanted her to go away and refresh herself. She did too. And this time, Sadie knew the way to act.

The best way to take Hannah's place was for Sadie to keep her mouth shut and follow a routine: the paper, the park, the return home to the front door in a carriage, meals in the window, lights out at nine thirty. Sadie, now Hannah, was a Central Park West denizen and nothing more.

TWENTY-ONE

Cornelius stood for arraignment before the grand jury in the Court of Special Sessions. Cornelius's hearing took place in a large courtroom in the Supreme Court Building at City Hall Park. If the jury returned a "true bill," it could mean the electric chair.

"The rules governing grand jury proceedings," began the judge, "are very different from those governing trials by a jury of twelve. A grand jury can be from sixteen to twenty-three members. It receives complaints and accusations in criminal courts, hears evidence adduced by the state, and approves an indictment when satisfied that there is enough evidence against the accused to warrant a trial. Is that clear? The procedure is inquisitorial rather than adversarial; the defense is not allowed to call witnesses, and the prosecutor is not obliged to present both sides. Not only does he present only his side, but hearsay and other evidence that might be excluded at a jury trial may be introduced to justify the finding of an indictment," he concluded. "The grand jury must believe the accused is guilty. They must be convinced that the evidence before them, unexplained and uncontradicted, would warrant a conviction by a petit jury. No grand jury shall disclose any evidence given before it. Let us proceed," he said.

Jerome didn't want any of his friends to believe that he had any part in the possibility of a trial. So prepared nothing.

Williams's Legal Aid Society lawyer entered a plea of not guilty. Cornelius stood at the end of the long row of prisoners waiting his turn. His eyes shifted uneasily around the room, and he seemed to be half asleep as the clerk read the charges. At that moment Jerome rose to his feet and said, "It is the intention of the district attorney to move this case for trial as speedily as possible. The DA couldn't avoid the case, because so many people had seen Cornelius Williams shoot Andrew Green." Jerome had to pursue the murder, but he had no intention of winning against an obviously crazy man. He expected the grand jury to see Williams's insanity and dismiss the case.

"I think it is only fair to the people of New York that if Mr. Williams means to make a plea of insanity, he should do so now to prevent any delay in this case!"

"I see no reason for such a statement," replied the Legal Aid lawyer. If the grand jury ordered a trial, he could call witnesses, a roster of uptown associates of Andrew Green. The publicity for the Legal Aid Society would be priceless.

"I merely meant," stumbled Jerome, "that it would be desirable to make the motion now if it is the wish that the prisoner be examined immediately," added Jerome.

"Our plea will stand," repeated Williams's lawyer, smiling enigmatically. He wasn't pleading insanity just to please the DA, he thought. He knew Jerome was counting on an insanity plea before the grand jury so that Williams would never be brought to trial. But he had every intention of dragging this scandal into court with the public and the press as judge and jury and issuing subpoenas to every millionaire friend of Green's or Hannah's in New York high society. Jerome could attempt to protect his blue-blood cronies, but the lawyer was going to get to the bottom of Green's shooting by using all the power of subpoenas to create a circus where the poor and insane would be the stars.

Jerome knew there was more to Williams's case with Hannah. If he had the information, he'd use it. At this point he knew only that she was once Bessie Davis, married to a Negro man, which while distasteful in his eyes was not a crime. All he saw coming out of a trial was an attempt to muddy all the *Social Register* millionaires who may have been in the company of Williams or Hannah, probably at her recent grand party. He wouldn't get Williams electrocuted, and he would lose many friends.

Jerome hoped to thwart rumors that Hannah had relationships with several *Social Register* millionaires by not calling her to testify, either at the coroner's inquest or to the grand jury. One couldn't be too careful, he reasoned. Once a witness had taken the stand, there was no predicting what they would say. And it would be on the record for all to see. There was no proof that Andrew H. Green knew Hannah Elias other than what was contained in Williams's statement: that she and Green had slandered him. In his wildest ravings, Williams had made no hint of improper relations between Hannah Elias and any other prominent man except Green—and Jerome intended to keep it that way. His duty to fellow members of the city's four hundred demanded at least that.

The prosecution began with his first witness.

The testimony of a Black cabman from the Murray Hill Hotel, who was the main eyewitness, was deposed: "I was standing at the north-west corner of Eighty-Fourth Street in front of the Murray Hotel wait-ing for a customer. I heard a shot followed by four others. I ran across the street with another cabbie and saw two policemen running. I got there first, where I found a colored man standing in a daze weeping. He held a cocked revolver to his temple. He pulled the trigger, but nothing happened. The chamber was empty. He had pumped five bullets into Mr. Green, who was lying on the ground, and he probably had thought he had saved one for himself. I saw that Mr. Green was dead or dying, and Williams stood over the body cursing, 'There he is. I done it.'"

After additional eyewitness testimony from Green's servant and his niece, Jerome presented the forensic evidence and the coroner's report. Then the alienists took over. McDonald testified first, concluding that Cornelius Williams was insane and a danger to himself. Then he cited his interviews with Williams, his visions and hallucinations, his fanatic conviction that he had committed not one but two murders. Dr. Flint corroborated the expert opinions of the other doctor, adding that the accused in attempting to kill himself directly after the killing of Green showed evidence of temporary insanity. Rand then introduced a letter from Williams's brother in West Virginia stating he had experienced fits of insanity ever since he had been stricken by a mysterious fever at sixteen years of age. Jerome then rested his case.

The Legal Aid lawyer, unable to put Williams on the stand, introduce evidence, call witnesses, or cross-examine the state's witnesses, contented himself with a plea of not guilty and a request for a full jury trial and investigation into a possible conspiracy behind Williams's actions. Meanwhile, Cornelius watched the ghosts of Bessie and Green coupling in the corner of the courtroom.

Jerome then read a statement that completely countered his own case. "The state, after extensive conversations with alienists, is satisfied that the murderer is insane. The time of the court would be misspent to bring Cornelius Williams to stand trial when for the remainder of his life he would be committed to an insane asylum after any reasonable judgment." This was Jerome's attempt to subvert a trial that would be highly publicized and that he couldn't win.

Soon after, the jurors returned "not a true bill" by reason of insanity. After arguing forcefully that everyone was equal before the law, and that included children, the insane, and Negroes, the judge pronounced a summary judgment. He remanded Cornelius to the Matteawan State Asylum for the Criminally Insane until such a time as he was mentally competent to stand trial or until he was dead. There would be no sensational trial to embarrass the Green family now or in the future. The Legal Aid lawyer was frustrated. He did not get his newspaper headlines. But of course, Cornelius's life had been saved. That's what he had been hired to do.

The case was closed.

Still, Jerome plotted a sequel, one that he would carry out with McClusky. They had found out new information about Hannah Elias: that she used the alias Bessie Smith when she felt like it as the proprietress of a boardinghouse, which everyone knew meant a bordello.

Ill-gotten gains had propelled Hannah Elias into her wealth—and probably not just prostitution, not with the mansion he'd seen and her steady income. There was probably money laundering taking place between her and her benefactor—or benefactors—maybe extortion. He and McClusky would get to the bottom of this in a spectacular fashion.

First he had to speak to McClusky and then put pressure on August Nanz, who if his calculations were correct knew Bessie Davis, Bessie Smith, *and* Hannah Elias. Those were the big fish whom Jerome wanted to fry—the undesirable grifters and lowlife Negroes. Jerome didn't just want to catch little porgies like Williams, who when caught in the police net would take everyone with them, including the reputable East Side.

The next day, McClusky met Jerome at his country house so they could plan a strategy. The trip by train had taken a few hours. The stop in Tarrytown station was John D. Rockefeller's private telegraph terminal, the wire reaching to his house not far away. A carriage brought McClusky up the winding roads to Jerome's personal estate in the hills, a house made for entertaining on a wide patio in the summer and around a massive cherrywood table in the winter. The smoking room on the side had a fireplace and large leather chairs. This was where he and Jerome met.

"I just didn't want to have this talk in the office. Too many ears," Jerome said. "You never know how many are working with the hoodlums and their bosses."

McClusky stared at the gilded mirrors and hanging chandeliers while he held his coffee cup in his hand. He wasn't sure whether he could put it down on the table next to him until a butler appeared and set down a coaster.

Jerome had stopped talking anyway when the man entered. He resumed when the man pulled the massive drawing room doors closed.

"This Hannah Elias is Bessie Davis, we know now. And how she got to Central Park West, I can't figure out yet. But I smell a rat. I know she doesn't belong there."

"She certainly ain't who she supposed to be," McClusky volunteered, then was suddenly aware of his grammar.

"Cuban, my ass," said Jerome.

McClusky now felt more comfortable.

"So I want you to find the dirt," Jerome said. "Look at Bessie Davis's records. What were her addresses? Who are her associates? I think we're going to find something big, and probably unsavory."

McClusky nodded, knowing that he could do this job. His first stop was going to be Hannah's lawyer, August Nanz. McClusky had his suspicions that he'd been hiding a lot. He'd tail Nanz as soon as he got back to New York.

After the Williams hearing, Nanz wondered if the police had found the name of the man who was the cause of Green's murder. He would bet it was the same man he had seen getting into Hannah's carriage at Green's funeral, probably Platt. If the police knew, why hadn't they revealed his name to the press? They probably didn't know her benefactor.

This kind of information was power, he thought. Power over the highfalutin men at his former legal firm and power over Hannah, who seemed to have so many other dangerous secrets. There was one way to find out more—see how sharp Williams's mind really was and how much he remembered. August decided to make a list of possible candidates. He was sure the DA was doing the same thing.

August took the New York Hudson railway to Matteawan. The massive redbrick building was five times the size of the Tombs. It dominated the countryside of Dutchess County like a sprawling, drowsing dragon, visible for miles, belching smoke and staring with windowless malevolence at anyone approaching it. Inside, the madhouse was a box within a box within a box, each one closing in on the visitor like a telescope. As he walked in, August felt as if he had a steel band around his head exerting enough pressure to crack his skull wide open. It was the most depressing place he had ever entered.

"I seen you before."

Cornelius Williams was dressed in a red prison uniform, his hair and mustache neatly trimmed, his high forehead with its receding hairline beaming in the sunlight coming in from the single high window under which he sat, a solitary figure surrounded by a wire cage.

"Of course, you came to see my firm once, about suing Bessie Davis for slander, way back . . . we didn't take your case, remember? But now I'm Bessie's attorney. I want to talk to you."

"Bessie's dead. You can't be her lawyer, unless she's risen from the grave." Cornelius laughed.

August hesitated a moment, trying to figure out what he was talking about. Then he realized that Williams thought Hannah was dead.

"Bessie's alive. She's sorry about your troubles. She wants you to forgive her. She says she never slandered you."

"That lying Jezebel! I'm glad she's in her grave! I'll never forgive her. Look where I'm at! What do I have to look forward to?"

"Freedom," August said. "Sooner or later, you'll get out. Quietly, of course. We're working on it."

"You don't think I'm crazy?"

"I know you're not crazy."

Cornelius laughed. "I ain't crazy enough to get myself lynched."

"Right," said August. "How's that?"

"Yes, Lord" was Williams's response.

"Who did you think Andrew Green was?" August asked.

"Why, Andrew Green, of course. I used to see him go into Bessie's rooming house when I used to live there."

"How did you know?"

"I recognized him from the time he tried to push me around outside Bessie's. I never forgot him. His landau was parked in front of Bessie's mansion the day I killed both of them."

Cornelius believed he had killed Hannah. But how? And who knew? August suddenly felt surrounded by a hostile army. He even looked over his shoulder.

"No, Cornelius, the day of November twelfth you saw some other man come out of 236 Central Park West, not Green. He knew families on both sides of Bessie, but he didn't know Bessie at all."

"But I shot Bessie because of him! He was Bessie's lover!"

"I swear to you. You killed the wrong man, Cornelius, Green swore to that with his dying breath, and you're going to help me find the right one."

"I am?"

"Think back. Think hard back to when Bessie was married to Matthew

Davis and living on Fifty-Third Street. Who were the men coming and going to her apartment?"

"My Bessie didn't have no other men. Maybe that Granville was hanging around?

"Granville. Inventor. Adventurer. Wouldn't touch her!" Cornelius laughed again. "He was so churchgoing he ran away from her."

"He was a white man?"

"Black as coal dust under a furnace man's fingernails." Cornelius chuckled. "I should know!" He burst out laughing and slapped his knee at his own joke.

"Yea, but Bessie was a churchgoing woman," said Cornelius.

"Bessie lived a double life, Cornelius. She isn't even colored. Bessie's white."

"It figures."

"You still love her."

"Yea, Lord. I still love that gal. It's like a red-hot blade stuck in my head . . ."

"Well, she still has tender feelings for you. Remember how she loved you?" August said, gambling on his instincts.

"Bessie's dead."

"No. Bessie is Hannah Elias."

"No, Bessie is a ghost."

"Well, of course, Bessie is a respectable and rich woman hiding under the name of Hannah Elias." August tried to follow Cornelius's logic. "Even if she is a ghost, don't you think she owes you something for the tragedy she's brought upon you?"

"Sure."

"Well, how much would you say?"

"Enough to get me out of here."

"What do the alienists say?"

"How do I know you ain't one of them? How do I know you ain't a doctor that's going back to them and say I'm shamming?"

"Because I'm here for Bessie. Bessie doesn't want you to tell them what you know about her."

"But I don't know anything," protested Cornelius.

"You're sure?"

"As God is my witness. I'm glad I killed Green and I'd do it again. The angel made me do it."

"But Cornelius, it was the wrong man. Do you understand that you killed the wrong man in cold blood?"

Cornelius was fading. His eyes had glazed over as he retreated into his fantasy world and the past.

August realized Cornelius didn't have the name and hadn't recognized Green. He would get nothing more out of Cornelius this day.

"Cornelius, do you need anything? Sweets? Newspapers? Smokes? Can you smoke in here? Opium?"

"Get lots of laudanum but I crave some hop from Chinatown. I really do."

"Done. Don't let the doctors find it."

"They want to do an operation . . . an experiment."

"Don't let them do it, Cornelius. No experiments."

"What's that?"

"I'll explain next time."

"I can't stop them."

"Yes, you can. If they start talking about cutting your brain, you tell them you have representation, that you have a lawyer and rights. Don't, for goodness' sake, sign anything. Here's my card. Call me if they try any monkey business."

"Oh, no sir. I am crazy. Certified. I still see old Green's ghost and that black dog of a devil, too, and thousands of insects crawling out of my toilet. I see Bessie sometimes, too, making love. Sometimes they have to restrain me. I still have nightmares, but I don't take them pills anymore 'cause they make things even worse. I flush them down the toilet with the ants. They'll probably kill me one day. I jus' hope they get tired of experimenting on me and jus' forget about me—you know, lose me in this hellhole they call a hospital. I tell you they are some real crazy people in here." Cornelius grinned, then added, "It ain't hard to impersonate a crazy nigger . . . when you are a crazy nigger."

August left the asylum without an inkling of the man in Hannah's life Cornelius thought he had shot. He took the train back to the city and the subway down to City Hall. From there, August walked to the Lower East Side. The sun was descending over the Hudson, and the streets were almost dark. Men passed by going to night jobs, coming from work, leaning against steps and having a smoke.

Houses of assignation bloomed everywhere, cheap hotels, lodging houses, and tenements, attracting single men with money. There were long lines of them outside every door. It brought back memories, smells, and hatred of his childhood. August almost ran along Park Row to Church Street.

As he entered the Bowery, the scene got a bit rougher. The streetwalkers were getting into the streets, and they practically accosted him. Both sexes called to him from the dingy houses and narrow doors.

In the very heart of the Bowery, he lingered in front of Frank Stevenson's the Slide concert saloon, the most famous gay meeting place in New York. August found himself thinking about the few free years of his adolescence when he felt most comfortable with himself, when he realized who he was and pursued his life without shame or guilt. Those years were sandwiched between his horrible poverty and the realization that who he was would not get him anywhere. He had forgone the Slide years ago as too dangerous for his double life.

Still, like a reformed alcoholic, a surge of desire overwhelmed him as he watched the boys and men in evening dress entering the establishment. He even took several hesitant steps forward, then stopped. He simply nodded to the male prostitutes who solicited him. He decided to stop in to see Gallus Meg, the most colorful ex-prostitute and saloonkeeper in the neighborhood. Meg held up her skirt with suspenders and was expert at biting off the ears of roughhousing patrons. Over time she had garnered a collection of her trophies, preserved in bottles of alcohol that stood over the bar. Both her whiskey and her company were good, and at this time of night, the saloon was unusually quiet. Nanz sat drinking, trying to calm himself.

Gallus arrived and gathered him up in her embrace. She had always had a soft spot for Nanz's childlike and fraudulent nature. He was like a little boy. And so pretty.

"Want a little hop, baby?" she crooned.

"Yes, why not, Gallus?"

She lit two pipes, taking her time, preparing the soft white pill carefully. Everyone smoked in the Seventeenth Ward. There was a Chinese opium den two doors down. Two blocks farther was a drugstore where one could buy laudanum, cannabis, and cocaine hydrochloride over the counter. Morphine had been the drug of choice of the middle class since the Civil War, but it was the use of opium by immigrant Chinese workers that had spread to the working class. Cocaine, the poor man's high, was sold in drugstores for a few cents. Bayer, the same German company that had invented aspirin, had synthesized heroin and sold both home remedies.

Gallus cradled August and held her *yen tsiang* with the other hand, puffing delicately, her eyes closed.

August was not unaware of the irony of his situation. God knew he didn't want to hurt Hannah, who had the morals of an alley cat, the strength of a boxer, and the illusionist power of Houdini. She was neither the most beautiful, nor the most wicked, nor the most seductive woman in New York, although sometimes, he thought, she was the most intelligent. He admired the fact that Hannah had the ability to make people believe anything she told them—nothing was untrue. The most bizarre, extravagant lies were not untruths on her lips; they metamorphosed into incantations of hope, declarations of love, and manifestations of charity. She had all the gifts of a great courtesan. Sensuality was like sea within her. The tides lapped at her edges and mixed with the salt and sunshine of her, a body full of fascinating stories and men's secrets. Without guile or subterfuge, she was as wide and as wild as a gliding river.

August imagined the way Hannah used every part of her body to do anything: to walk, talk, sing, dance, play the piano, laugh, cook—how all of it moved.

Now he was getting foggy and overwhelmed with ideas. But he couldn't tell for sure reality from imagination because of the drug. He seemed to be under a shadow of a nearby man, watching him, lurking near him—then suddenly like a specter behind him. He swung in a half circle away from the bar.

Unfortunately, it was real. McClusky had been following him the whole time.

"Got a match," said McClusky.

August startled until he recognized the detective. "Hi."

"What are you doing down here?"

"This is my turf."

"And is the Asylum for the Criminally Insane your turf too?" asked McClusky.

"I beg your pardon?"

"You were there this afternoon talking to Williams. What were you trying to get him to tell you?"

"None of your business. It's a free country. I can visit whom I like, even in the lunatic bin. Besides, why are you following me? I haven't done anything illegal."

"Not yet."

"I just wanted to talk to him."

"And?"

"Crazy as a loon."

"Really? I always thought he was faking, you know."

"Well, if he was, those pharmaceutical treatments he's been getting have sent him round the bend."

"Couldn't get anything out of him, huh?"

"No, could you?"

"That's none of your concern. But just let's say that the DA despite the grand jury's verdict has not closed this file yet. And Jerome doesn't like amateurs snooping around his cases. Get it?"

"You met me at Mrs. Elias's. Mrs. Elias is my client. I'm not snooping around."

"Well, if Mrs. Elias is your client and she has something to reveal, you can get in touch with the DA's office. They'll be happy to speak to you."

"Fuck you."

"No, you're fucked, Mr. Nanz, if you continue to visit Williams and generally stick your nose where it's not wanted."

"Are you going to keep following me?"

"Yep."

"And watching Mrs. Elias's house?"

"Yep." McClusky looked August up and down. "Well, why not see what you can find out. We need to collaborate. Don't try to do it alone. You'll only get hurt and complicate an already complicated case."

I'll report back to you when hell freezes over, you Irish bastard, August thought, but he nodded and started to leave.

"So let me put it this way: the case will get much more complicated when everyone finds out what you really are."

At that, August slumped. How long had he been followed? Had the detective seen his hesitant steps toward the male brothels or his wistful looks at the men entering dance halls arm in arm? McClusky could ruin his reputation, his life. He could end up in Five Points again, all his years of pretending wasted.

August turned and looked McClusky in the eyes. "What do you want?"

"The truth," said McClusky, "the truth about Hannah Elias or Bessie Smith or whatever you call her. Or else everyone will hear the truth about you."

"Leave me alone and I'll get back to you," Nanz said and walked to the exit.

"I know you will," McClusky called.

The next day, Nanz began to collect information for McClusky. He began at the Wing. The proprietor there remembered Bessie's house on Fifty-Third Street. His saloon was not far away, and he remembered quite a few white gentlemen who frequented her place.

"Do you think one of them was Andrew Green?" Nanz asked.

"The Father of Greater New York?" the bar owner asked. "Everyone knows he was squeaky clean."

The man continued: "But there was so many of them others." Several tall, white-haired, white-bearded, beautifully dressed scions of high society had repeatedly knocked at Bessie's front door. Sometimes they had wandered into the Wing for an early-morning draft beer—usually in pairs and in evening dress, with their cravats and cummerbunds undone, their flies open, and their eyes glazed from sex and cocaine. Yes, he remembered quite a few early-morning clients from Bessie's house. None, however, by name.

August realized then that he would need to go to the source. All prostitutes kept lists of their Johns for safekeeping. He could probably show that she—like all the rest—was subject to using blackmail. The irony was that now the police were also blackmailing him.

The key to Hannah was her clientele from '95. He wondered if there were police records—litigation or drunken brawls on the books with names, arrests, bail payments. McClusky would be trolling those documents for mention of every time Bessie Davis went to jail.

He might even come across an old photo. He had seen a few daguerreotypes back then, brownish-yellow, stiff-necked photos, which peered out from silver frames and spoke volumes. He even heard that now there was a fellow in New Orleans going around to the houses of prostitution photographing them—like Toulouse in the Moulin Rouge.

August turned up to Fifty-Third Street and walked the block to Hannah's old boardinghouse for inspiration. It was a handsome brownstone. Once there, he decided to ring the bell.

A woman appeared behind the imposing Black butler who opened the door.

"Smith, who is it?"

August was shocked. It was Leola Pershing. He had not been privy to the fact that Leola was also running one of Hannah's houses. Another of Hannah's myriad secrets! Who and what else had he not been privy to? She had kept him in the dark about Green, about Leola—who else didn't he know about? Leola knew about him. How was he going to explain his visit? In a burst of inspiration, he explained he had been sent to look for some stock certificates Hannah might have left on the premises.

"Nanz? Why didn't she tell me you were coming if she wanted them?" asked Leola, peering suspiciously at him over her pince-nez.

"Oh, I guess she must have forgotten. She needs them for Saratoga."

"Saratoga?"

"Yes."

"Hannah never forgets anything, Mr. Nanz."

"Well, she sent me," insisted August, hoping to brazen his way in.

"Well, only Mrs. Elias and Kato have the combination to the safe . . . unless you do? I don't know what it is," Leola lied.

"Not to bother," replied August. "She gave me the combination." So there was a safe. Thank God, he thought.

Leola led him to Hannah's small office. August wondered how he could decode a vault in broad daylight with Leola looking on—even though he had been an excellent safecracker when he had done petty thieving for the mob that ran the Lower East Side and worked for Pinkerton's National Detective Agency to pay his way through law school. As a poor boy, August had detested what he had had to do for money. But he'd never tried things in just this way—so publicly.

"Excuse me?" He nodded to Smith, and Leola. "The combination, you know . . ."

Leola, who had said she didn't have access to the safe, had no choice but to step outside. The lawyer fiddled around with the combination, his ear to the door, until he heard the characteristic click. The door swung open. He sighed.

August saw a triple folded document with several passports. He boldly took the papers out and held them to the light. There were three passports made out in the names of Bessie Davis, Bessie Elias, and Sadie Elias, aliases, he presumed. The other documents consisted of Hannah's New York marriage license as Bessie Elias and a letter from Bankers Trust with an unreadable signature but a banal content.

Nothing here, thought August. Hannah's real office was uptown, in her head. *Find something, anything!*

Then August spied a brown paper bag, all the way in the back of the safe. It was full of hundred-dollar bills, perhaps ten thousand dollars' worth, with a rubber band holding a packet of letters on which was written, "—John P."

Who was John P? Ironically, John was the name prostitutes gave their tricks. Was this the man in whose stead Andrew Green had died? There was no way to tell how long the cash had been in the safe. August opened the first document. It was a statement of Gwendolyn's paternity. The name listed under father's name was John Rufus Platt.

"Jesus Christ," whispered August. He had made the arrangements to take the miscarried infant's body to the funeral home without ever suspecting Platt as the father. She had told August that the burial was already arranged, and he asked nothing else. One more of Hannah's bloody secrets. She was full of lies and deceit. This paper, though, was what McClusky needed.

Additionally, there were love letters, which Platt had written many years earlier. Nanz decided to keep them for himself. He might need them for leverage at some future point.

Leola must have wondered why August Nanz was snooping around and lying about it. If Hannah had wanted something from the safe, why hadn't she asked her for it? Or come down and gotten it herself? Or gotten her to open the safe and bring it to her? She hadn't spoken to her since Cornelius had been sent up. She had put the letters Hannah had given her the day after Green's murder in the safe.

Leola watched as August turned west toward Fifth Avenue. She wrinkled her nose at his natty figure. She had never liked August. She hadn't liked him on sight. His coiled vitality, his air of sweet efficiency and masculine propriety, had always put her out of sorts. She had never trusted him. The long, caped figure stepped lightly, even athletically at the crossing, darted in front of a lone hansom cab, which he hailed with his walking stick. His fashionable Prince de Galles tweed bomber disappeared into the interior of the carriage. *A poor boy with ambition*, she thought, as she closed the door.

August left the boardinghouse and made his way on foot. It was faster to walk than risk congested lower Broadway in a cab. He trotted along, coattails flapping. He had to cross the traffic-clogged thoroughfare where police patrols were sent regularly to unlock the flow of carriages and other vehicles. The pungent aroma of horse manure inches thick tainted the cold air. The electric lights would soon go on, illuminating the lowlife as it crept onto the street.

From paradise back to hell, he mused, as he was pushed and shoved by the proletarian masses right back into his place among all the other low-class blokes. He had seen heaven. He had the key to the pearly gates.

Why stay down here in the gutter, when he belonged up there with the one-ton mahogany table and the dead, dead quiet?

Nanz arrived at his office and he locked the door and opened his desk drawer. He took out the packet of letters he had retrieved from Hannah's safe. He laid them out carefully. Then he took off his Brooks Brothers overcoat and pin-striped jacket, rolled up his sleeves, and sat down. Although it was a brilliant afternoon and his offices were filled with sunlight, the lawyer turned on his desk lamp. He then proceeded to copy each letter twice. It took him until midnight.

The next morning, he walked to detective McClusky's office and gave him the document Platt had signed designating paternity. August kept the copied letters for himself.

1903
SARATOGA

In this world, sin that pays its way can travel
freely, and without a passport; whereas Virtue,
if a pauper, is stopped at all frontiers.

—*Herman Melville,* Moby-Dick

TWENTY-TWO

Saratoga,
November 30, 1903

H annah had returned to Saratoga the way a murderer returns to the scene of a crime, with a morbid curiosity of the event that had taken place and a desire to know whether anything could have been done differently.

She had sat in the drawing room of Mr. Pullman's train as it pulled slowly out of Grand Central Station, amid clouds of saffron smoke and hissing steam. She waved goodbye to August as he stood on the platform, almost hidden by belches of vapor.

Despite everything, she was excited. She loved trains and especially Pullman trains, which had never lost their fascination for her. She wore a traveling suit of sable brown uncut velvet, trimmed with a fringe of silk and crystal beads made by Virot, Paris. Hannah smoothed her skirt in satisfaction. The handsome detective with the bedroom eyes named Mc-Clusky had asked her only if she knew Andrew Green. He had not asked her if she knew the men who knew Andrew Green and socialized in his circle, and had visited her bordellos over the years.

Cornelius was locked away for the rest of his days, she thought. He would never bother her again. There would be no public trial. John's name would never come out. The newspapers would forget. Her friends in high places could sleep the sleep of the just. Getting out of town was a wise decision. Her name had surfaced again just that day in the *New York Times*. The public and her neighbors now knew that Bessie Davis and Hannah Elias were one and the same. People had doubts about her race.

Her little trip to Saratoga Springs would not be a bad thing, she thought, while Sadie stayed home. Hannah was looking forward to the snow, the silence, the barren yet beautiful landscape, returning, so to speak, to the scene of the crime of twenty-seven years earlier.

Hannah sat looking out the window at the ice-cold white landscape racing by and thought of her father, who had sold her virginity and peace of mind for a house, never obtaining justice for his daughter. She despised him for that, yet her adoration had never completely died. He was the man who headed her childhood family, the strong man who reined in horses, spoke to animals, and was desired by all the racetracks and stables around New York. Yet he had allowed another man to take her innocence. She had never accepted his apology, not that he had said anything in words.

She had seen the change come over him. He was sullen in their new home, instead of proud. He went into rages. He cried. He acted as if he was losing his mind. Maybe she was too. Maybe her life had been one loss after another.

When Monarch committed suicide, Hannah's belief in any happiness disappeared. Her trust evaporated. Her tenderness turned to dust. Her natural affection and sunny disposition turned to ice.

> *I've got a ragtime dog and a ragtime cat,*
> *A ragtime piano in my ragtime flat;*
> *Wear ragtime clothes, from hat to shoes,*
> *I read a paper called the* Ragtime News.
> *Got ragtime habits and I talk that way,*
> *I sleep in ragtime and I rag all day;*
> *Got ragtime trouble with my ragtime wife,*
> *I'm certainly living a ragtime life . . .*

The song could be interpreted in so many ways, like her. She was both darkness and light.

Hannah stepped off the Pullman car onto the platform of the Schenectady and Saratoga Railroad station, only a few steps from her hotel.

She hardly recognized the silent, lifeless terminal that in August was bursting with porters, baggage, children, animals, and tourists, as well as regular summer residents, the richest of whom was Commodore Vanderbilt. Even the color of the station seemed changed, although she knew they hadn't repainted the light blue columns.

Hannah stood on the train platform. It had taken eighteen hours from Grand Central Station in New York to reach this "Queen of Spas." Other passengers alighted, several of whom, with their bowler hats and shabby overcoats, seemed not to belong there. But she knew Saratoga had been invaded by Italian immigrants, who mingled with the Irish and colored, who supplied the servants for the thirty or so first-class hotels in the village. The silver engine exhaled steam and crystal fog, against which Hannah stood, draped in a full-length astrakhan cape, a veiled military hat, and an outsize muff.

She intended to spend her time here between her suite at the Grand Union Hotel and the casino. It had recently been taken over by John Morrissey, who had christened his new acquisition "the world's second-greatest gambling casino" (the first being Monte Carlo), and had built a new racetrack for thoroughbreds and trotters. Along with Churchill Downs, it was the favorite haunt of American millionaires. A muffled-up man hurried past Hannah, bowler hat pulled down to his eyes. It gave her a start.

Hannah carried her derringer strapped to her calf. She hadn't gone around armed since her Tenderloin days. She looked forward to being alone, while she dodged the newspaper reporters and the officers from the Detective Bureau, who had not stopped calling the house since their last interview and the grand jury verdict, in vain. The affidavit she had signed was the only statement they would ever get from her, she thought—unless they arrested her for murder. She turned on her smile as the assistant director of the hotel appeared on the platform to greet her with a large bouquet. She walked toward him on the ice-covered platform.

As the slippery surface creaked under her shoes, she moved steadily forward. She was conscious of the fact that at any minute her feet could slide out from under her. Walking on thin ice was her vocation. Hannah had always lived dangerously, and many of the twists and turns in her life had come about because of that one false step that she always seemed destined to take.

Hannah continued walking toward the hotel director, carefully placing one foot in front of the other as if she were already skating on the lake, careful not to think about the terrible currents and icy depths beneath. The wet cold seeped into the soles of Hannah's new beautifully made boots just as she arrived close enough to the hotel assistant to take her hand out of her muff and place it on his arm.

"Oh, Mr. Watson, I'm so happy to see you."

"Welcome, 'Mrs. Jones.'" He winked. "Your visits are always a pleasure, summer or winter."

Mr. Watson gestured to the bellboy to load the suitcases and trunks onto the hotel trolley from the cart. She took Mr. Watson's extended arm to steady her walk to the hotel entrance. She had remembered to pack fur-lined galoshes but hadn't thought far enough ahead to have worn them.

Saratoga Springs was a ghost town of lovely frost-covered landscapes and a frozen lake. The palatial hotels were mostly closed, the racetrack deserted, the stables boarded up for the winter. It was a town of horse trainers, horse owners, and jockeys, and for this reason Hannah felt at home. In the days that followed, she skated on the pond, had dinner in the deserted dining room of the hotel, and went sleigh riding. Mr. Watson noticed that she drove a sulky with blades over the frozen lake like a madwoman.

Hannah received only specific New York calls from Sadie and gentlemen whom she classified as business associates. They were the Mr. Xs who were greatly relieved that Hannah had left town and that her name no longer appeared in the *Times*, the *Herald*, or the *Post*. Sometimes they traveled incognito with bodyguards, taking the overnight train out of Grand Central, spending a day or two discussing their business, and leaving their secrets behind like the new plans for the extended IRT subway stations. They also brought news from New York about the police, who were still, they assured her, watching her house, inquiring about her past, and investigating the murder. They all agreed that Hannah had made the right decision to leave New York and stay where she was out of the reach of the press and where they could talk business. It took only a few meetings with these gentlemen to finalize the deal. Hannah had no more business to take care of but herself.

Mornings were spent in the Turkish baths, or she would swim in the heated pool, or stay in her suite practicing her handwriting in her blue-lined copybooks. In the late morning, she would go skating, wearing a coat of cocoa-brown duvetyn edged with mink, decorated with tor-toiseshell buttons, with a matching mink muff—a familiar sight, always veiled, sometimes all alone in the rink, swirling and turning, pivoting and speed skating, her skates throwing up little clouds of white crystals that caught in the movements of her skirts. When she returned to her rooms, she would have a massage, a bath, and a light lunch.

Then she read the newspaper, looking first at the business section. She knew about the plans for the extended IRT subway stations. Hannah already had the plans of where the new stations would be in the Bronx, Brooklyn, and Queens. Her early paramours gave her this information as they lounged after their assignations. They didn't know she listened and held the news in her photographic memory. She bought property nearest to these new train stops, or rather in their path, so that the city would need to pay her for the right of way. In the evenings, she indulged her fantasies, eating fresh strawberries and caviar, and walking around her suite smelling the fresh roses in every room.

As the weeks passed, the murder became yesterday's news. The greedy reporters who watched Hannah's house gave up and went back to work. The police detectives stopped tailing Sadie. Best of all, Jerome left Han-nah's financial affairs alone.

TWENTY-THREE

Saratoga,
January 1, 1904

On New Year's Day 1904, Hannah stood in Saratoga's deserted bleachers watching expensive horseflesh through her binoculars. A jockey was driving his trotter along the muddy, snow-covered racetrack. Hannah stood alone in the immense horseshoe surrounded by the powdered-sugar landscape, the hot springs bubbling up through the ice along the edges of the lake. On the lake itself, horse-drawn sulkies with blades instead of wheels slid across its frozen surface, a crystal mirror.

Hannah's spirit had settled somewhat after the months of isolation and self-care. She had loved observing horses ever since her father explained to her how a 1,500-pound thoroughbred with impossibly fragile ankles was a perfect motion machine that could accelerate to 42 miles per hour in just over two seconds. Over time, she had slowly met stable managers, shed foremen, grooms, jockeys, and the "horse whisperers" lodged in town for the winter. She began to feel that the man who had abused her when she was a child was not like the others. He was an aberration. He was a man who would have taken advantage of a girl no matter his occupation—as so many coaches and doctors, ministers and priests, did when entrusted with children. Hannah's only regret was that with all her money, she could not put him in jail. Nor could she return to innocence.

She had something more now, though: the maturity of a woman who had seen many sides of life and come to peace with every part of herself.

She heard the Black trainers and jockeys complaining sometimes when she sat wrapped in a blanket at an outside café. The owners were no longer hiring them.

"The stakes is so high, they want to give it to the white boys," she heard one jockey say. "Like being white makes you better. A horse don't know the difference."

The men laughed a sad, ironic laugh.

She saw them carry their bags to the train, at least one more every day.

In the deserted quietness of the off-season, Hannah would have dinner in the half-empty dining room just to wear one of the dresses she had packed. Then she might have the hotel landau take her over to the casino, which stayed open all year round. Women were not allowed in the public gaming rooms, neither to watch nor to bet. But there were private rooms upstairs where wealthy women rubbed shoulders with the demimondes and ladies of easy virtue. Every weekend, trainloads of "actresses," showgirls, courtesans, and their sporting men descended on the casino, located next to the mineral water source that had brought fame to Saratoga, along with Saratoga's other famous invention: the potato chip. It was the only gambling house or hotel in Saratoga that didn't defer to the placard hung in almost every other: JEWISH PATRONAGE NOT SOLICITED.

The private gaming rooms upstairs had no limit as far as stakes were concerned, nor as to females or Jews, which suited the professional gamblers who took the Pullman train on Fridays to play with the big society gamblers on Saturday nights. Everyone at the casino believed Hannah to be a rich Spaniard traveling incognito. Sometimes during the weekend, she would appear with a tall, white-haired gentleman, and they would dine quietly in a corner. He then would spend an hour or so at the tables while Hannah waited for him in the lounge, but that was all. Hannah was an uninspired gambler—the idea of losing great sums of money in order to possibly win back more was to her a stupid idea, when one had Wall Street to play with. She had never learned to play bridge, *trente et un*, or even poker, considering card playing a waste of time. She detested roulette, which she knew was only for suckers.

Hannah was happier to talk to the horse whisperers. There was even one, Maurice Ducasse, a West Indian, who remembered her father from the war. He worked winters at the racetrack as a stable hand and sulky cracker, and summers at the casino as a doorman and oddsmaker. He looked to be 101 but actually was only in his sixties. His hair was dead white, and he wore tinted glasses so thick they looked like the bottom of a beer mug. He had huge, yellow horse teeth that eerily resembled those of his equine boarders. He was immense, perhaps six foot five with big hands, the palms of which were as yellow as his teeth. He was coal dark, with great bulging shoulders and a barrel chest that also seemed more equine than human. Most of all, he was a first-class horse whisperer.

When he found out Hannah was Monarch Elias's daughter, he promised to tell no one.

"When Monarch talked to horses," reminisced Maurice, "he was a poet—'What a horse is this?' he used to say. He had shoulders as broad as the horse but his eyes were kind. It was like he was flattering the animals."

He went on about how a stallion stood slightly over at the knee, a rare quality, and that he had character. "'A more unassuming, kind, modest horse character I've never met,' he would say. 'No human being I know can compare in goodness and affection.' And he was always right. He was always right about horses." Maurice's eyes shone behind the thick lenses. "About men too."

"You remember him that well?" asked Hannah.

"I knew him and loved him," said Maurice. "I knew him during the war forty years ago, and afterward in Jersey and Saratoga. Spent many a day talking horseflesh—he loved you children. If I remember, he had a peck of them—"

"Eleven in all, but not when you knew him. I and my brother David were born after Appomattox."

"For an Indian, he was well liked," said Maurice. "But he was standoffish and prideful—scared others away a lot. I, however, had his friendship and held on to it for many a year. Then he disappeared . . ."

"He died," said Hannah, "when I was thirteen—twenty-five years ago."

"What he die of? He was a young man twenty-five years ago . . ."

"Did you know," she said, "that he committed suicide way back in '78?"

"No!" replied Maurice, shocked. He shook his head. Then for a moment, Maurice looked off into the distance. "I'm going to tell you something that he didn't want anyone to know. But now that he's gone and you're a grown woman and, from the looks of it, a rich one, I'm going to tell you something."

Hannah leaned forward.

"I know about that guy who took advantage of you. I was around and the track is a small place. If ever anything happens here, everybody knows. After what happened to you, happened to you—" He didn't want to use the word.

"I was molested," Hannah said, her voice breaking. "I was raped." Tears welled in her eyes. Something that hadn't happened for a long time.

"Well, your father sent you home. And he and a bunch of guys went to find that man." Maurice looked up to see how Hannah was absorbing the story. She was teary, but OK.

"Your father was a good man, a gentle man. You remember that?"

Hannah could remember him being so kind when she was little. She nodded.

"So he and the others, but not me"—Maurice lied about his presence, as Hannah was soon to guess—"they went and picked up that white jockey Magnus Hirschfeld one night and they locked him in one of the stalls and beat him to death. They beat him so bad, pummeling him so that you couldn't recognize his face—just a mass of decomposing, formless meat. He tried to buy his salvation by giving all his money to your father, but Monarch, your father, took a gun, like the gun that they use to put a horse out of its misery. And then he shot the man dead. 'He's not going to do that to another child, never again,' your daddy said."

Hannah knew then that Maurice had been there.

"He said, 'Not another little girl or boy or anyone will the likes of him ever touch.'" Maurice lowered his head. It was the first time he'd admitted that he knew about the crime. None of the other jockeys and trainers ever breathed a word. When they encountered one another on the road, they were like the Pullman porters, a secret society of Black men who had one another's backs.

"Them men dragged the body out in the field and stripped it, they burned the flesh off his hands, feet, and face; transformed him a white murdered man into a Black lynched man by disguising him so he was un-recognizable with a noose around his neck, hanging from a tree." Maurice laughed now, tears in his eyes as well. "We couldn't string him up. That was going to be too hard on all of us. I mean them. But we knew those crackers would keep the death quiet. And sure enough the sheriff of Saratoga County found him, decided he was a Negro, and proceeded to ignore the disappearance of Hirschfeld. In the *Saratoga Gazette* there was a three-line notice of a 'Negro lynched in Meadows Field, found suspended from a sycamore tree disfigured by burning, no clues to the colored man's identity were found. The case as far as the sheriff was concerned was closed. Just another dead nigger in the dark."

Hannah's mind was spinning with this incredible information. All these years, she had hated her father for betraying her. But he had avenged her in the only way he could. And keeping that secret was too much for him.

"If ever there was a man to whom self-murder would be impossible, that man was Monarch!"

"I think he was looking for peace," Hannah said.

"Men have mysterious reasons," murmured Maurice, "that they don't even know themselves," shaking his head slowly.

Hannah didn't know whether to laugh or cry more. She had traveled all the way to Saratoga and found out more about her father and herself than she could ever have imagined. Why?

That evening at sunset, Hannah stood at the edge of the frozen pond and had a long talk with her dead father.

"I think you can hear me because I came here, the only place you really loved, the stables. You could whisper to horses, but you couldn't talk to me. Why, Monarch? Why? Didn't you see I was hurting?"

Maurice had said that Monarch didn't talk much because he was an Indian, but she knew it had been false pride.

"You could whisper to the horses but not to your little girl. I idolized you. I never wanted you dead. No matter what you did. Even when you left us! Eleven of us and Ma. She was never the same either and she blamed me. Do you know we had to clean you out of Mr. Sewyer's stables! The fire department made us do it—They said they weren't cleaning up after no nigger—not that mess. The Odd Fellows helped, but the damage you left was already in all of our minds." Especially Mother, who never forgave me!

Maurice had told her, "Monarch was a strange man, prideful like all Indians, secretive and ornery as they come. But he knew horses. Said they had souls like people and special ears for the gods. Lot of people didn't like him. Too smart. Too strong. Too indifferent. He didn't want too many people too close to him, especially women. Didn't have much respect for the women who hung around the racetrack. Prostitutes most of them. He didn't respect none but his wife and daughters. He believed they were different from other women."

Remembering those words now, Hannah began to shout and cry.

"Look what I became!" she shouted into the frozen air. "One of those whores. That's what I was—a whore." Then she felt something inside her give away. "Yes, I was a whore. Madame? Perhaps, but a damned filthy rich one, richer than you could ever have imagined. For all your pride, you starved us." Hannah began to smile. She thought about how far she had come and how she had survived, and she felt the peace she had always sought. "This is who I am. You were misguided, Monarch. So was I. But now here we are."

The only answer Hannah received was the silence of the icy landscape. This was the silence of peace.

Hannah saw Maurice a few times after that day.

"Call me Mau-Mau," he said. "You're out here by yourself. If anyone tries anything with you, just let me know. I pack a rod."

So did Hannah.

"Oh yes. Thanks, anyway. Thanks, Mau-Mau."

It seemed that just being in Saratoga and meeting Maurice had brought her the message she had needed all her life.

"I've found something I love even more than horses," said Maurice the last time she saw him.

"And what's that?" Hannah asked, trying to guess to herself.

"Automobiles! Horsepower on wheels . . . Slick, yellow, faster than a goddamn racehorse, a son-of-a-bitch whore of a machine called the automobile . . . It's made in Reading, Pennsylvania, and it's called the Duryea!

"Yaaahoo!" He laughed, as if he were taming a wild horse.

"Yaaahoo!"

Hannah got word in an electrical telegraph from Leola, carried by a man on the train, that the photographer E. J. Bellocq was in New York. He had been spending time in the boardinghouse that Leola maintained, and she knew Hannah's ardent desire was to have herself photographed. The girls in the brothel had posed in their underwear and on the plush sofas. "In an artistic way," Leola wrote. "They looked prettier than ever." She was even thinking of hanging the photos in some of the rooms for the big patrons as inspiration. "It's the new art form, said Leola." Not that Leola knew anything about art; she just knew that she liked the pictures.

"Tell him to come and see me," Hannah telegraphed back, and gave the note to a Pullman porter, who dropped it off at Leola's on his way to a gambling den.

Hannah had always wanted a photograph of herself. Everyone told her that she was beautiful and so did her mirror. But this was a gift to the man who had taken care of her all these years. She would have a fully nude image to give Platt to admire when they were apart. He might even notice, as she did now, the small swelling of her belly, and the picture would be even more precious to him. If he didn't recognize her pregnancy, she would send the photographs to him as his birthday present on top of the gift their summer days together had produced.

Bellocq moved into Hannah's hotel and spent hours in her room. He was an odd-looking man with a pointy head, which he covered most times with his hat. For this reason, Hannah felt completely at ease with him. He told her he enjoyed seeing her so perfectly comfortable in every light. He took pictures of her by the window with the sun illuminating her still-youthful bosom, or sliding down her sculptured backside. Once she draped herself across a daybed as Bellocq said the French women posed. Her smile was dreamy and mysterious. She was beautiful.

The daguerreotypes, once developed, rendered every niche and corner of Hannah's anatomy: hips, belly, sex navel, breasts; the curve of a haunch, the sweep of upraised arms, a rounded shoulder; a raised knee, a violin-shaped back, a landscape hip, a bottom; an elbow, a knee, a toe, a foot; legs opened, legs crossed, reclining, standing, sitting, kneeling; and finally, reminiscent of her time at Mrs. Truitt's house, her entire body covered with scintillating granulated sugar, glittering like snow crystals on the cypresses of Saratoga landscape, clustered like diamonds. The photographer was transfixed.

He then suggested a series of portraits taken with Hannah's finest gowns and most sumptuous jewels. Which of the two was most beautiful: Hannah as nature made her and men loved her, or Hannah as the world knew her and men bought her? Hannah had no idea what role these photographs would play in her future; for her they were simply souvenirs for John.

Back in Manhattan, Platt began to think about their relationship. Visiting Hannah in Saratoga was getting to be difficult for him. She was forty-six years his junior and would be thirty-nine in 1904. The years were catching up with him but not with her.

She was as beautiful as ever. She shined when she accompanied him to the gambling table in Saratoga, and she glowed by the candlelight when they returned to her room. She was not one to ask him to address her physical needs, but he could see her want when they slept together.

Still, he was willing to accept his age, and their days together had fallen into a routine—one made all the more beautiful by Hannah. She brought him a breakfast of fruit and croissants in bed. She read the *New York Times* to him. And she kissed him passionately after dinner—whether they would make love that night or not. He now depended on her smile to cheer him after a few weeks in New York surrounded by men of means and their greedy talk. She was as refreshing as Saratoga in winter.

So when the district attorney came to his house with his signed letter of paternity for Gwendolyn, their daughter who had not survived, Platt almost fainted. He had done it to please the despondent woman, to show her she mattered to him. "But no," he told the district attorney when asked, "I'm not sure that the baby was mine. Still, who else might it be?" The old man's hands began to shake as the DA told him that prostitutes never have only one John.

"Sit down, Mr. Platt; this is not your fault." Jerome spoke in a gentle voice. After the butler delivered some water and coffee for the district attorney, he continued. "You're not the first person to become ensnared by this ebony enslaver." It was a phrase he'd soon feed the newspapers. "I don't know if you understand her background, Mr. Platt." Jerome began running down the list of Hannah's arrests and the places she worked, the loss of her child, the other pregnancy. Who knew what had happened to the child she delivered in the first jail . . . Platt had known only a fraction of her past, although by his own uninterest.

When he was with Hannah, nothing else mattered. Her charm made the world go away. Even her race meant nothing to him when they were younger. But now, hearing about her color from Jerome's mouth, and her visits to Little Africa even when they were dating, made him feel stupid, as if he had been taken for so much money by her.

He had given her money to start her first boardinghouse—which Jerome now said was a brothel—and might have been even when he financed it. (It was a hidden threat that if he didn't cooperate, he might be implicated.) He had given her money for living expenses, and to take care of her pregnancy, and the elaborate funeral of Gwendolyn, attended by only a few of them. He and Hannah, Nanz and Leola. Now he began to wonder if Leola was part of the blackmail scheme, as Jerome explained that she was secretly a madam.

"Did you see the baby, Mr. Platt, if it was yours? Rarely does anyone bury a fetus. I'm not sure the hospitals even keep them."

Platt's stomach lurched.

"We need to get the whole bunch of them, Mr. Platt. Men like you—and Mr. Green—should not have their reputations sullied by women who came up from the gutter. If you don't watch out, she'll take you there with her."

Was it another threat from the district attorney? Or had Hannah tricked him? Platt wondered. His head spun.

"Think about it. I'll come back. We'll probably find more soon. We've been trying to chase down her bank accounts, as supplied by her lawyer, Mr. Nanz." Threat number three that could implicate him, Platt counted. "Seems like she came in to close down her accounts recently. She's left only the required amount in each one. When is the last time you saw her?"

"I couldn't say." Platt was by then screaming inside of his head. He had just left after spending the week with her. She hadn't mentioned anything about closing bank accounts and going abroad. What was she doing behind his back? He certainly wasn't going to tell the district attorney that he'd seen her in Saratoga the week previous. When did she have time to go to the bank? He had been right not to trust her.

Platt himself let the district attorney out instead of Arthur.

Platt thought of all the men Jerome named, and all the dirty downtown bordels. Maybe Gwendolyn wasn't even his. Hannah had made him feel like he was the only one.

John Platt stood in the two-level private library he'd had built in his mansion on Fifth Avenue, surrounded by the ten thousand volumes of his collection. His butler entered with a large envelope on a silver tray; the letter had arrived that morning. Platt was already dressed in a silver-gray smoking jacket, black cravat, and black shirt but was still in his black velvet slippers. When he opened the envelope Hannah had sent him for his birthday, and pulled out the Bellocq photograph of his mistress in all her magnificence taken by another man, his face broke into a catalog of disbelief, rage, outrage, despair, grief, shame, and fury. It cracked into a thousand pieces like a smashed Chinese porcelain vase on marble. Who had sent this picture? What man had seen Hannah like this? And how many others had seen her? What had she done? His Hannah—his most precious and beloved possession . . . This is what Hannah had been doing in Saratoga! He tore the photograph into pieces and threw it into the fireplace. Then he dissolved, like the gelatin print that curled and burned along with the unread note from Hannah . . .

For your birthday Papa! The New Art Form! The photograph of a genius Mr. Bellocq!

I love you,
Hannah

1904
THE ROBBER BARONS

We live in a world of chance, yet not of accident.
God gambles, but he does not cheat.

—*George Wald, Nobel biologist*

TWENTY-FOUR

Fifth Avenue and Sixtieth Street,
New York, May 14, 1904

Seated in comfortable leather armchairs at the Metropolitan Club, the bankers Henry Clews, Jacob Schiff, and J. P. Morgan, Mayor George McClellan Jr., John R. Platt, and August Belmont discussed the next stage of construction for the IRT subway, which would extend beyond the borough of Manhattan to the Bronx, Brooklyn, and Queens. The men had finished lunch and were enjoying cigars and brandy in the commons room.

The Metropolitan Club had been designed by Stanford White to keep women at bay. This included both private (wives, mothers, sisters, and daughters) and public (mistresses, showgirls, and ladies of easy virtue) members of the weaker sex. The rules of New York gentlemen's private clubs were fashioned after those of British clubs like the Players and the Athenaeum. Women were not allowed on the premises except in the lobby, the dining room, and the ladies' toilet. Women could not enter the commons room, the library, the reading rooms, the billiards room, the taproom, or the bar. The same restrictions applied to domestic animals, Jews, and Negroes. The Metropolitan Clubhouse posted rules that announced as much, where the new building stood in sublime architectural arrogance on Fifth Avenue facing Central Park.

It had been founded by J. P. Morgan in a pique the year before because John King, the president of the Erie Railroad, had been blackballed from New York's exclusive Union Club. When the board of governors rejected his friend, Morgan organized a hundred members to walk out in protest and commissioned Stanford White to build them a new club. The press dubbed it the Millionaire's Club. The members called it the Metropolitan Club, located on Fifth Avenue and Sixtieth Street.

"The IRT already belongs to the great tradition of civic projects like the Erie Canal, the Croton Aqueduct, and the Brooklyn Bridge," said Morgan, lighting a cigar.

"It was built by a genius. Why, the British can't hold a candle to our subway. It is one of the great engineering achievements of the age, and beautiful. The City Hall station is a work of art, with its Guastavino arches, leaded skylights, and crystal chandeliers."

"Wasn't it McKim, Mead, and White who designed the powerhouse and the cast-iron kiosks?" asked Henry Clews.

"Our trademark," replied Belmont, "is not only a signpost so that people can find the subway; it also shields the passageway so that they aren't drenched in rainstorms as they emerge."

"Of course, the public outcry about advertising in the subway is unfortunate," added Mayor McClellan. "Nevertheless, the commission *always* intended to permit advertising, we just didn't announce it *before*."

"Well, they pay." Belmont was the commission chairman and the originator of Contract No. 1—which was to build, equip, and operate the New York City subway for fifty years, with a renewable option for another twenty-five—and had paid for the cars, equipment, and electric signals from his own deep pockets.

"They are rather unsightly, these billboards for Baker's Cocoa and Cake Dandruff, not to mention Hunyadi János and Coca-Cola," complained Morgan.

"The Interborough earns five hundred thousand dollars from these ads and they're here to stay—we have contractual rights," Schiff responded.

August Belmont remained silent. In signing Contract No. 1, he had hoped to make a great deal of money, as well as win popular acclaim as a benefactor to the city. But he had no stomach for the rough give-and-take of urban politics; all the catfights and dogfights and real estate speculation, and these arguments over billboards, upset him. He began to regret his decision to finance the IRT single-handedly. He slumped into the deep leather armchair that was the trademark of the Metropolitan Club.

Belmont's temperament was his main failing. He sulked if not accorded the treatment he thought was due a gentleman of his station. He had financed dozens of candidates in local, state, and national elections, including the president of the United States, but did he get any thanks or pull any advantage? Politicians soon forgot on which side their bread was buttered. Or maybe they knew that he would keep quiet because he didn't want anyone to know he was a Jew. It was a kind of social blackmail that kept him paying but not getting entrance. Now they were talking about his billboards for the subway that *he* had financed as if he weren't there!

The new Interborough Rapid Transit, called the IRT, started at City Hall, with stations going northward toward the Brooklyn Bridge, Canal Street, Twenty-Third Street, Thirty-Third Street, Times Square, Fifty-Ninth, Seventy-Second, Seventy-Ninth, Eighty-Sixth, on up to Ninety-Sixth Street. Then the lines split. The Broadway stations went all the way to Bronx Park beginning at 103rd, through Columbia University and 145th Street to Prospect Avenue and 180th Street and north to Riverdale.

"The subway," continued J. P. Morgan, blowing smoke rings, "is the new Statue of Liberty. It's the new symbol of New York's wealth and power." Morgan had at one time put a lien on 1.9 million acres of land and the mineral rights on 2.4 million more acres when the Northern Pacific Railway had fallen into receivership some years earlier. Belmont's measly twenty-two miles of subway tunnels, he thought, were pocket change. Morgan controlled the Erie, Chesapeake and Ohio, Philadelphia and Reading, Santa Fe, Northern Pacific, Great Northern, New York Central, the Lehigh Valley, the Jersey Central, and the Southern Railway. The Morgan Company's combined revenues approached half of those of the United States.

"It guarantees New York's status as a great city," said Mayor McClellan, "and it makes us sons of the mightiest metropolis the world has ever known."

"I'll drink to that," said Henry Clews.

"Here, here," replied Jacob Schiff.

The waiters were now serving coffee (except to Belmont, who took tea), the cigars were lit, and the golden Dupeyron Armagnac poured. The "Lords of Creation," "the vital few," congratulated themselves on a sublime exercise of power—not to mention a great real estate boom in properties they owned along the subway line.

"It is to be greatly regretted that our colleague Andrew Green, who did so much for this endeavor, is no longer with us."

"Indeed. An incomprehensible tragedy."

"That we hope is closed forever."

"Well, why shouldn't it be? The Negro was crazy."

"And they did an admirable job. It is William Jerome who has still not classified the case as closed. His detectives are still snooping around looking for dirt."

"More dirt than the fact that a bloody Negro can murder an eminent white man of the highest social standing in broad daylight and not be strung up? What is New York coming to?"

"Alienists," said McClellan. "It seems a modern democratic society must protect the insane."

"Even the colored?"

"Yes, even them."

"What is the world coming to?"

"This Williams is being treated almost as if he had Andrew's social status instead of that of a Black man."

"It's called transference. Alienists use that word all the time to explain everything from sodomy to strangulation."

"Father's to blame, I suppose."

"Of course!" said Morgan. "Father's always to blame."

"Well, if Jerome doesn't take the bull by the horn, somebody should," said John Platt. "Why hasn't Jerome closed this case and stopped it from bubbling up in print every few weeks like a backed-up toilet?" Platt had tried to keep his voice even, but it had risen in panic as he spoke. He had not visited or corresponded with Hannah since he had received the photograph. In fact, he had called Jerome to say that he would cooperate in prosecuting the woman who had blackmailed him for so long.

The fact that Hannah hadn't sought him out frightened him even more. What was she up to?

"The tabloids love the story. They love Hannah Elias. She's terrific copy. As long as the books aren't closed, the reporters aren't going to go away."

"What will it take to get him to classify Andrew's death as an accident?" Platt added plaintively.

"It's the Elias woman. Jerome isn't convinced she's telling all she knows or that she isn't involved in the death."

"How can that be, if it was a case of mistaken identity?"

"And suppose it wasn't?"

"What do you mean by that?"

"An assignation gone wrong, a blackmail demand refused—there are lots of possibilities."

"Blackmail? Andrew? Andrew was as honest as Abe Lincoln, as straight as the proverbial arrow. Why, he didn't have a crooked bone in his body or an unpleasant word."

"You know, once the police are involved in *anyone's* life, the one sordid thing that ever happened to them, that one unethical lapse, is sure to come out."

John Rufus Platt was in no mood to argue. He sat alone in his mansion most nights seething at the way he was treated. The memory of the photograph made his blood boil and it stuck in his mind constantly, with a mixture of lust and longing, anger and fear. Who had sent the photograph and why?

He'd been physically ill since he saw the image. He cried himself to sleep some nights. His angry telegrams went unanswered. Platt looked up at the ornate ceiling with its crystal chandelier, and then around the room in which the glory and power of New York wealth, politics, and culture were concentrated. Without women.

It was such a relief, Platt thought, to be able to escape from the female sex, with their curves and cavities and bumps and softness and headaches and deceptions and sexual demands. To tell the truth, he was tired of Hannah—of what she evoked: feeling, desire, jealousy, rage. He wanted to be free of her. He had to cast this lust out of his heart. He was too old for these emotions.

"New York has finally achieved its ascendancy over both London and Paris," he added.

"Not quite yet," remarked Morgan, "but we're working on it."

McClellan said, "The IRT is having a tremendous impact on land development and prices; every real estate promoter in the city is begging for new stations. The only way to keep the pressure off is the way we did for the first contract—keep the plan and locations secret until the expansion is built."

"We don't need expansion; the profits are in the straps," said Belmont. "There's a very fine line between success and failure. Crowding during rush hour is inevitable. If a day ever comes when transportation during rush hour is done without crowding, the company doing it will fail. The last thing we need to do is to establish the city's needs too far ahead."

"You oppose expansion?"

"Our revenue is already huge. The IRT is a gold mine at eight percent pure profit. That is truly remarkable. I predict an earning rise of twenty percent and a dividend rise from two to nine percent in a year's time. I'm not going to let anyone push me into unwanted expansion."

"It's not expansion so much as a wider net of investors and certain democratization we need," added John Platt. "After all, US Steel has done it. So have American Tobacco and United Fruit. Now that thousands ride the subway every day, the average New Yorker has a stake in the IRT—decisions can no longer be confined to a tiny group of blue bloods."

"Democratization!" hissed Morgan. "Do you want to bloody lose control of this city?"

"It's impossible for us to lose control of this city barring a revolution," added John Rufus. But Hannah was of a different stripe, he ruminated. If he didn't get ahold of himself and his emotions, slay this squalid lust at its roots, he would ruin what was left of his life.

❧

Granville Woods stepped out of the Nassau Street offices of Warren, Warren, and O'Beirne, his wide shoulders even more set than usual with indignation and frustration. A year after his arrival in New York, Woods had tested his "Multiple Distributing Station System" for his American Engineering Company in a public demonstration on Coney Island,

Brooklyn. The demonstration had amazed the crowd and impressed the railway magnates present, men such as Vanderbilt and Morgan. The system represented a dramatic departure from any previous method of distribution of electric railway power. It allowed for the wireless transmission of current, utilizing the principles of electromagnetic induction instead of the overhead wires that had been banned since the New York blizzard of 1888.

The power system Woods had invented was known as the "third rail," a method of providing electricity for the subway trains without overhead wires, allowing the trains to fit into smaller tunnels and providing more electricity with less friction. The third rail was located either between the two running rails or to one side of them. Electricity was transmitted to the train by means of a sliding "shoe," which rested in contact with the rail. The return current flowed through one or both running rails, and physical contact with the rail was fatal.

Woods had been to see his lawyers because Thomas Edison's Engineering Company had stolen his patent and was attempting to market his invention as its own, without paying him a cent. After more than three years of complaining, he was suing the bastards. Granville had sold several of his patents to Edison and his trust, but others Edison had simply appropriated. Edison was determined to control any and all electromechanical inventions, including all the basic patents on movie cameras and projectors. He had filed such a stream of lawsuits against the film companies that they had all fled in desperation to California just to get away from Edison's lawyers.

Granville had been assured he would win his case, but the anguish was not just monetary, he thought; it was the experience of being bilked and humiliated, of having one's very soul defiled.

Defilement. The last time he felt this strongly, had been about Bessie. She had come on to him while she was married, and then afterward. Matthew had been right to divorce her. She was a whore, and Matthew couldn't ignore that. She had a lover, an official white lover, the whole time. Why then, thought Granville, did the image of her in his bed still come to his daydreams? He found himself longing for her still. He hoped to never see Bessie again. He felt lost.

Granville stopped at the bottom of the stairs and lit a cigarette. He pulled his fedora down over his eyes and, with his roll of blueprints under his arm, he began walking toward Wall Street. His dreams, he thought, were better spent with a new method of electrifying the subway in New York City than his old and lost forever love.

TWENTY-FIVE

The Metropolitan Club, New York,
May 27, 1904

E dward Estel sat at a corner table of the breakfast room of the Metropolitan Club, one of a roomful of breakfasters. Each had his ironed copy of the *New York Times* or the New York *Sun*. Edward opened his and choked on his orange juice. He let out a guffaw so loud it shook the crystal and made everyone look up. But since everyone was reading the same headline, no one protested. There was only silence in the room.

JOHN R. PLATT SUES HANNAH ELIAS
FOR THREE-QUARTERS OF A MILLION DOLLARS
129 MERCHANT BANKS NAMED AS CO-DEFENDANTS

A murmur of excitement and disbelief swept through the sedate white-and-gold breakfast room like a summer breeze. People spoke in the same hushed voices as at Andrew Green's funeral.

"Platt's suing every bank on Wall Street over Mrs. Elias's—"

"Let me get this straight: Mrs. Elias is a hooker who blackmails her rich clients?"

"No, she's a real estate speculator who takes the money bankers give her for screwing them and puts it back into their banks, for which they then pay her interest. Platt claims her money is his. And the banks have it."

"It's a ploy, of course, but brilliant. I wonder who at Warren and Warren thought it up."

"It's disgusting. Pathetic."

"It's unbelievable."

"The tabloids are going to have a field day with this."

"Mrs. Elias says she invested her money."

"The *Sun* says the old man gave her nearly $700,000 because, first, she said she liked him, and, second, that she would blackmail him. She says it's all baloney and she's done nothing wrong—"

"At least one good thing will come of it: Platt's action will clear Andrew Green's name for good from any suspicion of being connected with her, which his murder implanted in many minds."

"Kind of brutal, isn't it? Waking up in the morning to find your name smeared all over the newspapers a second time," said one of the bankers to another.

"Oh, really? I notice that your bank is on the list."

"She has how many bank accounts?"

"One hundred twenty-nine."

"Nobody has one hundred twenty-nine bank accounts!"

"She does."

"Then she is fronting for others—a straw man?"

"Perhaps, but who?"

"I expect she is diversifying," Edward joked.

"Then Platt has every merchant bank on Wall Street by the balls."

"Or is it Mrs. Elias?" intoned Estel.

"Platt is simply doing it Wall Street style. Destroy her financially, bankrupt her, and make her leave New York and go back to where she came from. I hear that would be the slums of Philadelphia. And she brought Platt with her. He is ready for revenge."

"Mrs. Elias has started a one-woman panic on Wall Street, I see," he said, laughing despite himself. "If there are one hundred and twenty-nine defendants, there are at least four hundred Wall Street lawyers with their dicks out pissing on their clients' checkbooks!"

"Edward, you'll be pissing blood when your name gets attached to this scandal. Isn't your bank a codefendant?"

"Perhaps, but maybe it's worth it," said Edward. "The same men who are screwing Hannah are screwing the United States out of its gold and silver, its land and mineral resources, its oil and water. Maybe if the banks are sued for money deposited in them by fraud and financial crime, we could wipe out the mob and tax evaders in one fell swoop. We are the ones who take their money, keep their money, use their money, invest their money, and pay them goddamned interest on their money. We are a heartless bunch, full of ourselves, ruthless, hypocritical, and without scruples.

"Mrs. Elias is only a player in the system. Besides, I believe she's innocent. I don't believe for a moment she blackmailed Platt. In fact, I know it for a fact. I hope she wins. We run the world. And Hannah is one of us. And we hate her because she's a woman and a renegade who has upset ever so slightly the balance of power.

"You, sirs, had better get down to your offices and start fielding telegraphs and phone calls!" he said over his shoulder as he left. The suit was all over Wall Street in seconds.

J. P. Morgan's assistant Belle da Costa Greene opened the morning edition of the *New York Times*, which she always read in the sanctuary of her head curator's office in the Morgan Library at Thirty-Sixth Street and Fifth Avenue. She gasped and almost knocked over the silver coffee urn sitting on its tray that had just been set down by Charley, the butler.

PLATT'S OWN STORY:

WHY HE GAVE HANNAH ELIAS NEARLY 700,000 DOLLARS

From behind a closed door that led from her office to J. P. Morgan's, she heard an explosion that could only be the Big Chief himself reading the selfsame article. Everyone had assumed that the Green murder scandal was over, thought Belle.

But this changed everything.

John R. Platt, millionaire glass manufacturer and member of an old New York family, listed in the Social Register, has brought a suit in New York Supreme Court against Hannah to recover the sum of 685,385 dollars of his money he said she squandered between the years 1896 and 1904.

Belle da Costa Greene's eyes scanned the article in disbelief: John R. Platt, millionaire, was suing Hannah Elias, courtesan, for $685,000. In a civil suit, "Platt's complaint said that he had been paying money to Elias for 17 years and stopped only last Wednesday. He was the man Cornelius Williams had meant to kill, he confirmed, and Elias' houses, furniture and jewels all came out of his pocket." Belle was appalled. What in heaven's name was John R. Platt, of the Platts of Park Avenue, thinking of, even if it was true?

Eagerly, Belle perused the article. It was on account of a fancied grievance with the woman that Cornelius Williams, certified madman, had murdered Andrew H. Green, the Father of Greater New York, on November 13 last in front of his home. The murderer had confused Mr. Green, who regularly visited a nephew at the house next door to 236 Central Park West, with Mr. Platt, who regularly visited Hannah.

According to papers filed in court the day before, "Mrs. Elias blackmailed Platt out of nearly three quarters of a million dollars, and she had received $15,000 from him since the murder. He had still paid her money the previous week. Mrs. Elias threatened to charge publicly that he was the father of two illegitimate children of hers. She threatened to tell the tabloids that Matthew Davis, her ex-husband, a Negro, had sued him for alienation of affection. She threatened to let people know that he was the man whom the murderer Williams was seeking when he killed Andrew Green. The Negroes with whom Hannah Elias associated before she became Platt's mistress knew Platt as "Mr. Andrews."

Just why Mr. Platt is trying to get his money back no one could or would tell. There are several coincidences connected with the suit behind which no one cognizant of the facts could explain. For example, about seven years ago, Hannah Elias was sent on behalf of a prominent person to the law firm of Warren & Booth, of which Lyman G. Warren was the senior partner. The chief clerk of that firm was August A. Nanz, who became Mrs. Elias's most trusted friend and legal counsel. He lived with her in the house that Mr. Platt now claims to be his, and he represented her in the troubles that followed the revelation of Andrew Green's murder.

Nanz stated yesterday that he no longer represents Mrs. Elias and has not communicated with her directly or indirectly since November last.

"But the lawyers now representing Mr. Platt in the action brought against Mrs. Elias are Warren, Warren and O'Beirne, of whom the senior partner is Lyman G. Warren. Furthermore, Mr. Nanz's office at 488 Broadway released a statement saying that if Mrs. Elias receives any messages purporting to come from Mr. Nanz, they are forgeries unless Mr. Nanz sends word that they are genuine. The murderer Williams said at his grand jury indictment that he had been commissioned by Satan to kill three men, one of which was Andrew Green, another was John R. Platt, and a third whose name has thus far been kept out of the scandal.

"Mr. Platt's complaint covers 27 typewritten pages and contains 36 clauses besides the prayer for relief, and names 34 trust companies, 26 savings banks, and 69 other banks as codefendants. In fact, the title of the suit reads like a Who's Who of New York banking. Mr. Platt claims that Mrs. Elias has an account in each of these banks."

"That makes a hundred and twenty-nine banks!" gasped Belle.

JOHN R. PLATT, PLAINTIFF, VS. HANNAH ELIAS,
DEFENDANT & CODEFENDANTS

The 129 codefendant banks were named. The list read like Mr. Morgan's private address book, thought Belle. Shocked, she realized that J. P. Morgan's National Bank of Commerce was codefendant with Hannah.

"Oh, my God!" cried Belle, not one to raise a hair on her immaculate head in the face of any emergency, and certainly never to swear. "Is John R. Platt out of his bloody mind?" She looked up just as her boss and surrogate father burst into her office.

"Belle! Have you seen this? Is Johnny Platt out of his mind?"

Morgan's eyes were incandescent, and a vein throbbed in his temple.

"One hundred twenty-nine merchant banks as codefendants in a civil suit—that's unheard of!" Morgan's voice shook the timbers of Belle's oak-paneled alcove. "You tell Warren and Warren to reduce their complaint to a half-dozen banks and to take my bank off his list, or they'll be Tomb lawyers and pettifoggers defending pickpockets at the Bowery precinct station!"

Belle couldn't believe her ears. A little Philadelphia jezebel had upset J. P. Morgan, who had personally saved the United States of America $20 million in interest by refinancing the Civil War debt! Morgan's National Bank of Commerce was the largest bank in the United States.

"Coffee, Mr. Morgan? Let's not exaggerate." But her heart was racing. This could go very far, she thought, even into the deepest secrets of her own personal life. Hannah Elias, if she was not mistaken, had been found to be a high-class mixed-race courtesan to the rich and famous, a *fille de joie* in interracial Five Points in her earlier days. Belle had already planned to do what JP now requested.

"Call William Jerome and tell him to get his ass to my office at the bank immediately. I'll meet him there. And call the mayor."

Belle's hand shook as she picked up the phone and asked in her steely yet girlish voice for the district attorney's office. Men, she thought—what they wouldn't do to ruin a woman. Didn't the poor fool realize he would be the laughingstock of all New York? That he would be struck from the *Social Register* if he went through with a public trial like this; that his friends would desert him and his children would probably have him committed?

Her boss, John Pierpont Morgan, had been personally responsible for changing the law that taxed imported works of art at 200 percent, making it possible for him to bring his fabulous European art collection back to New York. The banker had gone in person to the US Senate to argue that since pedigree dogs were allowed into the United States tax-free because their breeding improved the canine race in America, the same benefits should be given to works of art for the same reason. He had prevailed, and the law had been changed to suit him—all works of art would henceforth be allowed into the US tax-free. He had then taken advantage of the new law to import his entire collection in London to New York—partly for his mansion, partly for his library, and partly to fill the empty exhibition halls of the Metropolitan Museum of Art in

Central Park. The exquisite, illuminated books and porcelains Belle had bought in Europe now paid no duty at all. Other rich New Yorkers who followed his lead brought other European riches back home.

This crisis had to be managed. God only knew what might come out in the course of a public trial. Platt had pissed all over his social world with his ridiculous accusations. Why would he expose himself to such ridicule over a common woman? She had heard of Elias's antics in Far Rockaway a few years earlier, and of her feud with Lillian Russell, but nothing, nothing like this. Mrs. Elias revealed as a client of Morgan trust! And what else? A stockholder in August Belmont's IRT subway contract? And what else? A Morgan bank link to the underworld and the mob?

"Oh, Jesus," she moaned. "And what else?"

The phone rang. Belle picked it up absentmindedly and, in her distraction, handed it to J. P. Morgan without speaking. It was the director of Morgan's National Bank of Commerce, which had been named in the suit. They had been fielding questions from the *New York Times'* reporters all morning, as well as hysterical affiliate banks. The Bankers Trust had called. The Equitable Trust had called, and the Harlem Savings Bank had called. The Union Trust was on the line. The Astor National Bank had tried to get through to the library. The Bank of America's lawyers had already contacted Magistrate Alfred E. Ommen. It was as if John Platt had stamped on an anthill.

In William Jerome's office, there was unmitigated glee. "We've got Elias by the tits this time—blackmail and extortion. She'll never walk out of the courthouse a free woman." Jerome was on fire. His hatred of Hannah Elias was palpable. She had outsmarted him once. She was an affront to Anglo-Saxon society. Women like her got away with murder. He needed to set an example of her by punishing her to the limit of the law. What he detested more than anything was that she had made a fool of him and his detective brigade from the moment she first spoke to him—when she innocently said she was Bessie Davis. He still couldn't figure out her angle for letting that slip out.

Now he might even get a chance to reopen the Green murder case.

There may have been a conspiracy after all. Jerome seemed oblivious to what everyone in the Detective Bureau already suspected: With defendants who constituted the entire banking system of New York City, was Jerome insane? The calls and telegrams had already started pouring in; the newspaper reporters were already camping just outside the Detective Bureau's door. Jerome intended to make political hay out of convicting Elias, but had he really thought it through? Jerome would be taking on Hannah's lovers, of whom there were at least as many as she had banks.

But sure enough, the district attorney was crazy enough to risk his reputation in a case in which socialites' sex lives were the centerpiece. Platt was angry with Hannah. But Hannah possessed the address book. Her lovers would desert her, sure, but could Jerome really sink Hannah Elias without drowning a good number of his own class? The American public had taken a turn toward the Christian evangelist Right. It was awash with reformism. There were reform groups against prostitution, gambling, alcohol, and child labor. Did people really want their betters' dirty laundry washed in public?

Jerome even contemplated issuing a warrant for Hannah's arrest. As usual, he insisted on being judge, jury, and executioner in a dangerous game with some very powerful men.

McClusky tried to reason with him. "This is a civil case, after all. There is no basis for a criminal warrant."

"She's been blackmailing Platt. That's a felony. I can arrest her. I intend to issue a criminal warrant, and you will serve it. Let the criminal case supersede the civil one. We'll get ours in court first."

"But there's no proof of blackmail except Platt's suit, and he hasn't accused her of that."

"Can you imagine Platt remaining nine years with Elias without coercion? She threatened to expose him; he paid her not to."

"That's a fairy tale, not a case."

"I think I can get a warrant for her arrest from Magistrate Ommen in the Jefferson Market court, on the basis that she might skip town."

"He'll set bail maybe, but she'll be out free in a couple of hours. She's rich. Rich people don't go to jail, Bill. You should know that."

"She's a Negro, and I'm going to put her right down there in Coon's

Row where she belongs. How do you know Cornelius Williams wasn't part of her extortion plot and something went wrong? Was Cornelius after Green or after Platt or after her?

"We're going to get Williams, too. Williams has been giving interviews to the press that demonstrate he is perfectly sane. He even admitted that he made a mistake in killing Green.

"It wouldn't be the first time a person was declared insane and then brought back from the madhouse and put on trial for his life. The stupid bastard is just asking for it."

At nine o'clock that night, Jerome and his district attorneys, accompanied by a stenographer, met Police Magistrate Ommen and L. G. Warren at the Plaza Hotel. After a short consultation, Jerome's men left the hotel and returned to Platt's mansion.

Jerome had remained cloistered with John R. Platt and his son-in-law all night, insisting that Platt must also sue Hannah in criminal court.

"I didn't expect you to act without me after my visit," Jerome told him. "I thought you would call. Now we have to follow through on your case. If you want your money back, we need to charge blackmail in a criminal case. Then your civil case against the banks and Hannah will be smooth as butter."

Jerome beleaguered John Platt at length. If Platt was right in his complaint, he did not propose to let so great a matter pass without criminal charges. A crime had been committed; it was the duty of the complainant to aid the authorities in prosecuting the guilty person.

"It must be remembered that your lawyers started the prosecution of Mrs. Elias in the civil case, Mr. Platt," he continued. "As the district attorney, I follow up. *I* have to act. A criminal with a police record is at large."

"But we don't think that Mrs. Elias is a criminal," argued Platt's lawyer. "We only want the money or some of the money back. Besides, a large part of the money that we wish to recover would be eaten up by a drawn-out procedure! Mr. Platt would recover nothing!"

Jerome sniffed. "That is not my problem. My problem is crime and punishment. Mrs. Elias is a whore. Mrs. Elias is a felon. Mrs. Elias is a threat to American society."

Save for a glimmer of light on the second floor of the mansion at 7 East Fifty-Fourth Street, the house was in darkness. For the rest of the night into dawn, Jerome and his men interrogated Platt, who cried with anguish, and forced him to sign a criminal complaint that charged Hannah with blackmail.

1904
THE SUIT

JOHN R. PLATT, PLAINTIFF, VS. HANNAH ELIAS
DEFENDANT & CO-DEFENDANTS:

Bankers Trust Company, Bowling Green Trust Company, Broadway Trust Company, Central Realty Bond and Trust Company, Central Trust Company, City Trust Company, Colonial Trust Company, Continental Trust Company, Empire Trust Company, Equitable Trust Company, Farmers Loan and Trust Company, Fifth Avenue Trust Company, Guaranty Trust Company, Guardian Trust Company, Knickerbockers Trust Company, Lincoln Trust Company, Manhattan Trust Company, Mercantile Trust Company, Merchants Trust Company, Metropolitan Trust Company, Morton Trust Company, New York Security Trust Company, North American Trust Company, Real Estate Trust Company, Realty Trust Company, Standard Trust Company, Trust Company of America, Trust Company of the Republic, Union Trust Company, United States Mortgage and Trust Company, United States Trust Company, Van Norden Trust Company, Washington Trust Company, Windsor Trust Company, America Savings Bank, Bank for Savings, Bowery Savings Bank, Bronx Savings Bank, Broadway Savings Institution, Citizens Savings Bank, Dry Dock Emigrant Industrial Savings Bank, Empire City Savings

Bank, Excelsior Savings Bank, Greenwich Savings Bank, Harbor and Suburban Building and Savings Association, Harlem Savings Bank, Irving Savings Institution, Manhattan Savings Institution, Metropolitan Savings Bank, New York Savings Bank, Union Dime Savings Bank, United States Savings Bank, North River Savings Bank, Bank of America, Bank of the Metropolis, Bank of Washington Heights, Bowery Bank, Bronx Borough Bank, Colonial Bank, Century Bank, Central Bank, Corn Exchange Bank, Fidelity Bank, the Fifth Avenue Bank of New York, Fourteenth Street Bank, Gansevoort Bank, Germania Bank, Greenwich Bank, Manhattan Company, Mechanics and Traders Bank, Mount Morris Bank, Mutual Bank, Nassau Bank, New York Produce Exchange Bank, Nineteenth Ward Bank, Oriental Bank, Pacific Bank, Plaza Bank, Riverside Bank, Twelfth Ward Bank, Varick Bank, Wells Fargo and Company's Bank, West Side Bank, Yorkville Bank, American Exchange National Bank, Astor National Bank, Bank of New York, National Banking Association, Butchers and Drovers Bank, Citizens Central National Bank, Chase National Bank, Chatham National Bank, Chemical National Bank, Fourth National Bank, Gallatin National Bank, Garfield National Bank, Hanover National Bank, Importers and Traders National Bank, Irving National Bank, Lincoln National Bank, Liberty National Bank, Market and Fulton National Bank, Mechanics Exchange National Bank, National Bank of Commerce in New York, National Bank of North America in New York, National City Bank, National Bank of New York, New Amsterdam National Bank, New York County National Bank, New York National Exchange Bank, Phoenix National Bank, Seaboard National Bank, Second National Bank, Show and Leather National Bank, Fourth Street National Bank, United National Bank.

Defendants to the above-named defendants and each of them, you are hereby summoned to answer.

—*New York, May 27, 1904*

TWENTY-SIX

Upper West Side, New York,
May 28, 1904

Hannah learned of the suit just like everyone else, in the morning edition of the *New York Times*. She had returned from Saratoga months earlier, after getting letters and telegrams from Platt that were so upsetting. He accused her of taking his money, of sneaking around New York while telling him she wanted to be alone for her mental health. He told her that the photograph she'd sent him was just the calling card of a whore. That hurt her badly. She realized that he never really saw her as anything more.

After coming to so many realizations in Saratoga, and finding a deep well of peace in herself, she decided to let him go. She was done with the drama of men who accused and abused her. She didn't answer any of his communications.

It was as if the suit was his final way of getting her attention. How sad, she thought, that he didn't understand. She was almost ready to try to love him.

"The fool!" she shouted. "The fool doesn't know anything." She realized that she was crying. "Bastard!" she screamed. "It's because of Saratoga! It's Saratoga!"

Suddenly her feet seemed not to touch the parquet floor. She flew around the bedroom, her arms lifted, her dressing gown billowing behind her. The Egyptian statuary stared down on her rage. The eruption Hannah emitted was a repeat in even shriller terms than the mayhem that had landed her in jail almost seventeen years earlier. Except that this was her house, and she was free to do within it what she wished, including creating mayhem. Her shrieks brought the servants running and provoked the alarmed cry of her nursemaid, Francine. "Madame, you'll curdle your milk!"

What Platt didn't know, and what she wasn't going to tell him, was that she had become pregnant. She had decided to wait until the baby was born this time to tell him. But by then he had called her names and abused her emotionally. She wouldn't give him paternity over this daughter.

"That Judas! He *gave* me that money. He begged me to relieve him of it. He literally threw it at my feet, and now he's accusing me of extortion! Of embezzlement! Of all the nerve! When his friends make millions with their illegal dealing and inside trading, their trusts and speculation and contracts and mergers! If Mr. Platt thinks he can simply steal it all back, he has another think coming!"

Hannah had pulled the support out of her Gibson girl pompadour, and her hair, charged with electricity, sprang loose like the Metropolitan Opera's Medea. She swung around, looking for something to smash, and saw a row of Chinese vases lined up on the mantelpiece.

"I am *not* a thief! I am not a thief!"

"No! Madame! Not the new Mings!"

Before Kato could put himself between Hannah and the precious porcelain, she had seized two of them, one in each hand, and dashed them to the floor.

"Madame," he said. "No use. No point."

Realizing the irony of the situation, Hannah burst into frustrated laughter. It swelled through the mansion and awakened one-month-old Muriel Consuela. She laughed at the absurdity of life. She had everything she had ever dreamed of. She had a new baby. She had Sadie to watch the Central Park West house. Her family! And the trip she and Kato planned to his home in Yokohama was still going to happen. She had life and she had adventures just like the queen of Egypt.

And now she would fight John Platt to the death—his, not hers, she vowed. She was not a thief! She had never robbed anyone of anything!

She was not a blackmailer! She was not! She was *not*! Everything, everything, had been given freely out of love, out of sex, out of need.

When she finally came to herself, and focused her eyes and calmed her voice, Hannah asked for the baby.

The petrified servants scattered like marbles, returning to their chores, shaking their heads in dismay, and wondering what had riled up Hannah so early in the morning. Only Kato remained, silent, immobile.

The nursemaid entered with the wailing baby. "Ma'am, your pinafore," she whispered as she handed the baby to Hannah, along with an embroidered towel.

As soon as Hannah felt Muriel's small mouth on her breast, she calmed down, settling in the window seat to watch the child take nourishment. She had to think. Why after so many years was Papa doing this and exposing himself to disgrace? Was it revenge for staying so long in Saratoga? Had it something to do with Andrew Green? Was it Papa's guilt over causing the death of one of his own?

The newspapers had done an even more thorough job on Hannah than last time. *The Sun*, *The World*, *The Evening Star*, the *New York Times*—all had front-page stories. Hannah's entire life in all its details was splashed all over the newsprint pages. There were photographs of her house, images of John Platt, illustrations of Cornelius in jail, and several portraits of Hannah, including one of her nude portraits by Bellocq. There were even photos of her other houses on Sixty-Eighth Street, and Fifty-Third Street, and the facade of John Platt's mansion at Fifty-Fourth. There were detailed descriptions of the interior of 236. From *The World*:

> Mrs. Elias's theatrical imaginations have given an ingenious twist to somber upper-class decor, adding her fantasies of Ancient Egypt and Africa. . . . She pays her servants extravagantly and treats them well, for which they reward her with honesty, loyalty, and strict discretion. There are upstairs maids, downstairs maids, her personal maid, a cook, two kitchen maids, a stable boy, two lackeys, a coachman, and a Jap butler.

There was nothing New Yorkers would not know about her. It was far worse than the hullabaloo the murder had caused. Then she had been unknown. Now she was—what was the word she was looking for? Infamous—that was it—infamous.

NEGRO WOMAN WHO LIVES IN REGAL MAGNIFICENCE ON CENTRAL PARK WEST ALSO SERVED TERMS IN MOYAMENSING PRISON AND ON BLACKWELL'S ISLAND

Hannah had gotten pregnant in the Rockaways, when she and Platt were relaxing near the beach. Muriel was now one month old. She had told Platt only that she needed a raise in the monthly money he gave her. Their relationship had been smooth then; it was before the Green murder and all the chaos that created. Platt had given her $15,000 outright instead of a higher allowance, and a diamond necklace. Hannah wasn't even sure of the accusations, but she knew she couldn't trust Nanz anymore, since Leola had told her that he had taken papers out of her safe. She also couldn't trust any of the New York lawyers, who all tended to support the white, rich, upper class.

She decided to pick one of the eight colored lawyers who existed in New York City.

She kissed Muriel, held her up, and burped her. As she rocked the baby, her thoughts turned to Clara and that Christmas Eve in 1885 when she had left her, the same age as Muriel, in the arms of Mr. Hudson. Hannah had never recovered from that first sacrifice. It had haunted her all her life, tainted her every thought and dream, ruined every snippet of happiness she had ever had since. Platt was trying to steal back his own daughter's inheritance!

The best Black lawyer practicing in the county, state, or boroughs of New York was Washington Brauns. Hannah watched him mount the steps of the mansion. When he entered, having given his straw hat to Kato, she was surprised to see how young he was. He was high yellow and dapper, with attractive features. He wore a diamond in one ear and another on his right hand. He had graduated second in his class from Columbia Law School, only because Columbia had refused to graduate a Negro at the top of any class.

The first thing he said was that he had thought his associates were playing a joke on him when he had received Hannah's request for an interview. But he had obtained a copy of Platt's complaint, which he handed to her. Hannah liked Washington immediately. He was visibly taken aback by his surroundings, but Hannah hoped he would see through the gilded atmosphere to her innocence.

"The plaintiff has been supporting me for years, and there has never been any fuss about it until now."

"So, would you say you were his common-law wife?"

"Well, I suppose you could say so. Mr. Platt was named in my divorce from my first husband, Matthew Davis, in '01. I knew Mr. Platt before my marriage. I haven't done anything wrong and I expect that I have nothing to fear. I have a month-old baby here. I'm still weak from the delivery. I don't suppose I'll really have to go down to the police precinct."

"You have nothing to fear," said Brauns. "This is a civil matter, and I'm sure a transaction, if necessary, can be arranged."

"Transaction, my foot! I'm not paying Mr. Platt a dime. This is money he gave me in good faith and I accepted it in good faith in return for our mutual affection for each other."

"I understand. Three quarters of a million dollars is a lot of affection. I'll be in touch with his lawyers tomorrow morning, and we'll keep you informed."

"Oh, I know you'll take care of it. May I call you Washington?"

He went flushed, impressed. He had succumbed like all the rest.

"You'll have to tell me everything if I am to represent you—in confidence, of course. And you'll have to be honest with me, to avoid surprises. If there's something I should know about your past, let me find it out from you, not the opposing law firm."

"You'll have everything you need."

"Well, for starters, Mrs. Elias, tell me what your real name is."

Hannah began her tale, which to her amusement left Washington breathless and spellbound. She told the young lawyer of a life that had careened from the depths of Addison Street and Five Points to the heights of Delmonico's and Central Park. A life that for Washington was barely believable and astoundingly immoral. He thought of the alternatives if the abuse had happened to his mother or sisters. What choice would they have? Hannah was a woman warrior without scruples or limits, a woman driven by ambition and one single act of despair.

Several hours later, Washington accepted her case. He stood on the front steps of the mansion and held his first press conference.

"There has been no service in the case yet," he told the reporters camping outside, as Hannah watched from the ground-floor salon.

"The plaintiff has filed his petition and Mrs. Elias has decided I will accept service for her.

"I want to say that there is no inclination on Mrs. Elias's part to evade service. She is not running away. Had she wished to do so, she could have disposed of her real estate long ago. I will say that so far as I have gone into the case, I have found nothing to substantiate the charges of blackmail or wrongfully obtained money. Mrs. Elias has known Mr. Platt for many years, and I believe she always knew him under his own name. I have no reason to believe that Mrs. Elias ever knew Andrew H. Green. She says she did not."

"How colored is Mrs. Elias?" someone shouted.

"I do not know whether or not Mrs. Elias is colored," said Washington coolly. "I want to emphasize the fact that she does not intend to leave the city, and has not dismantled her Central Park West home with that end in view. I may or may not act as advisory counsel. She, however, will fight this case."

When asked if the district attorney would take any action, Washington replied, "If they cannot make a civil case against Mrs. Elias, how can they make a criminal case against her? I assure you Mrs. Elias has made no overtures for a settlement."

Washington started down the steps into the crowd of journalists. He

believed that because of Platt's advanced age, his lawyers would move for
an early trial. Ordinarily, it took two to three years for a civil litigation to
reach court, but Platt's attorneys had already applied to the court for an
immediate date in the criminal case.

To Hannah's great surprise, a letter from her twin, David, came in the
mail the next day.

Philadelphia May 31st, 1904

My sister and twin Bessie,

    Imagine my shock and grief in opening the <u>Philadelphia Ga-
zette</u> *and finding your episodes of lewdness, lawlessness, and luxury
revealed under our family name as this made-up, passing-for-white
Hannah person. I thank the Lord Mama is not here to witness such
sinfulness! Mama's laid next to Dad in peace, and Katie your baby
sister, is dead at thirty—from an asthma attack.*

    *But your other siblings, including yours truly, survive, although
we are scattered to the seven winds: Sam and Lizzie are in California, and Emma is in Kentucky. Maggie and Mary are in Boston,
Abigail's in New Orleans, and Hattie lives in Baton Rouge. As for
your favorite sister, Sadie, I have not a clue or a word as to where
she is. She grieved greatly for a while over your disappearance, taking on your way of walking and talking, imitating your airs and
comportment, resembling you in appearance as well as temperament, as if she, and not I, were your twin. She seemed to want to
follow in your footsteps. Then she too disappeared from the face of
the earth. Said she could no longer tolerate Philadelphia or the absence of you and Mama. Only I have remained here, so more than
likely I am the only one of all your brothers and sisters to know the
truth about you.*

    *Mama always said you had substituted prison for slavery, and I
could add felony for pride. God knows I tried my best with Frank*

as my witness to save you from a life of sin and perdition. But this is beyond my ability to comprehend, let alone control— The sporting life you so admired has taken over your soul so completely that even if we met face-to-face, I doubt I would recognize you in the flesh.

Remember how we played together when we were children? I would dress up in your clothes and you would dress up in mine and no one knew the difference, we looked so much alike. Then Dad borrowed this idea for you to dress up as me—when I had scarlet fever to go with him to Saratoga and treat Mr. Sewyer's horse— remember?

"You could be him," Dad said to you—and you said, "I could never be David, I'm not brave enough." And then Dad, he said, "That's not true, because you are one and the same coin—the only thing that separates you is your sex." And you laughed—but I was as mortified as if we had been naked, the both of us, because at the time we were too big to be going around naked in front of each other. And so, Dad took you to Saratoga instead of me—I stayed home, hacking away, looking as if I wasn't long for this world, and you said, "David, don't worry, I'm as strong as a boy—I can work like a man—I even look like one." But of course, you didn't look like one. You were the most beautiful thing anyone had ever seen. You got your head turned all around in Saratoga; I remember. You came back a changed girl. You were never the same after that. You acted like you hated me and Dad and we never exchanged clothes or places again. We got a new house—the trinity house on Addison Street. Then Dad killed himself. We lost it, you know, after Ma's death. The bank repossessed it and we were all out on the street with all the children: Maggie's and Emma's and Hattie's. That's when everybody except me decided to quit Philadelphia for good. Why, Bessie? Why?

I told Clara Hudson where you were but not what you were. But by now she's read it in the papers anyway. I discussed it first with Trevor because that much I knew. After you had been released from the poorhouse, Trevor told me how you had arrived on

Christmas Eve and handed him Clara. Now he says he is going to have to tell Clara her mother is alive and living as a white person in New York.

Poor Clara is the most injured. When Trevor told her the Hannah Elias of the newspapers was none other than Bessie, her prodigal and errant mother, she cried for a week. I backed him up on this reluctantly, but I insisted that there could be no doubt. You were Bessie my twin, Clara's mother, and Monarch Elias's Sugar Pot, his favorite daughter.

I imagine you expect me to ask to share in your ill-begotten gains, seeing that your wealth is immense and mine is that of a Rittenhouse Square hotel porter. I have no intentions of selling my story to the journalists now knocking at my door offering me money for telling what I know about you. Never, never will I reveal in act or word anything of your past life. In recompense, I expect my silence to weigh on the scale of what you owe to your family out of your fortune after all these years, beginning with a decent headstone for Dad and Mama instead of the one they've got, which was not carved by a real stonecutter but only a bricklayer.

I imagine you can also afford to settle a stipend on me that will enable me to quit my job and retire. I have no wife, no children, only a cat named after you.

Oh Bessie, Bessie, why have you walked down the road to perdition? A white whore—a hussy, a public woman? Why, when you were my heart—the best part of me. Half of my heart, my twin! I would have done anything for you— We too could have left Philadelphia and gone West like the others—Oklahoma, Tennessee, Arizona—if only you'd come home . . .

I am your baby brother born twenty minutes after you. Remember how we used to read each other's thoughts? Finish each other's sentences? Used to drive Mama crazy. "Stop that," she'd say. "Stop that witchcraft of talking like you're one person instead of two. Bessie, you can never be a man and David can never be a woman, so just you stop pretending it's so!"

I rescued you from your worst instincts! I tried to save your life and now you won't even recognize me—my heart beat next to yours in Mama's womb for nine months and now, I am like Clara to you—a stranger— Except that I was more to you than Clara—I was your better half—I was the male half of your soul. Who am I now and who's you? I . . .

Hannah let the pages drop. Her heart was a hard, cold ball in her chest—like indigestion. She didn't hate David. He simply didn't exist for her anymore. Had he ever existed? She sat in her window seat overlooking the park, no longer reading the letter. Her eyes took in her beautiful boudoir and searched for pen and a piece of paper in her escritoire.

New York, June 2, 1904

My brother and twin,

I acknowledge your letter of May 31st and your harsh words on my account even though my lawyers tell me not to. I am Bessie and you are my flesh-and-blood brother with the right to think what you will of me, but not to chastise me. No man can do that now.

I promise you nothing, but I acknowledge a family debt if you do not speak any more to reporters or policemen or come to New York and try to see me or opportune me. This is the condition for the recompense you demand of me. You judge me harshly but with an eye to the truth as well as your own pocketbook. I have neither apologies nor excuses to give you. Frank Satterfield was a no-good lying wife beater, and no vow would have made me remain at his side. As my own family had deserted me, Clara would have died had I not given her away. It is true that my ambition set me on a road as straight and narrow to hell as the straight and narrow road to salvation— redemption. Perhaps in all, I've never wanted either. I have never searched for happiness—I have reached for success. Twenty years ago, you washed your hands of me in disgust. Mama followed suit and disowned me. I in turn, changed my name and passed for white. I missed you more than the others, for I believed you indeed to be the best half of myself and that we could no more dissolve that tie than shatter the union of the United States of America. It is now too late to reunite and we can only separate and go on our own ways. I am what I am. You will have your hush money, but I am Bessie no more.

Hannah Elias

1904
CLARA

Give her as much torture and grief
As glory and luxury she gave herself
In her heart she boasts
I sit as queen: I am not a widow
And I will never mourn.

—Revelation 18:7

TWENTY-SEVEN

New York, June 3, 1904,
9:00 a.m.

It was just after dawn. Twice, Clara Elizabeth Hudson had taken the new IRT subway to Eighty-Sixth Street, carrying a little satchel containing a change of underwear, a gun, a copy of her birth certificate from the Blockley Almshouse, and the worn gunnysack she had been wrapped in when Hannah had given her away. She was a pretty, eighteen-year-old, copper-skinned girl with her mother's carbon eyes and coal-black hair.

Clara looked up at the five-story mansion with the chiseled and carved white stone cornices, the sweeping curved steps flanked with its intricate wrought iron handrail that led up to the massive oak door. The second floor had a graceful bay window that wrapped around the facade in stained-glass elegance. To the girl from the Seventh Ward, the house was from another planet.

The New York newspaper articles about Platt's suit had been printed in *The Aurora* and *The Philadelphia Gazette*. Her father, Trevor Hudson, had figured out the rest, and David Elias had corroborated it. The mother who had abandoned her was Hannah Elias, alias Bessie Davis.

Clara rang the bell, unaware that there were two process servers lurking in front of the house watching her, waiting since dawn to serve Platt's civil complaint against Hannah and a criminal one. Hannah could avoid them only by remaining inside. Kato, who could see Clara from the vestibule, had orders not to allow anyone into the mansion under any circumstances. Clara didn't look like a process server to Kato, but one never knew. He was, however, too curious not to open the door a few inches, leaving the latch on.

"Yes, Miss?"

"I would like to see Mrs. Elias, please."

"Who's calling, please?"

"My name is Clara Hudson, and I'm her daughter."

"Mrs. Elias is ill. She cannot see anyone."

"I've come," Clara's girlish voice broke, "all the way from Philadelphia. She must see me."

"Sorry, Miss, but Mrs. Elias has left strict orders."

"My name is Clara Hudson and I'm her daughter, don't you understand—her own flesh and blood!"

"You have a calling card, Miss?"

Clara had attempted to enter her mother's house twice before and had been turned away by servants. She had practically thrown herself in front of her mother's carriage as she came back from her drive in the park, but to no avail. Both times, she had actually encountered Sadie, who of course didn't recognize her.

When Kato refused her once again, Clara took the revolver out of her purse and aimed it at Kato's nose, her hand shaking wildly.

"Let me in," she said.

For Kato, the scene from the previous year came back to him. He felt regret that he hadn't acted to protect Hannah. He had gone over the possibilities in his mind many times. He swiftly snatched the gun from her hand.

"Oh no," he said, "there are too many guns around here."

He held the gun in one hand and had a steel grip on Clara's arm.

"Go home, Miss. This is no place for you. Not now. And this is no place to come with a gun. Don't you see police at the corner?"

"Please, give me my gun back."

"No, Miss."

"I wrote her a letter." Clara slipped her free hand into her coat pocket.

"I'll take that, Miss."

"You don't understand. I am her daughter. Her real daughter." Clara sobbed.

"Miss, you must go. I'll give her your letter. Now go."

"My gun," Clara said.

Without answering, Kato closed the door.

Clara stood pale and agitated on the front steps.

Kato slumped against the interior side of the door. The events of the last year flooded his mind. He blamed himself for Hannah's being shot. He should have opened the door. He had been in the kitchen making tea. The doorbell rang. He stopped to put the teapot on the tray before mounting the back stairs to open the front door. In that minute his mistress had come downstairs, probably thinking Mr. Platt had returned, and opened the door herself. He had heard the report of the gun. By the time he reached the door, Cornelius had fled, and Hannah had fallen backward, unconscious. Kato had had to make a split-second decision: to run after the man and try to capture him, or make sure his mistress was alive. He had held Hannah fast against his chest, checked her pulse, and realized her heart was still beating. He then had had another decision to make: to call the police or not. His mistress had a past to hide. She knew people in the underworld and so many prostitutes. What would she have wanted him to do?

Kato had loosened Hannah's dressing gown and found the bullet lodged in the steel stays of her corset. He opened the corset quickly and saw a dark, ugly bruise. She was seriously stunned by the bullet, and shocked by the event. She had fainted. That was all. Tears of relief stung his eyes.

"Mistress, Mistress," he whispered. "Hannah." There was no time to chase the assassin, he realized. He lifted her in his arms and carried her upstairs to bed. He sent one of the servants, a Chinese girl, to Chinatown with a note to an unlicensed surgeon from Shanghai who specialized in underworld gunshot wounds, asking him to come quickly. He told Francine, who had rushed to the scene, that Hannah had taken a bad fall on the stairs. He decided not to call the police.

The doctor passed smelling salts under Hannah's nose and woke her. He examined the bruise and pronounced her a lucky woman. Her life had been saved by her corset, which had acted as a bulletproof vest. Her ribs would hurt for a few days, he explained, but she would be on her feet in no time. Kato had escorted the doctor to the door. He had handed over a large packet of greenbacks and spoke to the doctor in Mandarin:

"We need protection, the same as last time. We need to find out who did this and why."

But by the next afternoon, everything was clear. The man who had shot his mistress had also shot Andrew Green.

"Cornelius!" his mistress had whispered when she had seen the newspaper headlines. "Now I remember. Cornelius." She repeated his name over and over. She was as shaken as if she had encountered a ghost. When Kato had asked her if she would call the police, she had answered, "The police will call me, never fear. Don't tell them about last night. It never happened. Do you understand, Kato?"

"Yes, Madame. It never happened. Nothing happened." He had cleared it from his mind. And that's how it had stayed all those months, until Clara's pathetic gesture had brought everything flooding back. He would have gladly taken the bullet that had struck his mistress. Hannah was the only one to rescue him from a situation that was practically slave labor when he first arrived in New York. He loved her.

When Kato peeked out of the first-floor window to watch Clara's back recede beyond the wall of the carriage lane, he noted that the summons servers, three of them, still lurked across the street near the park. He pitied the young woman. Maybe his mistress was indeed her mother. Not everyone wanted girl children. That is, until they got older and found themselves alone.

Kato knocked on Hannah's bedroom door and handed her the letter.

Dear Mother,

Your troubles have led me to your side after all these years. I am Clara, the daughter you left with Trevor and Sadie Hudson eighteen years ago.

My desire to see you has nothing to do with monetary claims. I

claim only your recognition and affection as a daughter. I hope you,
too, will claim me at last as your flesh and blood. I am staying with
my father at the Bradford lodging house on Twenty-Third Street. The
telephone is 3119. I have tried to enter the mansion several times
without success. Perhaps we could make an appointment at a place
of your convenience.

    All these years make no difference to my love and need for you. I
beg you to consider this plea. I do not hate you for what you did, and
I hope you do not hate me, even if you cannot love me.

Your obedient daughter,
Clara.

Hannah put the letter on the window seat and stared across the
room, wondering whether there could be any reconciliation now.

With no answer forthcoming, Clara went with her father to a lawyer. They
initiated a suit against Hannah for abandonment, nonassistance to a person in danger, and child abandonment, requesting five thousand dollars.

Soon Clara was ordered to appear in the magistrate's chambers of
the Mercer Street police station before a judge who would issue such a
warrant. Clara had hoped to the very last that she would be greeted with
tears and pleas for forgiveness and open arms at her mother's door. But
the judge wanted proof that Clara really was Hannah's daughter, and that
she was in danger of becoming a public charge, before he would issue a
warrant commanding Elias to open the doors of 236 Central Park West.

Clara's parents were not poor and had been very good to her. She
had lacked nothing growing up, including a mother. She had finished
high school and had attended Dillard Nursing College in New Orleans.
She seemed a sensitive, balanced, and happy young woman. If there were
scars because of Hannah's act, they didn't show.

The magistrate Ommen studied the composed face of the girl who
was suing her own mother. It was as hungry and expectant as the faces in
the crowds that gathered outside the courthouse to get a glimpse of a celebrity, criminal or otherwise. Ever since the Green murder, the details of

Hannah Elias's life had been morning reading for all of New York. Clara's demure, effacing manner standing beside her guardian plainly showed that she was not predatory, nor was she after money. She was just a lost little girl looking for her mother. The judge felt great compassion for her. How could Hannah have abandoned her own child like this?

The judge sighed, shook his head sadly, and signed a warrant for Hannah's arrest.

The case made the morning's headlines in the New York papers:

HANNAH ELIAS'S CHILD IN COURT

Clara had taken the train from Grand Central Station to Duchess County, New York, and the Matteawan asylum. She trudged up the long, pebbled driveway on foot and lied to the director, telling him that she was Cornelius Williams's daughter. For all she knew, it could have been true.

When the guard told him that his daughter was there to see him, Cornelius assumed she had been supplied by the devil. But this sweet, beautiful girl was an angel. She had the prettiest face he had ever seen, with the exception of Bessie. Was this another alienist trick to get him to talk? Or was it a sign from Jesus that he had been washed clean? Cornelius clutched his Bible tighter. He tried to arrange his thoughts, but all he could think of was that the young Bessie of long ago was staring at him with those same devilish black eyes a man could drown in.

Clara sat down and took off her gloves. All the inmates at Matteawan wore red uniforms, which consisted of a loose, one-piece shirt worn outside a pair of wrapped drawers and a small, square pillbox hat like the Turks wore. No suspenders, belts, shoestrings, buttons, neckties, or other dangerous accoutrements were allowed. She took a good look at Cornelius seated on the other side of the lacy steel wire screen that separated them. The thousands of x's made his contours imprecise, fading and then coming back into focus.

"You say your name is Clara Hudson?"

"That's correct. You don't know me. I'm . . . I'm Hannah Elias's daughter. I came all the way from Philadelphia to see her, but she won't receive me. That's why I came to see you. You must know I'm telling the truth. You are the reason I found her after all these years of searching. If you hadn't killed Andrew Green, I would never have found my mother."

"You mean . . . Bessie?"

"Yes, sir."

"What are you doing here?"

"Trying to see my mother, but I've been turned away three times now."

"You mean you haven't seen your mother since you were born?"

"I was born in the poorhouse outside Philadelphia. My mother gave me away to my foster parents, Mr. and Mrs. Trevor Hudson of 1230 Wood Street, when I was a few weeks old. Then she disappeared. She never came back for me. Never. Then I read about Mr. Platt's suit in the newspapers and my father told me it was she. It was my mother. He recognized her picture in the papers after all these years. He had never forgotten her face."

Clara sat there in her white shirt and red bow tie, black skirt and straw hat with checkered streamers, as prim and determined a colored girl as Cornelius had ever seen.

"You aren't my father, are you?" she asked hopefully, her eyes wide and brimming.

"No, sweetheart," said Cornelius. "I ain't your daddy. I'm sorry. But then you wouldn't want an assassin as a dad.

"I killed your mother," he said. "You can't find her. Or you will find a corpse. Even now, her ghost is sitting up there on Central Park; sometimes she comes around here and torments me. I can't get rid of that terrible sick feeling I had the night I shot Bessie."

"You don't see my mother's ghost, Mr. Williams. You see her. She's alive."

Cornelius began to speak as if he hadn't heard her. "They fed on my love for Bessie, telling me she was still in New York, with a house on Central Park and servants and jewels all as a result of her whoring with white men. I remembered how she'd slandered me and mocked me with her yearning over Granville. I remember an old white man giving me an argument about being in Bessie's house. He told me to get out of his way and called me boy . . . just like he did when I shot him. I vowed to get even one day. This was my chance to get them both—Hannah and him, for in truth, I was your mother's only love, her only salvation, the only one of all the men in her life who truly loved her. Only she didn't know it. She didn't even know I was alive. She got a divorce from her husband and disappeared. She began to slander me and backbite me so I couldn't work anymore . . . couldn't find a job and if I found one, couldn't hold it for a minute.

"I knew a lawyer on Broadway I had gone to see about suing Bessie at one time. He was the same lawyer who had got her her divorce from her husband, Matthew, my friend. This lawyer provided me with money and revenge in a neat package. He gave me two addresses. I went to Bessie's first, on the night of November twelfth around nine p.m. I saw Green come out of her house and stand under the streetlamp for a second. Saw his face good and clear. I waited till he left, then I rang the bell. Bessie answered her own door. She opened it wide and stood silhouetted against the marble columns and the curved staircase of her vestibule. She hadn't changed at all. I think she recognized me. At least she suspected it was me. Before she could cry out, I shot her in the heart. "Farewell, Bessie. I'm sending you to hell," I said. She didn't fall at once but stood there upright, a bewildered look on her face. I saw a Jap fellow flying towards me. Then she slumped to the floor clutching her bosom . . . There was nobody on the street. I ran into the park, got into a carriage, and went to find Green at his address. I knew Bessie was dead.

"I paid off the carriage in front of the Murray hotel and parked myself near the Park Avenue subway exit once I got there and thought about Bessie all night grieving for her. I fell asleep and missed Green when he came out of his house to go to work the next morning. So I had to wait until he came home for lunch. Off I went on foot back to my room on Park and got myself freshened up. I went back and waited under the subway kiosk until he appeared and turned towards home. I accosted him and he mocked me, saying, "Get out of my way, boy," just like he had done that day in front of your mother's house. I shot him. His hat flew off. He crumbed into a pool of his own blood and tried to crawl home. I stood over him and pumped four more bullets into him, saving one for myself. But I forgot I had already discharged one bullet at your mother as I sent her to hell. As I stood over him, Green swore with his dying breath that he didn't know any Bessie—didn't know your mother. I had intended to shoot myself after that and be done with it, but I didn't have a bullet left. You know like in a nightmare when you try to scream and scream but nothing comes out. Nothing! No bullet came out. I didn't know anything about John Platt until I read it in the papers, I swear. I regret shooting your mother and Green. I loved Bessie. She was a liar and a jezebel, but I loved the hell out of her.

"And now that you know everything, what do you expect of me?" added Cornelius.

"I want to know my mother. I want to know everything you know about her . . . about her life. What was she like? I want to know why she is the way she is. I want to know why she doesn't love me—why she never came back for me. I want to know why you killed Mr. Green for her. What kind of woman makes a man kill?"

"The way the light plays around your features," mumbled Cornelius, "your hair . . . there is such a resemblance—the way Bessie held her neck, those jet-black eyes. The first time I saw her was when she opened the front door of her boardinghouse at 145 West Fifty-Third Street and smiled at me. Lord Almighty. She was the most beautiful, most fascinating woman I had ever seen. The kind of woman you killed for or you killed, period. Maybe you should ask what kind of man kills another man over a woman," said Cornelius.

"Well, then, what kind?"

Cornelius hesitated for a moment. "A man kills for a woman because he has been made to understand that this is the only route to his own freedom. That without that crime, the woman will never be his and he will always be her slave. The blood you spill unites you both even if you never see her again. She is yours forever. The two of you are bound like when you were a kid and you and your best friend make a pact and seal it by pricking your two fingers and rubbing them together. Nothing can take Bessie away from me now. I killed for her. We are bound for eternity by that murder, Cornelius and Bessie."

"And what kind of man kills a woman he loves?"

"The same kind, Clara, the same kind. Only difference is this time it is to free both of you from love's harsh burden instead of only one. If you kill the other man, you still possess hope. If you kill the woman, you possess only despair."

"Are you crazy?"

"Clara, crazy people don't know they're crazy, otherwise they would drive themselves crazy wondering if they were crazy! Would anyone in their right mind, being a Negro in the United States of America in 1903, in broad daylight, at high noon, shoot a rich old white man five times as he walked toward home with twenty witnesses around? A white man, a millionaire, philanthropist, Christian? Of course I'm crazy."

"Did he say anything?" Clara asked.

"His last words were a lie: 'I don't know any Bessie Davis,' he said."

Clara should have been horrified, but she wasn't. She accepted Green's fate with a shrug, just as she accepted Cornelius's act. No death was real to someone who was only eighteen. The only thing that mattered to her was her mother.

"You make her sound like she is some kind of race apart. Not human like the rest of us all."

"Your mother was a kind of magician, Clara. I've always known that."

"You've known her a long time?"

"Since she was twenty-nine years old. She was always full of stories about Cleopatra and the Queen of Sheba and Jezebel. Know who Jezebel was?"

"Of course."

"Always full of tricks and magic . . . and surprises. No man could resist her, if he was in his right mind. I was crazy and I couldn't resist her."

"You felt sorry for her."

"No one ever felt sorry for Bessie Davis. She had this air of being untouchable, invincible, as if she were protected by a magic spell—or a curse. She never seemed quite real to me. Even now that I've ruined my life for her, she's little more than a dream.

"I expect to go to hell, Clara. I want to go there; I'm going to meet my pa in hell, my cruel, animal-torturing, son-of-a-bitch dad. He'll be there burning. Hell, for a Black man, is probably better than life on this earth anyway. Crazy, I'm not, because I know something crazy people don't know. The devil got to those alienists and put the idea into their head that I was crazy to save my life. He put it in their heads that I would never stand trial. And I didn't stand trial. Man, the devil's the smartest damned angel. He speaks every language, and, strangely enough, I can understand him, even when he speaks in tongues. I can understand him when he speaks French, or German, or Russian or Japanese. Man, if Lucifer told me to go to the electric chair, I would go gladly. I'm not afraid to die."

Clara half rose in her seat, thoroughly shocked. But what had she expected in an insane asylum? She was relieved to see two burly prison guards dressed in long white smocks approach. As they led Cornelius away, he bared his two gold teeth in what passed for a smile. "Bye-bye, my sweet Clara," he called out as he disappeared into the long corridor of the hospital.

An identically clad guard took Clara's trembling arm and led her through a maze of bile-yellow hallways, back to the visitors' station, where she recovered her purse and valuables. She had been unable to bring even a timepiece into the visitor's cage: no jewelry, hatpin, money, tobacco, or medicine. After she signed out, there were more corridors, locks, chains, and iron doors barring her way to the outside world. Cornelius would spend the rest of his life there, she thought in terror. Forever. It was worse than death. An insignificant madman had changed the history of New York because of her mother. Or was it her mother who had changed the history of New York? Clara was shaking uncontrollably by the time she reached the grounds outside.

She tried to fit the pieces of her mother's past together. It wasn't pretty. It had a big hole in it. There were horrible questions, terrible secrets. Did she really want to find out any more about Hannah? Why couldn't she leave her dead? There were accidental deaths, weren't there? And acts of God, and natural disasters? Wasn't her mother like one of those natural catastrophes no one predicted? An act of God? It was not her fault. It wasn't Mr. Green's fault. Neither was it Mr. Cornelius's fault. Was it all because she had been born in the first place? Clara burst into tears.

Clara's father met her at Grand Central Station, and together they took the IRT to Eighty-Sixth Street. A large crowd was gathered in front of Hannah's mansion, with more and more people joining, as if it were a riot or a lynch mob. Then Clara heard someone say, "They're going to arrest Mrs. Elias today on charges of extortion and blackmail."

Upper West Side, New York, June 4, 1904

Hannah's appearance in court was requested in a second case as well.

First, John Platt's lawyers had obtained an injunction against Hannah's assets and a lien on all her bank accounts, which froze all her assets except for $500 in expenses per week. Then, the district attorney obtained a criminal warrant for Hannah's arrest.

Washington Brauns came to her house.

"Jerome has obtained a criminal warrant for your arrest for extortion and blackmail. They are going to arrest you."

Hannah gazed blankly at Washington. No, they weren't. She had vowed she would never serve time again. She was hurt that Platt would go this far.

"Arrest?"

"I would advise you to make a deal with the DA," said Washington. "I'm sure we can work something out even if we have to post bail to avoid arrest."

"You said there wasn't a chance in hell of his getting a criminal mandate against me—there's no proof. None."

"I know. Unfortunately, they must have really leaned on Platt. They are way out of line legally. Jerome is making political hay out of this for his own purposes."

"What can I do? How can I fight this?"

"As long as you stay within the house, they can do nothing. They can't serve the summons. I don't think they'll do anything tonight, and tomorrow's Sunday. They can't get hold of a judge on the weekend to arraign you. Nothing will happen until Monday."

1904
THE ARREST

It appears to be an all-devouring Nemesis, feeding as a hungry lion upon this ruck of wooden provender and this wealth of human life.

—Theodore Dreiser, "The Fire," in
The Color of a Great City

TWENTY-EIGHT

Upper West Side, New York,
June 7, 1904

For two days, Hannah was holed up in her mansion. On Tuesday evening, as the shadows of the trees lengthened in Central Park, she stood in her window, a dark, imperceptible silhouette with a Tiffany lamp unlit behind her, and watched a mob gather outside her front door. They came to witness the arrest and humiliation of the Negress Hannah Elias, who had dared to become the mistress of a rich white man. In Hannah's mind she was Greater New York's Cleopatra, barricaded in her gilded palace, staving off the encroaching Roman army after the defection of her lover. In every scenario, she had become a spectacle. The evening headline in *The Sun* said it all:

LOCKED IN—HANNAH ELIAS AT BAY IN HER HOUSE

Among the straining onlookers lurked summons servers; police detectives, including McClusky; District Attorney Jerome and his assistants; and Chief Hurley. There were out-of-town tourists from every state, and New Yorkers who had come from as far away as Harlem and Brooklyn. A circus-like mix of races, classes, and celebrities had amalgamated into what looked like a free concert in Central Park. A regiment of sporting friends from Hannah's bordellos rounded out the pack, although none would admit to it. They appeared as gentlemen out for a stroll who happened upon the scene and decided to watch.

Bowler hats, flat-top derbies, Borsalinos, fedoras, top hats, and working men's caps all bobbed and weaved among what was predominantly a bevy of multicolored feminine millinery.

Amazingly, in a show of support, women had turned out to bolster Hannah against what they considered a male chauvinist hunting party as scandalous as Cornelius Vanderbilt's fox chase. Their chanting and placard-waving seemed, at times, to overwhelm the police.

"Free love!" they shouted together, and explained as they pressed handouts into the open palms of the passersby that men judged Hannah harshly when they patronized her too. The double standard was unfair, they said.

Hannah's oak door remained closed and barricaded. As she had been instructed by Washington, she refused to come to the door to accept Jerome's arrest warrant. The multitude stood shoulder to shoulder, waiting for a glimpse of her in a shadow or in a fluttering window shade or drawn back drape. The neighbors, at first agitated by the noise, came outside to witness the event too. They were inhabitants of the princely houses along Central Park West, but now they mingled with ordinary people in their desire to know what exactly transpired at 236. Pedestrians and parked carriages blocked traffic. Passengers descended from the immobile trolley cars along with the conductors themselves to watch the circus. Voices from the crowd floated into the interior of Hannah's bedroom.

Clara and her father were also in the crowd, with more and more people joining in a lynch mob.

"They're arresting Hannah Elias today!" someone shouted with glee.

A pang went through Clara's heart, and she clutched her father's arm. This would be the first time that she would see her mother.

"She won't come out!" a voice shouted to no one in particular.

"She's not even in there. She's flown the coop to Mexico," another answered.

Strangers began speculating:

"No, London."

"No, Paris, I hear."

"Nobody there but Jap servants."

The taunts grew.

"Hannah, Hannah, Hannah, come out."

"Hannah, Hannah, Hannah, tell us what's this all about."

"Hannah, Hannah, Hannah, how much did you take old man Platt for?"

"Screw you, Hannah."

"No, screw old man Platt!"

People laughed.

"Platt, Platt, flaccid Platt, wants to get his money back!"

Hearing this one, Hannah put her face in her hands. Was there no end to their shame?

Mounted police attempted to seal off the approach to the mansion. Chief Hurley had sent 360 policemen to Green's funeral, and he needed the same amount to arrest Hannah Elias.

Kato offered the police and the two process servers who had been there since dawn some hot coffee. The deputy sheriff had been unable to induce her to submit to arrest with the understanding that he would immediately accept $20,000 cash bail, doing away with the necessity of Hannah being taken forcibly to jail. Clerks from Warren, Warren, and O'Beirne, who had stood guard all day, were relieved by a new detachment that might have better luck. But Kato had been well schooled by Washington, who had told him Hannah could defy arrest only so long as she remained in her house, and Hannah wasn't moving. The only person Kato was to admit was her physician doctor, de Kraft.

Then the sound of a megaphone took over the whole block. One of the many big electric coaches of the "Seeing New York" tourist company drove past in the thin lane of traffic allowed in front of 236. Over the loudspeaker, Hannah's troubles were described to the thirty or so curious passengers inside:

"On the right, ladies and gentlemen, that house there is where Mrs. Hannah Elias lives. You can see the deputy sheriffs waiting to arrest her on the corner. She is the lady who got $685,000 by telling Mr. Platt she loved him, then by threatening to expose him. Six hundred and eighty-five thousand dollars, folks—just think, that's more than all the folks on this here coach have got between them, and the man is eighty-four years old, too. And when we get down a little bit further to Fifth

Avenue, ladies and gentlemen, we will pass by the corner of Fifty-Fourth Street, the home of her victim, Mr. Platt. On the left, ladies and gentlemen, as you can see, we have beautiful Central Park."

The tourist bus specialized in excursions that drove by the mansions of the rich and famous, homes of celebrities like the Astors, the Morgans, and the Vanderbilts, and pointed them out. The tour operator made sure everyone on the bus knew Hannah was New York's "Grand Horizontal," who had gotten Andrew Green murdered.

At nightfall, the facade of the mansion was lit up like a theater with torches and electric strobe lights, like those used at railroad crossings. Kato was sure now that the police were preparing to storm the house, despite what Washington had said during the day. Then, he'd told Hannah, "The order of arrest doesn't carry with it the right of forcible entry. As long as you stay indoors, you are safe."

Now a winded and red-faced assistant in the district attorney's office arrived at the front door, waving a court order. "This warrant charges Hannah Elias with criminal extortion and blackmail. Arrest her, even if you have to break down the damned door to get at her! That's an order!" He barked through his megaphone, snorting and winking at McClusky as if to say, "Got the bitch at last."

McClusky didn't like what was happening. He was shocked at the violence being used against her. But he recognized it for what it was. Jerome's spectacular entrance. Jerome was meeting the charge of blackmail with his own type of extortion. He had overstepped the boundaries of his role as district attorney. He considered this vaudeville performance just one more of his grandstanding, headline-grabbing raids on vice and prostitution he hoped would land him in the governor's mansion one day.

It was eleven p.m., an ungodly hour to make an arrest of someone who was not going to flee, McClusky thought. One of the assistants in Jerome's office began to ring Hannah's bell, again and again.

After about ten minutes, a second voice shouted through the megaphone, "This is the police! We have a warrant for the arrest of Hannah Elias. If you don't open the door, we will break it down."

Despite herself, Hannah began to shake. From the safety of her sanctuary, she peered out of the window.

Now the crowds saw her. They began to yell and boo. Mounted police pushed and shoved the onlookers. Four detectives were now taking turns kicking in the front door. They broke the ornate glass entry door in front of the mahogany one. Then one of the process servers brought a crowbar from somewhere. The cursing men battered the door with it until the carved wooden panels gave way. By smashing in the remaining panels, they finally got sufficient leverage to pry the door open. The iron bar knocked the precious Tiffany glass out of the upper half of the vestibule door and the latch chain dropped off. The detectives entered; as the gaslights flared, their voices could be heard arguing with Kato downstairs.

"What do you want?" he demanded.

"I am a police officer. I am here to serve this 'ere warrant on Mrs. Elias."

There was a pause as Kato didn't answer.

"Where is Mrs. Elias?"

"She's up there," he said, "with her baby." Muriel Consuela now wailed with the interior noise.

The police shoved Kato aside, and he bounced against the entrance hallway. The men ran up the stairs and burst into Hannah's bedroom after hearing the baby's cries. They found Hannah sitting, while the baby's nurse stood on the side near the bassinette. Hannah was propped up on lace pillows in a dressing gown, hands neatly folded on top of the satin coverlet, staring dry-eyed straight ahead, her perfectly coiffed head thrown slightly backward. Alone in the splendor of her boudoir, she finally resembled her Egyptian queen. Her stillness and eerie calm defied not only the clumsy detectives but even the wild circus going on outside. She felt a disconcerting and sublime otherworldliness, as if she really were a deposed and defeated monarch facing capture and death.

"We have a warrant for your arrest, Mrs. Elias," the officer announced flatly.

"Yes, I've been informed. I must get dressed." She nodded to Kato, who pushed his way through the throng of police, and went to her armoire to find an appropriate outfit. The arrest took place at 11:35 p.m.

❧

The police stood outside the door while Hannah got dressed. Together, they walked down the interior steps and to the front door.

Hannah gasped at the sight of the beautiful mahogany wood in pieces on her foyer floor.

When the people saw her step to the entry, a loud cheer went up from the crowd, which had waited since morning for a glimpse of her. She raised both bejeweled hands, which were handcuffed, in victory like a boxer and started down the steps. Now, with her arms down, she leaned on McClusky to steady her as she walked. He hadn't thought the hand-cuffs were necessary, but Jerome had insisted. After doing his interviews, he stood across the street to take in the entire scene. He grinned.

Kato returned with the victoria, which the detectives objected to because it was open. So Kato trotted off again to find a closed carriage while the detective squad swore and cursed. Despite herself, Hannah clutched McClusky's arm tightly as she waited quietly on the steps, and blinked blindly into the lights.

The *New York Times* reported in the morning on Hannah's outfit: "She wore a long-trained skirt of light gray, a white silk shirtwaist, and a stock of brilliantly checked material with long flowing ends at her neck. On her head was a wide picture hat, trimmed with long drooping feathers, in which were set three big, red roses. Over her gown, she wore a three-quarter-length silk coat of black. From her hat hung a flowing veil which reached to the point of her chin. Her hair was much curled, and was worn in a high pompadour." The paper added, "A single glimpse, and there was no room for doubt as to her race."

As Hannah left in the carriage taking her to the precinct jail, the crowd had begun to disperse. It was 1:15 in the morning. Hannah spent the remainder of the a.m. hours in the precinct jail, since it was too early to take her to the Tombs. She had left Kato sitting forlornly in the vestibule, holding the arrest warrant on which was scrawled: "To be served tonight." He stared at the triple-folded document incomprehensibly. Another of Hannah's servants took a carriage up to Washington's house to alert him of the occurrence.

As Hannah rode in her carriage to the station, she was philosophical about her arrest. The difference between celebrity and criminality, between fame and disgrace, between notoriety and prison, between life on the outside and death on the inside, was a very fine line indeed.

Downtown, New York, June 8, 1904

A livid Washington stormed into police headquarters as soon as he heard. By the time he had received the message from Hannah's servant and gotten dressed and arrived downtown, the sun had risen.

"I am Mrs. Elias's lawyer," he told the desk sergeant. "I want to see her immediately."

"Wait here," the policeman said, pointing to a sitting area a distance away. He hardly looked in Washington's direction.

While he sat on an outside bench, Washington spoke aloud to anyone who passed, "You are really something, you cops. You never would have treated a white woman on Central Park West in the same manner. You have one kind of justice for whites and another for Blacks." He continued to voice his opinion to all within earshot, knowing that they would hardly pay attention to him.

Finally, a detective approached him.

"Where's Mrs. Elias?" Washington asked.

"Oh, Mr. Brauns, *sir*, looking for your *client*, are you? Well, your *client* ain't here, took her down to the Tombs just before dawn this morning."

"But I'm here to post bail," Washington said, alarmed.

"No bail for Mrs. Elias, Mr. Brauns. Direct orders from the DA." He smiled.

"What?" Washington became more agitated.

"Just kidding, counselor!" The detective laughed at his own bad joke. "She's here all right, a little worse for wear. Take your bail issues up with the magistrate's court downtown. The little lady's right in her cell in any case—glad to get rid of her, too hot for us to handle. There's a crowd of reporters and New York citizens outside of here, and there's an even nastier group waiting for her outside the Tombs! I wish you luck, counselor. Don't want any lynching on our watch, do we?" The sergeant beckoned to the guard. "Get Mrs. Elias out here. This is her *lawyer*."

The intended irony was not lost on Washington. But he had seen jackasses like this before many times. So he turned his back and sat again, waiting for Hannah to be brought out.

If some in the crowd the previous night had been pro-Hannah, there were none outside now. He wondered what he would find downtown. Jerome had declared full-scale, all-out war against the woman. Washington could guess the reason. She was pitted now against an entire judicial system rigged against her because of her color. An insignificant feature in the world of the very poor and the very rich—who only knew greenbacks—Hannah's race meant so much to the supposed guardians of culture and morality.

Other women in her profession had been able to slip through the judicial system and continue their assent into the rarified air of white society. None other than P. T. Barnum had gotten the ball rolling with his pure Jenny Lind, a Swedish opera singer put on a pedestal as the epitome of grace and domesticity. Strange to Washington that this scheme worked as Barnum sold it—women should be the silent keepers of the morality of the home—when females were a third of New York's workforce. But these white, middle-class aspirations gained traction and predominated as reformers like Jerome tried to wipe out any vestiges of "working girls"—that is, prostitutes—and God forbid if they were colored.

When Hannah came out of the holding cell and greeted Washington, she looked tiredly into his eyes. She gave him a wan smile, and he shrugged. They walked together with a detective toward the front door of the precinct. Hannah emerged from the building leaning on Washington's arm as newspaper reporters scribbled and photographers' powder flashed in the gray early morning.

Lodged between her lawyer and the detective, Hannah was led down the precinct steps and to the waiting Black Maria. Washington entered with her. Before the lorry started to thread its way through the trucks and buses loaded with sightseers, and as the police were trying to close the prisoner's door, a rush was suddenly made on the vehicle. Arms and hands and faces pushed themselves through the opening. A man grabbed Hannah's sleeve. She screamed. Washington pulled the door closed as the van pulled away from a ragtag band of laughing boys who chased them down the street.

Inside the police van, Washington apologized profusely to Hannah for having left her alone to face arrest and for having underestimated the duplicity of Jerome.

"I'm going to take care of this. Don't you worry," he said.

"I'm not sure this is possible. The circus has already begun," she replied. To herself, Hannah worried about Muriel. Would the baby remember last night—the fear in the air, the invasion, and the sound of the broken glass door and the voracious hordes in the streets? Was she alone with the nurse, crying from nightmares?

Hannah forgave Washington. She knew how inadequate he felt. But then, who would have imagined that John would have betrayed her? Men, Hannah decided, did strange things for money, just as they did strange things with money, like buying women. Yet women gave themselves to be purchased. Men and women in love were even worse, their passions taking over their logical thoughts. At least when money was exchanged, everyone was aware of the bargain. Hannah suspected that both she and Platt had become too enamored of one another to make their relationship work.

Only once had she allowed a conversation with him about his affections.

"You know, I could grow to love you," he told her when they were in the Rockaways.

"You're sweet, Papa. But we live in different worlds."

"I just want you to be mine alone and forever."

She looked at the man so many years her senior, and her first instinct was caution. If she was his alone and cut off from her friends and her world, where would she be when he was gone? She would be lonely and adrift. Would she even have her own house, her fortress against the whims of society—one year a celebrity, the next a criminal? She was safe in the kingdom of her own making. She was free. Platt was sweet but he was still an old man, apt to find more in common with his children and his elite friends as the years passed.

"No thank you, Papa. Let's keep things just as they are."

And now, she knew she had made the right choice. She belonged to no one.

The suit now really concerned Platt's pride, not his cash. He did not want the return of his money, but his dignity. Well, she wanted hers back too. She had vowed long ago never to spend another night of her life behind bars—which was what she had just done.

And that morning, inside her beautiful lingerie, her bosom hurt for her baby. She unwound the scarves around her neck and draped them in front of her chest so that her pain wasn't visible.

She only half-listened as Washington read the warrant out loud, his voice cracking, his hands trembling as they rode down to the Tombs:

> John R. Platt, being duly sworn, deposes and says, "I reside at East 54th Street, borough of Manhattan, city and county of New York. I am eighty-five years of age. I know one Hannah Elias now residing at 236 Central Park West. I have known her for the last seventeen years. All the facts herein related took place in the city and county of New York. In the month of May 1904, Hannah Elias told me she owed some sums of money to persons whose names I do not recall. She also said that unless I advanced these sums whereby she could pay the sums she owed them, she would be sued for said amounts and that she would take the stand upon the trial of such suits and testify that I gave her money and that such testimony would be printed in the newspapers. She then said that if I gave her the sums of money mentioned, she would not say anything about my relationship with her.
>
> "The said Hannah Elias is a colored woman and I was afraid that unless I gave her said sums of money, she would expose my relations with her and I feared the disgrace of such exposure and, induced by such fear and in order to prevent such exposure, I paid Hannah Elias

in the month of May and in the city and county of New
York, among others, the sum of 7,500 good and lawful
dollars of the United States. Wherefore, I charge the said
Hannah Elias with the crime of extortion in violation of
sections 552 and 553 of the Penal Code of the State of
New York."

John R. Platt
Sworn to before me, the 4th day of June 1904
A. E. Ommen, City Magistrate

Hannah finally felt the weight of the last twelve hours. She let out a
string of curses that reddened the ears of Detective McClusky, who sat
with his partner across from her.

Washington reached out his hand and placed it over her wrists shack-
led together. "This will pass, sister," he said. She almost let down her
guard and began to cry. When had she last felt such tenderness? Maybe
never from a man who knew her as a person. Leola and Sadie had always
come to her defense, but a man? Never.

Calmer after taking a breath, Hannah could almost see the gears
of Washington's extraordinary brain, *first*, not second, in his graduating
class at Columbia, as he began to calculate the necessary strategies to get
her released, then exonerated.

When they arrived at the Tombs, as the sergeant predicted, another multitude had gathered.

"Here comes Hannah!" voices yelled, and a couple of missiles hit the
lorry as she descended.

A howl rose from the mob, and for a moment Hannah thought the
police were going to let the crowd lynch her. The police escort had allowed the sightseers to get so close to her that several small objects struck
her head. Everything now hurt. The blows just added to the misery in
her chest. She couldn't breathe as the detectives elbowed their way toward

the entrance and pushed her through the packed bodies. Here too the police had not anticipated the curiosity seekers, and as she mounted the steps of the prison, the crowd sent up a bloodcurdling roar that made her shudder.

"Hannah, Hannah!" they cried together.

Individuals in the mob hollered their own frightening witticisms: "Well, Hannah, how's it going in the jig, Jig?" A group of men laughed.

"A bit different from your palace, ain't it?" someone cried. Hannah closed her ears to the taunts and the shouts of "nigger" and "thief" and the flood of familiar profanity that washed over her. She had heard it all before, she had *mouthed* it all before, in the Seventh Ward and Five Points. She was back on Addison Street as if she had never left, where the world thought she belonged.

In the back of the crowd, however, were a handful of women. Some of them had been at Hannah's house the previous night. They linked arms and chanted.

Hannah could hardly hear their words, but Washington knew them by heart. "Fair Wages. No Rages. No Love Found in the Newspaper Pages."

"So are they with me or against me?" Hannah asked Washington.

"Both, I think," he answered. "They want women to get good-paying jobs so they don't need to become prostitutes."

Hannah thought maybe if she had been able to stay on as a housemaid after her first stint in jail, perhaps she would not have had to sell her body to live. Then again, now she was rich.

When she looked in their direction, they waved their signs in solidarity. The lettering said, WOMEN'S TRADE UNION LEAGUE.

Their presence did make her feel better.

The arraignment courtroom was packed, and police reinforcements were lined up in front of the doors to turn people away. As Hannah stood before the magistrate, leaning on the railing, there was no Cleopatra magnificence about her except the diamond rings on her hands.

William Jerome himself argued for a $50,000 bail to be posted, explaining that criminal proceedings had been brought following the discovery of the extent of the scandal, which he, as district attorney, intended to uncover once and for all.

"If this woman's story is ever told," he said, "there will be *nothing* talked about for days. The $7,500 mentioned in the warrant is only a very small part of a vast conspiracy and fraud. Mrs. Elias should not be allowed to go free. I insist the court demand a bail of $50,000."

Washington exploded, "That's ridiculous! Even Mr. Rothschild's bail was only $30,000! My client's money and real estate have been tied up by an injunction in connection with the civil case. She cannot raise such a bail. I promise to produce her whenever necessary. There is absolutely no proof that this woman has blackmailed anybody."

"I intend," said Jerome, "to present this case to a grand jury, to get an indictment and proceed to trial. So much ink has been spilled over this affair, it has become a public infamy. It threatens to bring the administration of justice in this city into contempt. It has become a farce and a moral disgrace. If this woman is found guilty, I shall demand that the heaviest penalty be imposed."

"Your Honor, I beg you not to fix this bail at $50,000. It is prohibitive. This is persecution, not prosecution."

"They held Bill Tweed on $1 million bail," said Magistrate Ommen. "I shall set the bail as I see fit."

"Fifty thousand is only proper," insisted Jerome. "Anything less and she'd skip town."

Her lips trembled, but Hannah was determined not to let these men see her cry. The hell with all of them.

Magistrate Ommen set the bail at $50,000. Washington was furious. He had already paid a $20,000 bail in the civil suit; this meant a total of $70,000, at a time when a one-pound sirloin steak was 20 cents and a loaf of bread was a nickel. And plenty of people didn't have enough to eat.

Washington, breathing fire, left to obtain a writ of habeas corpus from the New York Supreme Court, charging the award as excessive. Hannah, he argued, was being denied her constitutional rights.

As Hannah exited the arraignment, the news went around the crowd that she was going to jail. Some cheered and shouted at her even louder. The trade union women lowered their signs and blew her kisses and raised their fists.

Hannah was taken across the Bridge of Sighs to the Tombs, where she expected to be taken. But instead Hannah was handed to "Coon's Row," the same place as Cornelius, in another attempt by Jerome to humiliate her. Hannah walked into her cell like a queen, albeit one whose young daughter cried for her at home. Hannah's heart and body ached with every imagined wail.

1904
THE ESQUIRES

How often does it happen that where two individuals are transacting business of vital importance, where fate hangs upon every syllable and upon every moment—how frequently does it occur that all conversation is delayed, for five or even ten minutes at a time, until these devil's-triangles have got out of hearing, or until the leathern throats of the clam-and-cat-fish-vendors have been hallooed, and shrieked, and yelled, into a temporary hoarseness and silence!

—*Edgar Allan Poe, "Doings of Gotham,"*
June 12, 1844

TWENTY-NINE

Downtown, New York,
June 8, 1904

The detective bureau was deserted except for William Jerome, who sat at his desk under an old-fashioned gas lamp, which cast eerie shadows on the walls and his handsome features. He was not alone; August Nanz was sitting opposite him. They were both smoking and the air between them was blue with it, but that wasn't the only poisoned atmosphere between the two men. Neither of them could stand the other.

August was mortified that Hannah was in the Tombs. He hadn't believed she would actually be arrested.

"Platt is bringing all of her bankers into the case too," Jerome told Nanz, who had supplied the account numbers. "All I know is that board members of the most prestigious banks in New York have been calling this office, making 'inquiries' and shaking in their patent-leather boots so hard I could hear the squeaks on the telephone."

The district attorney put his feet on his desk and crossed his ankles, encased in knitted black silk socks, leaned back in his chair, and stared at August with obvious distaste. What was he doing here? The lawyer, up until a few days ago, had been Hannah Elias's legal representative. His adversary. Now, evidently, he had been fired. Or had quit. Jerome didn't know that McClusky had blackmailed Nanz to get the information being used in the suit. All Jerome knew was he had gotten the information and documents he needed to destroy the extravagant Elias.

"I can't allow a clever courtesan to contaminate the reputation of public men like Green and Platt. Elias has subverted good Christian men of property! She is the embodiment of every vice and immoral act on the books. At least she's behind bars."

"What about Mr. X?" asked Nanz.

"Mr. X's name will never be mentioned in our police reports; neither will Mr. Y's."

"Mr. X's description fits Green like a glove and vice versa—same clipped white beard, same height and weight, same expensive tailoring, even the same bowler hat."

"But he is not generally known by the press and certainly the tabloids. It's not as if it was John Astor or J. P. Morgan. Mr. X came into his fortune late in life and has never made an effort to enter high society. He does, however, belong to several exclusive clubs, among them the Metropolitan, the Racquet, and the Cosmopolitan."

"What about the Mr. Green who paid Hannah's millinery bills at B. Altman's department store? Is that still another?"

"Maybe there's a Mr. XXX?"

"Who belongs to J. P. Morgan's Metropolitan Club?"

"They all do, and that's why none of their names are going to hit the newspapers. Believe me, I have every intention of destroying Hannah Elias and disassociating her name from that of Andrew Green, Messrs. X, Y, and Z and any other socially prominent name that comes up!"

"That's why I'm here to help," said Nanz.

"Whatever happened to attorney-client privilege?"

"I didn't know she wasn't white." In truth, he'd suspected that Hannah wasn't Cuban, but she could be whoever she wanted. He certainly was. He didn't know her ethnicity and didn't care. But he knew it mattered to the district attorney.

"You took her money, didn't you? You represented her in her business dealings with the financial world. For all I know, you could have been blackmailing her. Or Platt. Or Green. Or all three—"

"Did she say that?" Nanz suddenly got a chill. Jerome might implicate him even though he had given McClusky the evidence. McClusky was the real blackmailer.

"Might she have? I haven't cross-examined her under oath yet, sir. I'll let you know when I do, if her new colored attorney allows me to."

"As her ex-lawyer, you can't subpoena me."

"Platt's civil case lawyer, Warren, says *he's* going to subpoena Elias if I don't. If she takes the stand, I can cross-examine. There's no controlling her. No one will be able to shut her up."

"Maybe Warren can be persuaded otherwise. Jews can always be persuaded if it's a non-Jew against another Jew."

"And who is this other Jew?" Jerome asked.

"August Belmont. He is named in the case, yes?"

"He's not Jewish."

"His father was Simon Schönberg, from Prussia," Nanz said.

"What's his connection with Hannah Elias?"

"The subway, Mr. Belmont's new subway," Nanz explained, "runs where Mrs. Elias owns three apartment buildings. They sit directly on entrances to the Interborough Rapid Transit, priceless parcels of real estate bought when no one was supposed to know where the exits or entrances would be, to prevent speculation. Andrew Green knew. As the major underwriter, August Belmont knew. As a former bond insurer, John Rufus Platt knew. John Jacob Astor's mansion is on the IRT. So is Andrew Green's, as well as Platt's. If Hannah takes the stand in her own behalf, she will have to make disclosures which will involve a lot of other persons whose names have not yet been brought into the matter publicly."

"Like yours, Mr. Nanz," continued Jerome, "but then I can't tell you if you are going to be cited at the hearing or not. As Mrs. Elias's former attorney, you should know better than I what she's going to say."

"I want to set the record straight on rumors that I was one of the people blackmailing Platt. I was not! You can expect almost anything from that woman. There's no telling what she may say. It would be her kind of trick to bring me into the matter in revenge for my having introduced Platt to my ex-law firm, Warren, Warren, and O'Beirne."

"Is that why you came down here? To tell me you introduced Platt to Lyman G. Warren?"

To the patrician William Jerome, first cousin to Lady Randolph Churchill, nothing was more important than appearances and good breeding. August A. Nanz, despite appearances, had neither. What did Nanz know that he didn't, despite all the investigations of his detective department? He had enough headaches keeping Andrew Green's name clear of any association with Elias. That would be impossible if she went to trial and testified under oath. Jerome had to consider the risk and whether August could help.

"Mrs. Elias is being railroaded," whined August, as Jerome's hand paused over the papers he was signing. "Fifty thousand dollars is prohibitive, and you know she cannot provide it, since all of her money is impounded. You want her to stay in jail forever?"

"So much the better," said Jerome, irritated. "This case involves almost one million dollars. This woman lived by blackmail. I have said it before and I'm saying it now: this is a very serious affair. Mrs. Elias has been levying blackmail on a prominent citizen of this city. Who knows? Maybe more. I reiterate, the harsh bail was necessary. This woman has tried to circumvent the law. Society demands that she be severely dealt with."

"You have no case, Jerome, and you know it. There is not a shred of proof that she blackmailed Platt—not a witness, not a letter, not a confession. She has cooperated with your office and what did it get her? Her door battered down."

"Whose side are you on, Mr. Nanz? If you have information concerning this case, or something you want to get off your chest, do it now or get out. I have no interest in you or your problems except as it concerns protecting Green's name and destroying your former client. May I ask why you no longer represent her, sir? Did she fire you?"

"Yes." Nanz lied again. He hadn't spoken to Hannah or Leola since he took the documents and letters.

"Really? Before or after you introduced Mr. Platt to his present lawyer, who's suing your client for three-quarters of a million dollars? You're a goddamn Aaron Burr."

Nanz started to speak, then thought better of it. Yes. He was a goddamn Aaron Burr. And he had Platt's goddamn love letters too if he needed to use them.

Nanz sat back. The soft leather armchair encased him with bourgeois comfort, even in this hellhole. Jerome could never guess at the enjoyment he took in such a simple thing as leaning back in a comfortable glove leather, deep-smelling armchair. Nanz had been in heaven decorating Hannah's mansion—the pleasure of precious objects, paintings, tapestries, Tiffany glass, Sèvres porcelain, silks, antiques, had given him more pleasure than even sex could have afforded him. In that way, he perfectly understood Hannah. In objects, they found peace, never in other people. Other humans were untrustworthy, unpredictable, and asked questions.

Everybody rich or poor longed for immortality . . . The rich attained it in monuments, medals, decorations, busts, honors, gold, portraits, elegies. Yet they too soon vanished into the dunghill. Ashes to ashes. Everything died except money. Plants, animals, men, stars, worlds, galaxies died. But money never dies; it perpetuated itself into infinity with interest. And the holder felt safer and safer.

Jerome had accused him of being guilty. Of what? Of deserving the good life he was about to partake of? Nanz contemplated his social superior, wrapped as it were in his golden gaslight and his cocoon of privilege, where money took a back seat to morals. How lucky he was!

"My own opinion," intoned the district attorney, his round glasses glinting in the lamplight, "is that a vast system of blackmail in this city is known to everyone but the district attorney's office. I intend to root it out. When you have a situation like this, a man does not sit and wait for crime to rub up against him—he goes out and *finds* it." Jerome fiddled with a folder marked CLASSIFIED on his desk.

So, thought Nanz, this was a real vendetta.

Hannah Elias had pricked his ego and his class pride. He would hound her, but the district attorney didn't know Hannah as he did.

And Washington Brauns was brilliant. If anybody could get her out of this jam, he could. Nanz had betrayed her just to save himself, and now his actions made his stomach feel sour. He was ashamed. She had been a friend.

Nanz rose and left the district attorney sitting alone at his desk. The Tombs, that somber pyramid of darkness where Hannah lay awake on her bunk, was less than a twenty-minute walk away. It loomed, he thought, over vice-ridden, merrymaking Gotham like a great beached whale.

Nanz left the building and started up Broadway toward his office, apprehensive and haunted by Hannah's arrest. When he arrived home, it was late, after one a.m., and he was tired. He entered the foyer of his building. Suddenly, he turned on his heel as a shadow approached him. He scuffled with a man and grabbed him by the lapels. It was McClusky.

"Take your hands off me," said McClusky coolly.

"What the hell? McClusky, you scared the piss out of me! You following me?"

"Just doing my duty, Nanz. I'm assigned to you, you and Miss Hudson, Mrs. Elias's daughter. Jerome has half the Detective Bureau still working on the Hannah Elias case."

"I'm no longer Mrs. Elias's lawyer. So what does this have to do with me?"

"You're going down, Nanz, at the trial."

"But I gave you the information you wanted!" Nanz pleaded.

"I know, but they'll call you as a hostile witness. That, kid, is in this subpoena. There you go." McClusky gave him the papers. "And if I were you, before I went to trial, I'd ask myself why, when you earned good money in legal fees from Mrs. Elias, you decided to double-cross her. And you'd better be ready to tell the DA or else.

"Jerome's got your number. If you lie on the stand or take the Fifth, I guarantee you'll be disbarred. If you *don't* lie, you'll probably still be disbarred. He's reading the report right now. You better pray Jerome doesn't get you on the stand, but you better be in that fucking courtroom on June tenth or I'll have an interstate warrant out for your arrest."

"What? What are you talking about?" Nanz passed the subpoena from hand to hand as if it were on fire.

"Extortion. Blackmail. Fraud. Mrs. Elias may be smart as hell, but she has put dumb faith in the wrong people. She's trying to pass herself off as a high-class white woman. You trying to make people believe you are a man."

"But I gave you what you asked for," Nanz begged.

"Yes. And the fact that you could put your hands on her papers so easily shows that you were involved. You took Platt's money. You double-dealt Hannah. There must be other skeletons in your closet."

Nanz's head spun. Of course, Hannah had other lovers in her lifetime. She ran a bordello. Probably every rich white man in New York passed through her places at one time or another. But everyone knew that and didn't care. "Why are you coming after us now?"

"Haven't you heard? We're cleaning up New York." McClusky laughed.

Nanz turned his back and pulled out his key to the inner door of his brownstone, with McClusky chuckling in the background. Nanz stepped into his apartment and cried.

THIRTY

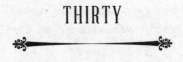

Upper East Side, New York,
June 9, 1904

H ave you ever been mistaken for Andrew Green before?" asked a reporter, in a press conference called by Jerome after Elias had been
put in the Tombs. John Rufus Platt sat dejectedly between his lawyer,
Lyman G. Warren, and his son-in-law. Platt looked up, his clear blue eyes
edged with tears, then shook his head no.

"I don't know that I have, but I probably owe my life to the fact
that Mr. Green was mistaken for me by the Negro. I can't get over that.
I feel so guilty about that." Platt shook his head sadly. "I'm so sorry, so
sorry. His family must hate me. Both Mr. Green and I have white hair
and white beards, about the same length. We both have blue eyes. We
probably wear the same flat-topped derby when we don't wear a top hat.
My barber is on the Upper East Side and so is his. Either on the night
of the murder or some previous occasion, this Negro must have seen me
near Mrs. Elias's house."

"You say 'Negro' with such distaste. Isn't Hannah Elias a 'Negro'?"
the reporter asked.

"Why, I don't know if Mrs. Elias is a Negro or not. I never thought
of her that way. I never questioned her origins, which she said were
Cuban."

"But you have eyes, Mr. Platt."

"I . . . never saw her that way. She was just Hannah to me. I didn't
know what race she was; it never bothered me, it never occurred to me."
Platt looked over the reporter's head to the distant side of the room. Then

he returned to the shooting. "Williams, if you like, probably caught a glimpse of Mr. Green just as he left his family's house at 235 and, supposing it was I who was coming away from 236, followed Green to his own house at 91 Park Avenue. In that way he located what he assumed to be my house. It is evident that the Negro thought it was me when he killed Mr. Green."

John Platt had a hard time pronouncing Cornelius Williams's name, though he didn't know why. He just thought of him as he had been described in the newspapers: a crazy Negro. But, he thought suddenly, this man had a name, this man had a mother, this man had loved Hannah Elias. How many men had loved her and probably still did? This made his heart sink.

Platt had married well and for love. If someone had told him when he was thirty that at the end of his life, he would be involved in a murder, blackmail, fraud, and mistaken identity because of a Black prostitute, he and his late wife, Dottie, would have laughed until they cried. But he wasn't thirty. He was eighty-five, and involved in unfathomable trouble, trouble that did not belong in his world, just as Hannah didn't.

"I'm certainly much obliged to the Negro for not killing me," Platt continued. "It's unfortunate that he should have killed an innocent man."

The reporter asked, "Did Mrs. Elias use the murder to ask for money, saying she would let the public know that it was you, not Green, that her admirer had intended to kill? I understand that she did tell District Attorney Jerome those were the real circumstances."

"I don't know what she told the DA. I don't know what she told anyone." Platt's voice was weak. "I haven't spoken to her for a long time." Here his voice cracked. There was silence in the room because of an uneasy awareness that this was an intensely private man baring his soul in the most public way.

Jack McClusky and Chief Hurley stood in the back of the room, taking notes and hoping they would pick up some information that had been overlooked. *Poor son of a bitch*, thought McClusky.

The reporters continued to press Platt. "Do you feel that she messed up your life?"

Platt had a fleeting thought of her smooth skin under his hand, her perfume. He smiled slightly. He didn't regret knowing her. Then he realized that he was smiling before an audience and he would never see Hannah again. His emotions flipped. "When I realized that I had been taken for a fool. And I was totally alone." Platt glanced at his son-in-law, then continued. "I considered killing myself. I'm an old man. I didn't want my reputation sullied by this scandal at the end of my life."

"What stopped you?" someone shouted from the back of the room.

"I decided, 'I'm going to see it through. Yes, for Andrew Green's sake, I'm going to see this through.'"

"Hannah Elias," he continued in a raspy whisper, "pretended to be fond of me and in love with me for many years. The documents—" Here he looked to Jerome.

The district attorney said, "Since December 8, 1887, to the start of our suit, May 15, 1904."

Platt added, "And during that period she was having relations with her estranged husband and with other men, and she gave birth to two illegitimate children, one supposedly mine and one whose father she did not know." There was strength in his voice now, although he had been given the proof by Jerome, whose techniques were dubious at best— taking testimony from women in jail who claimed Hannah had spoken to them. Hannah herself had said nothing.

The gnarled hands folded in front of his knees hung there helplessly, the fingers entwined. A gold wedding band glinted on his left hand. "I hate this exposure beyond measure, but as long as it had to come, I decided that I would save my family all I could of the $700,000 Mrs. Elias wrested from me. One of my married daughters is living with me at my Fifty-Fourth Street residence, and I have another married daughter living out west, and grandchildren."

"Could you tell us where that is?" asked a reporter.

"I won't tell where or what her name is. I won't drag any more of my family into this scandal."

"Isaac Platt is your brother. Do you have any other brothers or sisters?"

"Yes, I do, but I won't mention who they are. Isaac is my youngest brother and I'm sorry his name got out. I am grateful for his support, for my family's support, and my children."

"Yeah," whispered McClusky to Hurley, "and delivering his bloody mistress to bloody hell on earth."

"I was born in New York City on Cedar Street in 1820. My wife died many years ago and I always tried to lead an honorable life. I was for seven years a member of the Seventh Regiment. I was one of the individuals who raised a company of Zouaves during the Civil War. I was the last president of the old volunteer Manhattan Company firemen, so I've been a soldier and a firefighter all my life. It comes pretty hard for an old soldier to be disgraced at the end of his career."

"Bull," said McClusky, who turned away in disgust.

"He'll make a great witness," said Jerome, who'd come to stand beside the detective. "There won't be a dry eye in the courtroom. Let's hope he isn't a cadaver tomorrow."

John Platt rose, and, supported on either side by his son-in-law and lawyer, left the Plaza Hotel suite, which had been rented for the occasion.

McClusky opened the evening edition of the New York *World*. There was a huge headline with a photograph of Hannah Elias's bejeweled hands. It read:

MRS. ELIAS HELD ON $50,000 BAIL. WOMAN MOBBED!

The other reporters were at their desks working on evening deadlines so that all the newspapers in all Greater New York would have headlines screaming Hannah's name.

The flood of publicity from Andrew Green's murder and Platt's blackmail suit had made Hannah a celebrity. The affair had become a cause célèbre for New Yorkers white and Black.

Both Platt's and Hannah's lawyers were angry and bitter, but for different reasons. Lyman Warren was angry because District Attorney Jerome had practically taken over the case, deciding everything there was to decide, bullying Platt, and giving interviews to the press. Warren had objected to criminal charges being brought against Hannah in the first place.

As for Washington Brauns, he was appalled at the miscarriage of justice and procedure going on: the bandit bail, the raid on Hannah's home, Jerome's refusal to inform him of any action against Hannah when he had specifically telephoned to say he would deliver Hannah to him any time or place as requested.

He was especially outraged at the affidavit of Platt used as the excuse to have Hannah arrested. It was vague, it did not state when and where the "crime" had been committed, and it contradicted Warren's civil suit complaint. But Washington's only hope now was a direct confrontation in court, under oath, between Hannah and John Rufus.

The new bail hearing was a fiasco. Bail had been set at $50,000 in the criminal case and $20,000 in the civil case, making a total of $70,000. It was reduced by $20,000 by the presiding justice. The crowds in the courtroom roared their approval or disapproval. A fistfight broke out in the hearing room, along with a chorus of insults. It was the first time in the history of the old Tweed courthouse that a sitting justice had had to rise from the bench and yell at the top of his lungs to restrain the mob, which seemed determined to overwhelm the prisoner.

Hannah was allowed to dress for her bail hearing. She wore a soft blue silk skirt and gold-colored blouse with a print. Her long-sleeved jacket looked smart and professional. Her hair had been coiffed by a fellow prisoner before she left.

Now, with the bail hearing over, a new demonstration broke out as Hannah rose to leave. The court officers tried to make way for her, but they were outnumbered, twenty to one. In the struggle, she got knocked from side to side in the narrow lane police provided her. The judge, furious, jumped to his feet and fairly shrieked for order in the court. She was finally bundled out, and the doors shut on the public still left inside.

Hannah had hardly reached her cell when half a dozen people begged for permission to visit her. There was Kato with fresh clothes, carpets, linens, a picnic basket, and soap. Francine was there with kimonos, slippers, and hairbrushes. There were several ex-employees who remembered her kindness. There was Leola in her best hat, and there was Clara Hudson clinging to the arm of her father. She carried a satchel, a bouquet of flowers, and a large box of chocolates. But she was turned away.

"But I'm her daughter," cried Clara. "I have a right."

"Nobody has any rights here, Miss, unless the warden says so," said the guardian, "and he says only Mrs. Elias's domestics are to be admitted. Period."

"But I'm her domestic," shrieked Clara hysterically. "I am her slave, do you hear me? Her flesh and blood."

But the guard turned a deaf ear, and the others turned to look at her curiously.

"Oh, God!" sobbed Clara. "I am her slave. I am. I am!"

Standing by, Leola was shocked. Hannah had told her Clara was dead. Why had she lied all these years? And why hadn't she claimed Clara when she had the money to do so? The two eyed each other like two ends of a question mark, but neither of them broke their silence. Clara, out of ignorance, and Leola, out of knowledge.

Hannah agreed to receive only one person that day. She asked for Leola, but she deferred to a veiled stranger wearing a spectacular piece of millinery and carrying a picnic basket. She swept past the last coterie while guardians carried Hannah's lunch. The woman's identity was revealed immediately to Hannah, and later to her lawyer.

Just as the story of Hannah's outrage at the Minnehaha soda fountain had taken on a heroic spin among the Sisterhood, her recent headlines in the New York papers made her a larger-than-life figure. She was the woman they all wanted to be, especially the Philadelphia girls in Mrs. Truitt's establishment. Hannah had played the game with the rich men of New York and won.

When they saw the amount of money that Platt wanted returned, they laughed and said that he had given it to her in the first place. "No take backs," the younger ones called to one another over the dinner table. The women who had been longer in the business dreamed as they went through the motions of sex that they too could find a rich benefactor. But the prospects were slim and far between, as were their energies to pursue Hannah's goals.

Mrs. Truitt, out of curiosity and pride that one of her girls had gone so far, told the women one night, "Let's go and visit her."

She instructed everyone to turn faster tricks and hustle up more customers for a few days. The bordello was a hive of activity where men came and came and went out of the door. With this motivation, Mrs. Truitt also cashed in. Hannah's fame was good for all—except perhaps the clients who felt rushed. The women, however, were proud of their work ethic and their possibilities and, soon, of their wardrobes, which Mrs. Truitt picked out as meticulously as a girls' school headmistress.

With the money they earned, after her cut, the madam went on a shopping spree for hats, skirts, blouses, and traveling coats for all her charges. The demure outfits made them look like students from Vassar.

They were within the crowd yelling at Hannah when she left her arraignment and went to the Tombs. Some of the younger women cried at the words she was called.

"Dry your eyes," Mrs. Truitt told the tearful ones. "Don't let them get the better of you. Did you see Hannah moping? This isn't her first time behind bars."

"But what if she loses?" one of the women asked.

"She never loses," Mrs. Truitt replied, knowing full well that Hannah had a way of often ruining the good chances she was given.

Leola met Mrs. Truitt and her girls downtown when Hannah was taken away to the Tombs the previous day and, afterward, took them uptown to see Central Park and Hannah's house. As they stood in front of the building, now empty of newspapermen and police, they watched Kato directing the workmen to repair the door.

"This way," he directed them as they carried a new glass entry, even more ornate than the last, this one reinforced by iron filagree. Then for a moment, someone appeared behind the door, a shadow that darted out, then disappeared.

Mrs. Truitt noticed. "That's Hannah herself!"

"It can't be," said Leola, knowing full well that Sadie had exposed herself momentarily, then left after seeing people staring at the building.

"It's Hannah. I know her figure, her height, everything." Mrs. Truitt grew louder and louder.

"Sisters," Leola called to the women from the bordello. "Do you see that pathway into Central Park? It will take you into the most beautiful arboretum. Mrs. Truitt and I will wait for you here."

The young women went off with mouths agape to promenade through the park, pleased by the attention of the strolling male patrons.

"Come with me," she told Mrs. Truitt. Then she took the woman to the front door of Hannah's house, said hello to Kato, and they entered.

"Do not be surprised," Leola said.

But the old woman gasped anyway.

"This is Hannah's sister, Sadie."

Sadie stood quietly with her hand out to greet Mrs. Truitt, who gawked as Leola picked up her hand to shake with Sadie.

"Let's go upstairs," Leola said.

The three women went into Hannah's bedroom. Mrs. Truitt had never seen such extravagance. She began counting to herself the amount of money necessary to decorate a room with such gilded mirrors, antique furniture, and plush rugs. Then she gave up. She had arrived at a sum that was impossible to imagine.

She sat down on one of Hannah's peacock settees, and Sadie and Leola perched on a facing sofa.

Leola spoke first, "We need your help."

"Of course. Bessie was one of my best and a good girl at that," Mrs. Truitt replied. "I thought she might get married. But seems like she did better on her own."

"Except that she is in the Tombs now," Leola added. "And she needs to get out. For her baby and for her life. Muriel has cried nonstop since she left. I know that she has complained to the lawyers that it is unusual punishment to take a mother from a nursing infant. But most of these men don't care and don't understand. They want her behind bars."

"What can I do?" Mrs. Truitt asked, leaning forward.

"You can take Sadie with you when you visit the prison tomorrow."

Sadie, obviously already in on the plan, nodded her head.

"Sadie is going to go into prison for her sister. Hannah is going to come out and take care of the baby and her business."

"What if she is convicted?'"

"We'll cross that bridge when we come to it."

Then Leola turned to Sadie and asked, "You're not afraid, are you?"

The young woman shook her head.

Mrs. Truitt wondered how she would survive: Sadie was so obviously not a sister in any other way but family.

On the same day that Platt gave his press conference, Mrs. Truitt rounded up her group from Leola's boardinghouse, where Sadie met them. None of the young girls with Mrs. Truitt had ever seen Hannah, so when she introduced Sadie as another working girl taking the trip with them to the Tombs, the others paid no mind to her.

Sadie was dressed plainly and modestly, her face painted so that it hardly resembled her sister's—only her height could give her away. Sadie made up her face like a church girl on an outing, very carefully and poorly so that she would not resemble the woman now in the Tombs. She put on lipstick in a color that Hannah never wore and reddened her cheeks so much that she looked silly and overenthusiastic. Her face was powdered white. No one would readily look at her at think, "She looks like Hannah on Coon's Row." Still, Sadie wore a large hat and a thick veil.

The women set off to visit Hannah. Leola had obtained a note from Washington that identified them as a church prayer circle. It seemed a little bit odd that these women would carry a basket of food from Delmonico's.

Still, when they got to the prison, Mrs. Truitt explained that Hannah Elias was accustomed to the best and they wanted to placate her—before inviting her to worship. Then the guard said they could not go through.

"That will be one visitor at a time," he said.

Mrs. Truitt pleaded, but to no avail.

Finally, she squeezed Sadie's hand, looked her square in the eye, and said, "She'll bring the food."

The guard made Sadie lift her veil, and Mrs. Truitt took a breath. She could see that Sadie's overly powdered demeanor made him groan a little in disgust and look away. She looked very unattractive.

The veiled lady in the splendid millinery opened the picnic basket carefully, spreading the dazzling white napkins and settings of silverware and glasses on the concrete floor of Coon's Row. She arranged the fruit, foie gras, salmon, lobster, and wine in the middle.

"There's one thing I can't do for you, dearest—nurse Muriel."

Sadie Elias leaned forward and whispered the plan that Leola had created. Hannah put her hands together in prayer, making sure not to clap. She was so grateful.

Sadie continued, "At home, I managed to do everything. The monies have all arrived. The last transfer to London was made a while back. It went as well as if you had been there. They never questioned anything. Mister X, Y, and Z are expecting you."

Hannah leaned over and kissed her. The sisters dressed exactly alike, walked alike, and talked alike. They could wear each other's shoes and clothes, gloves and hats. It was impossible to tell them apart.

Sadie and Hannah together devoured the contents of Delmonico's picnic basket just as they acted as coconspirators to Delmonico's best patrons. The masters of the world, the Wall Street barons, the princely bankers, and the captains of industry thought by patronizing Hannah that they had purchased the time of an empress horizontal, unique au monde. Those three most expensive words, which characterized jewels, horseflesh, mountaintops, art—the one of a kind—as applied to Hannah, however, was a ruse. They may or may not have, depending on the day of the week, the circumstances, Hannah's disposition, a whim, or simply commerce. They believed that because they could possess anything they desired, they could possess the Hannah of their dreams, when they may have had only a counterfeit company or had dinner with Sadie, a stranger.

"Have you seen Clara?" Hannah asked her sister.

"That's one substitution I won't make," said Sadie. "I'm her aunt, not her mother."

"That's just the point. You could explain everything."

"She'll forgive you, Hannah. Children are hard, even brutal masters, but they're still children."

"She's brought suit against me."

"Well, what would you have done in the same situation?" Sadie said.

"I became a survivor," Hannah said. "And, in all fairness, Clara is dead to me. I had to believe it was so. I cannot resurrect her now."

"But Hannah. You saved your daughter by giving her away. You've actually done a lot for others in your own way."

Hannah sighed and wondered if Sadie might have been telling the truth. She did do a few things right, even if she'd started out wrong. Giving her daughter away was one of them.

"Find her, talk to her," begged Hannah.

"No, Bessie. I won't do it. Not now, not ever. You're her mother. You talk to her. That's all she's asking for, I imagine. A word from you."

"Maybe when this is all over."

Hannah changed clothes with Sadie. She left the same way that Sadie arrived and said nothing to Mrs. Truitt until they were inside the front door of 236 Central Park West and the group of young women were waiting in front of the park.

In the foyer of Hannah's house, she heard her baby cry. She ran up the stairs and into the nursery.

Francine cried out when she saw Hannah, her eyes filled with tears. Hannah took Muriel in her arms.

Downstairs, Kato bowed deeply to Mrs. Truitt as he let her out the front door to join her group of Sisters. Mrs. Truitt knew how to keep a secret, and she loved Hannah as much as she loved anyone. So there was no doubt that the police would not get the true identity of either sister from her. She worried that Sadie might get stuck in jail forever. What if Hannah lost the case? But for the moment, she put that out of her mind.

❧

Because Sadie was privileged to have her own cell, even if on Coon's Row, she didn't need to worry about being found out. Once she washed her face with the cloth that she'd brought in the picnic basket, none of the guards knew the difference between the women. All colored women looked alike anyway.

❧

There were other allies who came to Hannah's defense once the story appeared in the newspapers.

To many in New York, the word "Negro" was a badge of honor.

That afternoon, J. Frank Wheaton, one of the seven other Black lawyers licensed in the borough of Manhattan, sat in Washington Brauns's Nassau Street office next to Leola Pershing. He had come to work as a community representative in Hannah's defense.

"Colored people are very angry at how Mrs. Elias has been treated," said Wheaton. "They are outraged at the attack on her house and the excessive bail imposed on her by Ommen and Jerome. Hannah's Fifty-Third Street brothel employees, her butler, her cook, and her maids had come to offer their aid to her lawyers.

"Ms. Pershing and I are here to introduce two witnesses in defense of Mrs. Elias: Mary Scott and Richard Smith, who have been employees of Mrs. Elias's for eight years."

"Mrs. Scott is the cook, and Mr. Smith is the butler at Mrs. Elias's West Fifty-Third Street establishment," added Leola.

"Mrs. Scott and Mr. Smith will be made the complainants in a suit for bribery against three men," said Wheaton. He would bring the suit as the representative of two "Negroes," Richard Smith and Mary Scott," clarified Wheaton.

"Let's call them for the moment Mr. X, Mr. Y, and Mr. Z. One is a real estate developer, one of the most prominent in the city; the second is a politician who is a national figure; and the third is a Wall Street banker and financier."

"Some months ago," intoned Leola, "a number of Hannah's employees who knew the names and faces of prominent men who had, in the past few years, visited either Mrs. Elias's Sixty-Eighth Street or Fifty-Third Street mansions or were regular customers at such establishments were approached by an agent of Mr. X, Mr. Y, and Mr. Z and were promised large sums of money for their silence. The cook and the butler at Fifty-Third Street were singled out as having particularly dangerous information. They were offered a large amount of money by these men to maintain their silence. The sons of bitches. I only found out a day or so ago," she added.

"Unlike the numerous white show girls and actresses who received their hush money through their lawyers, Mary and Richard have not been paid this money," continued Wheaton, "and it is these two counts for hush money payment that I, at Madame Pershing's and the colored community's request, am going to pursue in court as a bill of complaint, where the names of the men involved will be made public in the course of the proceedings."

"True," said Leola, "it is a bit unusual, and Hannah might not approve, but it certainly is going to raise hell on Wall Street. They will mention the names of all the men who visited there and tell many things." She grinned.

"I will make them tell of the visits of men who are respected not only in New York for their commanding positions in the social world, in trade, or in politics, but known also throughout the country," continued Wheaton.

"Whew," whistled Brauns. "This is the most bizarre and Machiavellian scam I've ever heard of." Washington Brauns was shocked into awed silence. Then he exclaimed softly, "I'll be damned. This is the smoking gun. Thanks. Thanks a lot. You have the names?"

"Of course, we have the names!"

"Moreover," continued Leola, "the wife of one of these men did considerable business with Hannah, real estate deals from which Hannah derived a commission as well as jewels and clothes. Those blackmailing, backstabbing sons of bitches deserve no pity!"

"Oh, my friend—" Washington laughed until tears came to his eyes. "This, this is truth. This is justice. *This* is help! Wait till I tell Hannah . . ." Then he set back for a moment, thinking.

"No, I don't think I will tell Hannah. Not for the moment . . .

"Hope you'll be in court at Hannah's table with me, Frank," he continued.

"I'd be honored to carry the ticking bomb," said Wheaton.

"And I'll be there for the detonation," said Leola. "Hannah made a promise never to reveal the names of her lovers. But Mary and Richard didn't."

"You know the names, don't you, Mrs. Pershing?"

"Most, not all."

"But you would never go against Hannah's wishes, is that it?"

"Yes, unless . . ."

"Unless it was to save Hannah, isn't that right?"

"Yes, that's perfectly right," said Leola.

"And they didn't approach you earlier?"

"Of course they did. Do I look like someone who would betray her best friend for money? There's not enough money in the world."

After a brief pause, the diminutive redhead Leola added, "Well, I have other news." The two lawyers looked at her and wondered what more she could tell them.

When she explained there was no way that Hannah was going to be convicted, because she was not even in jail, they almost fell out of their chairs. It was an outrageous defense, but this was a crazy case.

THIRTY-ONE

All throughout Manhattan,
June 9, 1904, Evening

T hat evening, Sadie had dinner quietly with the other prisoners and went to her cell. It was tolerable, considering her past. When Hannah had lived at home and taken care of the younger children, they had slept sometimes in a barn, or four to a bed. They were cold and hungry often. She could tolerate the Tombs. At least, she could keep to herself.

The other women in the cellblock noticed a difference in her comportment.

"She's not acting so uppity, you think?" one asked another.

"I think she is just sad. Leave her alone."

They were impressed at how, in less than twenty-four hours, a rich celebrity had adjusted to prison life. She even seemed to find it interesting.

"I think she's nutting up," said an older cellblock mate. "I'm keeping my distance from her $70,000 ass."

"Big difference from your two-dollar can, huh?"

"Shit, you fifty-cent bitch!" the last woman said, and they all laughed.

Clara sat in the window seat of her hotel room on Nassau Street. She was weary but wide awake. She and her father had spent the morning at the Tombs trying to get permission to visit Hannah. They had gotten further today than ever before, and for a moment Clara thought that the encounter was really going to take place. Their lawyer had accompanied them to the warden's office, where Clara explained her dilemma. The warden had been quite sympathetic and had sent a prison guard to Hannah's cell with another note from her.

> *Dear Mother,*
> *We are in the Tombs waiting for a chance to meet with you. Please let us in. Please. Whatever quarrel we have between us is annulled by the gravity of your situation and I want only to assure you of my loyalty in this time of trouble. I don't care if it is here, in this time and place, that we must meet. What is important is that we must meet as mother and daughter.*
>
> *Sincerely,*
> *Clara Elias Hudson*

But Hannah had refused her as a visitor, just as she had as a daughter. She had been turned away with a look of pity by the warden.

And now, before the next day's trial, Clara lit a candle and got down on her knees. She prayed for her mother's freedom, for her mother's soul, and she prayed for her mother's sins. She also prayed for her mother's arms.

Clara always carried a Bible with her, and she opened it and read randomly until she fell on Moses's commandment to honor your father and mother. She did not even know who her father was. Perhaps her mother knew, or perhaps she did not. She had no one to honor except the parents who had raised, loved, and protected her. She chided herself for wanting more love, but she did.

Nanz had the letters delivered to John Platt's palatial mansion on Fifth Avenue into the capable hands of Arthur. He placed them on a silver tray and took them to Platt in his two-story, cathedral-shaped, oak-paneled library, which looked out onto the park except that the windows were so high one didn't see Central Park filtered through the stained glass. Platt descended the wrought iron steps that led from the second-floor gallery to the ground floor dressed in a pearl-gray silk smocking jacket with a black ascot instead of a white shirt. Arthur recognized his employer's own handwriting but like the good valet that he was, he showed no emotion as John Platt's eyes widened in recognition. They were his letters to Hannah, delivered into his hands so that they would never see the light of day.

All afternoon he read and reread them, sitting in front of the huge renaissance-style fireplace that blazed with hickory wood.

> *Dear Hannah,*
> *You are probably the most beautiful woman I have ever met. My time with you is magical. I feel alive again.*

Platt wondered why his lawyers hadn't prevented the criminal suit. Why had he allowed the district attorney to bully him into an accusation that might send Hannah to the penitentiary for years—over money? Even for three quarters of a million dollars. He had enough money. There was still plenty left.

> *Dear Hannah,*
> *The moonlight becomes you. I love the way your skin shines. And the sugar! Oh my!*

For a moment, Platt laughed aloud. Then he began to cry bitterly.

Hannah had been a young girl when he met her, and he had been in the shadows of old age. She had given him pleasure and life and laughter. True, he had suffered the constant damnation of jealousy and ridicule. But her affection for him, he was convinced, had been real. The brazenness and the lewdness of the anonymous photograph with no return address had driven him insane. To save his pride, he lost himself.

> *Dear Hannah,*
> *Take this cash and buy something pretty. Let me see you in it, and then out of it.*

He read until late in the afternoon, tears often rolling down his cheeks, a sob catching in his throat. He grabbed for a pen and paper and placed them in the pocket of the suit he would wear in the morning to court. Platt made a plan so that he could save his dignity and hers. He sat in his winged Moroccan leather armchair and wept tears of regret and relief, of love and hatred, of despair and loneliness, his head thrown back against the soft, smooth leather. His Yale signet ring glittered in the penumbra as his head tilted slightly onto his left shoulder and he dozed off.

Arthur came in and closed the drapes. On the table beside Platt was another package that had come in the mail: books he had ordered from Paris from the publishing house Bibliothèque Charpentier. Among them was a book that had made a sensation on the Continent by a writer named Émile Zola, entitled *Nana* . . .

Hannah had walked out of the Tombs at 11:45 a.m. and into Leola's waiting carriage, leaving Mrs. Truitt to occupy herself with the Sisterhood girls downtown. They drove like madwomen uptown to 236, arriving at 12:45 just in time to feed Muriel Consuela. Hannah then bathed and dressed in a black-and-white striped silk dress with an embroidered short vest of grosgrain, and a large black hat with white ostrich feathers and a chiffon bow.

She called on her new telephone the office of Mr. X to say that she would be stopping at the office at approximately 3:45 that afternoon. She then called Mr. XX to propose a closing meeting on their deal at the Plaza Hotel at 4:45. She set another appointment for cocktails with Mr. Y at 6:00 p.m. at the Waldorf, and, finally, she invited Mr. Z to join her for an early dinner at Delmonico's on Broadway at 7:30. This was her last real estate deal. She had already transferred most of her capital out of New York to London, leaving only nominal balances in all her current accounts. This was real estate and the subway, her whole empire of interlocking deals she had made in Saratoga and the gentlemen who had traveled upstate to see her in their Pullman cars. Hannah decided to take her own carriage and coachman, who were the fastest in New York, slipping back out of her house to the stables by the secret passage.

At the bank, she convinced Mr. X that she had no intentions of sharing her little blue notebook with anyone. However, she could not guarantee the actions of Mr. XX would be as discreet. She then complained to Mr. XX at the Plaza Hotel that although Mr. X was his friend and partner, she had doubts about his ability to withstand the interrogations of the Detective Bureau. At cocktails with Mr. Y, she complained about Mr. XX's inability to keep everyone's secret life secret, but she would do her best to make sure no leaks occurred on her side. Finally, in one of Delmonico's private dining rooms, she assured Mr. Z of her undying alliance and faithfulness come what may. Everyone was terrified.

None of the nervous men, all of whom had thought Hannah was imprisoned in the Tombs, could figure out how she was standing there before them as a free bird. Their red socks burned with panic and humiliation. What on earth was Hannah going to say on the stand the following day?

A collective tremor went through their balls. This was unthinkable! White as flour and trembling in their white-spatted black patent-leather shoes, they all signed their previous deals with her, which she then countersigned.

"Oh," she said, "they let rich people out on parole at night so they can sleep on their own furniture."

She added, "I will be in court tomorrow morning as sure as the sun rises in the east and sets in the west."

And she was. She was also home to feed Muriel Consuela at 10:30 that night, having completed all her business. The next day at dawn Kato and Leola would bring Sadie her outfit and millinery for the trial. Hannah would be dressed in a duplicate hat and veil except that over her dress she would be wearing the nondescript white collared smock of a Saks Fifth Avenue saleslady, name tag and all, and none of her jewels under her gloved hands.

At eleven p.m. Hannah collapsed into her beautiful bed with plumped pillows and French linens. The richly colored kimono she wore glowed. She pulled the hair away that had fallen into her face and gazed at her child nestled under her arm near her side. Beautiful Muriel Consuela— with the Spanish name of her mother's intended Cuban identity. Who knew the way Muriel's life would unfold?

Even though the trial was the next day, Hannah was not afraid. With Muriel next to her for a few hours, all was right in the world. She hoped only that Sadie would not have to get up and speak on the stand. That might be a problem.

Cornelius Williams had decorated his cell at Matteawan asylum by pasting newspaper articles and illustrations of himself and Hannah, her houses, Platt, and all the other actors in this melodrama, given to him by the guards, onto the walls. The newsprint screamed their headlines across his cubicle like ticker tape ready for a parade.

SOUL'S SALE TO DEVIL TOLD BY GREEN'S SLAYER
GREEN'S SLAYER PUZZLES EXPERTS
ELIAS WOMAN IN TOMBS
POLICE SMASH IN DOORS WITH AXES

Photographs, sketches, and magazine interviews papered the walls from ceiling to floor. The guards had given up trying to keep him neat.

"Let him have this pleasure," one told another.

"Yeah, he don't have any mind."

Cornelius had talked to more than two dozen reporters in the past seven months. He loved nothing better than reading about himself. He had cheated death, or so he believed. He had prevailed over fate and a Black man's annihilation. The Bethesda angel had saved him, and he was grateful. He was delighted to be crazy. Cornelius tore out still another newspaper article in the illumination of the moonlight flooding the barred window. He thought about Bessie—everything about her, the way she dressed, the way she smelled, the sound of her voice, her touch, her hypnotic eyes, the texture of her skin, its incredible color, and her incandescent, unbelievable smile.

His thoughts turned to sitting behind her in church, blowing on the boa feathers of her magnificent red-plumed hat. Music, he remembered, had always moved her—gospel and ragtime. At one point in his life, he had wanted to be a bass player. Bessie had played the piano. He imagined the two of them playing a duet together. She played and laughed with him, sitting close, her scent invading him like a regiment in step.

That was in another life, he reasoned. That was yesterday. Cornelius decided it was time to sleep. He sat on the side of the bed. He nodded curtly to Andrew Green's ghost sitting in the corner, he then fell back, flinging his left arm across his face as if he feared some kind of blow from that white, immobile figure.

Matthew Davis sat on the strap seat at the end of the dark, red-carpeted corridor of the Pullman car train on its way to Cincinnati. The corridor seemed to stretch on forever as he counted the pairs of shoes left outside the compartments that still had to be polished. They reminded him of tombstones in a cemetery, the dim light reflecting off patent leather, calfskin, and alligator. He held his brush and one shoe loosely, unable to set his hands in motion. Finally, he buried his head in the crook of his arm and closed his eyes. All the papers that the passengers had brought into their rooms had his wife's name in the headlines. The steam engine seemed to hiss "Bessie" each time the train stopped at a station, and the lights outside the moving train window seemed to flash images of her in a sparkling evening gown over and over again.

He still hungered for her, even though he had given her up so long ago. He had never remarried. Never had a steady woman. Bessie hovered like a spirit over everything he did or said, over this train and the next station, over Pullman, Illinois, with its Pullman hours and its Pullman stores, its Pullman schools and Pullman hospitals. He was a Pullman man.

He saw a red light go on beside compartment number 12 and he hurried down the hall and knocked sharply on the door. "Can I be of help, sir?"

"Oh, yes, boy, I'd like a bottle of whiskey and a bottle of soda water."

"Right away, sir. Anything else, sir?"

"Not a thing." The man winked and indicated the naked woman within. "We're just fine."

Matthew flushed and averted his eyes. How could this fellow allow a strange man to view his wife? Mistress? Harlot? But then he realized that the rider didn't see him.

To the Black people in his community, he was put on a pedestal. He was a Pullman porter, a steady man with a good job. But on this train and every train and every street in America where whites looked at him, he was invisible. He was simply any Negro. He didn't have eyes and ears, a brain or a dick. He was simply the Pullman porter.

Granville Woods sat at the large oak table the hotel director had installed for him in his suite, at the new Gilsey House Hotel at Twenty-Ninth and Broadway. It was one of the few first-class hotels that accepted Negroes, Jews, and ladies' lapdogs. But Woods stayed there when he was in New York because the twelve-story hotel had the most magnificent elevator in New York. It was a cast bronze ornamental cage of arabesques, flowers, and palms, twelve feet by twelve feet, with inlaid hardwood floors and an exquisite system of electrohydraulic pulleys and weights that was a marvel to behold. Several times a day it carried him upward to his suite on the twelfth floor swiftly and silently, or downward to the quietly spectacular lobby.

The table at which he sat working was covered with annotated blueprints, and to one corner in a neat pile were stacked all the New York dailies that had accounts of Bessie's trial the next day. He had learned more about Bessie's life from the tabloids than she had ever told him, including her alias, Hannah Elias. He now knew the name of her lover, the number of her bank accounts, the trajectory of her crimes, and about the suit of her daughter. He also knew she slept in the Tombs that night. He thought constantly of her, yet he found her image fading despite all his frantic efforts to remember. The tabloids brought her back in all her ambiguity. He felt ill.

He reached over to the carafe of water nearby and poured himself a glass. Then he rose, went to the window, and looked down on Broadway.

His heart raced. Sweat had broken out on his forehead and on the small of his back. The nausea hadn't eased. Slowly, he lit himself a cigar and blew smoke rings into the air. He watched the elegant crowd from Daly's Theatre spill out onto the brightly lit street. Was Bessie to finally have her just deserts, he wondered, or would she rise above this and walk away as usual, smelling like a rose? He bet on Bessie. He was astounded that he had remained so passionate about her that her name in print would arouse such violent emotions in him.

She was a beauty and a devil. An innocent and a liar. She was much too complicated for any man to call his. Even though she promised to love him, he couldn't believe her. How many men had she told this to— all at the same time?

He felt sorry for Platt. Sorry, but with a painful spike of jealousy that Platt had uninhibitedly had Bessie for all those years. The desire that she created in Granville was exceeded only by his devotion—for himself, for who he was. There were no more Granville Woodses to go around. So he had to protect himself to make a mark on his field, for his country and his people. He was a race man.

Still, perhaps this was the last time he would see her free. So he decided for once to follow his heart. He would go to Judge O'Gorman's courtroom. He would go even though he knew that he would face not just Hannah, but his own longing, his own loneliness, and his desire for more of her tarnished, sordid, filthy ragtime kisses. She would not fill his heart, but he'd keep her in his dreams.

August Nanz couldn't sleep either. Jerome's subpoena to appear as a hostile witness for the prosecution in the day's trial was more than enough to give him a difficult night. He knew now that Jerome intended to charge him with conspiracy. At least conspiracy to defraud, but maybe also extortion and private theft. Hannah had turned against him, so there was no hope of getting her help. She had guessed that he'd stolen the documents and the letters and given them to the district attorney. She just didn't know why, and there was no telling her now.

Nanz was no longer protected by attorney-client privilege. He would have to risk perjury or take the Fifth. He was drenched with sweat. Had Jerome told Hannah's lawyers that he had been stealing from her for years—not out of malice, but out of the need to pay his own blackmailers to protect his own double life? He had passed for straight just as Hannah passed for white. His fate seemed more consequential, somehow.

At any rate, he was dead on Wall Street if he testified. He would spiral right back down to the Lower East Side, back to his roots.

Nanz crossed the room behind his Broadway offices and washed his face in the basin that stood next to the bed. At least he had tried in this last day before the trial to make one thing right.

He had dropped off the packet of Platt's love letters at his mansion, hoping that the man would understand how much he had loved Hannah at one time. It was not right to give them to anyone but him. Nanz tried to, at least, save his own soul, if not his skin.

1904
THE JUDGMENT

She is monstrous, thy daughter, she is altogether monstrous.
In truth, what she has done is a great crime. I am sure
that it was a crime against an unknown God.

—*Oscar Wilde*, Salome

THIRTY-TWO

*New York,
June 10, 1904*

T he bright morning sunshine brought a multitude of people to the Tombs for a glimpse of the "enchantress." Hannah's scandal was once again headline news. Crowds milled around the Hall of Justice, waiting for her to be led across the Bridge of Sighs to its entrance. A small contingent from the Women's Trade Union League stood near representatives from the Colored Women's Clubs, talking shop. Some Black people in their best clothes—thin suits and print dresses—stood by other Blacks in linen suits and tailored summer jackets.

People had brought placards, American flags, balloons, white parasols, and black umbrellas. The crowd was rowdy but cheerful under the panicked watch of thirty extra police officers. Some of the spectators had been there since before dawn.

Platt was still at home, although he had been awake since four in the morning. This was no nightmare from which he might wake up to find himself saved. At three o'clock that afternoon, he and Hannah would meet face to face. Jerome was determined to put him on the stand. He could either drop dead or appear. He wasn't sure which he preferred.

No one knew what bombshells Hannah intended to explode on the witness stand. He knew that there were other elderly millionaires who visited Hannah's bordellos, who quaked in their socks that morning. Bankers and investors hoped their money would not be affected.

Platt's panic began to mount, and his heartbeat rose alarmingly. He felt his pulse. He began to moan softly, clutching his stomach. His valet entered to ask if he would dress or have breakfast first. Platt was so confused that even this simple request was too much for him. "Do as you like, Arthur. Run my bath or fry my eggs."

The servants at 236 had also been up since dawn. Kato was to take what Sadie would wear for the trial down to the Tombs. Francine had chosen a wide black hat with a rose-embroidered black veil; a black two-piece tailored Worth suit of twill edged with black soutache with a lace vestee; a green waist clincher; and a necklace of jet and pearls. She had packed black gloves and red gloves, black stockings and red stockings, and earrings to go with her mistress's diamond brooch. Kato collected all the morning newspapers, each of which had four-inch headlines screaming Hannah's name.

Hannah was going to accompany Kato and Francine. But she would be incognito, wearing a plain outfit and no jewelry. She was going to attend as a Saks Fifth Avenue saleslady on her day off.

The trial was not scheduled to occur until three o'clock, but several thousand people were already gathered. The Special Sessions courtroom at the southwest corner of the first floor of the Tombs was cordoned off. Innumerable squabbles broke out among the bluecoats and would-be spectators who tried to enter. When the doors were finally opened, there was a stampede through the corridor in which people's clothing was torn and women had fits of hysteria.

The Tombs warden, remembering the mayhem of the bail arraignment, had changed plans at the last moment and secreted Sadie pretending to be Hannah out the Elm Street entrance to make the short trip to the courthouse that way instead.

Hannah had added one more lawyer. The urbane and obese James W. Osborne was a dashing, socially connected, former assistant district attorney who had been involved in most of the important criminal cases of the past few years. He would carry the brunt of the defense and the cross-examinations. Osborne, square jawed and aggressive looking, as if he were pursuing a serial killer, sat within the rail, along with Washington Brauns and Frank Wheaton. The latter two knew about the identity switch. Osborne did not.

At the prosecution's table sat Assistant District Attorney Rand and his team of lawyers. Rand looked uncomfortable as he scanned the door opening every few seconds, searching for Jerome, who had not yet arrived from his country estate. Rand was nervous, sorely needing Jerome's backup. Close by were the detectives who had presented the evidence on which Hannah had been arrested.

Judge O'Gorman entered a little before three o'clock. He ordered the doors to be locked. "We must have absolute order here," he said, "and those who wish to leave the room must do so immediately." Not a soul moved.

August Nanz took to a fit of nervous coughing. He did not want to be in this courtroom, but he had not dared defy Jerome's subpoena. He wanted to leave this room, the city, the state—even the goddamned United States. He still wheezed when an eerie hush fell over the packed courtroom.

Sadie had arrived.

An excited murmur went up. "There she is!"

She entered the courtroom on the warden's arm; the large-brimmed hat and veil hid her face until she sat down beside Washington and lifted the gossamer lace. A trail of scent followed her, which reached several rows into the public. There was an audible gasp. This was the first good look anybody had had since the New York detectives had broken down her front door.

She bore no resemblance to the woman who had been taken into custody three nights earlier. She looked as rich as she was: jet jewelry topped with strands of pearls covered her crème lace bosom; expensive diamond and ruby rings covered every finger of her gloved hands. She had a Tiffany bracelet on one wrist and a Cartier watch on the other. Her tiny feet were shod in black patent leather. Her lace veil was held in place by a diamond hatpin. She was as expressionless as a Park Avenue matron shopping. Her skin glowed with luxurious cosmetic care and the serenity of one who never worried about the rent. Her heart-shaped face and darkened brows over the carbon eyes spoke of gentility, convent upbringing, Sunday churchgoing, ladies' luncheons, and Red Cross volunteerism. The plain, quiet woman of Coon's Row was nowhere to be seen. Sadie had so perfected Hannah's manner, composed and demure, that Nanz wondered if she hadn't calmed herself down with a dot of hop smuggled in by Kato. Hop had always had a way of ironing Hannah out, he thought, even as it revved up most cocaine users.

Sadie settled back in the chair meant for Hannah, her bosom rising and falling softly; she crossed her ankles, folded her hands, and prepared to stare John Platt off the stand. Nanz wondered if the millionaire had the guts to testify against her while she was in the courtroom. The newspapers had begun calling Hannah "the enchantress," the Queen of Sheba, Cleopatra—not all that far from the truth. Sadie looked neither right nor left, but straight ahead. Had she looked to the back of the room where Kato and Francine sat, she would have seen her sister. Leola sat in the front so she could give Sadie courage.

Sadie's ankles were uncrossed now, one small foot tapping. She leaned over, her pearls shifting, to whisper something to Osborne, who nodded and shuffled his papers.

"Aye, aye, all stand in the presence of Judge O'Gorman."

The courtroom spectators and players rose. Nanz noticed Sadie contemplating the judge as he took his seat. Damned if she did not make eyes at him! O'Gorman and Sadie locked gazes for a second. *Poor judge,* thought the lawyer, *she's got you already.* Never look straight at a cobra unless you have a very long stick. August could feel the woman size up the magistrate, lap around him like smoke, and weigh her chances. The judge signaled for the assembly to reseat itself.

Standing, Sadie was like Hannah, barely five feet tall, yet sitting, she took on a monumental grandeur, which she drew around her. August gazed down at his trembling hands.

"Let the play begin," he murmured, humming the tune that was on everyone's lips:

> *Hello, my baby, hello, my honey, hello, my ragtime girl*
> *Send me a kiss by wire. You set my heart on fire . . .*

The court illustrator began making sketches that would appear in the evening papers. It was Assistant District Attorney Rand who was the first actor onstage. He gave a summary of the history of the case as he saw it, and then said, "The district attorney has determined that a crime has been committed. Our sole purpose is to get to the truth of the matter."

Two assistant district attorneys presented the case for the prosecution. Attorney Rand summarized the evidence. The district attorney himself would deliver the closing argument.

"John R. Platt appellant," began Rand, "against Hannah Elias and others . . . The action has been discontinued against all the defendants except the Mercantile Trust Company, the Empire City Savings Bank, the Greenwich Savings Bank, the United States Savings Bank, the Lincoln National Bank . . ." He then named the lawyers.

"An action has been brought by the plaintiff to recover the sum of 685,385 good and legal United States dollars or the property in which it has been invested, which was procured by the defendant Hannah Elias by trick, device, fraud, coercion, pretended affection, and various other things by means of which she obtained almost absolute control and undue influence over the plaintiff, thereby enabling her to obtain from him without consideration, this sum.

"The principal defendant in this case, Hannah Elias, is now about thirty-nine years old, born in Philadelphia about 1865. The record of her life shows that at age of nineteen in 1884 she was convicted of theft and served a prison term in a Philadelphia jail for larceny. At the age of twenty, she was living in a house of prostitution in Philadelphia. Between 1885 and 1886, she was an inmate in Blockley Almshouse where she gave birth to an illegitimate child of which she accused a Frank Satterfield of Philadelphia of fathering. She became so troublesome that he left for New York City. She followed him to New York and so conducted herself that in 1887, she was arrested for disorderly conduct and sent to Blackwell Island for 120 days. This brings us to 1888, when she was twenty-three years old . . ."

The cold-blooded recital of her birth in the poorhouse brought a blush to Clara Hudson's cheeks. The large crowds, the screaming headlines, the swarming, shoving multitude, had badly frightened her, and now she sat at the back of the courtroom with her head down, not daring to look up at her mother.

"The plaintiff says he saw her for the first time at Pop Miller's, a bordello in the city of New York when he accompanied several visiting firemen from California. He does not remember the date or location, but it is fixed beyond dispute as December 8, 1888. Elias was twenty-three years old and went by the name of Hannah Wetherill. The defendant says that while at Pop Miller's the plaintiff began to shower money on her in sums of $200 to $1,000. Her first deposit was made in the Greenwich Savings Bank in 1894 and the United Dime Bank the same year. At these dates she was living at 12 East Fifty-Third Street. Her removal was to a little frame house on Forty-Fourth Street near Broadway. She then moved to a house on Third Avenue and Twenty-Fifth Street, where she remained two years, and at that point lost sight of the plaintiff and he of her. She advertised for massage treatments and the plaintiff replied to her advertisement with complaints of rheumatism when she was living in Corlears Hook, thus resuming their liaison.

"She next moved to 145 West Fifty-Third Street. She married Matthew C. Davis, a Pullman porter, in 1895. She then removed to 132 West Fifty-Third Street after which she divorced her husband in 1899. In March 1899, she also made the acquaintance of August Nanz, Esquire, who became her attorney at a time when Elias's extensive operations were very successful; that is to say that she realized as keenly as Mr. Platt the disgrace to him and the consequences resulting from exposure of his connection with her. She used this as a source of power to extract money from him—at times through her attorney. As the courts have said in cases herein after, 'We cannot see every step in her proceedings, but we can see the result.' From the beginning, the fear of disgrace was strongly impressed upon the plaintiff and constantly held before his weakened mental vision. Elias made false statements about Davis and others, all calculated to excite and terrify this weak old man.

"In 1901, Elias bought 236 Central Park West for $45,000, and in 1902 she bought 166 West Seventy-Second Street for $49,500. In 1902, she filed a certificate for another illegitimate child, naming Platt as the father of the child. She was thirty-seven at the time and he was eighty-two.

"After the tricks and devices she used and the lies she told, it is plain from his testimony—corroborated by her own affidavit—what means she used to obtain her immense fortune.

"Is it a wonder the poor, weak old man gave her cash to avoid notoriety and trouble? The defendant claims that the plaintiff's statement proves he was not personally afraid of her. He believed she was his only friend. He was duped into trusting her integrity and honesty and feigned love, but such lack of fear is absolutely immaterial. It is not a necessary ingredient of extortion. In 1896, the plaintiff was seventy-seven years of age. In that year Elias obtained from him $19,535. In 1897, $39,730; in 1898, $63,000; in 1899, $53,480; in 1900, $84,865; in 1901, $87,067; in 1902, $124,706; in 1903, $181,909; and in 1904, up to the time this suit commenced, $31,233.

"It will be seen that as the plaintiff became weaker and more mentally unstable, Elias, under the shrewd counsel of her lawyer and her own hitherto successful experiences, became stronger and more confident in her deceptions. The amounts subsequently increased in size from $19,535 in 1896 to $181,909 in 1903. Yet the defendant claims the plaintiff gave it to her willingly without a comment on what made him willing. The question in this case is not whether he gave it to her willingly, but what influence made him willing."

Rand paused for emphasis, and breath. "The thing to remember is that Hannah Elias is not a white woman, and from 1885 to the present she was and has been a woman of bad reputation with a dishonorable character, an inmate of houses of ill fame and assignation. She is a convicted criminal. She has a prison record and had served two terms in women's penitentiaries for felonies and as a vagrant in an almshouse. She has given birth to illegitimate children, one of which she claimed was the plaintiff's, now deceased. She caused a certificate of birth to be filed, although she was not sure who the father of said child was—in all, a picture of immorality that would stop at nothing to create fraud, coercion, and duress."

Some members of the audience hissed at this statement.

"Order!" the judge commanded.

Belle da Costa Greene and several other upper-class New York ladies were sitting in the courtroom. Members of the Women's Trade Union League had found Hannah Elias to be a cult figure and a cause célèbre. They considered her story of prostitution and degradation the result of poverty and the powerlessness of working women. Although they themselves were not prey to that kind of abuse, they believed it was their duty to show solidarity with the feminine underclass. Hannah had taken what she had been born with—nothing—and created wealth and independence. Was it a crime, or simply enterprise? She was a rallying flag for women's suffrage, just as she was also a danger to public morals and law and order.

But Belle's interest wasn't philanthropic. Belle was fascinated by this woman who had declared herself free of other people's labels and made them take her at her word, when in fact anyone with eyes could see that she wasn't what she claimed she was. She was a bit overweight, a little frumpy and frizzy, but dressed in the highest style. But her power of illusion was stronger than any physical trait. Belle knew image to be a true intoxicant. She knew it from the great works of art she handled, acquired, and collected for J. P. Morgan. Works of arts traversed centuries and became immortal on the wings of illusion.

Belle wondered what had compelled all of Hannah's men to follow her siren song. It wasn't just sex, she reasoned. Hannah's true power was knowing that men searched all their lives for the illusion of omniscience, of trumping the odds, of invincibility and raw survival. Hannah had been born in a stable and by her own doing emerged into one of the most powerful women in New York. Men blindly paved the way for her entry into their banks, their clubs, their casinos, their houses. There was something so wildly exhilarating about Hannah's magnificence.

Hannah had made black seem white, evil seem good, theft seem generosity, crime seem like charity—simply by being true to herself and refusing the labels other people lived by.

Belle was seated beside a man who looked and smelled like a policeman. His demeanor was overly taut, and he was sweating. Still, he had a wide grin on his face, as if he were at a first-class vaudeville show. It was, in fact, Detective Jack McClusky.

Before Hannah sat down, she lifted her veil, and Belle was able to get a good look at her. She had even brought her opera glasses along. She raised them delicately. Hannah had slum eyes, feline and shrewd, and her mouth was wide and her lips too plump.

Belle took out a small notebook and began writing in it as she alternated with raising her opera glasses to spy on the defendant.

During the assistant district attorney's opening remarks, Belle then turned her glasses on several men in attendance: one was a politician of national prominence, one a merchant who held a leading position in the city, and another who was a famous banker. She recognized them from J. P. Morgan's invitation list and from photographs in newspapers. What were they all doing here in the middle of the day? A weekday? This was pulp fiction, at its best, but still a dime-store novel for maids—not millionaires. Nevertheless, Belle noticed that Mark Twain himself sat alongside the court illustrator and busily scribbled in a blue lined notebook.

Granville Woods sat not far from Clara, but he could hardly have guessed she was Bessie's daughter. His eyes were fixed only at the back of Hannah's head in the first row. He had melted when he saw her enter. His desire for Hannah coupled with his bitterness against everything she represented had brought him to this courtroom and fused him to his seat. Now, all his ambiguous feelings returned in the pit of his stomach. She really was not good for him. His head spun a little, as if he had stood too long in the sun.

Bessie, he believed, had spied him in the courtroom when she entered, and had recognized him. He had felt the electricity, though her black eyes had met his for only a second; it had felt like eternity. He didn't realize that like so many men in the audience, he labored under Hannah's illusion. The woman he watched, lusted for, hated, and prized was, in this moment, not her.

"I call to the stand Mr. Platt, the complainant," said Rand, his voice resonating through the electrified courtroom, buzzing with spectators who craned their necks to see him.

Hannah, sitting alongside Kato and Francine, sighed a little when

Platt walked to the witness box. She saw that he stumbled. His head and hands shook with a palsied motion. His eyes were dim and bleary, with baggy wrinkles under them, and his face was puffed and flushed. His whole appearance had changed overnight to one of infirmity.

"Oh, Papa," Hannah whispered, "what has happened to you?" She wondered how he had fallen so low in her absence. The last time she had seen him in Saratoga he had still been vital, alive, and well—before she had sent him his birthday present of Bellocq's photograph. She had sensed the tension in herself as he wanted to touch her. They were kind to one another. That tenderness had kept him young.

This was the world of money, Hannah thought. She had sought it all of her life, but this was the real outcome. Money without love produced nothing of value.

Francine, hearing Hannah's mumbling, grasped her hand and held it to steady her. Hannah realized then that she was the very rich person to be envied she had always wanted to be.

As Platt awkwardly limped through the courtroom, there was a silence like that of a sickroom. Relatives waited for the patient's last breath and anticipated more than the end of his life—the reading of his will. The only sound was Platt's shuffling feet as he mounted the podium. He settled back in the chair slowly and folded his hands in his lap. He was dressed in a black business suit and wore a starched collar with a Yale tie clip, in which a diamond sparkled. His heavy gold watch chain and his enormous black jet cufflinks were old-fashioned and in strange contrast to the showy ring on his little finger.

Hannah saw that his face was seamed with deep lines and his eyes had the leaden, lifeless expression of encroaching senility. She felt sorry for him. He had been a powerful man, a hopeful man, only months ago. Platt finally raised his eyes to the woman who sat facing him, not twenty feet away, without any outward sign of recognition. For a moment, Hannah wondered if he really did not recognize her sister, or if he was ignoring the defendant as his lawyer had coached him.

Sadie felt a thousand pairs of other eyes while she stared ahead directly at Platt. Washington had told her, "You stare him down until you make him scared."

The young girl summoned her will against his and her strength against his weakness, while Hannah noted from her seat in the back that she had survived his betrayal. She had pitted her rage against his flagging devotion. She was Cleopatra against the Marc Antonys of the world. Now they sat all around her, millionaires and bankers, not even knowing that she was actually among them—physically nearby as well as matching their wealth. They were all around her, sweating in their morning coats and clutching their top hats—the scions of capitalism, the barons of industry, the princes of New York. They were bowed low by a girl from Five Points and her sister, impresarios of female power.

When District Attorney Rand began the examination, he asked Platt his name five times without eliciting an answer. Platt held his hand to his ear and looked puzzled. Rand went closer to the stand and shouted. Finally, he replied, "John Rufus Platt." He went on to say that he was eighty-five years old and retired.

"How long have you lived here?"

"In this city since 1863."

As soon as Platt took the witness chair, Sadie leaned forward, elbows on the table in front of her, and rested her chin on her two hands. She raised her eyes to Platt's. She would make him her slave.

Platt returned her gaze, then looked away, as if blinded by the headlights of an oncoming train, only to see a woman in the audience remove her hat and veil. Hannah in the audience now stared at him. Platt grabbed his head with both hands for a moment. The audience gasped. His eyes rolled as if he were about to faint. Then he took a breath and sat a little straighter. He looked from one woman to the other.

The audience watched him closely, unaware that Platt now saw double. Two Hannahs. Just as Cornelius had said. But only the judge and the prosecutor from their vantage could view the sisters. They were identical. One woman sat among the onlookers and one at the defendant's table. Who exactly was Platt suing? Did he know himself?

"Holy shit," Rand said, and he glanced at the judge, who sat stone faced, although his eyes had been wide a minute earlier.

All three men were thrown into confusion. Still, they proceeded with the rote inquiry:

Platt was asked by the assistant district attorney to identify Hannah. "Do you know this woman?"

"Yes," he answered in a voice so low that the courtroom scarcely heard him. "Well, yes. I think so."

The assistant district attorney continued, even though he knew that Platt's age and the spontaneous revelation made her identity suspect now. He had to follow the legal first line of questioning. "Who is she?"

"Hannah Elias," Platt said. "I think. I mean I'm sure. Hannah Elias."

"Hmph," the real Hannah grunted aloud from her place in the audience.

People around her twittered and chuckled, not realizing the problem, simply thinking she was another woman making a judgment about Platt.

"Order!" the judge said, banging his gavel.

Rand took a deep breath and tried his questions another way, using her name. "When and where did you meet Hannah Elias?"

"In a house on Twenty-Seventh Street. A man named Miller kept it."

"When was this?"

"When the volunteer firemen from California came here."

"How long ago was that?"

"I don't remember."

"You don't know how long ago that was?"

"No, I don't."

"Wasn't it fifty years ago?"

"I can't remember how long it was."

"See if you can try to remember when the firemen came here."

"I can't remember. Well, it was 1800 and some time."

"Was it within ten years?"

"It was less than ten years."

"Do you mean it was within those ten years?"

"I can't remember when it was."

"You met Hannah Elias in a house of prostitution on Twenty-Seventh Street?" asked Rand.

"Yes, but not exactly." Platt said. "She wasn't Hannah. But she was also Bessie."

The audience gasped. He had finally said it. Just as Cornelius had screamed as he shot Green. She was Bessie Davis.

Only the defense lawyers Washington and Wheaton—as well as the assistant district attorney—knew that the prosecution's case was falling apart as he spoke. Rand now had two women, two names and identities, and a feeble witness. What the hell was he going to do?

"Did you set her up in housekeeping as soon as you met Hannah Elias—er, Bessie?"

"No."

"Have you been supporting Hannah Elias, the woman you met, ever since you met her?"

Now the audience was beginning to chuckle. The prosecutor and the witness seemed daft, both fumbling awkwardly and looking around the room as if the heavens could give them an answer to win the case.

"No."

"But, you paid her money, didn't you?"

"Yes."

"How much?"

"I haven't the figures with me."

"You paid her money from time to time to support her, didn't you?"

"Yes, sir."

"You paid her money in large amounts."

"Yes, sir."

"At her solicitation or of your own volition?" Now Rand was getting somewhere.

"What do you mean?"

"Did she ask you for the money?"

"She asked me for money, and I paid it."

"Did she ask you often?"

"I don't remember."

"Did you pay her a total amount of $700,000?"

The listeners gasped again. One shouted, "Wowwee!"

"Order!" said the judge, as people in the room laughed. "Order!"

"I did."

"Did you pay her any money recently?"

"I did."

"How much?"

"Seven thousand five hundred dollars."

Nanz started to sweat. This had been his little courtesy fee. Hannah knew nothing about it. He hoped no one would find out. He'd be on his way to jail, just like her. Maybe even quicker. He looked around the room for McClusky. He was seated near J. P. Morgan's collection curator, Belle. Nanz nodded his head at McClusky and gave a big fake wink to send a message.

"Why did you pay $7,500?"

"Because she said she was going to be sued and if she went to court, she would expose me."

"Ha!" Hannah said audibly. She had never said anything of the kind. Nanz was a sneaky bastard. She needed to sue him.

"Did you really believe that if she went to court she would expose you?"

"Yes."

"And did you believe that by paying her the money you would induce her to conceal your relations with her and not give you away?"

"Yes."

"Did she tell you why she had been sued?"

"I don't remember."

"Did she tell you the name of the man who sued her?"

"I don't recollect. She didn't tell me exactly. It was her lawyer."

"Was he a man named August Nanz?"

Nanz winced at the mention of his name.

"Yes."

"What were the secrets that her lawyer said that she would expose?"

"I do not want to repeat them. Can I write them out?"

"Mr. Platt, you are here to testify in your own words. We do not expect you to write out what you have to say. Was that woman your mistress?"

"She was not."

"You have paid her very large sums during the last ten years."

"I don't know. Ask my lawyer."

"You mean to say now that you don't know you have given her a large amount of money? Did you not sign a complaint that she had extorted hundreds of thousands of dollars from you?"

"Ask my lawyer about that."

"No, I want to talk to you, not your lawyer."

John Rufus pulled a pen and paper out of his pocket and began to write. It was the old man's plan, hatched the previous evening, to avoid revealing too much embarrassing information.

Rand interrupted him, telling him that what he wanted to know now was evidence by word of mouth. To test Platt's memory he asked, "Do you know what day of the month it is?"

"I don't remember just now."

"Do you know what day of the week it is?"

"Yes. It's Friday, isn't it?" There was an outburst of laughter from the courtroom.

"You began your court actions about two weeks ago, didn't you?"

"I don't remember. Wasn't it a few days ago?"

"I am talking about the civil suit. You wanted a civil suit and then you decided that hers was a criminal act. So you pursued this case as well. You know the difference between a civil suit and a criminal action, don't you?"

"I suppose so."

"You recall signing a complaint in a civil suit then criminal, don't you?"

"I don't remember that exactly."

"Don't you know anything about these suits?"

Platt paused for a second. He looked out at the courtroom as the public fell silent. He could see the pity in their eyes, or their looks of anger. He focused on the woman in the audience who might be Hannah, then he turned his gaze to the Hannah that was at the defendant's table. He looked again at the first woman. A slight smile rose to her lips. That was her, Platt felt now. Only Hannah knew his foibles, his jealousies, his pride, and she still accepted him. That was his Hannah. It was the only thing he now knew.

Rand was now repeating the question: "Mr. Platt. Mr. Platt, what do you know about your civil suit against Hannah Elias?"

"I don't remember . . ."

The real Hannah kept her eyes fixed on Platt. She didn't want him to be humiliated like this—as she had been. His testimony was turning the trial into a fiasco, but Rand wouldn't give up.

It was now impossible for Platt to take his eyes off Hannah's face. Several times he made a supreme effort to turn away, but a moment later he would be back again as if his life depended on it, drawn back into those dark eyes, the seat of his soul.

Tears of effort began to fill his gaze. But his total expression was worse than tears, Hannah thought. The money had ossified his spirit and his social position had stolen his heart, and she could see his dismal future, alone and unloved.

The courtroom was perfectly still.

Rand began to perspire in frustration. He wiped his brow.

Washington squirmed with glee. He looked around just as Jerome quietly entered the courtroom. Washington motioned to Sadie to look at Osborne sitting next to them. He shook his head and winked. For him, this was going to be child's play.

As a last resort, Rand handed Platt the criminal complaint that had brought him to court that day and asked him to read the first paragraph.

"That's all right," Platt said.

"Then you were afraid of something when you gave her the money?"

"I didn't think of that at the time I gave it to her."

"Why did you give her the money then?"

"To avoid trouble."

"Did Mrs. Elias threaten you with trouble?"

"It depends what you mean by the word 'trouble.'"

"I mean the normal meaning of 'trouble' as in 'public disclosure' . . . as in 'to avoid trouble.' She generally told you things like that, didn't she, when she asked you for money?"

"I wouldn't say that. 'Trouble' is a general term. As a general thing she didn't say anything like that. I gave her the money willingly."

The entire audience exhaled with a sound halfway between a groan and a sigh. Platt had just absolved Hannah with his own words.

"If she had stood pat, I would have stayed pat," Platt added, explaining that he came forth only because people told him that Hannah would admit the relationship.

Rand held up his hand as the judge was about to lift the gavel. "Wait," he said. "Wait, your honor."

Rand knew that he had failed to evoke the slightest damaging evidence against Hannah. During the hour and a half that Platt testified, the woman at the defendant's table had maintained her sphinxlike composure that had aroused looks of admiration in the courtroom and helpless confusion in Platt.

In the last few minutes of the case, Platt had been staring into the courtroom audience like a madman, a smile on his lips and his early courtroom tension washed away, as if he had nothing left in the world to worry about.

Hannah in the audience blew Platt a kiss as he felt one of his own tears slide down his cheek.

Sadie dropped the haughty composure of her sister and relaxed her shoulders and took a breath.

The audience realized that Platt was a weak, helpless man who could not even remember the day of the week and who could never substantiate the charge of blackmail against the woman he had accused of grand larceny, more than to say that he had made some payments to her to avoid trouble. No one had expected his total collapse except Hannah herself.

The district attorney was furious as Osborne rose and disdainfully declined to cross-examine Platt. "You can dismiss this witness. I think that all that has to be said has been said."

Judge O'Gorman called the prosecuting and defense attorneys to the bench.

"What the hell is going on here?" he asked.

"Your honor?" said Rand.

"You know full well what I mean, counselor. Your main witness, upon whom this case rests, is incompetent."

"But isn't it more reason that his interests should be protected?" Rand asked.

Osborne stayed silent.

"It fucking seems to me that Hannah Elias was taking care of him better than you," the judge answered.

"We have more witnesses," Rand said. "August Nanz."

"The man who represented Hannah Elias until a few weeks ago?" O'Gorman asked. "The man who claimed Mrs. Elias was going to spill the beans but she never did? I've known that little rat since he was chasing ambulances. You know he was just trying to shake down Platt. Make a case against him."

The judge continued, "Please do not put us through any more circus. You have whipped up the public, brought the damn newspapers and every kook east of the Mississippi into my court. You have single-handedly brought the suffragettes, Colored Clubs, the 'working girls,' and the secretaries together. Against who? Not Hannah Elias. Me. Just get the hell out of my face."

The judge sent the parties back to their respective tables.

Osborne spoke as soon as he returned, "I demand that the case against Mrs. Elias be dismissed herewith on the grounds of coercion and insignificant evidence."

Realizing the hopelessness of the prosecution's case, Rand murmured his assent.

People in the audience began to cheer and shout.

"Order!" said O'Gorman. "It does not appear that the district attorney, Mr. Jerome, has a competent and willing complainant, and while in criminal cases this is not necessary, unlike civil court, the state still does not feel the necessity to bring evidence for a blackmail in which the person blackmailed is not particularly damaged and does not feel offended. This seems a waste of resources and time. In addition, this evidence so far does correlate to that which was given to me as a warrant for Mrs. Elias's arrest. This warrant was issued on the witness's statement that he had been defrauded and threatened. It appears today that he is not in any danger, nor was his money put to a use he did not intend."

As the judge spoke, the audience could see the fury rising in him. He had been made a fool of by the district attorney.

Voices began to rumble through the room.

"Order," the judge said loudly. "It is the hope that no court will ever be used as a stepping-stone for notoriety of any kind." Here the judge looked at Jerome. "And all parties will behave in a legal and orderly manner." Now he looked at Sadie and Platt. "Let everyone in this miserable scandal go their own way," he hissed.

Magistrate Ommen, who had issued the warrant for Hannah's arrest only because of the district attorney, was violet with indignation. He leaned toward Rand and almost shouted, "Do I understand that this recommendation is made on the authority of the district attorney, William Jerome?"

"On the authority of the district attorney," was the sheepish reply.

"Who has just bestowed upon this court his exalted presence?"

"Present, Your Honor," croaked William Jerome as he rose in his seat.

The crowded courtroom grew silent as a tomb. It was witnessing one of the most sensational climaxes ever played out in a New York court of law. The angry magistrate thundered, "There is not a scintilla of evidence before me in this case. Hannah Elias, you are discharged. This case is thrown out of court."

At that point, both Sadie and Hannah rose to their feet in the silent courtroom. People all around did a double take, then the room exploded with applause, as if they had just witnessed the best Broadway show possible for free.

Then, allowing an expression of triumph to spread across her face, Hannah smiled her smile, still without a word. Sadie turned, facing the courtroom, and raised her hand in a small salute. The entire courtroom continued to clap, which soon turned into a standing ovation. Hannah's eyes swept the courtroom and settled on the looming figure of Granville Woods, who was applauding Sadie. She regarded him with the usual pain in her heart.

Washington shook hands with and then hugged Wheaton, who was a little disappointed that he hadn't had the pleasure of putting Sadie Elias on the stand and asking Platt to differentiate her from her sister. Osborne, the expensive lawyer, stood with his mouth agape because no one had let him in on the punch line.

"Too bad," Wheaton whispered under his breath.

"Not bad," said Washington. "Those fools will drop the civil suit out of court before you get past the magistrate's door, Frank. They'll probably want to donate to your favorite charity to avoid being sued for slander."

"You know, you're right, Washington." Frank laughed. "They'll be standing in the damned corridor, waiting for me with their pants down!"

"Damn right, I'm right. They'll deem themselves lucky."

"The money could go to the Negro orphanage in Five Points. It's Hannah's favorite charity."

Osborne was still awestruck and trying to find the humor in his winning a case while remaining in the dark about his client. He realized now that he had been used, hired to be the token white Upper East Sider, perceived as an equal to the prosecution. He imagined the way he would tell the story to his lawyer peers: "Talk about a two-faced colored woman!"

August Nanz stepped into the aisle as Jerome tried to storm out of the courtroom. He had never even given the closing statement.

"Get out of my way, Nanz."

"Gladly, Jerome! Thanks to your blundering, I won't have to take the Fifth."

"You are a liar and a thief and a blackmailer, and you should be disbarred from practicing law. I'd like to drag you before the New York Bar Association."

"Listen, Jerome, your persecution of Hannah Elias was unpardonable. And the use of the old man was cruel. It's you who should be answering to the Bar Association."

"Don't push your luck, Nanz. Be grateful and stand out of my way before I have you cited as associating with malefactors."

"I don't think you'll ever have evidence on me. People who live in glass houses—you know the saying—even glass mansions or dirty little apartments like your McClusky." Nanz practically sang the saying.

Nanz continued: "Platt's lawyers say they never intended for the trial to be anything except a civil one. They say they never asked for any criminal action. Warren says he had nothing to do with Hannah's arrest and he is furious at what Rand did to Platt today in court. All he was after was the money."

"I made the decision to arrest Hannah Elias, and I don't need anybody's sanction to do so except my own."

"Well, you lost. There won't be a civil case. It's totally prejudiced now and you know it."

"The civil suit is not my affair. Crime is."

"Or punishment?" asked Nanz.

"I might have lost this case, counselor, but I was defending the highest values of our American society!"

"Yes, I know what that means. It's hard to have high values with no scruples, isn't it?"

Nanz stepped aside, and with as much dignity as he could muster under the circumstances, Jerome marched out of the courtroom a subdued but unchanged man.

The judge's decision reached the street outside, and a great hurrah went up among the New Yorkers. Hats were thrown in the air; slogans were shouted out. Hannah was hailed as a heroine, and John Platt was booed and hissed. A roar went up like the sea outside:

"Hannah! Hannah! Hannah!"

Hannah had uttered not one word in court. It was as if she had been watching one of those silent Edwin Porter motion pictures she adored. The only thing missing was Scott Joplin's piano music. Sadie had disappeared while the crowd applauded loudly. She stepped into Max's parked carriage waiting discreetly and glanced over her shoulder at the courthouse entrance and the crowds. She had her transatlantic passage on the Cunard Line for London booked for the following night.

Hannah looked around at the noisy, cheering, smiling crowd. They were the same people who purchased tabloid newspapers and read every word of the terrible articles that had maligned her body and soul. Perhaps now the American public would stop believing every lying word.

1904
THE HEROINE

Cunt in all its power; cunt on an alter with men offering up sacrifices to it . . . the poetry of cunt . . . women and men before that supreme apparition, Cunt. . . . Nana dissipates gold, devours every sort of wealth; the most extravagant tastes, the most frightful waste. She instinctively makes a rush for pleasure and possessions. She devours everything; she eats up what people are earning around her in industry, on the stock exchange, in high positions, in everything that is profit. And she leaves nothing but ashes.

—*Émile Zola, 1880, reference card for* Nana

THIRTY-THREE

Lower Manhattan, New York,
June 10, 1904

Hannah had been sure there were to be no more surprises in her life, but she was amazed at how New York women had rallied around her. They took her fate to heart and made her a heroine. Hannah was famous.

Hannah listened to the cheering and shouts, hardly daring to show her face. It could have been the Fourth of July. People of all colors, all classes, and sexes waved American flags. She let the people leaving the trial flow past her, leaving an eerie silence in the courtroom. Only one lone man, who stood ramrod straight at the back of the visitors' gallery, was left.

It was Granville. Her Granville. The only man she had ever loved, for whom, now, she was unattainable. Hannah walked slowly past unseeing Granville and through the courtroom door, down the wide corridor toward the exit, without looking back.

Clara waited for Hannah in the courthouse rotunda. The soaring marble pillars and the ribbed, multicolored glass dome shed a celestial light on the inlaid marble floor encrusted with the seal of the United States of America, which said, IN GOD WE TRUST. As Hannah crossed the deserted hall, Clara stepped out of the shadows. Mother and daughter stared at each other for a long moment, and then Hannah said, "You're Clara."

"Yes."

"My other suit."

"I've dropped my suit."

"Really?"

"Yes, ma'am." Clara held out her hand.

"How do you do?" Hannah said.

Yes, thought Hannah. That was she. That was she. Clara hadn't died and she wasn't dead. Clara was alive. Clara had survived. Clara was standing.

Silently, Clara reached into her satchel and pulled out her birth certificate and the neatly pressed and darned gunnysack in which she had been wrapped on that Christmas Eve in 1885.

Tears came to Hannah's eyes.

"You are, unfortunately, my mother," Clara said.

It was the saddest commentary Hannah had ever heard outside a bordello.

"I had often dreamed of this moment," Hannah replied.

"I, too, have dreamed of this day, Mother," replied Clara. Clara was about to faint with emotion. But she steadied herself, a deep sob shaking her shoulders.

"You have a baby half sister called Muriel Consuela," said Hannah, shaken.

"That's a beautiful name," replied Clara.

"Yes," her mother said, "for a girl, a beautiful name . . ."

Hannah looked into the identical cast-iron eyes of Clara. There was no way to resurrect this daughter, she thought. Clara had died the moment she had placed her in the arms of Trevor Hudson. Her daughter was in heaven along with Gwendolyn, she reasoned. There was no room in her heart for a living Clara. It was too much to bear.

Hannah saw Clara's eyes fill with pity. She stepped forward and pressed her cheek against her mother's. Hannah felt the soft smoothness and inhaled Clara's baby scent from eighteen years ago. It took all her strength to pull away.

"Adieu, Mama," whispered Clara. "I don't want your money nor your love anymore."

Hannah was voiceless.

"Goodbye, Clara," Hannah finally murmured.

A sea change had occurred in Hannah. She was not subdued, but absent, as if her great victory was of no significance, as if she had something else on her mind. She was also very angry. She'd been promised protection by the many men who had claimed to love her, but in the end she had found herself back in the same prison she had inhabited when she was nineteen. They had all failed her.

Hannah walked through the courthouse door into the sunlight. At the wide opening Hannah greeted the surging crowd of working people, who had taken time off to come to the courthouse to cheer her on. There were colored women in the crowd. There were women of ill repute from the Tenderloin district elbow to elbow with high-society women from Fifth Avenue. There were suffragettes, working girls, businessmen, and homeless men. Parents had brought their children. Vendors sold balloons and popcorn and candied apples.

> *Hannah, Hannah, in her red bandana,*
> *Skinned old Platt like a ripe banana . . .*

Women had stood chanting her name outside her mansion as Jerome had smashed down her door. Women had followed her to the Tombs and linked arms and voices to protest her imprisonment. Women had started a riot at her arraignment and her bail of $70,000, and had set off an angry, noisy march on the New York Supreme Court building.

And, she realized, it hadn't been just the underclass from Five Points and the Bowery. There had been working-class people, schoolteachers and secretaries, clerks, cleaning ladies, housewives, nannies, maids, cooks, waiters, bartenders, policemen, butlers, valets, cabbies, waitresses, hairdressers, seamstresses, milliners, cigar makers, factory workers, bakers, auto workers, jockeys, street cleaners, garbage men, taxi drivers, deliverymen, truck drivers, teachers, telephone operators, strippers, nurses, wet nurses, window washers, plumbers, glove makers, shoe shine vendors, Pullman porters, laundresses, cloakroom attendants, theater ushers, box office attendants, chauffeurs, firemen, florists, milkmaids, and hotel managers. All came out to cheer Hannah.

Colored women of all classes strove along with sensation seekers and

newspaper reporters. They chanted for Hannah Elias, but also for freedom, for women's right to vote, for equal pay and birth control; against
poverty, commercial sex, and child prostitution. They wanted independence from the domination of husbands, fathers, and brothers. They saw
in Hannah a renegade and a revolutionary. Hannah was a call to arms.
Women cheered her as a self-made woman who had bested the robber
barons and Wall Street at their own game, no matter how she had started
out or what she had been. Hannah had thumbed her nose at the oligar-
chy of male oppression, exploitation, and hypocrisy. There were respectable women who knew that they would have done what she had done
to feed their children. These women asked only for decent work, a living
wage, and the vote.

Women had begun to say, "Keep your hands off my body, unless I
give you permission. Get judges, policemen, priests, and ministers off
our backs. Get male hypocrisy out of our lives. Free Hannah Elias."

Hannah had never thought about anyone but herself. But now she
contemplated all those masses of women at the Tombs, at the courthouse, at the house on Central Park, and realized she had ignited their
thoughts and dreams—that her plight had touched some chord of recognition in them that was universal. These women desired independence as
strongly as she had fought for it and were just as filled with hopelessness
as she had been.

All of New York had gathered. Before she stepped into her automobile, Hannah answered several reporters' questions.

"I knew," she said, "it could not have been otherwise, since I am an
innocent woman. If I was composed in court it was because my conscience is perfectly clear."

"Are you considering bringing charges against the district attorney
and the City of New York for false arrest?"

"There has not been time for that yet," interrupted Osborne. "We
have been on the defense until now and the question of reprisals has not
yet been taken up. Mrs. Elias is simply grateful that this whole astounding tale is over and she can get back to normal life."

And what, Hannah wondered, was her normal life? Did it have any normality about it at all? Her eyes locked with those of Frank. "Thank you," she said. The strangest look came over his face. Then he simply shook his head without saying a word, bowed low over Hannah's outstretched hand, kissed it, and backed away.

"I must get back to the courthouse. We have some unfinished business to attend to," said Washington.

He handed Hannah into her open Duryea automobile, nodded to the driver at the wheel, who was Maurice Ducasse in livery, cap, and riding boots, and slammed the door. Hannah sank into the soft, white leather of the superb vehicle.

As the car sped away, Hannah could hear the crowds in the distance, still cheering and chanting her name.

Washington had already begged Hannah to consider a countersuit for false accusation and false arrest against the City of New York and Platt. He had explained that in Roman times a person convicted of falsely accusing another was punished by branding on the forehead with the letter "K," which stood for "calumny." Hannah tried to imagine a burning red "K" on the forehead of John Rufus, or on the high, smooth brow of the district attorney.

Hannah had never really pretended to be what she was not. She was a woman of the bordellos and jails. She had never "passed" for white behind her heavy veils and disguises. When a person was rude enough to ask, Hannah said Cuban—a nation full of descendants from Africa. Mostly, Hannah had simply forged a declaration of independence from all racial labels. It was New York society itself that had decided that her riches could not possibly belong to a Black woman or to one of her profession. It was America that had decided, not her, Hannah thought. Calumny? Wasn't that the crime made against every woman of color in the United States?

Hannah knew she would have to leave New York and take the names of her lovers with her into exile. She could change her name again, she thought. But why should she change her name? Why couldn't they change theirs? She could leave for Yokohama with Kato and Muriel, never to return. There was California, where she could buy gold mines and speculate in land. She could join Sadie in London, where most of her fortune was now.

Hannah had lost her fear of the material poverty that had haunted her all her life. But, as the plum-colored, chrome-plated automobile sped northward, there came upon her for the first time a deeper sense of poverty than she had ever felt in the almshouse. Once again, she would be forced to move from a home, to run along, to step back, to disappear. Once again, she would be forced to forego all identity.

Tomorrow, there would be headlines in every newspaper in New York City:

HANNAH ELIAS EXONERATED

HANNAH ELIAS WINS SUIT

HANNAH ELIAS KEEPS FORTUNE

Rich as she was, she had no name. She had returned to her anonymous, stateless invisibility. Hannah felt swept away, all alone, uprooted like a fragile plant in Central Park. She would have to renounce the mansion, since everybody now knew she lived there. Yet her heart clung to it. Her rise from the Seventh Ward to Central Park had not been without plan or reason. It had been a steady, single-minded march out of oblivion, fueled by her ambition, energy, and desperation to be a woman of property.

Everything seemed preternaturally silent. The traffic noise had disappeared. The late-afternoon sun and street reflections from the plate glass shopwindows first shadowed, and then lit Hannah's face under her veil. She thought of poor, crazed Cornelius. She had paid for his lawyers, the alienists, and his gilded madhouse from which he soon would be free. She felt no anger against his stupidity. It had cost him his freedom and his sanity. Crazy in love, Hannah thought. It could drive you mad. She forgave him. She forgave them all: her enemies, her friends, her lovers. Hannah blessed the only man she had left standing. Her Granville. She let the warmth and light of that name carry her home to 236 Central Park West.

"Drive through the park," she told Maurice. The soft hum and purr of the yellow Duryea, the fresh peaceful breeze off the park greenery, took them north to Harlem, away from the cheering crowds and toward the very same oblivion from which Hannah, the only woman I ever loved, had risen.

Acknowledgments

The Great Mrs. Elias was seventeen years in the making. I would like to thank everyone who accompanied me on this fascinating journey to find and portray the elusive and mysterious and sublime Hannah Elias.

Hannah Elias is, of course, a historical figure, the last of my quintet of "invisible" women of color that includes Sally Hemings, an enslaved woman; Harriet Hemings, a fugitive enslaved woman and daughter of the third US president, Thomas Jefferson; Nakshidil, an enslaved harem occupant and the queen mother of the Ottoman Empire; Sarah Baartman, a South African Hottentot Venus prisoner exhibited in Paris, who was the mother of scientific racism; and finally Hannah Elias, a courtesan and robber baron.

Hannah's portrait is based on a cache of microfilms in the New York City Archives that had been misplaced or lost until I found them. There were contemporary newspapers and articles, court transcripts of four different trials, police files and records, census and real estate listings, and medical files, but no personal correspondence. Hannah did historically disappear from the New York census in 1911, never to be heard of again, after gaining a reputation and fame as a New York philanthropist. Although Hannah Elias and Granville Woods were contemporaries, their encounter never happened.

I would like to thank my longtime New York researchers Sharon Morgan and Clarencetta Jelks. I would like to cite the nineteenth-century volume *Sunshine and Shadow in New York* by Matthew Hale Smith, published by J. B. Burr. I would like to thank my publisher, HarperCollins, which so enthusiastically brought Hannah to the great public. My thanks to my intrepid editor Tracy Sherrod who inspired the last line of this book by insisting that that last line which can make or break a book is the obligation of a good writer to her readers as well as recognizing the dangers and conspiracies that surrounded this manuscript and who silently always kept on going. I would also like to thank my brilliant editorial assistant of sixteen years, Marilyn Paed-Rayray, whose cool appraisal and uncanny ability to read my thoughts before I've thought them makes her invaluable as well as beloved. Thanks to professor Jennifer Wilks for her astounding reader's guide, first published in the Barbara Chase-Riboud issue of *Callaloo* (Johns Hopkins University Press, vol. 32, no. 3, Summer 2009).

Thanks to my astute curator and registrar Erin Gilbert, suddenly drafted as an accidental literary agent, who performed with exception and professionalism.

Thanks to my attorney, Alexander Blumrosen, who has been a blessing and a help and a brother for twenty-five years.

Thanks to my stylist, Marianne Mbama, who has kept my head on straight for twenty years.

Thanks to my two guardian angels, Vivian Mae Chase and Jacqueline Bouvier Onassis, who always seem to be watching over me and guiding my steps in the most preternatural way, performing celestial interventions and other miracles. Thanks to my adorable husband, Sergio Tosi, and my sons, David and Alexei Riboud, who have never complained of a working wife or a working mother, but who accommodated themselves to my needs unselfishly and cheerfully without complaint. Thank you, my loves.

Thank you to the anonymous New York City archivist in a gray smock who led me to the forgotten, lost, and miscataloged file of microfilm concerning Hannah Elias that is the basis of this book and that was not listed under her name at all but under nineteenth-century crime stories—which this surely was.

My thanks also to New York Bar Association Library and to the Costume Department of the Museum of the City of New York for the images of the clothes that Hannah wears.

Speaking of costumes, if you would like this book to become a movie, please write to me c/o HarperCollins with your dream cast. Mine includes Beyoncé as Hannah, Robert De Niro as John Platt, Charlize Theron as Leola, Idris Elba as Granville Woods, Jude Law as August Nanz, Tommy Lee Jones as J. P. Morgan, Mahershala Ali as Cornelius Williams, and Jay-Z as Maurice Ducasse.

And thank you, Hannah Elias, for being who you were, come hell or high water.

Barbara Chase-Riboud
Paris, France

About the Author

Barbara Chase-Riboud's first collection of poetry, *From Memphis and Peking* (1974), was edited by Toni Morrison and released to wide critical acclaim. For her second collection, *Portrait of a Nude Woman as Cleopatra* (1988), she was awarded the Carl Sandburg Poetry Prize for Best American Poet. She is the author of six celebrated and widely translated historical novels: in addition to *The Great Mrs. Elias* the bestselling *Sally Hemings* (1979), *Valide: A Novel of the Harem* (1986), *Echo of Lions* (1989), *Roman Egyptien* (1994, in French), *The President's Daughter* (1994), and *Hottentot Venus* (2004). She was awarded the Janet Heidinger Kafka Prize for Best Novel by an American Woman for *Sally Hemings*. In 1996, she received Knighthood in Arts and Letters from the French government in joint recognition of her literary and artistic achievements.

Chase-Riboud is an internationally renowned sculptor whose works belong to major museum collections around the world. In 2021 she was awarded the Simone et Cino del Duca International Sculpture Prize by the Institute of France and Académie des Beaux-Arts. She was honored with a rare living-artist personal exhibition at the Metropolitan Museum of Art in 1999. In 2013 a major survey of her sculpture and drawings was held at the Philadelphia Museum of Art, and in 2021 she exhibited forty sculptures in dialogue with forty sculptures of Master Alberto Giacometti at the Giacometti Institute in Paris. Born in Philadelphia of Canadian American descent, she is an MFA graduate of Yale University School of Design and Architecture and the recipient of numerous fellowships, prizes, and honorary degrees. She divides her time between Paris, Rome, and New York.